Windblown Clouds

THOMAS K. SHOR

Windblown Clouds

ESCAPE MEDIA

Windblown Clouds Copyright ©2003 by Thomas K. Shor. All rights reserved. Printed in the United States of America. No part of this book may be used or reproduced in any manner whatsoever without written permission except in the case of brief quotations embodied in critical articles and reviews. For information contact: info@escapemediapublishers.com

First Escape Media edition published 2003

Library of Congress Cataloging-in-Publication Data

Shor, Thomas K.
Windblown Clouds: non-fiction / Thomas K. Shor

LCCN: 2003 111511
p.cm
ISBN: 0-9661861-8-4

Cover Design: N-Z Graphics. All rights reserved
Author Photo: Isabel Antunes

First Edition

To the Rents, who got me here;

To Evthókimos, who gave me a place;

To Ed, now gone, who showed me a way;

and

To Isabel
who gives me a place to rest my heart
and with whom love is a daily renewal

I dedicate this book

The moon and sun are eternal travelers. Even the years wander on. A lifetime adrift in a boat, or in old age leading a tired horse into the years, every day is a journey, and the journey itself is home. From the earliest times there have always been some who have perished along the road. Still I have always been drawn by windblown clouds into dreams of a lifetime of wandering.

~Matsuo Basho

Windblown Clouds

Thomas K. Shor

Preface

This book describes a journey I took many years ago, when I was twenty-two. As with all good things in life, journeys tend to circle round to their beginnings. This journey was no exception. One goes off, one comes home again, and then one reflects. This journey began and ended in Vermont. During the two years following my return, I spent most of my time writing about my experiences. I wrote the story through from the beginning to the end without stopping to revise or correct what I had written. The resulting manuscript of over six hundred typed and hand-written pages was the first draft of the pages that follow.

Both traveling and writing are bugs for which I have never found a cure. Before I had time to edit the manuscript and shape it for others to read, I was stricken again with the travel bug and set off on other travels. I left the manuscript with my sister, who lives in Washington DC, for safekeeping. When I returned from that journey, I wrote of other things, and quite got on with my life.

About a year ago I started thinking about that old manuscript. It had been many years since I'd seen it. I didn't necessarily want to work on it; I was merely curious. I only wanted to take a look. Like the Indian shopkeeper garnering customers off the street with the call, "Looking only, no buying," I thought I could simply take a peek. So I called my sister and asked her to send it.

My sister had been carefully guarding the manuscript all those years, and she was not keen to give it up to the US Postal Service. She reminded me that it was the only copy in existence and insisted on sending it by overnight express delivery.

I live at the end of a very long driveway off a dirt road that couriers often have difficulty finding. So, just to be safe, I had my sister send the manuscript in care of a friend, Kate Jones.

When I gave my sister the address, she said, "Kate Jones,

what an unfortunate name."

I asked her what she meant.

"It's like Jane Doe," she said.

I assured her that Kate received overnight mail regularly and told her not to worry.

A week later Kate had received no package for me, so I called my sister again.

My sister lives a busy life. She apologized for forgetting to send the manuscript and promised again to send it right away. I must have only half believed her, for a good month went by and I hardly gave the manuscript a thought. Then it was her birthday and we were talking on the phone. I reminded her again, and this time she swore she would find the manuscript the moment she got off the phone and would send it the very next day.

Half a week later I called her again. I was beginning to grow tired of her promises and told her so. But she stopped me. She *had* sent it. It should have arrived four days earlier. She commented again on my friend's unfortunate name.

I called Fed-X, and they tracked the package. The driver claimed he'd been unable to locate Kate's residence, so he'd done what he always did when he had difficulty locating someone in our area: he went to Sam's Septic Service. Since Sam emptied every septic tank in town, he knew precisely where everyone lived.

Sam told the driver that there was a K. Jones living just around the corner. He pointed out the apartment building.

The Kate Jones I know is my neighbor; she lives on a farm, miles away from the village.

But I knew the building Sam had referred to. It had long ago been nicknamed—by its residents, no less—the 'Brown Slum.' It is known for its transient and more down-and-out residents.

So the news couldn't have been worse. And as if that wasn't enough, he'd delivered it not to the K. Jones who lived there, but to a man loitering in front of the building that claimed to know her. He'd signed his name 'J. Miller.'

I was horrified.

I rushed down to the Brown Slum and started knocking on doors. The first door on which I knocked was opened by a man who worked the graveyard shift, and he was decidedly *not* happy to be awakened at nine-thirty in the morning. He said he had neither seen the package, nor had he heard of the man who'd signed for it, but he told me that indeed a woman named Jones did live in the building, though her name was not Kate, it was Kay. He pointed to the door across the hall. "She lives there," he said.

Kay Jones herself answered my knock. She had the look of someone who hadn't seen the sun in years. The homemade tattoos that ran up and down her arms had a decidedly jailhouse look. She was haggard and tired, a woman apparently worn to the bone by life's vicissitudes.

I pictured this woman opening my package on the off chance that it contained something of value, discovering only pages and pages of my barely legible scribbling, certainly worthless to her, and hiding it under a bed, or throwing it out so as not to be caught having opened another person's mail.

She stood with the door half-open, her hand clutching the doorknob, blocking entrance to her apartment. I explained why I was there.

"I never seen a package," she said, eyeing me closely.

I told her about J. Miller, who had signed for it.

"I never heard of no J. Miller," she said.

I had to think fast. If I assumed that she was lying, then my best chance was to make her sympathetic to my cause. So I launched into a long plea, explaining how the missing package contained the only copy of a manuscript I had spent years writing, and how it had no worth to anyone but me. She relaxed a bit and stepped back from the door, allowing me to enter her apartment.

Taking her into my confidence, I told her how I would understand if one of her *neighbors* had taken the package—

just to see what was in it. I even said I might have done the same myself. I stressed that no questions would be asked. I even suggested that an anonymous phone call telling me the manuscript was sitting in a hall would suit me fine.

All I wanted was to have the manuscript back.

The entire time I was making my plea for help, I was moving around the room, trying to pick up some clue amidst piles of dirty clothes and overflowing bags of garbage. I was looking for the corner of a Fed-X envelope, or a box of the right dimensions.

Before the manuscript had been lost I was merely curious to see it. I had pictured myself flipping through the pages, cringing the whole while at my abuse of the English language, and perhaps recalling a few details of a journey that the years had swept from my mind.

But when I first heard the manuscript had not been delivered, its stock had risen a notch. And as the situation became more hopeless, I had even begun to see myself working on it again. Now that it was probably gone forever, I felt the full tragedy of its loss.

So I made a promise, a solemn vow. I vowed that if I could find the manuscript, I would complete it. Perhaps the manuscript had become lost only to extract such a promise from me. I felt destiny at work.

I left my name and phone number with Kay Jones. That was all I could do. She promised to call if she heard anything.

Then I proceeded to knock on doors up and down the halls of the Brown Slum. At every door I repeated the entire story, left my phone number if they'd let me, and grew more desperate as the word *gone* rose like a lump in my throat.

By the time I reached the last door, and delivered my story for the umpteenth time, this time to a middle-aged woman dressed in an old coffee-stained bathrobe, I was entirely discouraged and thoroughly depressed. Still I tried to remain upbeat.

But it was no use. Halfway through my impassioned plea

the phone rang. The woman answered it and started arguing with a man from a collection agency. He was threatening her with court and jail and worse if she didn't come up with a certain sum in short order. "I have no money," she said, "especially none to give you!" She argued desperately for a good ten minutes while I stood in the doorway. Finally I gave up.

I went back outside and started to walk away. None of the people to whom I'd made my plea seemed likely to go out of their way to help.

In my mind I went over again what must have happened. Someone must have gotten their hands on the package, (most likely Kay Jones but there was no telling), and thrown it out.

Then it hit me: if so, it would probably have ended up in the tenement's dumpster.

I went to the parking lot, lifted the dumpster's lid, and was almost blown off my feet by the stench of death. Holding my nose, afraid of what I might find, I looked inside.

There on top of dozens of plastic bags of trash were the remains of a slaughtered pig. Huge ball joints—the cartilage still white and glistening—leg bones, and whole sides of fat—from which, under happier circumstances, bacon would be cut—were all draped over the shiny black bags, slowly decaying beneath a thick cloud of flies that rose when I opened the lid, then settled again on their quarry.

Holding both my breath and my nose, I looked beneath the carnage for something resembling a box of paper. But I saw no such box. I thought of ripping the bags open, but the festering pig flesh and the flies turned my stomach.

I could not endure it.

So I closed the dumpster and walked away, riling against the fate of having lost the manuscript at precisely the moment I realized its importance. I tried to get used to the fact that I would never see the manuscript again.

I couldn't.

That dumpster was my only chance.

I found a broken broom handle lying underneath a bush and returned to the scene of the carnage. I opened the dumpster again, held my breath, and started poking the bags of trash, ripping them open, and trying to see what lay beneath.

I worked my way systematically through the dumpster, from one side to the other. When I reached the farthest corner and moved the very last bag of garbage I spied a plastic grocery bag tied shut around something the size of a ream of paper. Catching the handle with the stick, I moved the bag to the side. Then I held my breath, leaned deep inside the dumpster, and snatched it out.

I opened the bag and there it was, hundreds of typed and handwritten pages that I hadn't seen in a decade. Someone had ripped open the box, taken the pages out, shuffled through them, and then stuffed the whole mess into the bag. Every single page was there.

Having literally saved the manuscript from the jaws of death, I walked away from that dumpster clutching the plastic bag to my breast.

And so it was, I had no choice but to finish the project I had begun so long ago.

Part One

Left to his own resources man always begins again in the Greek way—a few goats or sheep, a rude hut, a patch of crops, a clump of olive trees, a running stream, a flute.

—Henry Miller

Windblown Clouds

Thomas K. Shor

1

I was on a ferryboat making a night crossing of the Adriatic Sea, from the southern Italian port of Brindisi to the Greek island of Corfu, where I had once lived. The sun was about to rise and I was leaning against a rail, straining for sight of land, mistaking clouds on the horizon for mountains. The bow sliced through the calm, dark sea, peeling back wave after wave, each tinged with the glow of the eastern sky.

The mountains only appeared when they were quite close, their peaks having been hidden in the clouds, both cloud and rock having been washed pink by the early dawn light. The rising sun dispersed the clouds, leaving the rock gray against a blue sky.

The sun had risen fully by the time we drew close to land. The mountains were too high and wild to be those of Corfu. We were off the coast of Albania. Nowhere had I seen mountains as rugged as these. We steamed south and entered a strait between an island and the mainland. As we rounded the island's northern shore I searched for some sign by which I could know the island was Corfu and not some other. For so long I had been traveling through unknown lands, never seeing a familiar sight, never pausing long enough to grow accustomed to a single face, forever the stranger passing through.

Villages of whitewashed houses lay nestled along the green strip of shore. Behind the villages the land rose to steep mountains. Following the stony slopes up from the coast, a spark of recognition shot through me as I saw one final towering peak, a stony cone I would have recognized anywhere as belonging to Corfu's northern mountains. Seeing that mountain was like seeing an old friend.

~

When the boat docked I was the first one off, leading two-dozen other disembarking passengers down the pier and toward the customs building. Opening the door to a long, wide corridor of low customs inspection tables, I realized there wasn't an inspector in sight. The boat had docked a few minutes early, probably catching them on their morning coffee break. Knowing they were supposed to be picking out the more suspicious of us for inspection, I wondered whether it was all right to pass through so blithely. But I was excited to be back on Corfu. I strode on as determinedly as a tour-guide leading his innocent charges.

I swung open the door to the noisy waiting room, but before I could take another step, a large and imposing customs man, standing two inches in front of my face, blocked my advance. I stopped, shocked by his sudden appearance. The suitcase belonging to the lady behind me jabbed into my ribs.

The customs official had a big black mustache, a chest full of medals, and stripes on his shoulders to prove his authority. He spoke English with a thick Greek accent. "Where you come from?" he demanded.

"Italy," I replied.

"How you get here?"

"On that boat," and I pointed to it.

"Oh!" he said, and his face lit up. He tipped his hat. "Welcome to Corfu!"

Making my way through the clamor, I cut inland onto the narrow, winding streets and alleys. An old woman riding sidesaddle on a donkey came toward me. She smiled and said, "*Kali mera,*" good morning, as we passed. Young children in blue uniforms, eyes big as almonds, went by like schools of tiny fish. An old man sat on a chair by his door with a coat thrown over his shoulders, a cup of Greek coffee balanced on his knee, and a cigarette in his hand. He smiled as I passed.

Every sight, smell, and sound brought back memories; past experiences flashed through my mind like crystals forming around a nucleus. I recalled the first time I'd arrived on Corfu six years earlier. I was making the same passage from Italy to Greece, only that time I was headed to the boat's

Windblown Clouds

Thomas K. Shor

final destination, the city of Patras on the Greek mainland, from where I would go by bus to Athens. I had met some other travelers on the boat and we had talked late into the night. Long after the moon had sunk below the horizon, I had fallen asleep on a bench on deck. The boat wasn't due to dock at Patras till afternoon.

The next thing I knew the sun was beating on my closed eyelids. I heard the tooting of a car horn. I heard the braying of a donkey. In the distance voices were raised in song. I opened my eyes to see hillsides covered by whitewashed buildings shining brilliantly in the sun. Passengers stood around me, looking at the town and waving good-bye to people on shore. As sailors loosened ropes, I realized I had but seconds to get off the boat. Running down the gangplank, I jumped to shore just as the gangplank was raised.

Clearing customs, and still half-asleep, I stumbled onto the street and stepped unwittingly into a parade. I had arrived on the morning of Greece's highest holiday, the Orthodox Easter.

The parade was a magnificent affair, with priests in their finest black robes followed by musicians and singers. Then came dancers dressed in traditional costumes. Children shook loose from their parents and joined the growing procession, many leading goats and sheep. Everyone was being swept into the parade, and I couldn't help being swept up as well.

Noticing that some of my companions from the boat had also joined the parade, I asked if any of them knew where to get the bus for Athens. They laughed at me as they realized I wasn't kidding. To my dumb stare they explained that we were on an island. The island's name was Corfu. I had never heard of Corfu before, but what I had seen of it so far, I liked.

Peter, a wiry Englishman, had been to Corfu before. He suggested we all go to Kontokali, a village up the coast some five miles away, where he knew of a taverna with rooms to rent. So we went, four or five of us, to Kontokali.

After settling at the *dhomatia*, we borrowed bicycles and

took a ride down a dirt road through a grove of olive trees. We came upon an old van parked off the side of the road in the shade of a huge olive tree. Bouzouki music blared from a radio, and an old man with a glass in one hand and a cane in the other signaled us over by waving his cane above his head.

A party consisting of a huge family, ranging from an old woman wearing a weathered peasant dress to her great grandchildren who were barely old enough to walk were having their Easter dinner. They invited us to join them. We hadn't a language in common but that mattered little: this was a day of festivity, celebrating the risen Christ.

The old man handed each of us a small glass filled to the brim with ouzo, Greece's clear, anise-flavored liquor. He motioned us to empty our glasses in a single gulp, which we each did in turn while the others cheered and laughed. We repeated this ritual three or four times until the old woman snatched the bottle from his hand. She was afraid we'd be unable to ride our bicycles home. After a meal of spit-roasted lamb, rice, bread, feta, and olives, someone turned up the music, and we attempted to learn Greek dances under the twisted boughs of the olive trees. We were not very good pupils: the ouzo was still coursing through our veins. We staggered more than danced. With hugs and laughter, we mounted our bicycles and rode back to Kontokali.

Corfu is a world set apart. Time moves with a lazy fluidity, and magic sweeps through the air. It is a land where anything can and constantly does happen. My first visit there stretched into a two-month-long stay. I rented a house in the hills outside Kontokali with one of the people from the boat. We rarely planned what we did from one day to the next; it was enough to allow the events of the day to come to us. It was to this house that I was now headed. Now, my brother Andy and his wife Ann lived there.

~

The course I took through the streets of Corfu Town was determined by no particular rationale; recollection and intuition were my sole guides. I had never completely mastered navigation in Corfu Town; I knew portions of the town as the New Port, the Old Port, the market street near the Church of Saint Spiridon, and the bus square. Winding, narrow streets connected these places. When to go right and when to go left were decisions made spontaneously. Often it was a slight detail that triggered recognition, a place where the road turned to cobbles or where an old woman fed stray cats. I knew the town not entirely, but intimately.

Near the bus stop in Corfu Town was a small dairy and bakeshop, a place I had thought of often since I'd last left Corfu. Eating a raisin bun and a bowl of *crema,* a goat milk pudding, I had often sat at a corner table for an hour or more watching old Greek men talking and smoking and telling jokes. The place had an atmosphere akin to a family hearth. Walking through the narrow streets, I remembered Spiros, the elderly proprietor who presided over the scene with the kindness and concern of a shepherd. He was a large man with protruding eyes. Stretched taut over his ample frame, his skin was as pale as the milk he sold.

Inside the bakeshop, above the moneybox and behind a glass counter that contained milk and cheese, was a small shrine fringed with multi-colored tassels. Olive oil lamps illuminated icons of both Christ the Shepherd and the Virgin holding the babe in her arms. The lamps also illuminated pictures of Spiro's parents, wife, and children. As I sped through the streets, I wondered whether the shop and the shrine were still there after all these years.

To my delight, the bakeshop was right where it was supposed to be. I ducked inside. The corner table—*my* table—was free. I sat. Nothing had changed. There was Spiros sitting on his stool behind the glass case. Above his head was the shrine. It glowed warmly. It was as if the scene had been frozen in time. I ordered a raisin bun and *crema.*

After breakfast, I rounded the corner to the bus square and took the bus to Kontokali to see my brother and sister-in-law. Arriving in the village, I found the well-trodden path that led through olive groves and up the hill. At the far end of the grove stood the house. Ancient trees overhung its clay-tiled roof; whitewash peeled from its walls; plaster crumbled to reveal the stone beneath; the shutters were broken. The house looked the same as it had when I'd first set eyes on it years before. I remembered that living in this house had been like living in a ruin; one constantly uncovered relics from the past.

Since neither Andy nor Ann had any idea that I was coming, I approached the house stealthily, with the intent of surprising them. But to my disappointment, the front door was locked. So was the back door. I tried all the windows, but the house was locked up tight. I sat down in the grass under the prolific, sagging grape arbor by the front door. Then I lay down. As my eyelids grew heavy, I wondered whether they might have left the island, perhaps gone away for a few days. After a time, I fell into a deep sleep.

~

I awoke with a start to find a donkey peering down at me and sniffing my face. An old woman held its leather lead, and I recognized her as the woman who lived in the house farther up the path. Somehow, her name flashed in my mind.

"Lefteria!" I called out as I jumped to my feet, startling the donkey. "Lefteria!" I called again. Lefteria was visibly shocked that I knew her name.

"Andy? Ann?" I said and pointed at the house.

A puzzled look crossed her face. Then she brightened and said, "Ah, Andreas, Anna," and she launched into a rapid and fiery monologue, gesticulating so emphatically that she upset the donkey, who started braying plaintively.

When she finished I rejoined with an equally long and rambling story of how I had come to the house only to find no one home and had been worried that they had gone or were called away because of emergency, but felt better now that she had known their names and didn't seem to be implying that they were gone. I used especially obscure words and complicated ways of saying things to heighten the sense of the absurdity I felt at having such an earnest discussion with this woman, whose vocabulary and my own coincided only on the words *Andreas* and *Anna*.

When I finished my side of the story she shrugged her shoulders. A smile crossed her lips. Then we both burst out laughing. She dug deep into her pocket and took out a handful of ripe figs. She gave me some, called to her donkey, and they continued up the path toward her house.

I fell back asleep and awoke when the sun was much higher in the sky. This time I awoke from familiar voices calling out my name. I jumped to my feet, Andy and Ann dropped their groceries, and we hugged one another. "How long have you been here?" they asked. "Where were you? I thought you had left," I said, and we all bubbled over with questions and answers. It had been a long time since we had seen one another and there was much catching up to do.

2

Within a few days we fell into a routine akin to the languid ways of Corfu itself. The house was surrounded with fruit trees over-laden with ripe fruit—figs and apples, oranges and lemons, pears, cactus fruit, and berries—and no matter how much we ate, even more fell to the ground to rot.

The first to rise in the morning would find the fig tree that had the largest number of ripe figs and pick a small basketful to spread on the breakfast toast, which we made by holding bread with a fork over a gas burner.

On Mondays, Wednesdays, and Fridays we took the bus to Corfu Town. On these days Ann, the only one of us who spoke Greek, gave an English lesson to the daughter of the people who owned a small vegetable shop where we shopped. While Ann gave her lesson, Andy and I visited various markets.

It was often humorous, Andy and I pushing our way

through the crowd of Greek women at the bake shop, trying to get the attention of the man behind the counter, handicapped by language, knowing only a set formula of three words to yell out to get the loaf we wanted. "*Ena mavro psomi.*" Those were the magic words, "One dark bread," and the man would weigh and wrap our whole wheat bread, then write a number on a scrap of paper to tell us the price. That was usually our first stop, after which we'd go to the vegetable shop where the couple whose daughter Ann was then teaching would greet us at the door to help us pick out our vegetables. Then we were off to the fish street, a narrow cobbled alleyway where fishmongers in tiny stalls sold yesterday's catch from wooden bins. We were usually after the small, minnow-like fish that the fishermen attract to their boats at night with gas lanterns hung off the boat's sterns. From the harbor, one could see the boats at night on the mirror-calm water. We'd point to these fish and say, "Ten grams," (which is very little), and they in turn would laugh at us until we explained, "*Gato,*" for the cat. Sometimes they gave us the fish for free. Then we'd go to the dry-goods store for rice, noodles, soap, and toilet paper.

We usually rushed through our shopping so we'd be free to go to the *kafeneo*—or coffee house—that we dubbed the Chess Café, where we'd play chess and drink coffee until Ann was through giving the lesson.

The Chess Café, much like the bake and dairy shop I had rushed to on my first day back on Corfu, was a place in which Greek men spent most of their waking hours drinking coffee, beer, or brandy, smoking cigarettes, and playing cards. Two or three heated games were always under way.

Greeks play cards like no other people I've seen. When it is a Greek's turn to put down a card, he doesn't merely pick a card from his hand and put it on the table; he lets a good amount of time elapse first. He deliberates so long and hard that all eyes are trained on him. Then he chooses a card from his hand with a look on his face that says he'll win the game within minutes. He holds the card high over the middle of the

Windblown Clouds

Thomas K. Shor

table and lets his hand quiver before slapping it onto the table, grunting as if to say, 'So there!' Then he quickly looks round the table to judge reaction, which invariably is loud and raucous. Never sure whether the reactions were due to the particular card slapped down or to the quality of the delivery, the game they played always eluded me. As far as I could judge, the rules were constantly changing, and cheating was an integral part of winning.

One day, Andy and I were playing chess, and Andy was taking a long time to move—I had just threatened his queen and he was looking for a way out without loosing his knight. I happened to be watching the card game at the center table, which had become quite rowdy, when one of the players stood up to go to the toilet. The moment the man closed the toilet door the others grew mischievous. Looking like a gang of eight-year-olds, they picked up the stack of cards before the empty seat and quickly rearranged them, placing them back on the table just as the door opened and their friend walked over, adjusting his fly. The looks that flashed round the table were priceless as the poor man lost hand after hand, and finally gave up the game in disgust. Yet another hand was dealt in this seemingly endless game, until another of the players went to the toilet. Once again, the moment he shut the door behind him, the others rearranged his cards and returned them just in time. The game resumed and the next victim of the rouse lost miserably, completely unsuspecting of the antics he had participated in only moments before.

The Chess Café was the perfect place for games. One moment Andy and I would be engrossed in the world of bishops, queens, and pawns, and the next we would be watching the card player's antics, or the son of the café's owner taking a metal tray of Greek coffee, tea, or ouzo to another shop owner down the street.

Our game was usually in its final stages when Ann arrived from her lesson. We'd have another coffee with her before leaving, and then make a few more stops to purchase items that Andy and I had been unable to buy without her linguistic assistance. After shopping, we would take the bus back to Kontokali, and by the time we were walking up the path into the hills, the sun was so intense that we'd feel ready to die from the heat. But we countered the heat by going to the well to pour buckets of cool water over our heads. After a lunch of bread, feta, tomatoes, onions, and olives would come a nap, necessary in such a hot climate.

Our days were, to put it plainly, lazy and idyllic. We were living in a paradise where our needs were both few, and easily met. Things were so perfect that they couldn't possibly last that way, though at the time we were naïve enough to think they could.

~

Andy and Ann first met on Corfu many years earlier and had now lived there together for over a year. After a few years back in the States they had returned to Corfu, hoping to live on the island permanently. The only way they could stay on the island was to acquire residence permits, and the only way to do that was to start a small business. Since Ann knew how to weave they decided to start a small weaving business, consisting of a loom and Ann sitting at it, making rugs and wall hangings to be sold at tourist shops in Corfu Town. It wasn't exactly a front—they *did* hope to gain a little income from the business—but what they really wanted was their residence permits.

When I arrived, they were ready to start. The only thing holding them back was the rain that fell with too much regularity in Ioánnina, a town across the strait in the mountains of the mainland known for its wool. They had bought wool in Ioánnina and arranged for someone to dye it. But the dyer could only dye the wool during a long stretch of dry weather; for after dunking the wool into the dye, he'd have to hang it outside, and if it didn't dry quickly the dye wouldn't set.

We always thought it odd that Ioánnina should be

receiving so much rain while Corfu was in the middle of its dry season; but Ioánnina was, after all, in the mountains. And in Greece such details as these, or delays of a few weeks, don't mean what they do elsewhere. If you hold someone to a deadline in Greece, then he often becomes indignant, as if you are breaking a code of Greek ethics. Just to spite you he'll slow down even more to prove the point. It is a matter of survival to accede and say, "If it's not done today, maybe next week it'll be done, or the week after that." In the mean time you continue picking your morning figs and taking afternoon walks through the olive groves.

In order to receive their permit to start a business, Andy and Ann had made a deep incursion into the labyrinthine world of Greek bureaucracy. Every weekday morning for the past three months they had presented themselves before a man in uniform they called—in mock affection—the 'Main Man.' Pinned to his chest was a badge surrounded by medals, and perched on his head was a crisp military cap. The Main Man worked out of police headquarters in Corfu Town.

A police headquarters in Greece is usually the last place you might want to end up. Not long before, military colonels, during whose regime the police were designated as enforcers, had run the country. During that time, the police were notorious for their nefarious ways. In those days, the police struck terror in the hearts of villagers and city-dwellers alike, enforcing the will of the colonels with gleeful and vicious abandon. And when they weren't busy fulfilling the colonels' will, they were busy imposing their own on whomever they saw fit. Local police chiefs held the same arbitrary terror over their villages as the colonels held over the country.

Now the colonels were gone, replaced by an elected government. But through this change of government many of the police had kept their posts. The same hated men to whom the colonels had given free rein, parliament supposedly had now reined in. But they still had tricks hidden up their sleeves, and evil schemes hatched in their brains. Their specialty was finding obscure laws to bring down their enemies.

One such law stated that every restaurant had to have a bathroom and that every bathroom had to have toilet paper. The penalty for running out of toilet paper was swift and severe: the police would instantly impound the restaurant and throw the owner in jail. This law struck terror in the heart of every restaurateur, for with this law the police could close down whomever they didn't like. The police were not above removing toilet paper from a bathroom and then conducting a raid. So restaurant owners who had spoken out against the colonels when they had killed the students at the university in Athens, or who didn't like giving free food to the police, or whose family had a land dispute dating back five generations with a policeman's family, all these restaurateurs had to protect themselves against toilet paper raids, which they did by filling their tiny bathrooms with cases of toilet paper. You could tell a restaurant owner's standing with the police by the amount of toilet paper in his bathroom. Sometimes you could hardly open the door, much less fit yourself inside and close the door behind you. Needless to say, one approached the police with caution.

Every day at nine o'clock sharp, Andy and Ann presented themselves at police headquarters well scrubbed and in clean clothes. The Main Man, despite his military demeanor and questionable background, was not, in the end, all that bad. From him they received their instructions. He would tell them which government office to go to for a particular form. Invariably, they'd have to take that form to another bureaucratic office for the signature of some functionary. The signed form would then have to go to a third office to be stamped. Every stage of their journey would entail a fee, some of which were legitimate, others not, though of course one never asked and therefore never knew. They learned early on to follow the Main Man's instructions to the letter and to complete all the steps he laid out in the morning before the

Windblown Clouds Thomas K. Shor

fall of night. They learned this the day they tired of government offices and decided to go back to Kontokali before getting the final stamp on the day's form. They figured they could do it the next day. But the next day they discovered the form had to be signed and stamped the same day it was issued. They had to start all over, wasting a day and paying all the fees twice. So they followed the Main Man's directions carefully, and in the end he was really quite helpful. He even pointed them in the direction of a good lawyer who pled their case for a business license before the district court.

It all went off without a hitch. All their forms were signed, stamped, duplicated, notarized, and blessed—all, that is, except one, the one that had to go to Athens for approval. That form was their residence permit. Since their business permit was approved and in hand, and since the Main Man considered the residence permits a mere formality, he said that as far as he was concerned they could start working. That was when they started designing and building their loom and traveling to Ioánnina to order wool, the wool they were waiting for when I arrived.

~

So the days wore on. Andy and Ann waited for their wool, as I awaited the next step on my journey. Limbo is fine as long as there is something at the other end to pull you out; I was continually trying to figure out just what that something might be. I considered where to spend the winter, and thought of possibly going to Crete or Turkey or North Africa. But as I considered each of these places I found myself gazing at Corfu's northern mountains, the same mountains that I had seen as the ferryboat rounded Corfu's northern shore. My thoughts of far away lands were continually preempted by speculations about these mountains.

Corfu is roughly hourglass-shaped, a narrow isthmus in the middle, widening both north and south. In the north are the island's only mountains. And these mountains rise toward a single stony peak, the highest point on the island, the mountain Pantokrator.

Corfu is one of Greece's most lush islands. But Corfu's mountains rise to an altitude that can support only bare and naked rock. The mountains stand solidly contrasted against both the blue sky and the verdant lowlands. The mountains are so massive that no matter where you are on the island, if you look up, there they are.

This omnipresence might not have struck everyone, but I was fairly hounded by it. I would catch myself staring up at the naked face of Pantokrator, daydreaming, imagining life amid so much stone. I might be thinking at any given time about going to North Africa, considering the relative cost of flying to taking a boat, when I'd suddenly realize that I was staring across the bay at the mountainside and wondering instead what it might be like to live upon that mountain. Or I might be wandering in the olive grove behind the house, where I sometimes took solitary walks, and my thoughts would turn to where I might go next. I would look down the hill toward the coast and dream of distant lands. And, in fact, I'd been going up there for some time before I realized that an opening in the trees offered an unobstructed view of Mount Pantokrator. And I even subsequently discovered that the very tip of the mountain was visible just above a rooftop when one looked out the window at the Chess Café. Pantokrator became a recurring theme, or image, in my ruminations.

~

The very ease of life in Kontokali, though seductive, couldn't hold me; in fact it compelled me to consider moving on. Had I stayed there, I'm afraid I would have grown stagnant. I'd always known that it was merely a point of rest from which I would launch my next move. Yet, no matter how much I thought of traveling to some distant shore, Corfu's northern mountains were calling. It was an uncanny feeling, one probably best described as intuition. It was a call I did my best to resist. I fully intended to leave the island. I was pricing tickets to Africa. I was trying to imagine myself in

Istanbul. But perhaps within its bulk the mountain hid a lodestone to which I responded, and it became increasingly difficult for me to deny the call.

3

It actually took some time for me to heed the mountain's call; in the mean time I was content to live in Kontokali in what was almost a state of suspended animation, watching the hot, dry days of summer turn into the cooler, wet days of fall.

The sky had been cloudless for so many months that when the clouds came, they built over the course of a week, slowly blotting out the deep blue sky by day, and by night obliterating the stars one by one. Each day threatened rain more than the last until the clouds became so heavy with moisture that they could hold it no longer. The sky cracked open and released a deluge on Corfu.

The threat of rain had hung over us so long that when it finally came it was a relief. But for us that relief was short lived, for when the rain fell we discovered our roof leaked. The worst leaks were right over Andy and Ann's bed. We had to move their bed and place buckets under the drips. The roof leaked elsewhere as well. We employed every bucket and pan in our possession.

On our way to town the next day we stopped in the village to see our landlord Giorgos. The house had been in his family for generations. Giorgos, his father, and grandfather had all been born there, and they had all lived there until Giorgos had bought a house in the village some ten years earlier and moved the family from the hill. When we told Giorgos about the roof he was apologetic. His wife Maria was concerned we'd all catch cold. Giorgos promised to find a roofer and get right to it.

A week later, after a few more rainfalls, we went to see Giorgos again. He was now a little less eager. He told us he was having trouble finding a roofer. Because the house was so old, he explained, and since tiles were missing, the beams under the tiles were sure to be rotten. He needed to find not only a roofer—there were plenty of roofers—but a small roofer, one whose weight wouldn't crush the beams as he crawled across them. "I must find a jockey-sized roofer," he said.

A few days later we were lounging under the grape arbor in front of the house, sipping coffee after awakening from a nap, when we saw Giorgos coming up the path through the olive grove accompanied by a man no more than four-and-a-half feet tall. They each held an end of a long wooden ladder.

Overjoyed at their arrival, we offered them coffee and ouzo; but Giorgos was all business. He must have been paying the roofer by the hour. We showed them where the roof was at its worst, over Andy and Ann's bedroom. They leaned the ladder against the building and Andy held the bottom of the ladder steady. The roofer climbed the ladder, Ann pointed out to Giorgos where the leaks were, and Giorgos shouted instructions to the roofer. The roofer took off a few tiles and stuck his head in through the hole.

What might have happened had Andy not been holding the ladder, I don't know. It probably would have been the end of the jockey-sized roofer. He recoiled so violently that he almost tipped the ladder back, and he let out a string of curses. Immediately, I thought of hornets. But as he didn't flee down the ladder, I assumed it couldn't have been that kind of danger. The condition of the roof must have horrified him. Or maybe something had died in there. Carefully, he put his head back through the hole, and there he stood for the longest time, his head under the tiles, transfixed by what he saw. When he came back down he was ashen and shaking like a leaf. He pulled Giorgos to one side and whispered something in his ear. Giorgos knitted his bushy brows.

"No!" Giorgos said in disbelief.

"Yes!" the roofer insisted. "See for yourself."

Giorgos climbed the ladder and repeated the roofer's long,

steady stare. When he came down, he too looked shaken. He quickly took the ladder away from the house.

Giorgos told us the roof was extremely dangerous. He said it could fall at any moment. He kept repeating the word *epikinthunos,* dangerous. The roofer agreed so strenuously that I thought his head might fall off his neck from nodding so forcefully. They said that Andy and Ann should take all their possessions out of the room and close the door behind them.

"Do not return to that room," Giorgos said, his voice quivering with emotion. And with that Giorgos and the roofer hoisted the ladder over their shoulders and set off down the path toward the village.

We thought it odd that the roof, after so many years of slow deterioration, should suddenly be in such danger of collapse—in fact, Giorgos and the roofer's reaction seemed more than just odd: it was really bizarre. We decided the repair job must have been beyond both their expectations and their abilities. This bothered us because instead of fixing the roof, Giorgos would be all the more likely to evoke that Greek turn of mind that says, *If it isn't done today, maybe next week*, and we'd be left emptying buckets and mopping the floor.

Meanwhile, Andy and Ann were becoming tired of waiting for the wool. Ann had some rather nasty exchanges with the wool dyer in Ioánnina. It became a new part of our routine: after shopping and chess and coffee, we'd stop off at the long-distance telephone exchange and Ann would call the wool dyer, a conversation that invariably ended in shouting—and no wool.

And I? I was busy studying maps of the northern mountains. At the base of the highest mountain, Pantokrator, which appeared uninhabited, was the village of Strinilas, the highest village on the island. I thought a mountain village would be a good place to live quietly and do some writing. So I decided to find a small house to rent in Strinilas for the winter.

One day in town, after shopping and before going to the

Chess Café, I went to inquire about buses to Strinilas. I had bought a small book entitled *Beginning Greek,* which I had been going over with Ann. I was always looking for opportunities to practice my Greek, and I thought my trip to the inquiries office would offer a great opportunity. I worked out exactly what to say, rehearsed it in my mind repeatedly, and walked up to the window. I gave my spiel, which in translation went simply, "When bus Strinilas?" (I've never been good at foreign languages). The clerk—he was actually a boy, no more than seventeen—answered in perfect English. "There are buses on Tuesdays, Thursdays, and Saturdays leaving Corfu at five forty-five in the morning and returning from Strinilas at nine-fifteen. Another bus leaves Corfu at one-thirty on those days and returns at four- thirty."

Although crestfallen at a lost opportunity to practice my fledgling Greek, I was glad for the information. I walked to the Chess Café where Andy was waiting for me. I told him I was going to Strinilas the next day on the morning bus, and would return in the afternoon.

That afternoon, after eating lunch, we sat on the front step of our little house, sipping coffee. Andy and Ann were discussing whether or not to go to Ioánnina to see if it really rained there. Half listening to their conversation, I gazed through the trees at the mountain, Pantokrator. Suddenly they stopped talking, and I saw that they were both staring down the path. It was Giorgos. But this time he came not with the jockey-sized roofer. This time, two uniformed policemen accompanied him. Panic flashed through each of us. What could they want? We were quickly working out alibis for crimes we had not committed in places we had never been when we noticed that the police were carrying over their shoulders the long wooden ladder.

Placing the ladder against the outside wall of the bedroom, Giorgos climbed slowly, as if he thought any quick movement might cause the roof to cave in. He peered inside, as he had the first time, then he came back down. Each of the policemen took his turn at what was beginning to look like a ritual: to climb the ladder carefully, peer inside through the hole in the tiles with the utmost concentration, and then climb slowly back down. Each took his turn; each went up twice. They refused to let any of us take a look. As they took the ladder down from the roof, Giorgos reiterated that we were not even to go into the room. We were to remove all of our belongings and shut the door.

"Do not open the door again," he said gravely.

"Stay out of that room!" the policemen concurred.

Then they lifted the ladder onto their shoulders and walked through the olive grove toward the village. They left us more mystified than before, wondering whether the roof would be fixed before the end of the rainy season.

4

Next morning I awoke well before sunrise and ate a substantial breakfast. Then I put together a lunch of bread, feta, tomatoes, and olives. The last sliver of a waning moon lit my way down the path to the village.

I hoped to flag down the bus to Strinilas when it came through Kontokali on its way north along the coast. This was not easy since at five forty-five in the morning a whole fleet of buses left Corfu for points north along the coast road. I had but a split second to discern the unlit destination sign—written in Greek lettering—before the bus rushed past. After flagging down two wrong buses, the Strinilas bus finally came and stopped for me.

As I ran to the front door, a young man stuck his head out the window reserved for the ticket collector. He yelled to me in English, "Hello, friend, do you remember me?" But it was too dark to see who he was. I jumped on the bus and it sped off. The ticket collector got up and insisted I sit in his seat so I could better see the countryside that we would be passing through. He sat on the vibrating motor cover between my seat and the driver's. "You don't remember me," he said. Although I knew we had met, I had to admit I didn't know where. "You came into the bus station yesterday," he said, "and tried to ask in Greek about the buses to Strinilas. You looked very upset when I answered in English." He told the story to the driver and they both had a good laugh.

We followed the coast road to the north of the island, and just as the sky was beginning to lighten in the east, and the mountains of Albania were becoming visible in the distance, we cut inland on a road that switched back and forth through groves of olive trees. We had entered the mountains.

Olive trees, with their slender silver-gray leaves, are particularly beautiful and mysterious during the early morning hours. The trunk of an olive tree resembles more a collection of thick vines interwoven and grown together than a solid and unified trunk. Even in the oldest trees there are passages to the center of the trunk, and sometimes you can see clear through to the other side. If ever a tree meant to be inhabited by tree spirits, it is the olive tree, with its ancient secret chambers.

Above the olive grove the terrain became steeper, and the road—obviously built long before the advent of buses—became narrow, the turns too tight for the bus to negotiate in a single attempt. At the first such turn, the driver spun the wheel and nosed the bus up to the rock face that the road cut into the mountain. Then the ticket collector ran to the back of the bus, looked out the back window, and yelled, "*Éla, éla, éla,*" come, come, come. He guided the bus back to the very edge of the road, which dropped off precipitously. Then he yelled, "*Endáxi,*" enough, just as we felt the rear wheels start to plunge. Then the driver rounded the corner and moved to the next turn.

We were traveling through an increasingly rugged and wild landscape devoid of settlements when a peasant woman, who was sitting upon bulging burlap sacks with a kerchief tied round her head, flagged down the bus. As the driver stopped for her, it was obvious that the sacks were too heavy for her to lift. The ticket collector and I helped her onto the bus, and then we hauled the bags on for her. She hadn't any shoes and her dress was dirty, as if she had been working in a nearby field all night. Sitting on the floor by the door and looking around the bus, she began to laugh for no apparent reason. Her eyes sparkled, perhaps betraying a slight madness. She took some nuts out of one pocket of her dress and a rock out of another. She used the rock to smash the nuts open on the floor of the bus.

Soon we came upon a few small farmhouses made of gray rock with red tiled roofs. Chickens, goats, turkeys, pigs and donkeys all ran free on the road. Then we passed a small school. We were entering the village of Spartilas. We stopped in the village center, across from a *kafeneo*. The ticket collector and I helped the old woman off the bus then leaned her sacks against a building. Plopping herself upon one of the sacks, she started laughing again at nothing in particular.

The driver, a burly man with a large and fleshy nose, invited the ticket collector and me to have a coffee. Inside the *kafeneo*, the driver bellowed to the man behind the counter, "Coffee for me and my friends." And when we were through with our coffee he bellowed again, "Ouzo. My friends want ouzo." When the man came with a bottle and three glasses, both the ticket collector and I declined. Greedily gulping down the ouzo, the driver smacked his lips and yelled out, "Ouzo. More ouzo!" The ticket collector was standing by now. He lifted the driver out of his seat and told the *kafeneo* owner, who was approaching with another bottle, to give him no more. To the obvious relief of the ticket collector, the driver didn't put up a struggle. As the driver took out a large note and paid the bill, the ticket collector told me that the driver had a problem with ouzo. "They like me to go with him on his route," he told me, "because he is my uncle, and though no one can make him stop drinking entirely, at least I can make him stop after one drink. Last month he crashed a bus."

Windblown Clouds   Thomas K. Shor

When we stepped back onto the street, the whitewashed houses and shops of Spartilas, perched precariously on the side of the mountain, were bathed in the pink glow of the morning sun. Far below and in the distance, Corfu Town shone like a white, multi-faceted jewel. Near Kontokali, where my morning's journey had begun, I could see fishing boats setting out for the strait between the island and Albania. It was all so far away, yet I could see it all so clearly, and a feeling of lucidity came over me. I knew this day would bare much fruit.

Above the village the landscape changed dramatically. It was here that the island's lush green growth gave way to the browns and grays of earth and bare stone. We passed a few farms, but they were no longer situated among flowers and fruit trees. These farms had an increasingly desolate look. The few trees that grew above Spartilas were stunted and gnarled. The livestock were lean. We passed a shepherd surrounded by his flock, the sheep grazing off the stunted brush growing out of crevices and fissures. The shepherd raised his staff in greeting as we passed.

A few miles above Spartilas, we turned right to an even smaller road that ran along a shelf cut out of the side of the mountain. There were no houses or farms on this road; there were few signs of life at all, only a short black stubble where bushes had once grown but had been claimed by wildfires that frequented the mountains and terrorized the few mountain villages and their people in the hot, dry summers. From the coast, one sees these fires as glowing red lines moving up the mountain slopes.

The village of Strinilas appeared, nestled in a fold of the mountain Pantokrator. As the bus passed the first few houses on the village's outskirts it became clear that life in this village was not easy. The stone houses, thick walled and solid, stout and low to the ground, were built to withstand wind and rain and snow. The road by which we entered was the village's only link to the outside world; but other than the bus on which we traveled, no vehicles were present. The villagers of Strinilas traveled on foot and by donkey on paths composed of dirt and ancient-laid stone. There was only one *kafeneo* in the village, and it was also the village's only store.

The bus dropped me off in front of the *kafeneo*. I went inside, ordered a cup of Greek coffee, and sat at the corner table by the door. A constant stream of people flowed in and out of the shop to buy milk and bread and other simple foods. As people passed, I was sure I was seeing brother, sister, aunt, uncle, and cousin greeting one another. They exchanged very little money; rather, the *kafeneo* owner, a kind-looking man wearing a white apron, marked each transaction on a piece of paper, a debt to be paid later or to be worked out in barter.

The three other tables in the little *kafeneo* were occupied by old men wearing baggy pants and tattered and patched coats thrown cape-like over their shoulders. Their deeply wrinkled faces and cracked, arthritic fingers spoke of a life of both soil and toil. They sipped coffee, smoked unfiltered cigarettes, and debated with conviction, as if the fate of Greece, both ancient and modern, hinged on their every word. Yet they were relaxed, almost playful in their passion, as if they knew that the mantle of their civilization had already passed to future generations, and that for all practical purposes they had already taken their place beside the Greeks of old.

I realized that at that very moment old Greek men were sitting in village *kafeneos* from the Albanian border to Turkey, from Bulgaria to Crete. They were meeting over innumerable tables with tiny cups of coffee balanced upon their knees. It was thus they greeted the day as they have, it would seem, since the very beginning of time. A tiny cup of coffee balanced on the knee of an old Greek man achieves a balance few of us can ever hope to achieve.

Before me on the table was a deck of cards. I stared at it, took a deep breath, and said aloud, "Ace of spades." I cut the cards, turned my hand over to see what card I had picked, and there it was—sure enough—the ace of spades. I paid for my coffee and stepped out onto the street.

5

The village of Strinilas moved with a rhythm of life deeply rooted in the past. I walked down the narrow, winding ways, past small courtyards laden with bright flowers. Children played in the street. As I walked past them, some ran to look at me while the more timid of them became frightened and ran to the shelter of their doorways or to hide behind their mothers' aprons. Soon the mothers called the older of the children to come inside: it was time for them to change into their school uniforms. Then the children, clean as whistles in their crisp silver-buttoned uniforms, their brown and glossy arms heavy with schoolbooks, came through the arched, whitewashed doorways to walk through the village toward the school. Once the older of the children had departed, their mothers could begin washing at the village well. There they met each day to wash and talk, and, on this day, to watch me, the stranger passing by.

Making my way to the edge of the village where the green patchwork of fields began, I watched the people work, plowing the earth and pulling out weeds. Beyond the fields the land dropped sharply, and all I could see beyond was the blue Adriatic, thousands of feet below. Walking along the road, I made a turn into the next valley, and there I sat with my back against a roadside shrine to the Virgin Mary that was lit by a small olive oil lamp. From this perspective the village was sharply contrasted against the dark barren earth. The towering rock above the village dwarfed the achievements of people upon this rocky slope. The rich green valley that lay before me seemed only a tiny consolation for a life eked out of a barren, lifeless place.

I walked back to the village, hoping to notice an empty

Windblown Clouds — Thomas K. Shor

house to rent, wondering all the while how I might communicate this wish to the people of Strinilas, and also wondering whether they would take well to having a stranger living in their midst. As I thought about this, I came upon an old and weathered sign nailed to a wooden post that was leaning so heavily to the side that I thought the next gust of wind or even a pebble thrown by one of the village children would knock it down. The letters, which were worn, looked like this: ΠΑΝΤΟΚΡΑΤΟΡ. Though Greek lettering was still new to me, I was able to mouth out the sounds. It said Pantokrator. A barely discernible arrow on the sign pointed up a steep and narrow rocky road. Since this mountain had beguiled me for so long, and since the day was still young, I decided to follow the narrow road up the mountain. I wanted at least once to set foot on top of the highest mountain on Corfu. I longed to see the island laid out as on a map, to stand alone on top of the highest point and have an unobstructed view in all directions. Pantokrator is one of the Greek names for God. It means *all-powerful*.

The road mounted the slope above the village at an oblique angle. At the top of this slope, where I expected the land to rise again to the top of the mountain, a plateau opened out before me. Rocks jutted out at odd angles, their disordered array resembling ice on a river that had let loose then been dammed at a narrow passage. Titanic forces had once broken to the surface here, and the rocks looked so freshly surfaced that I expected to hear them rumble beneath my feet. But a profound silence laid thick over this landscape. This plateau seemed to be the very roof of the world. At the far end of the plateau was the final cone of Pantokrator. It rose from the landscape as if some god had let rubble slide through his fingers, or some heavenly hourglass had let its sands run out. The road wound its way across the plateau to the cone's base; then it switched back and forth to the summit. And on the summit I now saw what looked like a fortress or a castle with high stone battlements.

Windblown Clouds

Thomas K. Shor

About halfway across the plateau I heard a chicken clucking. Turning toward the noise, at first I saw nothing, just the same random array of rocks that surrounded me on all sides. Then a pattern arose out of the stones, much as a photograph appears in a tray of developer, and I realized there was a small farmhouse with outbuildings not more than twenty feet away. The buildings were made from the stone close at hand; the walls, which in places had caved in, blended in perfectly with their surroundings. Even more astounding than having a farm suddenly appear out of nothing was the presence of a chicken, indicating that someone actually lived there. But why? The village of Strinilas was nestled in a fold in the land where there was warmth and security, water and terraced fields. Here was nothing but stone, the plateau, the deep descent of land and, across the sea and in the distance, the wild and ragged mountains of Albania.

Farther on I heard a faint tinkling of bells. The sound grew louder and softer as I followed the road up and down the small hills. Gradually the bells got louder until I saw goats jumping from boulder to boulder, searching out little bits of brush to eat. They jumped across the road before me, the bells around their throats ringing gently. A goatherd stood in the shade of a huge boulder. He raised his staff and beckoned me. I was glad for the shade; the sun was now high in the sky. We sat on a stone. I pulled out my lunch and offered half to the herder. He accepted wordlessly.

The sun had darkened the goatherd's face; his hands were rough and callused. His clothes were old and tattered, patched and ripped. His manner was rough. He seemed half-wild, un-tempered by the company of other men, his ways more in keeping with his four-legged companions with whom he roamed day after day. He tore large pieces from the loaf of bread and took handfuls of olives, spitting out the pits carelessly. We washed our food down with water from a flask the goatherd had slung over his shoulder. He gave me a cigarette. We didn't speak a word; we didn't even try. He knew I didn't speak his language, and I knew he didn't speak mine. Replete, we sat in the cool shade and watched the goats in their endless scramble for food, their melodic bells ringing softly.

Leaving him to the companionship of his flock, I continued toward the cone of Pantokrator. At the base of the cone next to the road was an old, solidly built house nestled between the edge of the plateau and the steep land behind. Its shutters were locked, the front door padlocked shut. A small oasis, consisting of a few trees and small patches of grass surrounded the house. Some earlier inhabitants had leveled the slopes of the mountain to create a few terraced fields, which time had tried to efface: the rock walls that held the terraces up were crumbling and the little fields themselves were overrun with weeds and stunted trees. Yet the house itself looked tended. A bucket stood beside a stone-lined well. I drew some water and poured it over my head.

Above the house the road rose steeply through a series of switchbacks to the final summit of the mountain. In places the road was washed out; in others, stone and rubble had tumbled off the mountain and blocked the way. The elements were obviously in variance with this road; left to itself, in time, the zigzagging scar would be obliterated.

What would take longer to obliterate was the stone fortress on top of the mountain. As I mounted the final switchbacks its high stone wall towered over me, and I saw a quick flash of black material billowing above the wall. When I looked again, it was gone.

Turning the last corner in the road, I came upon a closed metal gate of the high stone wall, above which was a bell tower. As I peered through the gate I realized that what I had thought was a fortress or a castle was actually a monastery. Stepping away from the gate, I stood on a boulder overhanging the steep back side of the mountain. The wind rode the slope of the mountain and howled in my ears. I looked at the villages below and at the boats in the water.

Suddenly, I heard the creaking of the metal gate and jumped back from the boulder. Turning, I saw a black-robed monk. Shutting the gate, his back was turned toward me, his robe fluttering in the wind, causing his form to shift and change shape.

When he turned I saw that his long beard was mostly white, and though he was old he seemed to radiate strength and vitality. He gathered the ends of his robe in his hands and came toward me.

"*Yasas*," I called out to him, hello.

He returned my greeting. Then he said something in Greek that I did not understand. So I recited one of the few sentences I knew in Greek.

"I do not speak Greek," I told him. It pained me to have to say this, to have come to this man's lonely mountaintop and not be able to speak his language.

He shrugged as if to say it didn't matter.

It was then that I noticed the monk's eyes. At first I thought they struck me because they were dark as coal yet shone with a light that seemed more than that reflected by the sun. But then I realized his eyes did not both look in the same direction. His left eye was fixed on me, his right eye directed somewhere over my left shoulder, as if he were seeing something hovering there. And his dominant eye switched. He fixed me first with one eye then the other. It was an odd feeling, as if he were seeing something just on the periphery.

He came up beside me and looked out over the vista that fell away below our feet. Words were not necessary. Silence suited the place well. It was a good place for a monastery. Modern civilization had too often crowded in on other monasteries in Greece, such as the one on Corfu's west coast, surrounded now by tourist beaches. This place was different.

6

The monk turned to me, smiled, and asked if I wanted coffee. I said yes, and we walked through the ancient stone gate with ironwork doors and entered the monastery's courtyard.

A few stunted trees grew in the middle of the courtyard, on either side of which were long low buildings built right into the monastery's stone wall. Along the length of the buildings were doors that led into separate cells. Each cell had a single window, crosshatched by iron bars. At the far end of the courtyard a set of stairs ascended to a smaller courtyard and to the monastery's church. Obviously older than the other buildings, its walls were smooth and newly whitewashed and its roof was rounded in the Byzantine style. Higher than the older buildings, the church stood out sharply against the sky.

The monk's long robe played gracefully with the wind as I followed him across the courtyard. He led me into a simple, Spartan kitchen. A few pots and pans hung from nails driven into the whitewashed walls, and a large cupboard held cups and plates, bowls and silverware. A half-eaten loaf of bread lay upon a roughly hewn wooden table. Braided garlic hung from the ceiling. There was a two-burner gas stove, and over a stone sink was a single faucet. A window overlooking the courtyard provided the only light. Through the kitchen and into a narrow room with a low ceiling, he motioned me to sit on a bench before a table. Then he went back to the kitchen to brew coffee.

In the meantime, I took out my pocket English-Greek dictionary to work out a few simple questions to ask him about his life on the mountain. I could tell by the way he had looked out over the mountains that his love for the mountains mirrored my own. I wanted to know more about this man.

Soon he returned with two small cups of Greek coffee and sat down across the table from me.

"How old are you?" I asked.

"Sixty-one."

"How many years have you lived here?"
"Forty."
"How many other people live here?"
"None."
I looked up the word *alone*.
"Alone?" I asked.
"Yes," he replied.

The process of speaking with him was laborious. He knew not a single word of English. But he had patience. Once, when I couldn't understand one of his answers, he pulled out a pair of thick reading glasses from his robe, squinted into the tiny dictionary, and looked up the word. Then he pointed out its English equivalent.

After we drained our tiny cups to the thick black grounds, he brought out a bottle of ouzo and two small glasses. He filled each glass half-full with the clear liquid, then we clinked our glasses together. As we sipped our ouzo I asked him more questions, and though it was difficult, neither of us flagged. As I spent more time with him it became clear that he had a different relation to time than most people: for him, it seemed, time was unlimited. He drew patience from a well that knew no bottom.

This is what I found out from him: he was born and raised in Strinilas where two of his brothers still lived. He had a sister in Athens. His parents were dead, buried in the village cemetery. When he first moved to the monastery another monk lived there, a man whom he referred to as his teacher. They lived ten years together on the mountain. Then the older monk died. Since then he'd lived there alone. He was a *monohós* and a *papa,* a monk and a priest, the priest for Strinilas. He received money from the Greek Orthodox Church, but it wasn't much. The condition of his robe and the simplicity of his kitchen attested to this. He relied on the help and goodwill of the villagers. The people of Strinilas were good people, he told me, and his life had been good.

The man was as singular as the mountain; in fact, they

Windblown Clouds
Thomas K. Shor

shared certain features—some superficial, such as the furrowing lines that crossed his brow, so reminiscent of the well-worn fissures carved into the mountain's twisted rocks, and others that ran deep, as if the deeper the foundation, the wider and broader both the mountain and the man. Yet there was nothing grave about him. The lines on his face were not the lines of worry; they were not written in stone. Nothing seemed hardened in him. He was fluid. More than anything, he was full of life.

Once, when I chose a word that rendered my question an absurdity, he laughed so hard that I too couldn't help but laugh. When I found the correct word and put the question to him again, a knitted-brow concentration came over him as he sought an answer so simple that even *I* could understand. His face, like a child's, reflected directly the emotion he felt. When he told me his parents were dead, I saw the pain he felt at the loss, and when he said the people of Strinilas were good people, I saw the pride he felt for them.

I asked how old the monastery was. He waved his hand with his fingers outstretched as if to say the monastery's age was beyond reckoning. Then he crooked a finger and told me to follow him. Outside, we walked the length of the monastery's waist-high wall—a wall that dropped thirty feet before reaching the mountain's slope. Looking out over the plateau at the winding road I had just traversed, I realized it was from here I had seen the black figure, the monk I was now following.

He brought me to the brilliantly white church. Inside, my eyes at first were useless in the dim interior. I groped after the monk, our footfalls echoing hollowly. Shafts of light streamed in through high, slit-like windows, casting woven patterns of light upon the floor's cool stone slabs. The body of the church was empty, the arched ceiling painted with cracked and water-stained frescoes that depicted scenes from the life of Christ. From the walls hung icons, old and yellowed. Upon the altar, elevated by a single step, stood metal racks for candles. At the center of the altar an old and finely made wooden stand held a large, leather-bound Bible. The monk lit some candles, muttering a prayer beneath his breath.

Outside, we leaned against the wall near the kitchen. Below us, the mountain twisted and fell to the sea. I wondered how many monks had spent their lives contemplating this scene, one that I was seeing for the first time? I thought about the search for God that these heights had surely engendered in them. Certainly there are times when the very context of our lives is wider than everyday experience. And surely there are places that make this wider context manifest. From this mountaintop monastery I felt a glimmer of something vast.

Without really considering what I was doing, I looked up the words to ask the monk one very simple question: "Do you see God?"

I was young at the time. I still believed the answer to be within reach. I thought: If something underlies all-we-know, if there is a unity to be found within the diversity, and if it is possible to comprehend and experience that unity, then surely there must be people who have experienced it. These people would no doubt be rare, and they would have to have come to their realization by extraordinary means. And, further, it was reasonable to believe that they would have to live far from the distractions of a bustling world. It was my search for that experience, I then knew, that had drawn me to this mountaintop and why I was standing in the wind with this old monk.

I had put the words together from my dictionary. *Blepes Theo? Blepes,* you see; *Theo,* God. Do you see God?

My question caught him off guard. He flashed me a look like lightning. Then he waved his hands in front of him, as if to fend off the question.

I repeated the question. This time he pretended not to understand. I looked up the words again, and repeated each word distinctly.

He turned, looked steadily over the mountains, and let the silence speak what no words could communicate.

Suddenly I felt like the imprudent young American that I was, intruding upon ground I had no right to intrude upon. It was enough that he had shared the silence and peace of his monastery with me. I had gone a step too far in asking after the fruit of his many years of solitude.

I knew it was time to go.

I began the painstaking process of telling the monk I had to leave, that I had to go back to the village of Strinilas to search for a place to live. Again I felt badly for the intense concentration he had to maintain simply to understand me. But he was patient. He stumbled along with me as I looked up each word and constructed disjointed sentences. When he suddenly understood what I was trying to tell him his face lit up, he tapped a finger to his temple, and his eyes glimmered. He had an idea.

"*Éla mázi mu*," he said, come with me.

I followed him past the kitchen to the next door. He opened it and we entered a small cell. He made a gesture to encompass the room.

"You live here," he said.

I was sure I had misunderstood him. I tapped my chest. "*I*," I said. Then I held my open palm to the side of my head and inclined my head as if in sleep.

"Yes," he said, "yes, yes. You live here!"

He was speaking rapidly now. Greek flew over my head as my legs almost buckled beneath me. I could hear my heart pounding as if I were riding the crest of a wave, the wave of certainty that had driven me up the mountain. So this is it, I said to myself: I didn't even have to ask for it.

He stepped aside so I could examine the room.

The room was about twelve foot square and sparsely furnished. To the left of the door stood a bed made of roughly cut wooden planks on which a thin foam mattress lay. Above the bed, the room's only window looked out over the courtyard. Running almost the entire length of the room along the back wall was a long table and bench. A chair stood at the table's head. The room's whitewashed walls were rough, as was the ceiling, which was quite low. I stumbled back out into the courtyard, my mind stunned by his offer, my eyes smarting from the sun.

The monk followed me. He could wait no longer. "You like?" he asked.

"Yes," I said. "I like. Much I like."

"*Éla mázi mu,*" he said again, come with me. So I followed him into the kitchen. He picked up a box of matches, pretended to light a match, and pretended to light the gas burner. Then he put a big frying pan over an imagined flame. He diced some imaginary vegetables then tested the pan to make sure it was hot. He put the cut vegetables into the pan, stirred them with an imaginary spoon, and then divided them between two imaginary plates. He then pretended to eat. All the while he hummed softly to himself, absorbed in his culinary arts and pleased that he had found a way to show me that we could eat our meals together in the kitchen. It was a great performance. I clapped. He took a bow. We both laughed.

Then he showed me the outhouse. It was perched so precariously over a steep abyss that the hole in the floor seemed to open to eternity.

We crossed the courtyard. I was overwhelmed. My mind was swimming. He stopped and waited till I was fully facing him. He fixed me with his left eye, his right eye looking over my shoulder. He asked, "You live here?"

"Yes," I said.

He clapped me forcefully on the shoulder with his open palm. "Good," he said. "Good!" He told me I could move in any time. I told him I'd return within the week. Standing at the gate, he told me to wait. He rushed to the kitchen and returned a moment later with a handful of shelled almonds. I filled my shirt pocket.

When the monk was out of sight I ran to an outcropping on the side of the mountain and let out the joyous shout that I'd been holding back since he'd first opened the door to the cell and said, "You live here." I jumped from boulder to boulder then ran back to the road. Stopping at the house by the unkempt terraced fields, I looked up and saw him leaning over the wall at the mountain's summit. I waved my arms over my head, and he returned my farewell.

7

By the time I was walking up the path to the house in Kontokali it was late afternoon. Andy and Ann were sitting on the front step, and when I reached them Andy said, "You'll never guess what happened to us today. Even when we tell you, you won't believe it."

"You won't believe what happened to *me*," I said. "Let me tell you first." So I told them how I had gone up the mountain, met the monk, and been invited to live there with him. They became as excited as I was over the events of my day. We made coffee, reestablished our perch on the front step, and Andy recounted his own story that seemed even more unbelievable than mine.

First he described the beginning of a typical, lazy day in Kontokali. They had slept late, eaten fresh figs smeared on toast, done a bit of laundry in the stone basin behind the house, then eaten lunch. After lunch they decided to take a walk. Calling their cat—who always enjoyed going on walks—they were about to leave when they heard voices in the olive grove.

It was Giorgos, and he was not alone. An army general, in full military regalia, and two Greek soldiers, each shouldering an end of the same wooden ladder, accompanied him. Approaching the house, the general greeted Andy and Ann in English, which they both took as a bad sign. What did an

Windblown Clouds

Thomas K. Shor

English-speaking general want with *them?* The general explained to them that he had learned English in the United States while visiting his brother, who owned a pizzeria in New Jersey, which put them at ease. While Andy and Ann and the general discussed pizza in the United States, Giorgos instructed the soldiers where to place the ladder.

The general excused himself. First Giorgos climbed the ladder and peered into the hole. He came down, muttered something to the general. Then the general climbed the ladder, peered into the hole, came down, and muttered something to the soldiers.

Unable to watch this strange ritual repeated over and over again, Andy and Ann went into the kitchen. But after almost half an hour, Andy began to wonder what was taking them so long. He went to the back door just in time to see the army general backing down the ladder, cradling in his arms an old and rusted metal cylinder. When the general reached the ground, he yelled out, "Hey, you! You better look out. I have a *bomb!*"

"*Right,*" Andy said, and hurried back into the kitchen. When Andy told Ann what the general had told him, Ann convinced Andy that he had misunderstood. A bomb—now *that* was absurd.

After another twenty minutes they decided to take that walk. They called the cat again and went out the front door. But as they rounded the corner of the house they heard a gunshot followed by an enormous explosion. The concussive wave that followed almost swept them off their feet. The cat screeched and shot off down the hill, (it still hadn't returned while they were telling me the story). Andy and Ann, shaken, hid behind the corner of the house, and when they dared to poke their heads around the corner they saw a mushroom-shaped cloud of smoke rising from the olive grove. Giorgos, the general, and the soldiers soon appeared, jauntily walking back toward the house, their faces flushed with triumph.

Giorgos explained to them what had happened: During

World War II the Italians occupied Corfu. The Corfiots resisted in whatever way they could, though being an unarmed civilian population there wasn't much they could do. The Italians camped everywhere and caused trouble wherever they went. Some camped in the olive grove in front of the house. Giorgo's uncle couldn't help but notice that the troops in front of his family's house were guarding a stockpile of bombs. So he did what any resourceful person might do under the circumstances: one night, after the troops had drunk themselves into oblivion, he stole one of the bombs and hid it in the roof. He then waited for an opportunity to use it on the foreign aggressors. But alas, the opportunity never arose. The Italians withdrew, and the memory of the bomb died with the uncle some years later, leaving behind a family legend that no one really believed. That is, until the jockey-sized roofer removed the tiles to examine the condition of the beams and discovered it.

This explained so much. It explained why Giorgos had been so adamant that Andy and Ann vacate the room. It explained why the police had come, then the army general. And it explained why the roof's condition was such a concern to all of them. The only thing it didn't explain was why Giorgos hadn't warned us sooner.

Giorgos explained: "I didn't want to scare you."

It was one hell of a crazy day.

While I prepared dinner, Andy and Ann walked to the village to buy cigarettes. When I heard them coming up the path I grabbed a lantern and greeted them at the door.

"Perfect timing!" I yelled into the darkness. "Dinner is ready."

Ann said, "Hold your horses, it can wait, you'd better sit down." I sat. "I'm going to London!" Ann blurted out.

"You're *what?*" I said.

"I'm London bound. I'm going on Monday. There was a guy hanging out at the kiosk, looking for someone to buy the return half of his airplane ticket. He came from London on a two-week holiday, met a woman on a sailboat, and now he is sailing off with her to Crete. He was desperate to sell it. He only wanted the equivalent of twenty dollars. It was an offer we couldn't refuse. We've been planning to go for Christmas anyway, to visit my mother and get more of our stuff. We won't stay as long as Christmas, but this way we can both fly."

"Both?" I said.

"Yes," Andy said, "it's so cheap that now I can get a normal flight—and we'll *still* be saving money."

"There is only one hitch," Ann said tentatively.

"Yes," Andy said, "there's just one favor…"

"Well," I said, "what is it?"

"We need someone to watch over the place and feed the cat."

"*Óxi problema,*" I said. "No problem. The monastery's been on the mountain for over half a millennium. It'll be there. I can wait."

After dinner we decided to go to bed early before anything else could happen.

~

The next few days went off without a hitch. Andy secured a seat on a plane to London the following Saturday; it wasn't as soon as he would have liked, but it would do. I went up the mountain to tell the monk I'd be delayed a few weeks. Luckily, I stopped off at the *kafeneo* in Strinilas. The owner guessed correctly that I was the *"filos tu papa,"* the friend of the priest. News of my coming had spread. He told me the monk was in Corfu Town for his monthly meeting with all the other priests and monks on the island. He promised to give my message to him when he returned.

8

Monday morning, the day Ann went to London, I awoke from a deep sleep in time to see Andy helping Ann with her bag. They went out the door at dawn. At nine o'clock Ann would leave Corfu. I fell easily back asleep as Andy and Ann walked to the bus stop where Ann would take the bus to town.

When Andy returned I stirred again from sleep. I saw him go back to his bedroom. The sky was brighter now—pink and red. I heard roosters in the distance. I drifted back to sleep again.

I awoke with a start. Someone was pounding on the door. Pulling on my clothes, I stumbled into the main room; Andy came out of his room as well, sleep still in his eyes. Together we opened the door.

It was Giorgos. He told us the police had just come to his house looking for Andy, and though we couldn't get his story straight, it sounded serious. We both wished Ann were there to translate.

Then it occurred to us that maybe something had happened to Ann. We tried to get more details from Giorgos, but we gave up. Thanking Giorgos, we reassured him that Andy would go to the police station in town. I made coffee as Andy washed, shaved, and put on clean clothes: he had to look presentable for the police.

We caught the bus to town, and while Andy went to the police station I went to the Chess Café to wait for him.

About an hour later I was sitting at our usual table, a game of chess set up before me, when Andy walked in, his face deadly pale. Slouching in the chair opposite me, he reached out his hand, lifted the king, and laid it on its side.

"The game's over," he said.

"What do you mean?"

"Just that," he said. "I'm being kicked out of the country."

"What?"

"Remember the last form, the one that still had to be approved, the one that had to go to Athens?"

"Yeah—what about it?"

"You know the one," Andy continued as if he hadn't heard me, "the residence permit, the one we were going for in the *first* place, the one that we were trying to *get* by starting a business? The Main Man explained to me that a residence permit must gain approval from many government agencies in Athens before it's issued, one of which is the secret police. That's where mine caught a snag. They rejected my permit. But it wasn't only rejected—it's not as simple as that—that would have been too easy! They sent word to the Main Man to kick me out of the country. 'You must go, you must leave Corfu,' he said. I asked him why the secret police wanted me out. He said he didn't know, or he couldn't tell me—I couldn't tell which he meant. The *secret police!* Apparently, they don't have to give a reason. That's why they're called the *secret* police. They do as they like. *They* answer no questions. They're like the CIA, but even more sleazy, more secretive. They're probably a holdover from the days of the colonels. Everybody is afraid of them. Even the Main Man. I could tell. It was strange, but he treated me as if I posed some kind of danger to the welfare of the country."

"But—" I said, unable to complete my sentence. "This is madness! Did he say when you have to go?"

Andy sighed. "He sure did, and here's how he decided: in a haphazard way, as if he were daydreaming, he flipped through his calendar and stopped at the page for Thursday. He pointed at it. I told him I already had a reservation on a plane for London on Saturday. But he said, 'No. You must go. You must leave Corfu—here,' and he pointed again to Thursday."

A wave of indignation swept over me, a flood of moral outrage. "They can't just kick you out like that!" I said. "What about the business, the time you've spent, all the forms, the stamps of approval, and the money you've sunk into it, all those lawyer's fees? Think of the loom—and don't forget the wool; maybe it's even waiting for you in Ioánnina. They can't *do* that."

But of course they could. What I said was absurd, wasted energy. Secret police, I discovered at that moment, dwell beyond the moral sphere.

Andy ordered a cup of coffee. We sat in silence till it arrived, staring dumbly at the old men slapping cards on the other tables. I could tell by the look on his face that Andy was asking himself if this might be the last time he would see the players' antics, if we had already played our last game of chess in the Chess Café.

When Andy's coffee arrived I said, "We've got to fight it."

"I know," he said, though his heart didn't sound in it. "But how?" Andy asked. "The worst part is that Ann isn't here. When I arrived at the police station, I had to wait for the Main Man to see me. I was standing on a balcony on the station's second floor. I looked at my watch. It was exactly nine o'clock. Then I heard the plane, *her* plane, taking off from the airport. It flew right over the police station. I think if Ann had been looking out the window, we could have waved to each other. An instant later the Main Man called me into his office. He sat me down. And then, with no preliminary, he said, 'You must leave Corfu.' His timing was impeccable. I think he planned it that way."

A look of despair crossed Andy's face. "God," he said. "Maybe—behind the smiling and helpful front he presented to us every morning during all those months—the Main Man knew that this would be the final outcome. Maybe he woke this morning with a smile on his face, knowing today was the big day." Andy sighed again. "I can tell you this," he said, "we have a battle ahead of us."

~

During the days that followed we spent most of our waking hours at the telephone exchange inside adjacent wooden booths dialing, dialing, and dialing, getting busy signals and then dialing again. Telephoning off the Island of Corfu was a horrendous task. There couldn't have been more than a single line laid under the sea to the mainland. It was like playing the lottery—or Russian roulette—but instead of our fingers pulling a trigger, our trigger finger went the rounds of the rotary dial, hoping for a happy outcome. I dialed the same number so many times that I feared the number would be etched forever in my memory. I feared the harsh and annoying busy signal would haunt my dreams till my dying day.

Our first call was to the American Embassy in Athens. When we finally got through, Andy described the situation to one of the attachés, who agreed to investigate. He told Andy to call back later that day.

Next we went to Andy's lawyer to see if there was any legal recourse. The lawyer said there probably wasn't. He offered to call the Main Man for the details of the ruling. The biggest hope he could offer was that *perhaps* we could appeal.

Back at the telephone exchange we attempted to call Ann in London. It took us almost three hours to get through to her. Andy told her the bad news. He filled her in on all the sordid details. He told her we'd call the next day.

A quick trip back to the lawyer offered no great hope. The Main Man, the lawyer informed us, was merely acting on orders given by the secret police, and their rulings were usually as incontestable as they were secret. The lawyer tried to get Andy to confess to the crime that the secret police must have uncovered. The lawyer told us that if he knew the offense, then perhaps he could help. But without as much as a single unpaid parking ticket to blight his record, Andy hadn't a thing to confess. This only seemed to raise the lawyer's suspicions.

Back at the telephone exchange, our fingers were becoming stiff from dialing. When Andy got through to the embassy, the attaché said he was still looking into the matter, and that Andy should call back the next morning. At this point, Andy became upset. He told the attaché he didn't have too many mornings left; he reminded him again of the Thursday deadline and implored him to work quickly. The attaché said he understood and hung up.

Exhausted, we walked out of the telephone exchange. We wandered aimlessly through the streets and alleyways of

Corfu. I remembered just that morning lying on my bed and gently falling in and out of sleep as Ann made ready for her trip to London. Already, it seemed as if a week had passed since Giorgos pounded on our door with the news that the police were searching for Andy. It was hard to fathom the level of concentration that we had maintained during the course of a single day. Bleary eyed, the busy signal ringing in my ears, my senses were still sharp, *too* sharp, perhaps, especially when we passed a small taverna and wisps of delicious-smelling smoke wafted through the restaurant's open doorway. Unable to resist the temptation, I tugged on Andy's sleeve and we veered inside.

We followed our noses to the kitchen, pointed out what we wanted from large, steaming pots on the stove, ordered beer, and sat down at a table near the front of the taverna. We drank our beer slowly, staring out the restaurant's open door.

Directly across the narrow street was a vegetable shop, next to which was a small shop that sold hardware. It was late in the day and business was slow. The two shop owners had pulled their stools onto the sidewalk. They sat talking to each other while smoking cigarettes, as a veritable parade of humanity passed on the street.

A boy no more than five years old came running up the street, chasing a puppy. First he and the puppy passed us from right to left; a moment later the puppy came running by again, the boy close behind. Then the boy and the puppy caught the attention of the shop owners across the street, and we could see them laughing at something just out of our view. Soon we saw what they were laughing at: the boy and puppy came back, but this time the boy was first and the puppy was nipping at his heels. The poor kid looked terrified, the puppy triumphant. We were still laughing over this scene when we saw the boy's angry mother march by with the puppy under one arm and the boy under the other.

The moment they were out of view an old woman appeared, leading a donkey over laden with burlap sacks.

Then a man on a bicycle appeared, holding a large bag crooked in his arm. Swerving around an old man walking with the aid of a cane, the man on the bicycle startled the donkey, and the donkey dropped its load. The bicyclist stopped, the old woman yelled, and the old man, oblivious to everything, hobbled away. The woman and the bicyclist began to argue, gesturing wildly with their arms, as a policeman came walking along the street. The woman appealed to him, pantomiming the entire story. With this, the two shop owners got into the fray. They pointed at the donkey and the sacks. Then the shop owners, the bicyclist, and the policeman loaded the sacks onto the donkey, and the old woman led the donkey away.

When our meal came, Andy and I spoke of what a wonderful documentary film one might make depicting life on Corfu by simply mounting a camera in this (or any other) taverna and letting the film role. It was our only moment of respite in an otherwise difficult day.

9

Next morning we headed straight for the telephone exchange and hammered away in our separate booths until we got through to the embassy in Athens. The attaché told Andy he had spoken to one of the officials at the secret police, who would only confirm the ruling in the case. He further speculated that, since Andy's background was clean, the decision to kick him out of the country was political.

The general election in Greece was only a few months away, and it looked as if PASOK, the socialist party, would gain control of the country. Since PASOK was anti-American, the attaché theorized that the official at the secret police responsible for issuing the order to deport Andy had probably wanted to secure his position under the new regime by having it on his record that he had kicked out an American. The attaché ended the conversation abruptly by stating that the

Windblown Clouds   Thomas K. Shor

embassy never interfered in Greek internal affairs.

We walked outside. Andy said, "It feels as if the noose is tightening. I think it's time we call in the reinforcements. We've got to pull out our trump card."

"What do you mean?" I asked.

Andy told me that Jordan, a close friend of the family, had been working with the Greek government, promoting American businesses in Greece. Jordan had told Andy that if he ever ran into trouble, he should call him. "I think it is time to make that call," Andy said.

We decided the best way to contact Jordan was to have Ann contact him first from London, where calls go through in a single dialing. When we finally got through to her, Ann told Andy she'd call him. Andy said to Ann that we'd call her back in a few hours.

In the mean time, we did some shopping and checked our mail at the post office. Andy received a note from the wool dyer in Ioánnina, which we had translated. The wool was ready and waiting in Igumenitsa, the port on the mainland about half an hour's boat ride from Corfu. How incredibly ironic, we thought, that the wool was finally ready just as Andy was being kicked out of the country.

We went to the port and studied the ferryboat schedule to Igumenitsa. We decided that Andy had just enough time to take the ferry to the mainland to get the wool before we had to call Ann. So he set off for the mainland as I went to Kontokali to put the food away and feed the cat. Andy arrived home with five big sacks of wool whose fate was as uncertain as his own. We rushed back to town to launch our next offensive at the telephone exchange, which was beginning to feel more like home than our quiet abode in the olive grove.

This time the telephone exchange was busy; we had to wait a long time just to get a booth. As Andy dialed, I talked to a Frenchman who had been trying to call Paris for three days. I believed him. His disheveled clothes and stubble beard attested to his struggle. Somehow, quite miraculously—and to the great distress of the Frenchman—Andy got through to London in less than half an hour. Ann told him she had talked to Jordan. She had the name and number of a high official in the embassy in Athens whom, Jordan had said, he would have briefed by the time we could get through to him. So we dialed Athens.

The official that Andy contacted said he would try to use his influence on the secret police and that we should sit tight. He told Andy not to worry about the Thursday deadline. Nobody, he said, would bother him if he stayed a few extra days.

So the war went on. We were in the trenches now, fighting the final campaign. We had called in the reinforcements and the special diplomatic teams. We made another trip to the lawyer to update him on recent developments. He agreed with the official at the embassy that Andy could stretch the Thursday deadline by a few days, but Andy was leery. It was fine that the embassy and his lawyer said he could stretch it, but what about the Main Man, the one who would come to get him? He might not agree. We went home. Andy packed. He left his bag by the back door just in case.

The next day was Thursday, Andy's deadline. We woke early and took the bus to town. Everywhere eyes seemed to follow us. At the edge of town, a man dressed in a dark business suit got on the bus. He was holding a hat under his arm, and he put it on. It was a policeman's hat. Both our hearts were pounding. The bus stopped at a light, and when the light turned green, Andy jumped from the bus.

We met at the telephone exchange. Jordan's mysterious friend at the embassy said he was unable to influence the decision handed down by the secret police. He said he was sorry, but there was nothing more he could do.

That was it. We had pulled our last string and it had failed. We went to a travel agent and changed Andy's reservation to the next day, Friday. Then we dialed London to tell Ann the bad news.

Ann had talked to Jordan again. He had one other friend in the Greek government who could possibly help us. Jordan said his friend was already 'working on it.' Ann gave us the man's number, though Jordan had refused to give the man's name. So we called our last hope in Athens.

If Jordan's friend at the embassy had sounded like a spy, this man, according to Andy, sounded like the ringleader of the entire spy organization. According to Andy, it had sounded as if he were talking from an underground bunker, his voice seldom rising above a whisper. His manner was curt. He told my brother that he was investigating the case and we should call back at three o'clock that afternoon.

So we wandered around town. Andy said good-bye to friends. At three o'clock we got through to the man in Athens. He said there was nothing he could do. Andy told him the Embassy's theory about the upcoming election, but the man in the Greek government dismissed it. "If that were the only reason," he said, "I would certainly have been able to intervene. But they have certain *information*." He would say no more.

Now the game really *was* over. We had called all the resources at our disposal, to no avail. Even the mysterious high official—the man we imagined speaking from the underground bunker—could do nothing. Later, we found out that he was Greece's finance minister.

I went home and Andy went to the police station to tell the Main Man he need not come to get him since he would be leaving the next day on his own volition. When Andy returned he told me the Main Man was apologetic to him. He also offered some friendly advice: he told Andy that if he stayed out of the country for a week or two he could return on a regular tourist visa. And although he now could not work in Greece, he could spend another three months on Corfu. Andy decided he would see how Ann felt about returning. In a few days, they would send me a telegram from London.

Windblown Clouds

Thomas K. Shor

Friday was a black day. We were both exhausted from the fight. Now that it was over we both felt deflated. I helped Andy down the hill with his luggage. We rode the bus to town in silence, and after a few words of farewell he was gone.

With a lump in my throat, I wandered aimlessly around the winding alleys of Corfu Town. At the port, I watched an old man sitting on a crate, fishing. Waves lapped gently against the landing. Across the bay, the mountain Pantokrator rose in its solitary gray silence.

Back in Kontokali, I felt strange to be alone in the house. I lit a lantern and cooked a meal. The cat came in and I gave it some of the tiny fish that it loved. I kept reminding myself that Andy and Ann might very well be coming back in a week or so. Now I just had to wait for their telegram.

~

Later that evening I sat at the table to read by the light of the lantern when the cat jumped inside through an open window and ran beneath the table. I started playing with it, rolling it around with my bare feet, when I realized the cat wasn't really playing with me. Something cool moved across my skin and slithered between my toes. I lifted the lantern, brought it low beside me, and leaned over. A shriek spontaneously burst from my lips as I fell backwards, my chair splintering beneath me. My cry and the sound of splintering wood startled the cat, but it continued to claw at the small green snake that was desperately trying to free itself from the cat's grip.

I took a leg of what was once my chair and brought it down with accuracy on the snake's head, killing it instantly. I fell back on the floor, and, gasping for breath, tried to remember what someone had once told me about snakes on Corfu. The ones no thicker than a pencil, I dimly remembered, were deadly poisonous.

I wrapped the snake in a piece of newspaper so I could show it to someone next morning. In the mean time, I tried to be calm and rational. I told myself that I had never seen a snake in the house before. I probably never would again. But my sleep was disturbed that night by dreams so vivid that I awoke many times unsure whether the snakes I saw crawling across the floor were real or imagined.

~

Next morning I took the snake in the crumpled piece of newspaper down the path to the pig farm. The farmer's wife was out feeding the chickens. When I approached her and unfolded the paper, she jumped back, gasped, and shrieked, "*Estreetas!*"

This brought her husband running from the barn. As the farmer's wife pointed to the mangled snake, the farmer put his hand to his forehead and exclaimed, "*Po, po, po,*" as if he were going to faint. He asked where I had found it. I pointed up the hill and said *spiti moo*, my house. "Inside?" he asked. I nodded.

His wife shook her head. "*Kako, kako, kako,*" she said, bad, bad, bad. Her husband joined in. They both stood there shaking their heads, saying, "Bad, bad, bad!" Then the farmer made a motion like a snake striking, and he said, "One hour and—KAPUT!"

I continued down the hill to the village. I had to investigate. I had to find out how the villagers kept snakes away from their houses, and what they did if bitten. Until I knew all there was to know, I couldn't sleep in that house again.

First I went to Dimitris, the man who ran the taverna where I had stayed during my first trip to Corfu. He spoke English fluently and had a good head on his shoulders. He was a real solid citizen. I was hoping he'd tell me that the people at the pig farm had exaggerated, that there were no snakes on Corfu that could do away with one with such haste. But when I told him that the farmer's wife at the pig farm had yelled *estreetas*, he winced. He translated the word for me: viper. He said one's only hope when bitten by one of these snakes was to get to the hospital for an anti-venom injection within one hour. Otherwise, that hour would be your last. It would also be your most painful.

He told me a couple of stories about snakes in general and vipers in particular. They were horrible stories, enough to make my blood run cold. He told me that snakes are attracted to milk. When he was a young boy, a woman in the village was working in a field with her infant child. She breast fed him and left him on a blanket at the field's edge. A while later she returned to see a snake slithering down the sleeping baby's throat, following the scent of milk.

After a while I implored Dimitris to stop. "OK, you've convinced me," I said. "These snakes are a menace, they kill children, little babies barely out of their mother's wombs, but surely there is something one can do to keep them away."

"You're right," Dimitris replied. "The women burn something at the beginning of snake season every year. I'm not sure what they burn. It's women's duty. Let's go ask my mother."

So we went across the road to the village well where we found Dimitri's mother along with other village women. They were drawing water in buckets to wash clothes. Dimitris spoke to the women in Greek, explaining what had happened to me the night before. They listened to him, their mouths gaping. Then they crossed themselves and gasped. Pushing past Dimitris, they surrounded me, shaking their open hands toward the heavens. They spoke to me all at once. I knew I was in trouble.

Dimitris interrupted them and translated for me. He said: "They say you should never kill the first snake you find in your house. You should show it out the door with kind words and a gentle request never to return. If you kill the first snake, all the other snakes will know it, and you'll never be rid of them. You have to make peace with the snake world, that's what they're saying; make violence toward snakes and that violence will be returned."

"Ask them," I implored, "what they burn to keep them

away." Dimitris asked them, and then he translated. "They say you must burn leather shoes, old leather shoes, shoes that have been worn for years and have been run right to the ground. The smellier and more filled with holes the better." As he told me this, the women nodded their heads in agreement and pointed at their feet.

I thanked Dimitris and the women and proceeded to take the bus to town in search of old leather shoes. My first stop was the shop of Giorgos the sandal maker. Although Giorgo's shop was no larger than a closet, he produced the finest sandals on all Corfu. A local legend, he was known to drink ouzo as if it were water. I walked into his shop and found him sitting on a stool surrounded by piles of leather and balls of leather chord. Before I could say *yasas*, he stood and asked if I wanted ouzo. Giorgos transacted no business before drinking with a customer. We chugged the contents of our glasses in a single slug, and then he asked what he could do for me.

Recounting the events of the previous evening, I told him the advice of the village women. I ended with a plea for old leather shoes. But I could tell what I said bothered him. "Those women no right," he said. "Burn old shoes, yes. But leather ones—NO!" He was roaring now. "Not leather shoes. *Plastic* shoes. You burn old plastic shoes!"

"Giorgos," I said, "how can this be true? Plastic is simply plastic. It isn't biodegradable." But Giorgos repeated his words as if they were a firm religious conviction written on a tablet of stone: "You must burn old *plastic* shoes."

I asked him if he had any old plastic shoes he didn't need. "No!" he boomed, bringing his fist down on his workbench. I had really insulted him now. Asking a leather craftsman for plastic shoes—an unforgivable blasphemy. I asked him for some leather scraps just in case they *did* work against snakes. He grudgingly gave me a few handfuls, which I stuffed into my pockets.

Slinking down alleyways, market streets, and behind buildings, I looked in dumpsters, trashcans, and gutters for old, worn out, and discarded shoes. I searched for leather shoes, plastic shoes—it mattered little to me. The more people I asked what material to burn to drive away snakes, the further, I knew, I would be drawing myself into the controversy of folklore, a fascinating study in itself, but not my present and immediate aim, which was to drive away snakes. Since I had broken the cardinal rule—namely killing the first snake found in the house—the mixture I burned would have to be particularly noxious. I found a surprising number of old shoes, both leather and plastic, and I rounded off my collection with miscellaneous bits of plastic and paper. Then I returned to Kontokali.

As I walked along the path to the house I shied away from low branches and bushes. Surveying each step for lurking danger, I was held in sway by that dark corner of the mind that harbors an instinctual fear of snakes.

We burned our trash in an old olive oil tin we left in the high grass behind the house. Lifting it now, I stood transfixed, staring at the spot where the tin had been. There, coiled in a perfect spiral, was another green snake. The snake lifted its head slowly, as if I had awakened it from an age-long slumber, flashed its tongue at me twice, and lazily slithered off into the grass. I stared at the flattened, matted grass where it had been sleeping, and I realized I could no longer stay there. The snakes had won.

I packed enough clothes and books for a long stay in town and left. I checked into the Cyprus Hotel. There, at least, I could go barefoot.

10

Andy and Ann's promised telegram arrived the next day. It said they would arrive on Corfu the following Monday. This meant I had to spend another week at the Cyprus Hotel. Once they arrived, I would go to live on the mountain.

On Tuesday and Thursday of the following week I went

Windblown Clouds

Thomas K. Shor

briefly to the house in Kontokali to feed the cat. On Sunday, the day before their return, I mustered enough courage to burn the anti-snake mixture. Bringing the smoking olive oil tin inside the house, I let it smolder for five minutes in each room. By the time I had extinguished the small fire in the tin, I had a horrendous headache.

Preparing to leave the house, I heard someone call my name. It was our landlord Giorgos, and the moment I saw the look on his face I knew there was trouble. He was speaking quickly. It was difficult for me to understand him. But then he said *astinomía,* the word for police. That word I knew. He insisted I follow him to his house in the village.

Inside his house and through the kitchen, where his wife was preparing Sunday dinner, he sat me on a straight-back wooden chair on a step outside the back door, and there he left me—alone, on the threshold, like a stray dog he'd decided to keep on a leash. If I leaned forward on the chair, I could watch Giorgo's wife tending to the pans of roasting meats. Wafting my way, the smell of her cooking drove me mad with hunger.

Guests began to arrive—Giorgo's parents, grown children, grandchildren, uncles, aunts, and cousins. Each one shot me a furtive glance before going inside the house. I could tell that none of them knew why I was sitting alone on a chair just outside the kitchen door. And indeed I must have looked as forlorn and unsure of myself as I felt. Anticipating the police at any moment, I just wanted to get it over with.

Giorgo's daughter spoke English. When she arrived, I implored her to ask her father what the police wanted with me. When she returned from the kitchen, she said simply that earlier that morning a policeman had come to the house looking for me. I asked her why, but she didn't know. Or maybe she didn't want to tell me. She did tell me the police would be back soon.

Then Giorgos came out with one of his ancient uncles, a living relic, no doubt, of an earlier age. A wild and unkempt shock of gray hair covered his head, and a huge waxed mustache his upper lip. Placing a chair next to mine, Giorgos helped his uncle to sit. He handed us each an empty glass then filled our glasses from a full bottle of ouzo. He put the bottle on the floor between us and left us to our own resources. The old man cracked a smile, lifted his glass, and said, "To life!" "To life," I said, and gulped down the ouzo.

When the meal was ready, Giorgo's wife insisted that Giorgos couldn't just leave me alone by the door. Since they didn't know what else to do with me, they invited me to partake in their feast.

Giorgo's wife had cooked a massive leg of lamb, small fried fish, moussaka, spinach and cheese pies, and a host of other dishes I couldn't begin to name. The smell of the roasted meat made my mouth water, and the juices in my stomach flowed in happy anticipation. I could not believe my good fortune. To top this, Giorgos showed me to the seat of honor at the head of the table. The plates and silverware were so fine and old and delicate that they looked like they might have been part of the dowry of someone who had died before Giorgo's grandparents were even born. Giorgos loaded my plate with food and set it before me. He filled my glass with a powerful homemade wine he had opened especially for the occasion. He made me drain my glass as he watched, then filled it again to the brim. After a few rounds, I had the distinct feeling that he was trying to loosen me up for my approaching encounter with the police.

Giorgos piled more and more food onto my plate, as if he were fattening me for slaughter. Every time my glass was half-empty, he filled it again, as the ancient uncle, with whom I had drunk ouzo, looked at me sympathetically. Even Giorgo's youngest grandson, who was only a toddler, pretended to pout as he gazed my way. They all seemed to say, gazing with sudden, sullen looks: It's too bad what's about to happen to you, but who among us can change fate? All the while, I had one eye on the front window, waiting to see the police car outside.

A car finally did pull up to the house, but if it were indeed a police car, then it was like no other police car I had seen before. From the unmarked, black Mercedes Benz, a middle-aged man wearing a gray suit and dark glasses approached the house. Giorgos stood up, motioned for me to follow, and we went out to meet my fate.

In perfect English, the policeman first asked me what I was doing on Corfu. Then he got down to business. He wanted to know whether Andy and Ann were planning to come back to the island. I couldn't lie to him. I told him they were due to arrive the next day. He said, "When they come, they may stay two days, maybe three. They can pick up their belongings—but then they must go. They must leave Corfu! They must leave Corfu, and they must never return! Is this clear?"

"Y-yes," I stammered.

With that he got back into his black Mercedes Benz and sped off.

I turned to Giorgos. He managed a weak smile. Saying how sorry he was for me and how sorry he was for Andy and Ann, he led me back to my place of honor at the head of the table. Filling my own glass now with the powerful homemade wine, I finished off the business Giorgos had begun. And while I could still lift myself from the table, I thanked my hosts and wound my way back up the hill to the house.

~

After sleeping off the effects of Giorgo's wine at the house in Kontokali, (snakes, at that moment, were not on my mind), I closed up the house and returned to my room at the Cyprus. I slept again and woke when it was dark. Then, wanting to take along books to read while on the mountain, I went to the library of the Anglican Church, which was only open on Sunday evenings.

Built when the English ruled the island, the Anglican Church of Corfu, as well as many of its members, were of a time, it seemed to me, more in tune with the past. During

Windblown Clouds   Thomas K. Shor

Sunday evening library sessions, the members, it seemed, tried to keep alive the air of their formal colonial rule over the island. From their conversations, it was obvious to me that they dreaded where they were, as if powers beyond their control had forced them to brave harsh conditions amongst a horde of simple-minded natives. Here they considered themselves elite; if still in control, they would no doubt set straight the backward ways of a country on the fringe of civilized Europe. Yet everyone at the church lived on Corfu by his own choice. Some worked in the British Consulate, others taught English, and still others had retired to Corfu where their pensions allowed a life of regality in villas with ocean views, not to mention a staff of gardeners, maids, cooks, and drivers.

That evening the gathering had a good turnout. Twenty-five to thirty people stood in tight circles, chatting. It looked like a cocktail party, and, like times before, I noted that not one person browsed the bookshelves that lined each wall. Books, in this library, were of secondary importance.

I approached the grandmotherly woman whose duty it was to bake cookies, make tea, and check books in and out of the library each Sunday evening. Handing her the three books I had to return, she opened a box of filing cards—which she guarded with as much zeal as a hen protecting its eggs—and began to search for my name. The only problem was, the books were filed under the author's name, not the reader's, a mistake, I noted, she made each week. I let her search for my personal index card until she was convinced it wasn't there then reminded her it was the author, not the reader that she had to look for. She tapped her forehead. "Ah, that's right," she said. "I always forget, don't I?" I smiled. She found the right cards and checked in the books. Closing the box, she said to me, "I want to introduce you to our new vicar. He's a *very* nice man." She brought me to the circle of people that had formed around the vicar then tottered back to her booth and her box of index cards.

Windblown Clouds — Thomas K. Shor

Because the congregation of the Anglican Church was not large enough to support a full-time vicar, one was sent each month from England. The vicar—and his family if he had one—occupied the apartment above the church and was treated like a visiting dignitary. For the visiting vicar, the one-month sojourn on Corfu was akin to an exotic paid vacation, the only official business being Sunday sermons, and the remainder of the time allotted to seeing the sights. Occasionally, a vicar felt it his duty to see to the well being of his parishioners, as well as the needy of the island.

Back from a recent visit to the hospital in town, this vicar was recounting to the wary group of tea-drinkers stories of unfortunate foreigners who had fallen ill or had taken accident on Corfu. For example: a German man, who, when given an injection—an injection for what I did not know— had had an allergic reaction and lost his leg. Amidst the murmurs, I asked the vicar the type of injection that had made the unfortunate German lose his leg. "The anti-venom serum, of course," the vicar said. "He had been bitten by a snake, a particularly nasty viper. It's the little ones, you know, that are dangerous." Then he told me of an even less fortunate man, a Greek, who had also been bitten by a snake but had arrived at the hospital too late. He had died before the serum had had time to take effect.

"I'm glad it was the Greek who died and not the German," the vicar continued. "I'd much rather have someone die in his own country. Then I don't have to deal with the box. The box is so messy. Too much paperwork. The letter to the family and all...

"It doesn't really matter to me what country a foreigner is from or what church he attends. If he's in hospital, I'll try to comfort him. And if he has to go home in the box, I'll see to the details and write the letter to the family. I don't like it, though. But it's what I must do. The church doesn't send me here just to loll in the sun." He stopped a moment to reflect. Then he said, "And what do you do here on Corfu?"

I was aghast at his matter-of-fact attitude toward 'the box,' especially since I had been so dangerously close to ending up in one myself. I was glad I didn't have to inconvenience him with all those nasty details—the letter home and all. It took me a moment to collect myself. Then I told him of my days in Kontokali and my upcoming move to the monastery.

Our conversation was interrupted by another round of cookies and tea. As the vicar engaged his circle of listeners about an unfortunate Dutch woman who had been thrown off the back of a motorbike, I combed the bookshelves in search of books to bring to the monastery. Since there were only a few hundred titles, I had already read or dismissed many of the books. That night, I hoped to find new acquisitions or newly returned books that would catch my eye. And indeed I did find a few new books, as well as some older titles that I had seen before but had put off until I felt desperate enough to read them. And so with a number of books in my arms, I bid the vicar, the old lady with the filing cards, and the others good-bye and walked back to the Cyprus.

~

Next morning, after checking out of the Cyprus Hotel, I went to the house in Kontokali to await Andy and Ann's return. I searched for a good way of breaking the bad news to them—the news that their return to the island would be followed by yet another hasty, unplanned departure. But I could think of no positive way of being the bearer of such ill tidings. For a moment, I considered delaying the bad news, allowing them a few hours of blissful ignorance before telling them of their imminent departure; but the moment I saw them coming up the path, I knew I could not feign ignorance of their situation. After greeting them, I let the cat out of the bag, trying desperately to temper the bad news with the story of the snake and how, even if it were possible for them to remain on Corfu, they would most certainly want to find another place to live. But that did little to mollify their disappointment; it merely confirmed their growing conviction that Corfu was a crazy place, fit only for madmen. In the end, they told me, they both felt lucky to be getting out relatively unscathed.

Two days later I helped them take their luggage to town. And as they got into the taxi that would take them to the airport, we bid one another farewell.

11

When I got off the bus at Strinilas the villagers greeted me at the gates of their stone houses. "Up the mountain to the monastery?" they asked me. "You're the friend of the monk?" Children ran after me with fruit.

Under the weight of my pack it was difficult to cross the great plateau. The sun beat down mercilessly, and I was drenched in sweat by the time I reached the final cone of the mountain. At the monastery gate, the monk, his face beaming with a broad smile, waited for me.

Outside my cell door I dropped my pack. Trying to lift the pack with one hand, the monk was impressed by its weight. He inspected the straps and zippers and felt the material. Then he motioned to me that he'd like me to place it on his back.

Together we hoisted it over his long black robe. As I adjusted the straps, he tested the weight by bobbing his knees. Then he strode off purposefully. He crossed the courtyard with sure and powerful steps, as if he were embarking on a pilgrimage. Striding back to me, his face was radiant.

"Together we go to Mount Athos!" he said and burst out laughing.

Leaving me to unpack, he went to the kitchen to make coffee. Soon I heard the monk shout from the kitchen door, "Thomás! Coffee! Come, come!"

On the kitchen table he had set two cups of coffee and a

plate of olives and bread. Over repast, we tried to converse, but it was still quite difficult. My command of his language still rudimentary, our conversation progressed more like an introductory Greek lesson.

"What is this?" I asked, pointing to the cup before me. The monk answered in Greek. Then I formed a short sentence using the new word. "Inside the cup is coffee," I said, to which the monk seemed truly pleased. He patted me on the back. Then we went on to the next word. Progress was slow, but the monk was patient—far more patient than I was. He was a good teacher, and after a few days we were able to talk to each other entire evenings in (fragmented) Greek.

Later that day, searching the courtyard for stones I could use as bookends, I came upon the monk bent over a stone tub. He was washing a robe, his arms to the elbows covered in soapy water. Curious about the large stones I had collected, he followed me back to my cell.

Standing in the open doorway, he watched me line books across the table, propping them up with the stones. I took out my notebooks and pads of paper, my pens, pencils, and envelopes. Neatly setting my writing materials on the desk, I put a chair in front of it and sat.

The monk came inside my cell to take a closer look, and then he said, "Thomás reads and writes much?"

"Yes," I said.

He touched the bindings of each book then picked up the copy of *The Works of Lewis Carroll* and laid it on the desk. Sitting on the bench, he dug deep into his pocket and took out his thick reading glasses. Placing them on his nose, he raised his chin while rubbing the cloth-bound cover between his fingers. "It is good?" he asked.

He opened the book and carefully examined the foreign script, his eyes following his fingers across the page. He felt the page as much as he looked at it, treating it as if it were a rare, old manuscript.

Carefully turning the pages of *Alice in Wonderland*, he

examined an illustration of the caterpillar sitting upon a tremendous toadstool, smoking a hookah. Peering closely at the illustration, he mumbled something under his breath. Then he noticed Alice looking up at the scene from between the blades of grass with a bewilderment matching his own, and he slapped the book shut. He looked up at me, and smiled uncertainly. I smiled back, wanting to explain who Alice was and what she was doing there between the blades of grass; but the thought of translating Alice's adventures in Wonderland into Greek seemed as fantastic as the adventures themselves.

~

That evening we shared the first of many meals eaten together. Dining at the monastery seemed to follow a well-prescribed ritual. The opening gesture would come with the monk's call: "Thomás! Come! Come here!" For the first few days, I thought something horrible had happened to him. Running in the direction of the sound of his shouts, I'd be ready to tear the sleeve off my shirt to make a tourniquet for his bleeding wound, or find a board to make a splint to set his leg. But always I found him unharmed, in the kitchen, busily putting food on the table as the rich aroma of garlic and olive oil, fish or chicken wafted through the room. Sometimes, his shrill dinner call would find me in my room, where I was absorbed in reading or writing. Other times, I heard his cries while sitting on the edge of the monastery wall, engrossed in contemplation. But suddenly his call would come, pulling me back to the present moment like the line of a kite being tugged back to earth. "Thomás! Come!"

By far, the dominant ingredients of Greek cooking are garlic and olive oil. I learned this at our first dinner together. The monk had cooked chicken and potatoes. Because he had cooked our dinner in a pan half-filled with olive oil, when we sat down to eat the oil oozed out of the food and slowly filled my plate. Then the monk, to my surprise, uncorked an old wine bottle and poured even more of the thick, golden-brown liquid over his plate. But what really shocked me was when he held the bottle across the table to me. I shook my head, declining politely. Staring at me, he kept his arm outstretched, shaking the bottle from side to side. I sighed, dropped my fork, and grabbed the bottle. Letting a few drops fall on my food, I put down the bottle, picked up my fork, and continued eating, not daring to look up to catch the disparaging gaze that he was no doubt casting my way. I had barely gotten one bite into my mouth when the monk, fully aware I was trying to avert his gaze, called out, "Thomás!" Shaking his finger at me, he laughed.

A few moments passed. Then he picked up a head of garlic, tore off half a dozen cloves, and peeled them with a sharp knife. He popped a few cloves into his mouth, put the rest on the edge of his plate, then held out the head of garlic and the knife to me. I stared at him and said, "No." No monk was going to push me around.

"It is good," he said.

"Yes," I agreed. I indicated how much garlic was already in the food. He backed off.

"Okay," he said cheerfully. "Tomorrow."

"Tomorrow what?" I cried.

"Tomorrow you have more garlic," and he burst out laughing.

Actually, the monk was correct in his assessment. The next day I peeled a few extra cloves of garlic and ate them with my meal. Within a week, I was drenching my food in olive oil and popping cloves of garlic like candy. A meal, I began to firmly believe, wasn't complete without liberal amounts of both garlic and olive oil.

~

One morning after breakfast the monk informed me that we were to meet Spiros, a mason from Strinilas, to work on a church they were building at the lower monastery. At first I didn't understand what he meant by the lower monastery, so he pointed to the building with the untended terraced fields at the base of the mountain's last cone. He said, "When storm and thunder and lightning comes, we go there." Then he went to the kitchen to gather some food in a sack, and together we walked down the hill to the lower monastery.

It is truly curious to observe the process of Greek construction. Though the Greeks are credited as the forebearers of our civilization, somehow, over the centuries, they must have lost the concept of the right angle. I've never yet seen a Greek building outside Athens that can boast a right angle. Objects roll and slide along the floors and the doors hang at an odd pitch. I had often wondered how the Greeks achieved such marvels, but then I met Spiros.

An elderly man, he carried a worn jacket draped over his shoulder, and a cigarette seemed to forever dangle out of the corner of his mouth. As he mixed concrete, he told me that the church, when completed, was to be a one-room stone and cinderblock structure. Already, he had laid an uneven stone floor, which rose in the back with the slope of the mountain, and built the foundation of the walls, which was composed of bits of broken rock mortared together into a uniform and level surface. Accuracy at the foundation level was important, because any mistake here would cause the cinderblock walls to curve inwardly or outwardly and leave spaces in the walls where no spaces should be. The holes would then have to be filled with bits of stone cut to size. Our job was to find these stones for Spiros.

I loved watching Spiros work, and it was obvious that the monk had recruited him for his expertise in stone work. Though the walls he had built were not straight, he could cut a stone to fit any size hole. He was a master at patchwork. He seized a stone, examined it from all angles, cracked it to size, and then tapped it into the hole it was meant for. His greatest satisfaction was when a stone slipped into the hole without resistance.

The monk, after determining that I could fetch stones on my own, went inside to prepare lunch. Occasionally, Spiros yelled to me, "*Megalos*" or "*Mikros*," large or small, then pointed to the place where he wanted the pile, and I went off to collect the stones.

During a break, I decided to explore the lower monastery where in stormy weather the monk and I would seek shelter. Before, it had been an old farmhouse, a place where people had once cultivated the surrounding fields and tended flocks of sheep and goats that grazed the mountain's slopes. The walls of the house were three feet thick, and the windows had wide sills. Because it was built so long ago, when people were smaller and shorter, I had to stoop to pass through doorways. Unlike the upper monastery, the rooms were connected from the inside. The hallway led to two rooms: on the left was the dining room; on the right was the kitchen. The dining room, in turn, led to the bedrooms. Off the monk's bedroom was a smaller room, a shrine, to which the monk retired for an hour in the afternoon to say his prayers. The kitchen, like that in the upper monastery, was furnished with basic cooking equipment, including a tin vessel above the stone sink in which we stored water from the well. The nicest feature of the kitchen, which made it far more comfortable than the one in the upper monastery, was a small fireplace. Sometimes it smoked horribly, especially when the wind blew hard, but normally it gave off a golden-yellow glow that warmed me to the marrow on the stormiest of days. An iron tripod held a big pot over the fire in which many fine meals were cooked. These were meals that held the delicate scent of wood smoke combined with the usual Greek seasonings of garlic, oregano, and olive oil.

Soon I heard the monk's familiar call, "Thomás, Spiros. *Ora ya fayitú!*" Mealtime. Spiros came inside, and the monk laid out a delicious meal of chicken, rice, and greens. The monk poured wine. I tried to follow their conversation but didn't have much luck, though I suspected they were talking about me most of the time.

After lunch I began to gather the dirty dishes, but the

monk told me to stop and follow him. In the hallway he handed me a note, which was written in Greek, and told me to go to the village to give it to the man in the *kafeneo*.

Armed with the monk's note, a good meal under my belt, and wine coursing through my veins, I set out for the village, the sound of Spiros smashing stones to fit holes fading behind me.

Assembled at the *kafeneo*, the old men of the village had set chairs out onto the street where the sun's rays could warm them. They were a motley crew, half of them leaning on canes and all of them talking at the top of their lungs. Finding the proprietor, I handed him the note, which he read carefully. Then he yelled something in the direction of an alleyway behind the shop. A woman, most probably his wife, answered his call. He handed her the note, and she went back up the alleyway. Then he showed me a seat in the center of the group of old men.

A ripple of *"filos tu papa,"* friend of the priest, spread through the crowd. An old geezer to my right, who had a cigarette dangling out of the corner of his mouth and a cup of coffee balanced upon his knee, stared at me then launched into a raving monologue, not a word of which I understood. Gesticulating wildly, he pointed up the mountain then at the sun then at the big tree in the square then down at me. He stroked his chin thoughtfully, and closing his eyes, he seemed to absorb himself in a deep prayer. And all the while words cascaded from his mouth like water from a waterfall. I became dizzy as the other men, so concentrated upon this man and his story, all but forgot me; that is, until the man suddenly fell silent and turned to me as if it were my turn to respond with an equal flash of wit. It was all I could do to stammer out the words, "I speak little Greek." With this there was a single burst of uncontrolled laughter from the men, except, that is, the man who had just finished his monologue. The cigarette fell from his lips. The cup of coffee, along with its delicate little saucer, crashed to the ground.

Wanting only to escape, I was saved by the proprietor's call from the doorway of his shop. Bringing me inside, he sat me at a table and poured us each a large glass of brandy. I was thankful.

After our drink, he pointed to a big bag of locally gathered wild greens he called *horta,* a loaf of bread wrapped in a fine linen napkin, and a bag of eggs laid out by the door. I gathered my bundles and bid him good-bye. I said farewell to the men outside; in response they only laughed.

I made my way back up the mountain.

~

That night after dinner the monk decided to teach me the card game I had observed countless times at the Chess Café. It was an easy game to play, or so I thought at first. Shuffling the cards, the monk placed four cards face up on the table then cut the deck. He gave me but a fleeting glance of the card chosen then dealt out the remainder of the deck. He went first. The first card in his stack was a seven. He matched his seven with another seven overturned on the table then took both cards and started a new pile by his side. Then I turned over my top card. It was a four and matched no card on the table. I showed it to him, he took up an ace and a three from the table, showed me that they added up to four, and thus I started my own pile of tricks. His turn; he had a six. Since only a jack remained, he left his six overturned next to the jack. Then it was my turn again. We played until he ran out of cards to turn over; it was time to count points to see who had won. My stack was bigger than his. I assumed I had won. Counting my cards, I told him I had thirty-five. He counted his, did some calculations in his head then wrote down an eight on a little scrap of paper. Then he took up my cards, counted them, did his mental calculations, and wrote down a four next to his eight. I didn't understand how this could possibly be, but I let it pass; I would get the hang of it soon enough. But as we played more hands and he consistently came up with twice as many points than me, I began to object.

I asked him, "*Yiatí?*" why?

He acted as if he didn't understand what my problem was. "*Yiatí?*" I asked again.

"*Yiatí? Yiatí?*" he responded.

As we played into the night he became increasingly smug. Finally, when I threatened to quit, he broke down and showed me how he scored. There were so many points for the jack of hearts, so many points for the card picked when cutting the deck, and so many points for going out first.

Finally armed with the rules, I won the next game. He acted as if it were luck. But then I won the next game and the next game after that. Finally he quit. We never played cards again.

~

I had begun to understand that no day on the mountain with the monk ended as I had pictured it at its inception. And the most common harbinger of digression was the monk's commanding call, "*Éla mázi mu,*" come with me. Whenever he said this, I became immediately attentive to his every move and gesture so I might have the best chance of meeting the challenge he was about to convey.

Though there were many examples of this, one in particular stands out in my mind. It was a quiet day in the upper monastery and I had spent the morning writing. Around noon, after eating lunch with the monk, I was sitting at my desk with a cup of coffee, ready to resume my work, when the monk came in, said "*Éla mázi mu,*" and walked out. I sprang to my feet and reached the door just in time to see the tail end of his robe going through the kitchen door. Inside the kitchen, I found him crouched before one of the cabinets. After a few minutes of rummaging, his head and half his torso still inside the cabinet, he came out holding several natural sponges and an array of rags. He grunted, signaling that I should take them; then he removed a bucket from the cabinet and I thought to myself, 'Ah-ha, we're going to wash something,' and when he finally stood and handed me a mop, a broom, and a dustpan my guess seemed confirmed.

Armed with these cleaning implements, I followed him across the courtyard to the church. Inside a closet, he rummaged through all sorts of junk—old candleholders from the church, broken pieces of statues, dust-covered wooden crates—until he came up with a long length of rope.

Back outside, he had me hold one end of the rope as he held the other end. He walked several paces then, without warning, tugged on his end, tearing the rope from my hands. "Thomás," he grunted. He motioned that I should hold on tightly. We pulled against each other until he was certain of the rope's strength. Coiling the rope, he slung it over his shoulder and walked back into the kitchen. I wondered where the rope fit in and became all the more baffled when he took off his robe and rolled up his pant legs and shirtsleeves. He took off his shoes and socks, left his hat on the table, slung the rope over his shoulder again, and stepped back outside. I followed him across the courtyard and behind the church. Tying one end of the rope around his waist with a secure knot, he handed the other end to me. Then he jumped up on the low rim of a stone well and pointed down into the darkness. I quickly took up the slack, and before I knew it I was bracing my feet on the well's rim, lowering the monk into the darkness, bits of broken rock and gravel splashing beneath him. I had given a good dozen feet of rope when I heard his feet splashing into water. Then the rope slackened.

Peering into the darkness, I saw the monk, knee deep in stagnant water. He untied the rope from around his waist and yelled up to me. It was a word I was unfamiliar with. He repeated the word, but, alas, an unknown word does not become intelligible through repetition. I told him to wait and ran to my room for my pocket dictionary. As I ran back across the courtyard I heard him screaming frantically, "Thomás! Thomás! *Éla!*" Come! The poor man thought he'd been abandoned, and he was relieved to see my head peering over the edge of the well once again. I said, "What is it you want?"

He repeated the word, which translated as *bucket*. I should have known. He thought so, too. I tied the bucket onto the end of the rope and lowered it into the well. He filled it with water and sludge. I hoisted it, dumped it out, and lowered it again. We extracted dozens of buckets of water in this manner until not enough water remained to fill the bucket. I then lowered the sponges, rags, mop, and broom to him. Then I sat down to rest. I waited for him to call me to lift the bucket out. The sludge became increasingly slimy and thick. Once, when he called me, I glared down at him in the darkness. "What do you want?" I asked. "Food? Wine? A blanket? Oh, you sleep down there tonight?" He got mad and yelled, "The water, the water, out. Now!" and I pulled up another bucket of slime.

I was resting with my back against the rim of the well, waiting for him to call my name, when he yelled out, *"Lepta!"* Money! I looked down the well and saw his hands digging in the mud. Between his fingers I saw silvery glints. The monk started dancing, and then he dug like a madman, deeper and deeper, coming up with more and more coins. He rinsed the coins in the last of a little puddle of water before putting them into the bucket. By the time he had cleaned the well to its smooth rock bottom, I had hauled out two buckets full of coins —almost one hundred dollars. The next day the coins were outside drying in the sun when some Greeks from the mainland came to the monastery. They thought we were making a collection and dropped spare change onto the pile.

12

It was well before sunrise as I sat upon the wall that overlooked the mist-enshrouded mountains of Albania. At this early hour, with the sun but a dim intimation, the Albanian coast was suffused in fading starlight.

The sun rose behind the range, its fiery rays striking first the distant peaks and then the top of Pantokrator. The valleys still slumbered in darkness. Slowly the fog cleared, and as the sun mounted the sky the valleys grew sharper and more defined.

Since coming to the mountain I had developed a heightened power of concentration. I had grown patient, as patient as the monk. But it wasn't the monk who taught me this patience. His was but an example. We drew patience from the same source: the mountain itself.

It was in times like these that the wheels slowed enough for the mountain to speak. The mountain was immobile, existing without a thought. The mountain was silent, and within that silence was an invitation to cast off all that is unnecessary; in silence all that is frivolous, inessential, and superfluous naturally falls away. What one is left with is the essential.

~

During lunch the monk told me he would spend the night in the village. The next day was Sunday, and every Sunday, early in the morning, he performed Mass at the village church. Shortly after we finished eating, I watched as he went down the steep switchbacks to the lower monastery then across the gray plateau to the village. Every step he took increased by exactly one pace the distance between another human being and myself, and with every step I felt that much more my elemental connection to the mountain. By the time he had disappeared over the edge of the plateau, that connection was complete. I was now alone with the mountain.

Late that afternoon, as I sat writing at my desk, I looked up from the page to see the room darkening. I glanced out the window, but the window had fogged over, and I could see neither the stunted trees in the courtyard nor the building on the other side. Opening the door, a blast of cold air rushed into the room. I felt my beard and it was wet.

As I stepped outside, a furious wind blew. The dampness penetrated my skin and burrowed deep into my bones. Walking to the low wall beyond the kitchen, I was met straight on with a full-force gale, a gale of pea-soup fog, of low cloud pierced by high mountain.

The fog defined a circle through which my eyes could not penetrate. Beneath me the wall faded before reaching the rocky slope, and even my hands looked less sharp than they had inside. Before, all had been keenly defined: my hand holding the pen, the pen's sharp point touching the paper, the letters forming into words on the page. It had all been so clear, so black and white. But that continuity had been broken. The light had dimmed. I had stepped outside into opacity, a world at once less defined and more immediate. Here, at the edge of a sea of nothingness, clutching a wall that faded into insubstantiality, my feet anchored in a ground that seemed no longer foundational, the mind bypassed by the marrow.

It was as if I were the lookout on a ship's prow, peering into obscurity, looking for something tangible by which to guide my ship. The mist, like a continual spray, drove the water deep into my clothes and made me shiver. I awaited the massive wave that would crash over me. I awaited the shudder that would resonate through the ship's hull. But no wave came. The rock beneath my feet remained firm.

Then came an opening, a break in the fog, and I found myself staring straight up the edge of a vertical column of cloud, a puffy cottony wall, towering, threatening to tumble hundreds of feet onto my head. The top glowed pink, red, and golden from the sun, which was, no doubt, setting peacefully beyond the tumult. Then the column closed, and the fog enshrouded me again.

I went inside to find my jacket. I put on my hat and gloves. The passing of clouds, which from a village along the coast was a fleeting phenomenon in the sky, was from the monastery an event full of immediacy. This was the layer of the atmosphere in which warm and cold meet and play out their battle.

When I went back out to the wall it was as if my ship had been dashed upon the shore: I was on an island surrounded

Windblown Clouds
Thomas K. Shor

by a turbulent sea, the cone of Pantokrator bathed in the last reddened rays of the setting sun. But my island illusion didn't last, for suddenly the sea lifted in great puffy veils and engulfed me, leaving me submerged once again.

Then, as the great sea of fog parted, hues of blue peeked out high overhead and the sky was revealed again, only to be obliterated a moment later by a wave of crashing cloud. From being a creature of the land, upon an island in an expanse of white, I became a creature of the seas. Then, as the clouds parted, I became a creature of the sky, an eagle soaring high over the island of Corfu.

Another line of clouds grew in the distance, boiling internally and mounting to terrific heights. Thunderheads drew near. The air became charged. And just before the wall of seething cloud slammed into the mountain, the wind, which had been rushing out ahead of the storm, suddenly switched direction and started rushing toward the cloud. The oncoming thunderhead was consuming the surrounding air, sucking the air into it, sucking the mountain into its sphere as well. Suddenly I was in the middle of the seething cross-currents of the cloud's interior, my skin bitten by rain driven horizontally now over the monastery wall.

The ferocity of the storm drove me from that wall into the courtyard's interior. Wind and rain buffeted me from all sides. It was all I could do to keep my balance in the whirlwind. I huddled against a wall just to feel something solid, something rooted in the earth, something unchangeable.

Gusts eddied around unseen corners, hitting me like the disembodied souls of the monastery's former inhabitants. They came out of the gray like cool hands upon the back of my neck, making my spine tingle with waves of sensation. With my mind unhinged by the tempest, I did not know whether it was from the cold and the wet or from these hands whipping out of the whirlwind that these waves of sensation flowed over me. I turned with a start, certain that someone had tapped me on the shoulder. But the same gray was staring back at

Windblown Clouds

Thomas K. Shor

me.

The rushing wind made the monastery's mute stone speak. The top of the monastery wall moaned with a hollow sound, and the buildings howled furiously, as if scores of multi-pitched and out of tune strings were being played with varying intensity by a thousand bows. No one string could be discerned out of the mismatched chorus. The droning in my ears never reached a crescendo, never found resolution as the ever-rising wind drove the cold and rain ever deeper into my bones.

The whole while that I was being tossed by the storm, enclosed in a tiny ball of gray, stumbling like a nearsighted fool, walking into walls and being buffeted by the eddies of wind forming off the corners of the buildings, I was aware too that I was over half a mile above the sea, over an hour and a half from the nearest human being, running around beneath thick walls, on a mountain in the center of a thunderhead. The whole while I was in the thick of it I was also strangely outside of it, aware—graphically, spatially, with the clarity of looking down on a topographical map—of exactly where I was. While never losing for an instant the sharp immediacy of my surroundings, I could practically see the great globe itself and where I stood on it.

The security of being surrounded by the high stone walls, which had weathered storms for half a millennium, faded when distant rumbles of thunder grew even louder than the howling wind. Fear overtook me as the thick fog became illuminated with blinding flashes of light that lacked direction of origin, flashes that illuminated equally my entire field of perception with a ghostly light. Flash followed flash, followed by echoing rumbles.

I decided to take my bearings and head inside.

But it was too late.

A crash of unimaginable magnitude shook the mountain to its very foundations, a crash that was concurrent with a blinding flash that rendered my eyes useless for a few agonizing moments, moments during which another clap of thunder crashed around me followed by another and yet another. The lightning bolts were distinct now through the thick fog, arching less than a hundred feet above my head. They were close enough to gauge their thickness—thick as a man's arm, thick as a horse's torso. Others originated *below* me and shot up the side of the mountain, branching directly overhead. Their zigzag paths were etched on my retinas, etched in burning red.

Panic seized me to the marrow, wiping out all sense of sport I had felt toward the storm. It was no longer a playful game to be walking in the tempest. So I ran, trying to anticipate the next bolt of lightning. I knew if I stopped I would be hit. I ran like a jackrabbit dodging the hunter's shot, all the while hearing the boom, boom, boom from all directions. I came to a high wall and ran alongside it until it turned a corner away from me. I missed it, ran straight on, and was again at sea without an anchor or point of reference.

The storm rendered my will inoperative; in its place was pure and raw instinct, an instinct as old as time itself, the instinct that calls out from the primal depths for shelter. I became a being in search of a cave, a niche, or a burrow in which to find protection from the storm.

And then, off in the distance, I heard, between claps of thunder, the eerie sound of something ringing. I ran toward the sound and it became more distinct. I recognized it: it was the bell that hung over the monastery's front gate. It must be the monk, I thought to myself. He has returned, found me missing, and now he's calling me back! I followed the sound to the gate. I stared into the flashing darkness, searching desperately for an outlined figure. But no figure was there beneath the bell, just the rope flying in the frenzy of the wind. Knowing now where I was, I quickly found my room and slid in through the door.

13

In the morning all the elements of the storm were still there: the terrific wind, the driving rain, the impenetrable fog. Thunder could be heard in the distance, echoing off the mountains of Albania. I wondered what the weather was like in Corfu Town or in Kontokali. I imagined that it was raining. Nothing more. I recalled the many rainy days I had spent in Kontokali, looking longingly at the mountain, its summit lost in thick cloud. It had always looked peaceful like that, rising above the turbulent and stormy weather.

I mused over the scene that was no doubt playing out at the Chess Café—old men arriving one by one, shaking their umbrellas outside the door and sitting down for a serious game of cards, the proprietor's son dodging rain puddles to bring ouzo to shop owners down the street. Yet everything that existed outside the confines of the monastery walls seemed a rather flimsy abstraction.

~

"Thomás. Thomás!"

My name rang out above the cry of the wind. I opened the kitchen door and admitted not only a cool and wet blast of fog, but also a rather forlorn-looking monk—*my* monk—speaking Greek at an alarming rate. I listened to him closely, but the only words I could understand were the words for cold, lightning, thunder, rain, and wind. In all, he summed up my sentiments exactly; what else was there to say?

I offered to make him coffee.

"No!" he boomed. "We go below. Down. Down. Lower monastery. Now! Thunder coming, lightning coming. Lightning bad, very bad. We go NOW!"

He whirled round the kitchen like a dervish, shoveling bread, coffee, rice, chickpeas, sugar, olives, garlic, and any other food he could find into a cloth sack. Then he buttoned his shawl-like coat and we burst out into the storm, each going to our own cells. I emptied my bag onto my bed and refilled it with what I'd need at the lower monastery. The monk burst into my room, the food sack in one hand and a sack of clothes in the other. Rain dripped from his robe, forming a puddle on the floor. His eyes flashed menacingly. "Now!" he yelled. "We go now!"

We closed the monastery gate behind us and started down Pantokrator's steep slope. Bending our bodies sharply into the cutting wind and rain, we kept our heads bowed as if in veneration to the storm.

When we reached the door at the lower monastery and closed it behind us, a cold wind followed us in through a crack beneath the door. It emitted a high-pitched and eerie whine, a whistle that rose and fell with every gust. The stone house was stone-cold, but it was solid; it was a safe refuge. Never has a sailor in a wild sea felt more relieved to set foot on solid land.

First we cleaned the room that would be mine. There was a single bed, a desk, a chair, and a large window. It was so dark outside that the monk had to hold a lantern while I swept the room. When the monk shook out the blankets on the bed, a dead scorpion fell to the floor. He kicked it under the bed, thinking I hadn't seen it. After that, I was always careful not to let my blankets dangle on the floor.

I followed the monk through the hallway toward the kitchen, the circle of light emitted by the lantern casting a grotesquely enlarged shadow of the monk's billowing robe on the walls and ceiling. It preceded us like a dark phantom.

In the kitchen, the monk closed the door to the hallway and let out a thankful sigh. He lit another lantern and placed it on the windowsill above the sink; the added glow of the lantern made the room actually seem warm. I watched as the monk built a fire in the fireplace. We pulled the bench up to the fire and stretched out our hands within inches of the flame. We stared into the crackling fire and let its warmth penetrate every pore of our bodies. Steam rose from our rain-drenched clothes.

Windblown Clouds

Thomas K. Shor

Outside, the storm was heightening. The monk donned his heavy black cloak, and I followed him to the front door where an old and patched cloak hung from a hook. He put the cloak around my shoulders and tied the drawstring tightly around my neck. He thrust a bucket into my hand and pushed open the door. He brought me to the well, and as I lowered the bucket he gathered an armful of wood piled under the roof's small overhang. Hauling the bucket from the well, I nervously eyed the overflowing metal tank for collecting rainwater that stood upon a scaffold towering above the outhouse. It was a perfect lightning conductor. I ran, the monk close behind me, back into the lower monastery.

Inside we sat on the bench, our feet and hands outstretched to the fire. Outside, violent claps of thunder shook the mountain as the howling wind traveled down the chimney in bursts, as if driven by a piston, filling the room with smoke. The monk put a handful of loose black tea into a battered teakettle. He added sugar and filled the pot with water. Then he put the pot directly onto the hot, glowing coals.

A little later, still sitting on the low bench before the fire, teacups balanced on our knees, the monk said, "Thomás, the fire is good. Yes?"

"Yes, it is good. It is warm. Outside is cold. There is rain, wind, thunder—and lightning. Outside is bad; here is good."

"Yes, Thomás. Outside is bad, but here it is good."

We were staring at the embers, occasionally adding a stick to the fire. The monk placed an iron tripod into the hearth. He filled an iron pot with water and put it on the tripod. We poured a bag of chickpeas onto the table and sorted out the sticks and small stones. He poured the chickpeas into the water as I sliced onions. Then he peeled garlic. When we added these ingredients to the boiling water, along with half a bottle of olive oil, the brew was complete but for a few hours of boiling.

"Thomás," the monk said, "when the storm is over you

come with me to the church in the village. I baptize you. You become Greek Orthodox, and one day you become *papa*. Yes, *Papa* Thomás. And you can live here, and when I am old you can take care of me. And when I die, this will be your monastery. It is good here, yes?"

"Yes, it is," I replied. "But Thomás no *papa*. One day I go home. I see my family. I see my friends."

"Eh, Thomás," he said and shook his finger at me. "I baptize you and all is good. You won't *have* to go home. You stay here and I teach you about Christ. We eat rice and fish and we build rooms, and on Sundays you come with me to village and I teach you. The people in the village like you. They think you be good *papa*. One day you have long hair and long beard and black robe like me. We walk together to the village. Everybody who sees us bows their head and says, 'There are the two *papáthes,* one old and one young. Long live Christ!' They give us food. When we bless the olive press they give us oil, and the best oil, too.

"Come, I show you."

He got up with a grunt, thrust the lantern into my hand, and I followed him out of the kitchen into the front hallway. He opened an old wooden door, which had rotted off its hinges. He had to lift it and lean it against the wall so we could enter. He lit a match and put it to the wick of a kerosene lantern, which sputtered and sizzled before taking the flame. The room was long and narrow and cold like a cave, yet it was dry. Along the walls were shelves from floor to ceiling packed with dusty tins, bottles, kegs, and urns.

"Look," he said, pointing at the dust-covered tins. He tapped one after another with his knuckle to show that they were not hollow, but full of liquid. "Olive oil, olive oil, olive oil—much oil. Too much oil. More oil than *I* can use." He found an old and rusted nail on the ground, pried the lid off a tin, and stuck his finger in. It emerged dripping with golden-green oil. He stuck his finger into his mouth.

"Mmm," he said, "very good!" He motioned for me to do

the same. The oil tasted delicious.

Then he moved deeper into the room and pointed at the big earthenware urns. "Olives, olives, olives," he said, shaking his clenched fist, his voice rising. "All full!" He uncorked an urn and scooped out a handful of dripping olives. "You like, yes?"

They *were* delicious, but I was afraid he would link an affirmative answer to my wanting to become a *papa* so I might receive these gifts from the villagers on a regular basis. He looked at me expectantly, waiting for my judgment on the olives and, by association, my decision to become a *papa* and live out his last years with him.

Of course I was flattered. Yet I knew I couldn't accept his offer.

"Yes," I said, "the olives are good, but '*Papa* Thomás' no. I don't want to be a *papa*."

He banged the big cork back into the urn with his fist and blew the lamp out.

~

"*Thélis na fáme?*" "Do you want to eat?" the monk asked. The bubbling water in the pot had caused the window above the sink to fog over, and drops of dew gently rolled down the windowpanes. With a wooden ladle, the monk scooped chickpeas into two ceramic bowls as I sliced a few pieces of bread from a loaf. He crossed himself and we began to eat. We looked at each other across the table as a downdraft sent smoke into the room. The fire crackled. Sparks flew.

"In Greek, what do you call these," I asked, pointing to the chickpeas in my spoon.

"*Revéthia*," he answered. Then he asked timidly, "And in English?"

"Chickpeas," I answered.

"Cheeek-pays," he said, trying to get his Greek tongue around the word.

"No, not cheeek-pays, chickpeas."

He tried again and said the word perfectly.

"Very good!" I exclaimed.

A broad smile crossed his face and he repeated the word over and over in a sing-song voice, "Chick-peas, chick-peas, chickpeas!" He triumphed in learning a new English word.

He often asked me the English word for something after I asked him the Greek, but usually he forgot it as quickly as he learned it. Not this time. After we had finished our peas and were sopping up the last juices from the bottom of our bowls with thick slices of bread, he suddenly yelled out, "Chickpeas!" and burst out laughing. His laughter was like a lion's roar; it came from deep down inside his belly, from somewhere in the center of his existence.

That evening, as the storm raged outside, we spent hours talking and roasting chestnuts over the coals. The chestnuts burned our fingers as we pried them from their shells.

14

The next morning a ghastly clap of thunder interrupted my peaceful dreams. As the receding rumble of thunder gave way to the sound of rain driving against the bedroom window, a relentless wind threw its strength against the stone house. Outside, storm clouds as thick as cotton rushed past my window. I couldn't help wondering whether the entire world was pummeled by the storm, or whether the storm sat over this mountain alone. It took an act of will to get out of bed and slip on my clothes.

In the kitchen I watched as the monk sat in front of the fire, boiling coffee. As thunder crashed outside, no doubt originating from a bolt of lightning that struck close by, on the mountain's flank, the monk moaned and shook his head.

"Bad," he said wearily. "Lightning is bad."

His hands trembled as he poured coffee into two cups. This worried me. I had imagined that the monk, having lived on the mountain for so many years, was accustomed to the raging storms that frequented the mountain. Somehow I had thought that the gods—or God—watched over him, and now that I was with him, that protection had also been extended to me. But to see him so visibly shaken shook my own confidence, especially when I realized I had to take a trip to the outhouse.

Amid a terrific crash of thunder, I announced I had to go outside. The monk, looking up from his cup of coffee, offered me some advice—mainly to make great haste—then handed me his cloak. He walked with me to the front hallway, and as he unlatched the front door a terrific blast of wind tore the door from his hands. Swinging back on its hinges, it hit the wall with a clamor. I stood a moment, poised, ready to run, waiting for a flash of lightning and a crash of thunder. I wanted to go just after one release of electricity and—hopefully—return before the next.

The lightning came with a nearly simultaneous crack of thunder. The monk bid me good luck. Actually, he said, "May God be with you!"

I ran as fast as I could to the outhouse.

I did my business quickly, thinking all the while of the metal water tank a few feet from where I now squatted.

As I ran back to the house, a presentiment of electricity came over me. Stopping, I turned to see a bolt of lightning as thick as a horse's hind leg kick out of the sky and strike the tank then branch out and splinter over the outhouse. Thunder crashed simultaneously, as if the heavens themselves were cracking open. Running back to the safety of the house, I stood trembling before the monk.

"The storm is bad, no?" he said.

"Yes, it is bad."

~

Two days later the storm let up. Only a light drizzle remained. The clouds lifted and once again we could see the upper monastery on the mountain's peak. It stood unharmed.

After breakfast the monk and I began work on the stone church without the aid of Spiros the village mason. The floor of the building, made of the mountain's rock, sloped with the contour of mountain, and we began to level the floor by pounding on the stone with sledgehammers. Barely yielding to our blows, the stone fractured into small pieces. Dust encased the room. We hammered away at one spot for an hour, yet we hardly saw any progress.

The plaintive braying of a donkey interrupted our work. Going to the open doorway, we watched as a man climbed off the donkey and approached the church. His face was contorted with grief, and as he spoke to the monk, the sorrow on his face shone on the face of my friend.

"Thomás," the monk said, "the storm has taken a life. A man from the village was bringing his sheep to shelter when lightning came out of a cloud and made him fall. It happened two days ago. They couldn't reach me because of the storm. Now I must go to the church to pray for him. I will not be back for a few days. Go to the upper monastery. I will meet you there."

The monk rushed inside and reappeared a few moments later with a sack of clothes. He sat sidesaddle on the donkey, and the man from the village led the donkey back down the mountain.

~

The clouds dispersed by late afternoon. At sunset, I leaned over the wall at the upper monastery and watched the sun sink into the sea. To the east the mountains of Albania glowed pink and red, and as the sun touched the horizon the shadow of Pantokrator crossed the narrow channel and clothed the Albanian mountains in darkness. Twilight deepened. Lights, twinkling from the coastal villages, mirrored the stars in the sky.

~

Two days later the monk reappeared. Hearing his footsteps in the courtyard, I ran to the door to see him stumbling toward the church, a stack of wooden planks balanced upon his shoulder. Over his other shoulder was his cloth sack, and looped through his arms were plastic bags filled with vegetables. In his free hand he held a large jug of wine. Helping him to remove the planks from his shoulder, we sat on the step at the front of the church.

"The man who died," the monk said, "was a good man. He was young, too. He left a wife and two children. It will be difficult for his family, but the people of the village are good people. They will take care of them. I spent two days in the church praying. I have not slept. I am very tired."

"What is the wood for?" I asked him, wondering how he had made it up the mountain under such a load.

"Building," he answered.

"Where did you get it?"

His eyes sparkled. He tapped a crooked finger to his temple. With a mischievous look he said, "To be a monk, Thomás, you must be *Ponirós! Ponirós* Thomás, *PONIRÓS!!*" and he roared with laughter.

I had my pocket dictionary with me. *Ponirós* means "sly."

"Eh," I said, "you *are ponirós*. You are the *Ponirós* Monk!" and I shook my finger at him, as he had shaken his finger at me so many times before.

Then he asked me what the word was in English. I told him.

"Sly," he repeated after me, getting it right the first time. "Sly, sly, sly, slyeee," he said, squinting his eyes at me. "Thomás, I am not sly, you are sly. You are a sly young man. You are a sly chickpea!" He almost rolled off the step, he was laughing so hard.

It was good to have him back.

15

A few weeks passed, a time of quiet study and wonderful meals eaten with the monk.

Then our larder grew thin, so I suggested I go to Corfu Town to replenish our supplies. The monk agreed. Instead of going to the village to take a bus to town, I decided to walk straight down the eastern slope of the mountain to the coast road, where I could easily catch a ride to town. I chose this route—more difficult by far—both in order to slowly ease myself back into civilization and because there was an abandoned village in this direction at the base of the mountain's cone I wanted to explore. My plan was to spend the night in Corfu Town, shop in the morning, and then take the bus back to Strinilas the afternoon.

～

The abandoned village was nestled in a little valley, a pause on the mountain's steep descent to the sea. It was surrounded by terraced fields now overgrown with bushes, vines, and trees. The silence of the graveyard hung low over the village, and the air was suffused with a forsaken desolation.

Roofs were caved in and stitched over with vines. The church stood on top of a little knoll near the village center, its simple white adobe belfry covered with vines that were slowly tightening their grip and making it crumble.

Jumping over a low wall, I found myself in the courtyard of a large stone house, in the middle of which stood a fig tree surrounded by brambles. I ascended the steps of the house, which had been worn smooth by untold generations of feet, and went inside.

Though time and weather had wreaked havoc with the house's exterior, the interior, though bare of furnishings, was intact. A huge fireplace took up an entire wall of the kitchen. Baking chambers with iron doors in which bread had once been baked flanked the fireplace. Above the fireplace the whitewashed ceiling was brown from the smoke and grease of cooking.

In the next room a thick vine had taken advantage of a broken window to grow inside. It clung to the ceiling, its rootlets penetrating the whitewash and plaster, leaving trails of white debris on the floor. The vine reached clear across the ceiling. Its leaves were ghostly pale for lack of light.

In one corner of the room stood a wooden chest whose every surface was carved with interlocking figures and geometric designs. Full of anticipation, I lifted the thick metal clasps, imagining a pirate's bounty of jewels and gold inside. Instead, I found a well-worn, rusty horseshoe.

I explored a few more houses and even found the village store and *kafeneo*. Most of the houses were in much worse shape than the first one I entered. Roofs had caved in and rock walls lay in ruinous heaps.

I aimed toward the church on the knoll, which had once been the center for the villagers who lived in the now silent and abandoned streets. But as I neared where the land rose to meet the church's door the way became so thick with brambles that I became entangled; thorns scratched my arms and brought blood. I gave up. The church had been the center of the villagers' existence. Perhaps now that the villagers were gone it was best if this center remained obscured and seen from a distance only, crumbling slowly under the hand of nature.

I walked to the edge of the village and climbed into the terraced fields so I could pick a route to the coast. Though I still couldn't see the coast I did see a stream that ran below the village, and I knew it would take the most direct route to the sea. I followed the contour of the land to where the stream dipped into a shallow ravine. There I turned to take one last look at the monastery, which loomed high on top of the rocky slope.

Following the stream until the ravine became too narrow to continue, I climbed the riverbank. There I came upon a small trail. At first the size of an animal track, it quickly widened as it followed the slope of the mountain toward the coast. Soon I saw donkey tracks and knew I was nearing a village.

Rounding a corner, I came upon an elderly peasant woman clad in an old and patched dress. She was picking wild greens and stuffing them into a cloth sack. When she saw me her mouth gaped in toothless wonder at one the likes of me descending the mountain. She asked where I had come from.

"From the mountain," I said, "I came from the monastery. I live there."

Her face lit up. "You are a monk?"

"No, but I live with the monk who lives there."

"The monk is a very good man," she said as she tied the sack with a piece of rope. "He is generous and wise."

She threw the sack over her shoulder and walked with me along the path.

"You are not Greek," she said. "Your words come too slowly."

"I am from America."

"Ah, America! It is very good there, no?"

"Yes, it is; but it is good here too."

"Yes, it is good here," she said after thinking it over. "I have my house and my family. I have olive trees and a donkey, and I can pick greens. My life is good."

I saw that she was feeling the strain of the sack on her back. So I took it from her and put it over my shoulder. "Thank you," she said. "You are young and strong. I am old now. When you are old it is hard to carry heavy loads."

As we passed the first house at the edge of the village she called out to a woman sitting under a grape arbor surrounded by young children. "Anna, look what I've found! He's from America, and now he lives at the monastery on top of the mountain."

Anna came to take a better look. The children hid behind their mother's dress, giggling, peering out at me from time to time. Never addressing me directly, Anna asked the elderly woman some questions about me, and the old woman answered, beaming as if I were a new possession. As we took our leave, the children, who hadn't yet dared to say a word to me, called after us, "*Yasas, yasas,*" good-bye. They ran back to their veranda giggling the entire way.

Soon we came upon a low, whitewashed house surrounded by fruit trees. "This is my house," she said. "Come, I will give you coffee."

I deposited the sack of greens by the front door. She brought out a chair and put it in the shade of a mulberry tree. She told me to sit while she prepared the coffee. Soon an old man appeared at the door. He was bent with age and his face was deeply wrinkled. His whiskers were thick and long, almost like a cat's. He dragged a chair next to mine and letting out a long sigh, he sat. Then he said, "You are from America, no?"

"Yes, I am."

"Good, very good," then he stared through the olive grove on the other side of the dirt track as if he were trying to remember something. Then his eyes lit up and he raised his hand, forming it into a make-believe gun. "Bang-bang!" he said. "Chicago? No?"

His wife brought out a small table, covered it with a tablecloth, and carefully smoothed out the wrinkles. She then brought a tray with two small cups of Greek coffee, half a loaf of homemade bread, and a plate of olives and feta cheese. Occasionally someone passed the house, old women leading donkeys laden with sticks gathered on the mountain, or children returning from school in blue uniforms dirty from a day's ware.

"Look, he is from America," my hosts called to passers-by. "We found him on the mountain!"

I finished my coffee in the shade of the mulberry tree then thanked them warmly for their hospitality. Promising to visit on my next trip down the mountain, I bid them good-bye. Then I walked down to the coast and hitched a ride to town.

~

The next morning I awoke to the sound of rain against my window at the Cyprus Hotel. Lingering over breakfast at the dairy shop, I hoped the rain would let up. It didn't. So at half past ten I started shopping—in the rain. I had stops to make all over town.

At the dry goods store I bought noodles, rice, beans, and—of course—chickpeas. At the butcher shop I bought a chicken and salted fish. Soon my pack was full, and my arms were full of bags.

At the vegetable shop, the old couple was glad to see me and asked about Andy and Ann. I told them about their return to London, and how I was living on the mountain. I took out my list and told the woman what I wanted: four kilos of potatoes, three of carrots, three of onions, and two of apples.

As I told her what I wanted a smile came to her face as if there was something to wonder at. I didn't understand what amazed her so, having only asked for some common vegetables.

Right then, another customer came into the shop, a woman I had seen there before. The proprietress turned to her. "This man," she said, "when he came to my shop a few weeks ago, he couldn't speak Greek. Now he speaks Greek!"

She gave me a big hug. The most amazing thing was that I understood every word she said.

The rain was falling so hard when I left the vegetable shop that I ducked into a *taverna* to have lunch and hopefully sit out the storm. I had only one more stop, the wine merchant's, before catching the bus. But as I ate, the rain came even harder, and as I lingered over coffee the wind started to blow the rain horizontally. Since it was late, I had no choice but to brave the weather. Dodging puddles and resting under awnings, I made my way to the wine shop.

The wine merchant, a short and rather rotund man, noted my long absence then asked what he could do for me. I told him I wanted one jug of white wine and one jug of red. He asked me what kind. I told him inexpensive. Going to a shelf and rummaging through an assortment of spigots and jugs and the other paraphernalia of his trade, he presented me with two clay cups. He led me to a cask in the back room. The casks were made of bowed planks held together with metal rings. At the end of each was a hole, some of which were plugged with corks (the wine in these hadn't yet aged) and the others were tapped with spigots. Turning the spigot of the cask before us, he filled each of our cups. The dark red wine had the consistency and taste not only of the grapes from which it was made, but the very earth that produced them. He motioned that I was not merely to sip what was in my cup: I was to gulp it down. He brought me then to another cask where he refilled my cup with another dark red wine. This one was sweeter than the last but just as delicious. By the time I had quaffed it, he was refilling my cup with yet another vintage. My ears were beginning to ring and my head was feeling light. We sampled two more wines and it was all I could do to keep the shop from spinning.

He asked me which wine I liked best. Since the earthy taste of the first wine was so distinctive, I chose it. He told me I had chosen correctly; it was also his personal favorite. He filled a jug, put a cork in it, and said: "Now we must try the white wines."

He started filling my cup from a cask of white, and although I tried to tell him I would trust his judgment, he wouldn't hear of it. He insisted I try samples of quite a few. After a while I started spilling the wine behind a cask when he wasn't looking. Finally he asked me which I liked best. Although I couldn't remember how many I had tested or the differences between them, I chose the second.

His grin suddenly vanished. "But the first, *that* was a wine, *that* had body and flavor," he said. After an awkward moment, I assured him I had meant the first. Grin restored, he filled another jug.

Back in the front room of the shop I looked at the clock and realized that I had only ten minutes to get to the bus. Paying him quickly, I tried to pick up my load, but the jugs were just too much for me to carry along with the other sacks and bags, especially with the quantity of wine coursing through my veins. My attempt ended in everything tumbling to the floor. I began to panic. If I missed the bus I would have to spend two more days in Corfu waiting for the next bus. The monk needed food. I couldn't let him down.

Finally the wine merchant came to my rescue with some lengths of rope with which he tied the sacks together and lashed them to my pack. This left my hands free to carry the wine. I thanked him and ran from his shop into the deluge.

When I got to the bus square I was drenched, breathless, and sure I had missed the bus. But I searched anyway for the bus with the *Strinilas* destination card, and much to my surprise and great joy I found it. I jumped aboard and sat near the front with my over-laden pack and jugs of wine beside me. Immediately I heard a ripple of voices behind me. "*Filos tu papa*," they were saying, Friend of the priest. I turned around and was met with many approving smiles.

As it turned out I needn't have worried about missing the bus, for the bus was going nowhere fast. We just sat there, everybody staring silently out the windows watching rain-drenched figures under umbrellas darting back and forth. The windows had fogged on the inside, so each stared through a tiny opening in the glass cleared with the back of the hand. Occasionally a bus would pass on its way out of the square, its engine roaring, the sound of tires plowing over drenched pavement, and the succession of uncomfortable wet people staring blankly through tiny cleared patches in fogged windows.

After half an hour I asked the man across from me what was going on. He told me that there were rumors from Strinilas that the road had washed out just below the village. But no one knew for sure. The driver was supposedly deciding whether to attempt it, but my neighbor suspected he was in a *kafeneo*, playing cards.

Then the driver got on the bus, stood in the front, and announced that the passengers headed for Episkepsis, a village on the other side of the mountains that was not as

Windblown Clouds   Thomas K. Shor

high as Strinilas, would be coming onto our bus. He would drive to Episkepsis first and if the road was good to that village he would attempt a trip higher into the mountains. Although some grumbled at this idea because it meant further delay, more driving, and only the possibility of reaching our destination, most kept their disapproval for the plan at bay. Our only hope was in humoring the driver. As the driver started the engine and awaited the arrival of the other passengers, an old woman hobbled up the aisle and gave him a piece of bread with some feta cheese on it. As she went back to her seat everyone patted her on the back and thanked her for her show of generosity on everyone's behalf. With this gesture came a deep sense of camaraderie among the passengers. Everyone began passing around loaves of bread and pieces of fruit. If we were to make it, it would be together. It was certain to be a long trip.

    The passengers for Episkepsis arrived and I was pressed up against the window with my pack and bags on my lap and the jugs on the floor beneath my feet. Three other people sat on the seat that was meant for two, and that was the rule throughout the bus. The last people on had to stand. We were a single mass of pressed flesh.

    The driver put the bus in gear and drove out of town and headed north along the coast road. The whole time my head was bent toward the window and locked in place by the man next to me whose arm was over my shoulders. Luckily my hand was just free enough to keep a little patch of the window clear in front of my eyes. Otherwise, I might have gone mad staring at the glass with beads of condensed human perspiration dripping down it.

    When we arrived at the fork in the road where the way to Episkepsis went one way and the way to Strinilas the other, the bus stopped and the driver announced that all those headed for Strinilas would have to get off and wait for his return. The road to Episkepsis was a rough one, he explained, and he didn't want to go over it with such an over-crowded bus. And since he might not attempt to go up the mountain when he returned, he suggested that we look out for rides. He also asked us to get reports from anyone coming down the mountain about the condition of the road. Being made to stand out in the rain brought many protests, but in the end everyone headed for Strinilas got off the bus.

The driver had left us in a forsaken, desolate place. The clouds were low and in constant motion, alternately obscuring and revealing the steep rock faces that towered high overhead. The scene had the ethereal quality of a Chinese landscape painting in which different scenes on a single mountain are set apart by strange twists of perception created by layers of fog and mist. We were as one such scene on the scroll, a mass of humanity huddled under umbrellas surrounded by packages on a road that forked and became lost behind boulders and around turns, a road seemingly leading from nowhere to nowhere but simply existing within its own coordinates of time and place. The cliff over our heads was another such scene with its jagged rock face becoming occulted and softened by rounded wisps of cloud.

After half an hour a car came down the mountain. The driver said the road to Strinilas was in bad shape, especially for a bus, but if driven with care it was passable. This lightened our spirits, as did the sight of a goatherd coming around a bend in the road who invited us to take shelter in a little stone building not far from where we stood. Leaving a sentry to flag down the bus, the rest of us went with the goatherd. The building was just large enough to accommodate us all, and the thick straw on the floor was dry and comfortable to sit on. We were so wet and tired that we scarcely said a word until we heard the drone of the bus's engine coming up the road. We ran from the building *en masse* and were waiting for the bus when it stopped. We told the driver what the man in the car had said and he agreed to try it, although he did so grudgingly.

The road was bad, gouged by deep diagonal gullies and

practically blocked in places by mudslides and fallen rock. Maneuvering around these obstacles proved dangerous, since to do so seemed always to entail passing within inches of a steep precipice, each of which was itself undermined by the rain. At a dangerous turn of the road we came upon such a bad rockslide that it appeared our journey had ended. We could neither maneuver around the large rocks in the road nor pass over them. Since Strinilas was just a few miles away, the more hearty among us—myself included—decided to set out on foot. But when we were ready to go the old woman who had brought the bread and cheese to the driver announced that we either all go or none of us go. "And since I am too old to walk that far," she said, "the only solution is that we clear the road!" Enthusiasm for her idea spread quickly, and within seconds everyone was on the road removing rocks according to his or her ability, the very young and old picking up little rocks and throwing them to the side while those of strength and agility banded together and rolled the large boulders out of the way. The entire while the old woman moved amongst us, offering encouragement and advice. She was a grand matriarch and road commissioner in one. Within minutes we had cleared a wide enough aisle for the bus to pass through. We reached Strinilas without further incident.

16

When the bus stopped in the village everybody scattered for their houses, leaving me alone in the heavy rain, feeling wet and forlorn. Hoisting the pack and looping the bags of food through my arms, I threw my poncho over my shoulders and picked up the two jugs of wine. The road that led through the village was deserted except for a few wet dogs curled up together in a doorway, shivering in their sleep. The wind howled, ballooning the poncho behind me.

As I reached the last stone house of the village, whose back door opened to the mountain's wild, untamed slope, an old woman came running out to me. She stood before me in the rain, her face wrinkled and her eyes large and soft with compassion. Her dress was the color of the earth; her apron had flour on it. She stared at me, taking stock of my situation. Then she pointed toward the mountain and said, "*Epáno?*" Up? I said yes, and she muttered something beneath her breath. She held out her hand, caught some drops of rain, and said, "*Vroní,*" rain. I nodded. Another moment passed. She turned. She took a few steps; then she stopped to see if I was really going *epáno*. Seeing I was, she crossed herself and scurried to the shelter of her house, leaving me alone to face the mountain.

By the time I reached the dirt track that led to the monastery the wind had reached a ferocious howl. As I climbed the trail, I entered the low clouds and walked in their midst. I heard no thunder; nor did I see flashes of lightning. Uncorking the bottle of white wine, I took some large gulps, and with renewed confidence pushed on through the boulder-strewn landscape. I prayed that the monk was at the lower monastery, and that there would be a fire and supper waiting for me when I arrived. I could just see the kitchen suffused with the fire's warm glow.

But that was all in my mind's eye. In the gathering darkness, two dark figures emerged from the thick fog. One figure was short and stout and bent almost double against the wind, and the other, taller and more erect, was wearing a long robe that billowed in the gusting wind. It was the monk and a man from the village.

"Thomás," the monk yelled, "eh, Thomás!"

Then he said, "A woman in the village has died. I must go to the church. The lower monastery is locked. Go to the upper monastery. I will meet you there in a few days. May God be with you! The storm is raging upon the mountain!"

And with that he was gone. He didn't even stop to tell me the news. He told me in passing, as he and the villager continued toward the safety of the village. I stood watching the two men dissolve into the darkening night, taking with them all hope of a warm fire at the end of my journey. Instead of the monk cooking chicken while I warmed myself before the fire, I now saw the cool and damp bed that awaited me. I cursed it all. "Eh, Thomás," I said aloud, donning the monk's raspy voice, "you are a crazy man!"

Ahead of me was nothing but storm and fog-obscured mountain. Putting my hands out before me, I touched the soft limits of what I could discern. The fog deepened. Opacity turned to night.

Nothing of what I knew would be of help here. Darkness had descended. I was alone with the mountain. Much of who I was fell away at that moment. I was both closer to the animal and to the divine. My senses sharpened. Into me flowed the raw forces of nature. The mountain stood solid and unmoving—a mass of bare rock pounded by rough weather. The air was thick with cloud and cold. Rain was falling heavily now. Everywhere rivulets flowed and merged together. Distant rumblings of thunder sharpened my awareness to a keen edge, and in the distance through the rain-filled fog dim flashes reached my eyes.

I felt strong, as if I too were an element along with mountain, cloud, rain, and lightning. We had all existed before in this heightened tension of warring elements. And strange as it may sound, I now felt completely at home so far from anything human. I came to know myself in elemental simplicity as the warring forces called me into their sphere.

I felt myself as one with every human being who has gone to the edge of the earth, to the bottom of the ocean, or to the roof of the world.

The thunder came closer and the lightning became more intense. But I was not afraid. I was behind myself, watching my eyes watch the world, hearing my ears listen to the whirl of the wind, and feeling my body weak from the cold and the weight of my load. I felt what Thomas felt, saw what he saw, and heard what he heard; yet I was behind it all, unmoved and unconcerned.

I would have felt with equal indifference if lightning had struck a tree on the slopes or a rock on the path, smashing it to pieces; I would have felt the same if it had been me who had been struck. It would have mattered little. Would the winds have ceased to howl? Would the rain have ceased to lash?

I was walking up a barren mountain road, yet I didn't know how long I'd been on it. Going from one turn of the road to the next, I felt like the sailor whose boat is being dashed by the storm: he cares little of his final destination. The trough of one wave and the crest of the next is as far as his senses will take him.

Finally I heard the bell above the monastery gate being rung by the gale. I went through the gate with the sense of relief that a sailor feels when his storm-racked boat comes in sight of land, and he recognizes it as his own harbor as he glides in through a well-known channel, knowing that his feet will soon touch solid earth. I opened the door to my little room, dumped the food and wine on the floor, and lay on the bed, falling instantly into a deep sleep.

17

The next morning I awoke from a dream that had the clarity of a vision and the immediacy of waking life. Sometimes a dream stands out like a clear signpost on a dark roadway. One drives one's car along these dark roadways every night and occasionally the headlights fall on something significant. Usually the headlights are dim, the messages obscure. It is the intensity of the beam that determines the clarity of the vision. And one can never be too sure. One never knows the origin of a dream. As the wise Penelope, wife of Odysseus, said,

Windblown Clouds

Thomas K. Shor

> *Dreams, sir, are awkward and confusing things: not all that people see in them comes true. For there are two gates through which insubstantial visions reach us, one is of horn and the other of ivory. Those that come through the ivory gate cheat us with empty promises that never see fulfillment; while those that issue from the gates of burnished horn inform the dreamer what will really happen.*

Occasionally one has a dream whose place of issue is clear, a dream that leaves behind a deep sense of a destiny, a potential to be fulfilled. This was just such a dream. Dreams like this reflect the deeper patterns of which we ourselves are but reflections.

I dreamed I was sitting at the desk in my cell surrounded by papers and piles of open books. I was writing in a blue notebook. Then a voice rang in my ears. It was an ancient voice, the voice of one as old as time itself, a voice more familiar even than my own. It was the voice of the Mother, not *my* mother—though her voice was reflected in it; this was a far more ancient voice, that of the Great Mother, the matrix of all.

She said to me, "Go look under the tree."

So I opened the door and there, where the stunted trees had always stood in the middle of the courtyard, stood a colossal tree, a tree whose branches swept the clouds and whose trunk would have taken thirty people to encompass. At the base of its great trunk, where its ancient roots twisted and turned along the ground before delving down to the very foundation of the mountain itself, was a fish. I bent down and picked up the fish.

Then I was plunged into darkness. I could no longer see

what I held in my hands, so I looked at it under a quick succession of lights of increasing intensity, beginning with a match, then a candle, then a lantern, then an electric light, until it was by the light of the sun itself that I was looking at it.

The scene changed and I was bringing the fish to the house where the Great Mother lived. She greeted me at the door clad in a flowing white robe. She was pleased I had recognized her voice and had carried out her instructions. She took the fish and went inside. A moment later she reappeared, holding out a goblet filled with a chalky white mixture she had made from the fish.

"Drink this," she said. "It will bring you good luck in your upcoming travels."

I drank it and woke up.

~

Opening the door to brilliant Greek sunshine, I saw that the violent storm of the previous evening had passed, leaving the air crisp and clear. I walked to the low wall beyond the kitchen and looked down over the slopes of the mountain.

For the first time I saw the mountain for what it was. Before, my view of the mountain had been tainted by my own personal stamp. I had been preoccupied with myself when I had looked at it. It took the storm of the previous day to shake me loose from that preoccupation, to be prepared to be struck down like a pine along its slopes. A subtle yet powerful shift had occurred in my center of gravity.

Something new flowed inside me, as if I had lifted a rock to allow a clear spring to gush forth. But this spring was not new. It had flowed before, deep in my past; and it flowed before any past I could call my own. It was far more ancient than that. It was as old and familiar as the Mother of my dream. I was gazing over the mountain with the fresh and immediate clarity and wonder I had experienced as a child.

And with this clarity came a feeling of fruition, as if something was complete. Every particular fit in place and the patterns they created merged with the universal. Each moment in time stood perfected, lacking nothing from the past and yearning for nothing in the future.

Then the wheels turned again; time moved a notch and there was something to be fulfilled. Like an undertow coming suddenly at the changing of the tide, I knew my time on the mountain was drawing to a close. The words of the Mother came ringing to my ears, "Drink this," she had said, "it will bring you good luck in your upcoming travels."

From the top of the mountain I could sense the roundness of the earth implicit in the encircling horizon. The horizon seemed not that far away, and the earth itself seemed rather small. I wondered which point on the horizon hid my next destination.

I looked south, past the island's southern tip, toward Crete. Crete would be warm. I could speak Greek there and still be with Greeks, of whom I had grown so fond. Beyond Crete lay Egypt and the rest of Africa, a whole continent of deserts, plains, and jungles, whose villages and towns were populated with people who spoke languages as strange and alien as Greek had been when I first arrived. I knew I could learn one of these languages, and I knew these people could become my friends. Then I looked east. Beyond the Albanian mountains—across Turkey, Persia, Afghanistan, and Pakistan—was India, whose ancient cultural and spiritual traditions had long drawn me to them. Intuition seemed to confirm the unity that the Eastern thinker sees behind the multiplicity of the phenomenal world. I thought perhaps it was to their land that my steps would tend. In the west was Europe. I had long wanted to go to Assisi, the town in Italy where Saint Francis had lived. And beyond Europe, across the ocean, were my family and friends. I thought of the soft rolling hills of Vermont and I knew I would return there one day. I knew my travels would circle back to their beginnings, but I also knew the circle was only partially complete.

It was an intuition that first brought me to the mountain

Pantokrator, and if that had taught me anything it was that conscious intentions don't always lead to the goal. The traveler leaves the known world—as well as all pre-conceived notions—behind, and opens himself to the world of chance. He takes a step into the world's flux. He must enter the flow and follow it.

Since I had to leave Greece—if only to step foot in another country to receive a new visa—I decided to take the boat to Italy, which was the closest foreign landfall. Once I arrived there I could decide what to do next.

~

I decided to leave the mountain on a Tuesday, two days before the monk had to go to Corfu Town for his monthly meeting with the other priests and monks on the island. We arranged to meet in a taverna in town for an early lunch before my ferry left. This made it easier to leave the monastery since I only had to bid the monastery and mountain good-bye. I would be seeing the man again. And having a full day on the coast would allow me plenty of time to return my books to the Anglican Church library, go to Kontokali to bid my old neighbors good-bye, and take one last stroll through Corfu Town.

~

On the day of my departure I awoke before dawn and watched the sun rise over the Albanian mountains one last time. Then I spent hours walking around the courtyard and sitting on boulders outside the monastery gate trying to etch into memory every sight, smell, and sound of the place. When it was time for me to go the monk brought me to the church and he lit a candle for my safe journey. We stood in front of the burning candle in an attitude of prayer with our eyes closed for some time. Then I walked down the switchbacking road under the same heavy load of clothing and books as when I arrived. I turned when I reached the lower monastery and saw the monk's black form above the monastery wall. He raised his arms and waved good-bye to me. I waved back, turned, and continued across the gray plateau with no backward glance.

~

Thursday morning I arrived at the taverna early, sat on a chair outside the front door, and awaited the monk's arrival. I first spied him some distance down the road. He was wearing a new robe. It wasn't the patched one he wore at the monastery, but one he must have kept packed away for these occasional trips to town. His progress down the road was slow, for everybody seemed to know him, and when they stopped to speak with him they showed him great reverence, a reverence that seemed deeper and more heart-felt than I had seen shown toward other priests and monks I had seen in town.

When he arrived we sat at a table and ordered our meals and some beer. The food came quickly. We ate in an awkward silence, both feeling the sadness of parting.

When we had finished eating the monk broke the silence. "Thomás, one day you come back. You bring your wife and your children and you all stay with me. I will still be on the mountain. You will travel by boat, plane, and train to see the world and I will see it from the mountain Pantokrator. It is not so different in the end. But remember, when you come back I will be an old man. I will have a cane and I will hobble from place to place."

"But my friend," I said, "I will always be able to recognize you. No matter how old you are you will always be the one with fire in his eyes!" Then we laughed our last laugh together.

We stood to leave and hugged one another with lumps growing in our throats. Then we faced each other in an awkward silence, neither of us knowing what to say. He turned and made for the door as fast as he could.

Just as he was about to step outside I yelled out in English, "Good-bye, you sly chickpea!"

He whipped around with his finger to his mouth, his eyes scanning the taverna to see if anyone else had heard, which of course they had for I had yelled it out, and they were all staring at us.

Then he realized I had spoken in English and no one else understood my words. It had been our little secret and it would remain so. Then, forgetting the presence of the others, he shook his finger at me as he had so many times in front of the crackling fire, and he said, "Eh, *Thomás!*"

~

Then I was on the ferryboat to Italy, leaning against the stern rail, watching the Island of Corfu recede behind the boat. Instead of fading out of view, it remained clear till the very end when it suddenly sank beneath the horizon. The earth's curvature had claimed it. The last thing I saw was the high cone of the mountain, Pantokrator.

Part Two

ho·ri·zon (hə-rīʹzən) n. 1. The apparent intersection of the earth and sky as seen by an observer. Also called apparent horizon. 2. Astronomy. a. The sensible horizon. b. The celestial horizon. c. The limit of the theoretically possible universe.

—American Heritage Dictionary

Windblown Clouds   Thomas K. Shor

1

When the boat landed I had no idea where I was going. Everyone else getting off the boat had a destination. They clutched train and bus tickets in their hands. Their minds were full of timetables.

My time on the mountain had left me in a peculiar state of mind. I felt finely tuned. Sounds, smells, colors—everything was extremely sharp. Within me I carried the silence of the mountain. Still, I felt a bit like a fool, wandering off without purpose. I was a clean slate. To consciously direct my steps would have been contrary to my state of mind. I had no destination. I was in a state of flux, a state of pure possibility. To decide upon one destination would have been to block out all others. All points on the compass were equal to me. Strange as it may sound, I was awaiting a sign, a glimmer of recognition—anything that would direct me. I knew it was preposterous, but it was just such a glimmer that had led me to the mountain. Leaving the mountain was like jumping over the edge of the known world. Hopefully the universe would uphold me.

Food on the boat had been prohibitively expensive, so the first urge that directed my steps was hunger. I wanted spaghetti. I was, after all, in Italy. So I stopped at a place not far from the port and ordered a bowl of spaghetti. When it came it was greasy in a way that just wasn't right. I couldn't get it down, thinking the whole time of Lord Byron, who caught the cholera that cost him his life—in Brindisi. When I couldn't communicate with the waiter I left the restaurant feeling angry that I had to pay for something I couldn't eat. Nothing about Italy seemed right. I walked back to the port and bought a ticket for the boat's return trip to Greece.

Thinking I was the first one on the boat, I went straight to the large passenger cabin to claim the same seat I had occupied on the crossing to Italy. Entering the cabin, I noticed it was empty except for an old man sitting in *my* seat. Many people were still boarding the boat or exploring the various decks before finally finding places to settle for the journey. There were probably a hundred seats in this cabin, and though some people came in behind me and were now stowing their luggage, the only person sitting was this old man, and the seat he occupied was the one I wanted.

His head was turned away from me and he was looking out the window, probing his teeth with a toothpick. Standing in the aisle, I looked around for another seat, wondering at the same time whether the old man spoke English.

He sensed my presence and turned. "Please," he said, motioning to the seat beside him, "sit down."

I wanted to sit alone and meant to refuse; instead I accepted his offer. With a sigh I heaved my pack from my back and propped it on the back of the next row of seats. And as I sat I noticed his pack, a small canvas daypack on the floor by his feet. It was bright orange and slightly frayed around the edges.

The man turned to face me fully. "My name is Ed Spencer," he said, holding his hand out for me to shake. His hand was large and strong. I introduced myself.

"Judging from your voice," he said, "I'd say we hail from the same country."

"Yes," I said, "I'm originally from Massachusetts."

"I once lived there," he said. "In Cambridge, not far from Harvard Square. But that was many years ago. I was raised in New Jersey."

His head was large and his white hair and beard were cropped short. The bones in his face were prominent, and I could see his collarbone beneath his shirt. He wore sandals, and his pants ended well above his ankles. His clothes had the look of clothes bought at the Salvation Army.

Beneath his left eye I noticed a small bruise. In the center of the bruise was a tiny opening in the skin in which a drop of thick white liquid had formed. He noticed me looking at his cheek. He reached into his shirt pocket and took out a piece of tissue, with which he dabbed the puss.

"What happened?" I asked.

"Oh, this? A few months ago I was hitching to Miami. I was just on the edge of the city when it started to rain, so I took shelter under a bridge. A homeless man had put an old tarp between the abutments, and he was living there. I thought it quite enterprising of him. I had an orange, and I offered him half. Unfortunately, he didn't like me taking shelter under his bridge, and he decided to use my face as a punching bag. The police found me unconscious, and I was in the hospital for a month. The doctors had to reconstruct my face, and they left a hole here for the discharge from my eye. They say it will dry up on its own. Sometimes I think it's infected." He pressed the tissue on the wound again and winced.

"You're coming from the States now?" I asked, again eyeing his tiny pack.

"Yes," he said. "I flew to England about two weeks ago. It took me two weeks just to get to Brindisi."

"You hitched?"

"Yes, though I've had pretty rough luck. Seems I've walked half the way. I wanted to take the boat from northern Italy, but it was too expensive. I thought of hitching through Yugoslavia; then someone told me about this boat, so I hitched down here."

I felt sorry for him. He was obviously down on his luck. He must have been pushing seventy. It is sad, I thought to myself, to see old people all alone and without money.

"Is that all you have with you?" I asked, nodding at his pack.

"Is that *all*," he said. "Usually I have less than that—far less. The best way to travel is with the clothes on you back and with what fits in your pockets. That's the way I see it. Anything more than that only gets in the way. Eventually you get fooled into thinking you need all sorts of possessions. And then you think you need even more. And then—well, then the straps that bind you to your pack are stronger than the straps that hold the pack to your back. The world has it wrong. Less is more, as far as I've seen it."

"Then why the pack?" I asked.

"Probably because I'm getting soft in my old age," he said. "Or maybe it's because I was walking by a dumpster in Upstate New York and saw it right on top and thought, Why not? One takes what comes one's way. I'll get rid of it by and by."

He put the toothpick back in his mouth and gazed at my pack with the same bemused smile he'd had when he first turned and saw me standing in the aisle. Under his gaze my pack did look ridiculously large. It was heavy and it slowed me down. It made me feel like a tortoise. It was like moving a house. My tent, cook stove, clothes for both hot and cold climates: all these conveniences bound me to their upkeep; I was their slave, carrying them around. I had never used three-quarters of the stuff. His pack couldn't have held more than another shirt and maybe a pair of pants.

He looked at my pack for a long time; then he turned and looked me straight in the eye. He locked me in his gaze with a probing look, as if he wanted to know whether I understood what he had meant. I could feel his eyes plumbing my depths. It was an uncanny feeling.

"Where are you coming from now?" he asked.

"Greece," I said.

"Greece!" he said, laughing. "But I was led to believe that Greece is where this boat is *headed!*"

He had a way of cocking his head to one side, as if to present his ear to my words.

"You're right," I said. "We *are* headed for Greece." I told him I had to get a new visa. I didn't tell him how uncertain I was about my destination. "I came over earlier today on this very boat," I said. "You're sitting on the seat I sat in on my way here. That's why I was standing here, eyeing your seat."

"What were you doing in Greece?" he asked.

"I was living on Corfu, at a monastery on top of the island's highest mountain."

With this I obviously piqued his interest. He probed deeper with his toothpick. "A monastery..." he said, letting the word hang in the air. "Why were you living at a monastery?"

"Maybe you'll understand," I said, "traveling as you do. Living at that monastery was like living at the edge of the world. Sometimes it felt as if I were at the edge of the known universe. You see things differently from there." My words, once they were out, seemed cryptic. But I sensed that he too was living on the fringe, on the outside looking in. "I left the monastery just a few days ago," I continued. "It is still strange to be around so many people. It was a very distant place."

"What brought you to this distant place?" he asked.

"I suppose there is a light that shines only when the light fades that holds us to our attachments," I said, aware again that I was speaking in the shorthand that one uses who has spent a long time in solitude. "Maybe it's the same as when you travel with only the clothes on your back."

"That's probably true," he said. "I know what you mean by that other light. I've known that light. It is only from the edge of things that that other light can shine through."

This man was obviously not what he had at first appeared to be. On first impression I had assumed that he was nothing more than a bum traveling with hardly a change of clothes, his face battered from a fight, a man with hardly enough money for his ticket. I kept expecting him to reach into his pocket, produce a bottle of cheap liquor, and take a slug. I could sense something broken in him. Yet his clothes, though shabby and miss fitting, were clean. His white hair and beard were neatly cropped. He thought before he spoke and picked his words carefully. I sensed in him a keen intelligence. All of which made me wonder what brought him to such an impasse.

But before I could ask him anything about his life, he

started asking me about my experiences on the mountain. His questions were probing and to the point. They forced me to express what I never thought I could have expressed. He was interested in the inner dimension and depth of my experience. He plumbed my depths, as a sailor plumbs the waters around his vessel to determine how many fathoms lay beneath his keel. He seemed satisfied by the depths of my waters. We ended up discussing the importance of developing direct intuitive intelligence, which lies beyond the conscious mind.

"It is rare," he said, "to meet someone who understands such things."

2

The boat lurched forward. The dock glided by the cabin's window as the din of many voices rose above the engine's drone. Ed Spencer looked out the window as our boat passed an oil tanker anchored in the harbor.

In the silence that grew between us I fell back into my first impression of him, the one I formed before he spoke. Looking again at his clothes that had obviously once belonged to someone else and the tiny pack he picked out of a dumpster, I wondered whether he was running from something, perhaps the law. He was obviously well educated. He must once have had a family, a home, and possessions. He seemed to have lost everything. He was too old, I thought, to be tramping the way he was. I sensed that he had endured much suffering. Something in him seemed broken. Yet whatever it was also seemed mended, and like a piece of metal that has snapped and been welded together again, the weld is always the strongest part. He possessed a great strength.

"Where are you headed now?" I asked, not sure if a man in his circumstances, whatever they were, would be *headed* anywhere.

"I am on my way to India," he said. He intoned the word

India with a deep reverence, as if it were the name of an old friend or lover. The word hung in the air between us a moment, then I asked whether he'd been there before.

"Yes," he said. "Many times. I've lived longer in India than in the West. India is my home, as much as any place here on earth can be."

"Why India?" I asked.

"As a child I dreamed of India," he said. "Whenever I could get my hands on a book about India, I devoured it from cover to cover. I suppose this was because my life didn't seem like much. Looking back now I can see that I understood from a very early age just how hollow and shallow the West is. Even as a child I knew this. I was not a happy child—unwanted and unloved. I've always been a fish out of water. I had to travel far to find my true home. Though I often dreamed of traveling to India, I never thought I'd get to go, transportation being what it was in those days. I came from comfortable circumstances—but still, India was very far away.

"Then World War II broke out. I didn't believe in taking up a gun to kill others who happened to have been born on the other side of an arbitrary political line. I'd heard that the American Field Service was looking for drivers for their ambulance corps in India. It meant a deferment from fighting. So I signed up. Most of the time I was in Bihar and West Bengal, in the east of India, north of Calcutta and what is now Bangladesh. Once, when I had some days off, I took a walk through the countryside. As I crossed a small village some people invited me into their hut for tea. On the mud wall was a picture of a man. I asked them who he was. 'A very great teacher,' they told me. 'A mystic.' They said he lived close by, in a neighboring village. They asked if I wanted to meet him, and I jumped at the opportunity. I was looking for answers, hoping India could provide solutions to my life's conundrums.

"We walked for an hour across fields and through tiny

settlements of grass and mud huts till we reached the village that had literally grown up around this man. They brought me to the central pavilion where he lived. They left me at the door and disappeared inside. Soon I was announced and led into his presence. The moment I saw him I felt as if I had come home after long wanderings. Tears came to my eyes as I felt his gaze fall on me. I knew he could see right into me. He was seeing me on a level more profound than anyone had ever seen me before. And I was probably cracked anyway; I was in need of healing. He saw straight through places where I could see only twisted paths. That is how I met Thakur, my teacher."

Ed stopped and again looked out the window. Puffy white clouds sailed over the Adriatic's gentle waves. Slowly he turned back. His eyes looked gentler now, almost misty.

"Did you stay there with him?"

"No, I couldn't. The world was still at war. Time wasn't my own. Though I did manage to see him a few more times before the end of the war. Anyway, I had a life to return to in the States."

"What kind of life was that?" I asked, trying not to let my curiosity seem too keen.

"I was a teacher."

"Where?"

"Harvard. I taught medieval European history. Though if before the war my studies—if my entire life—seemed shallow, upon my return from India it all seemed completely devoid of meaning. There I was at the highest seat of learning in America and I kept asking myself: Who is this serving? And to what end?

"The war had torn the mask of civilization from the barbarism that still lurked beneath the surface of Western Civilization. Harvard was self-serving and self-satisfied—a self-perpetuating institution whose sights rarely went beyond the world of academia. It excluded more than it included. Academia constituted a world set apart from the real world, the world of experience.

"Before the war I never felt at home—anywhere. I came back from India seeing more clearly why I had always felt out of place. I probably *was* cracked in the head. But I knew that the world around me was cracked as well. Healing cannot come from a society that itself is cracked. I had to leave. I had to leave or risk going mad. So I taught a while longer, and taught myself Sanskrit. The entire time I dreamt of returning to India. I was sure India could help put my twisted life in order.

"While at Harvard I got married. A few years later my wife and I set out for India. We went by boat. Oh, yes, and we took our dog, for we were moving there, you see."

He turned to look again out the window. A long time passed, so long that I thought maybe he was finished with his story. But then he turned again.

"This move upset my father. He said I'd be throwing everything away. What he meant was everything dear to him. He was right, of course. I would have had standing, everything that comes to a fully tenured professor at Harvard. I probably would have authored many books. A friend and I had worked out some new theories on education. We even spent an afternoon at the White House presenting our ideas to Eleanor Roosevelt, when FDR was president. I met with her once after that, when she was living in New York. She was quite a woman, Eleanor Roosevelt. She had a keen interest in India, you know.

"All that promise and more my father said I'd be throwing away. He called India the 'great intellectual graveyard.' He said it had claimed many great minds in the past."

Ed Spencer's words trailed off. Then he continued, almost in a whisper. "The spiritual life is one of purging, you know. That was my first renunciation. The next one came soon thereafter.

"The boat brought us to Ceylon. From there we took a train to Bihar to see Thakur. But from the very start my wife didn't like India. She detested the dirt, the poverty, the ragged millions—and the oppressive heat. And when she met Thakur she wasn't at all impressed. He didn't strike the slightest chord within her. To her, he was just another sordid piece of a sub-continent that was itself fetid and backward.

"Before long my dog died and my wife left me—two devastating blows. My wife returned to the States and divorced me. I never heard from her again.

"All my ties with my old world—the West—had been broken; yet a new center was beginning to grow within me. It wasn't easy: it was torturous most of the time—believe me. I left all comfort and security behind. I staked my life on following my will in my pursuit of truth. I was desperate. If I hadn't been desperate I never would have taken such desperate steps. But there was no turning back. I *had* nothing to return to, even had I wanted to. I had to continue stripping away at myself or perish. Thakur was instrumental in this. He saw the truth in me, buried beneath a lifetime's falsehood. I would have perished long ago if it weren't for Thakur, probably by my own hand."

"Thakur taught that the highest truth is love. What gets in love's way is the ego's selfish desires. I was full of ego, and my ego was full of cracks. I tried to love Thakur perfectly. I was looking for a human love to fulfill my destiny. But can any human love truly satisfy the heart?"

"How long did you stay with Thakur?"

"Years. Decades. But in the end we had a falling out. It was easier for the Indians. Indians are practically born believing their teachers are beyond fallacy.

Ed Spencer took a deep breath, and then continued. "Thakur's cook died. He committed suicide. I knew he'd committed suicide and I knew Thakur knew it too. But this was late in Thakur's life. The village that had grown around Thakur by the time I met him had turned into a small town. He commanded an empire of tens of thousands of followers. He was embroiled in politics and had to hold up appearances.

He was concerned with his image.

"Thakur said publicly that the cook had died by natural causes. I knew this was a lie. But when I confronted him he denied the truth. His eyes would not meet mine. All those years I had tried to aspire to *his* truth, only for him to prove false in the end. I felt betrayed.

"Where on this earth—amid all the disappointment and disillusion—where in this 'vale of tears,' as the Bible puts it, where even the highest proves false, is that to which one can aspire? I realized that Thakur was but another false attachment.

"So I hit the road.

"At first I had some money, not much. I bought a flute with some of it and the rest time wore away. I started off with a small bag, but soon that was gone. In the end I had only the clothes on my back.

"One evening I walked into a little mud and thatch village. All I had left was a twenty-five piasa coin—a quarter of a rupee, worth a few cents American. As I entered the village a beggar approached me, his hand outstretched. I reached into my pocket, but caught myself: I thought it unwise to give away my last coin. So I passed him by and found a place to sleep in a little courtyard that was overgrown with trees and bushes where no one would bother me.

"The next morning I awoke just before sunrise. And there lying beside me was the beggar from the evening before. On the previous evening he had looked pained and hungry; now, in his sleep, he was peaceful. His smile was like a child's. His head was propped upon his outstretched arm and his hand was half open as it lay in the dirt. I took that last coin from my pocket and carefully, so not to wake him, I put it in his hand. As I said, it was my last coin, and I gave it away. And the moment it was gone I knew I was free.

"As I walked out of the village a fair wind blew. My steps came effortlessly. The village still slept. I was as free as the clouds that floated across the sky. I was ecstatic. No money!

Free! The way of God is free! I danced in sheer delight. The birds were singing in the trees and a song came to me."
"Does that song have a name?" I asked.
"Yes. I call it the Road Song."
"Do you remember it?"
"Yes."
"Would you sing it for me?"
Ed Spencer laughed now. He cleared his throat and began to sing. His voice had the bravado of a midnight drunk:

> "A roamer, a rover, the whole world over,
> As happy as me, you'll seldom see.
> At the Lord's own boards each day I dine,
> From the Bearing Straits to Palestine.
> Each mile, a smile, from a man's pure heart,
> Jump in that truck or bullock cart!
> This nook, that brook, will ring the bell,
> No need of dough, it's God's hotel.
> No pills, no bills, no therapy,
> Sun, air, and sea are ever free.
> There's light and right in every code,
> And a heap of God on the open road.
> One shirt, no dough, was Christ's motto,
> Then do the same: let heaven flow.
> A roamer, a rover, the whole world over,
> As happy as me, you'll seldom see."

"Wonderful!" I exclaimed.
He smiled.
"What happened after that morning?" I asked, eager for more.
"I continued down that dusty road, and then I went down another and another. I went through village after village and town after town. I was free. Giving up that last coin had set me free. And I was at peace.
"I was filled to the brim, and the universe upheld me. Not

that I didn't lose what I'd gained that morning, not that I didn't fall from those heights. Not that I wasn't tested. I lived through incredible hardships. Nothing could sway me; I simply accepted whatever came my way."

His eyes took on a far away look. "I loved the very simple ones," he said, "the ones with dancing love in their eyes and dirt on their hands. I joined them for a while, lived with them. It was so easy, so good. But only for a while, for no one was perfect. No one loved me. They loved me for themselves. Even the poor. Eventually the desire in them would surface and I would depart. I came to understand what the Bible says about Christ: he committed himself to no man because he knew what was in the heart of man."

First I had thought that Ed was one of those who couldn't live up to society's standards; I now knew it was society that couldn't live up to his.

"How long did you travel?" I asked.

"About ten years," he answered.

"Without money? How did you eat?"

"When you exchange food—or anything else—for money, you compromise both yourself and the person you're dealing with. 'I'll give you this and no more if you give me that': is that any way to live?

"Christ said, 'Love ye one another.' Does money have anything to do with love, with the ideal? I was in search of Truth—at all costs. Though I didn't really know what I was looking for, I had no choice but to live by the ideal. Anything less would have been a compromise. I had given up too much to compromise."

"But still," I said, "how did you eat?"

"Whatever I needed always came my way. Sometimes people gave me food. Sometimes I found it. Other times I had no food. The body craves food every day, but it isn't necessary. I went days and sometimes weeks with little or no food. Once I lived on nothing but the leaves of the betel tree. They are rich in vitamin C. You don't need money. You're better off without it. Take the money out of your pocket and put yourself in the hands of the unknown."

"Perhaps in India you can travel like that," I said. "There's a tradition, isn't there, of wandering holy men? But surely you couldn't do that in the States." I tried to picture him rambling past shopping malls, or on freeways, trying to catch a ride without a penny to his name, but always a police car came into the picture. Having no money in America is a crime.

"I travel the same way everywhere I go," he said, dismissing my question with a single unequivocal blow.

I didn't think he was lying, but it seemed fantastic. His story reminded me of a line from William Blake's *The Marriage of Heaven and Hell*, and I quoted it to him: "The road of excess leads to the palace of wisdom."

Ed laughed. "I like that, though I wouldn't say I've been excessive. I've merely done what I've had to. But Blake is right: how else are we to find wisdom?"

"I've never been outside America and Europe," I said, "though now that I've lived on Europe's edge, I long to go farther. India—what another world altogether it must be."

Ed looked me straight in the eye. "I think you should come with me to India," he said.

A rush surged through me, the type you might feel if someone opened an airplane's hatch, revealing a mile of open space below. My stomach dropped. Immediately—as if ready made—fears welled up; they congealed and took form. One hears stories of people who go to India only to become so frightened by what they see that they jump on the next plane out. One hears about people who catch nasty diseases there, people who are never quite the same.

But then there were those like Ed, whose lives India had transformed in some mysterious way. They were the ones I feared most; since something had happened to these people I couldn't understand.

Ed was still staring me in the eye, awaiting my response.

"There are cheap flights from Athens," he said. "That's

where I'm headed now. If we can get a flight to Bombay, I have friends there. When you're a bit acclimated and your feet are back on the ground we could travel together, maybe to the south."

"Look," I said, "I have to think it over."

"Yes," he said, smiling, "you must consider it carefully."

"I need some air," I said. "I need air to think this through." I stood up. It was all so fast.

Ed realized what a shock his sudden offer had caused me. He laughed. "Yes, you do that. Take your time."

I went to the boat's stern and leaned over the rail and watched the sun sink into the sea. The sky was brushed with red. Italy was disappearing beneath the horizon. Seagulls rode gusts of wind behind the boat, gliding back and forth, first high against the fiery sky then dipping gracefully back to the ocean. They rode the air currents, making a passage across the sea to Greece. Did they know where this boat was leading them? Did they care? The gulls called to one another above the sounds of wind and wave. The sky took on deeper and deeper shades of red as the sun dipped beneath the horizon.

I could weigh forever the pros and cons of going to India with a man I hardly knew. There was no telling what might happen. I might get sick far from a hospital. I might be robbed and find myself halfway around the world without a penny to my name. I thought of myriad potential dangers that might take my money, health, or sanity.

But the birds! How did they know this boat wasn't going to sail out to sea and keep going farther and farther away from land till they dropped from the effort to keep up? How did they know? They didn't know, yet they flew out to sea behind the boat anyway, playing in the eddying wind, calling joyfully back and forth to one another as the fading light of the passing day engulfed them in darkness. My boat was leaving now. The next leg of the journey had been announced and I realized that I hadn't any choice. It was no mere chance that our paths had crossed—Ed Spencer's and mine. I knew I had to go with him.

3

When the boat landed in Greece we passed easily through customs and stepped together through the final gate. It was nighttime and everything was closed except the kiosk-like exchange bank. Walking just ahead of me, Ed passed this kiosk as if it were nothing. I called to him, "Hey, the bank. We'll be needing money." I had a money belt full of traveler's checks. He had told me that while in the States a friend had suggested he apply for Social Security. He had taught at Harvard just long enough to qualify, and I knew he had traveler's checks too. I also knew we hadn't a single Greek Drachma between us. It was a Saturday night, and money exchanges were closed on Sundays. Besides, we were in Patras, a city on the Peloponnese. Athens was a few hours' drive away. A bus to Athens was waiting.

Ed stopped and turned. He had a toothpick in his mouth, as he always did. He took it out of his mouth and asked what *we* needed money for. I was taken aback.

"For starters, we'll need food and a place to spend the night. This isn't Athens, you know. We'll have to get there. That's what the bus is for; it's taking people to Athens—and the bus isn't free. There are many things we'll need money for." It was like talking to a child.

Ed looked at me as if I were crazy. He knitted his brow and sighed. Hadn't I understood, he seemed to be saying? It was then I realized the gulf that stood between this man and me, between this man and the rest of humanity. At first I had been impressed by his stories of traveling with nothing, and relying on the goodness of humankind to see him through. I had nodded my head in agreement when he described an exchange of money as an unloving act, as an act that debases the human being into doing for others and having others do for you, always conscious of the rate of exchange, always calculating how much you receive for what you give. Ed believed in both giving and receiving freely. He wanted love to be the unit of exchange. But these weren't just ideas for him. It came right down to how one fills one's stomach or finds shelter for the night.

To pass that money exchange would have been to dive headfirst into an ocean whose depth I could not judge. I was sure my head would strike bottom. I was sure I would die of starvation that very night. The spaghetti in Brindisi had been inedible, and food on the boat had been expensive. I was hoping to find a taverna in which I could order a meal. I thought about a bed for the night. I thought about the comforts afforded by those printed-paper notes and those stamped metal disks.

We stood there in the night, the neon light of the money exchange illuminating our faces, as people from the boat lined up like a herd of docile cows. They were exchanging one piece of paper for another, the rate of exchange clearly marked on the window placard. Ed was watching me, his eyes questioning, gauging whether I was made of the right stuff.

I wish I could report that I passed muster, that I shrugged and laughed off the thought of possessing money in a foreign country. Instead, I did the prudent thing: I pulled out my traveler's checks. He did too, and we waited in line with the others. I felt dirtied by the affair, but still I felt I'd done the prudent thing. I didn't see how else we would put food in our mouths or shelter over our heads for the night.

We came away from the exchange window and Ed held out his hands, now full of banknotes and coins. "Here," he said. "You can be our official money carrier." He handed me the money, uncounted. He had no idea how much he had—or what it was worth. He treated the money with total disregard. I stuffed it into my money belt with a feeling of shame.

Then the bus driver approached us. He pointed to his vehicle and told us to climb aboard. Ed wagged his finger at him and said testily, "No. No. We will walk." The man didn't understand. I explained in Greek, *"Tha perpatísume,"* we will walk. "But everybody gets on the bus here," he said. "With boat ticket, only one hundred drachmae. Only one hundred drachmae! You can't walk to Athens." I started telling Ed how little it would cost to get to Athens, but Ed just started walking.

The urge came over me to jump on that bus and part ways with Ed Spencer right then and there. I thought maybe he really was cracked. But I had all his money. I couldn't just take off. I had no choice: I had to follow.

Adjusting the straps on my pack and trotting to keep up, I followed Ed away from the docks and into the unlit streets of the dirty port. Ed was a tall man, standing well over six feet. His stride was great; he was a powerful walker. There was certainty in his step, as if he knew exactly where he was going.

We passed boarded-up warehouses and derelict, old brick buildings. This port had seen better times. There wasn't a soul in sight. I kept looking behind me, expecting someone lurking in the shadows to pluck me off the street.

I wondered if he was trying to lose me, but something bound us together. He could no more lose me in those darkened streets than I could have lost him by simply jumping on the bus.

As he led the way down smaller and smaller roads, I could never quite catch up to him to ask where we were going. My pack grew heavier with every step. I stumbled. I tried not to lose him. I trotted, ever attempting to catch up. His feet hit the pavement with perfect regularity, the snap, snap, snap of his sandals echoing from the deserted buildings in perfect measure. He held his head erect, not stiffly on his neck, but proudly. He turned neither right nor left. His back was straight, his shoulders square and firm, as if nothing could stop him, as if an invisible force, a hidden source of strength, was leading him on.

Windblown Clouds   Thomas K. Shor

Ed was in his element. He had spoken of being on the road, of the years he had spent walking: now I saw him in action. He was indefatigable. He was tall and lean. His shortly cropped hair was shockingly white. In the darkest shadows it was all I could see of him. In the darkness I could imagine him as a clothed skeleton. I couldn't even remember his face. I had only known him a few hours. What madness. What total madness!

We came to a slightly wider street. A deep rumble and bright swath of headlights announced a huge truck rounding the corner. It was a tractor-trailer truck and it was working through its gears and gradually gaining speed. When it came abreast of us Ed put out his thumb, and the truck stopped with a loud hissing of its air brakes. We ran to the cab. Ed jumped up and grabbed the door. I was surprised by his agility. He opened the door to a blast of full-volume bouzouki music and jumped inside. I hoisted him my pack, climbed in, and slammed the door shut.

Icons of saints were glued to the dashboard, and from the windshield hung colorful fringes, talismans, and ornaments. Colored dashboard lights washed us in hues of pink and red and green. The driver was a large man, his face bony and angular and covered with stubble. He was pleased to have companions and hummed along with the radio as he shifted through the gears.

The driver offered us cigarettes and a half-eaten loaf of bread. Ed ripped a piece off the loaf and handed the loaf to me. I took the bread and caught his eye—or rather he caught mine. Without uttering a word he was telling me to pay attention. With his eyes he said, 'See, now we're humming along, we've gotten a ride and now we have something to eat.'

The bread seemed a feast.

It was as if Ed had brought me to his kingdom and now he was showing me its riches. He was the one who, possessing nothing, has it all. I was still unsure of his realm. It wasn't mine.

Then I realized we had no idea where this truck, and its driver, was taking us. Ed seemed to care less, as if the thought hadn't crossed his mind. All the normal concerns of travel seemed to elude him. Silently chewing his bread and following the headlights' beam in the darkness, he was happy just to be on the move.

When we came to a larger road, there was a sign for Athens. I pointed to the sign. "You go to Athens?" I asked the driver in Greek. "Yes, to Athens," came the reply.

Out of the corner of my eye I saw Ed smile. He was ruminating with his toothpick, deep in thought. He didn't say a word.

~

We had to spend several days in Athens while I secured a visa and we booked a flight. Ed would no doubt have lived on the street, but I insisted we do otherwise. We stayed in the Plaka, the old center of Athens, where we—and dozens of mostly young travelers—paid a nominal fee for a bunk in a house that had probably once been owned by one of Athens' leading families. Now the place was falling apart and there were rooms in the rear where the roof had caved in. The old kitchen, which had once buzzed with cooks and servants, was now communal. We all took turns buying food in markets and making dinners of Greek ingredients spiced by cooks whose home countries often spanned three continents. We were a band of gypsies, ever grouping and regrouping.

Only one door in the entire mansion had a lock, and that was the door to the front hall closet, which was reserved for left luggage. There I left my heavy pack and took with me to India only my daypack containing not much more than a change of clothes.

4

Our plane landed at Bombay's Santa Cruz Airport just before the sun set. As we taxied to the terminal, the sun dissolved into the thick air before reaching the horizon. The setting sun lent its color to the entire western sky, which was ablaze in shimmering heat.

When we stepped from the airplane's door we stopped at the top of the gangway to breathe deeply India's thick, fecund air. Nothing could have communicated more deeply nor directly how different a world I was entering than that smell, which was sweet, like the smell of decaying fruit. It was the smell of life at its fullness, at its very peak, which includes its dissolution, its decay, the preying of one form of life on another. The aroma of wood smoke hung in the air. I could even smell curry and incense, right there on the tarmac of Bombay's international airport.

By the time we cleared customs darkness had settled over the city. In front of the airport, dozens of taxi drivers descended upon us, each trying to coax us into his taxi. Ed waved them all away. He told them we would walk. But they persisted, thinking he was holding out for a lower fare. Ed spoke to them in their own language, which surprised them, but still they would not let us alone. They reminded me of the bus driver in Patras, and I found myself siding with them, and against Ed. It was ten miles to the city. Prudence sided with the drivers; beyond the airport's lights, India was a vast darkness. Ed was excited to be back in India. Nothing could stop him. I had no choice but to follow. The taxi drivers called after us in their strange tongue, but we had already plunged into the tropical darkness. I turned and saw them pointing us out to others. They were laughing at us.

The road leading from the airport was long and dark and straight. Ed walked ahead of me and again I sensed his indomitable will; again I questioned the wisdom of following this man—to where? To the other side of the world...

At the end of the airport road was a wide metal gate. Passing through that gate was like passing through the birth canal into a world as new and terrifying and fantastic as any through which a baby has ever entered this world. The barrage on my senses was dizzying: hoards of people in what seemed great migrations were streaming up and down the street, disregarding the distinctions we in the West make between sidewalk and street. As far as the eye could see were the bobbing heads of walking people. Trucks billowing huge clouds of smoke, their horns blaring, pressed through the human mass, scattering carts full of rags and vegetables. In the distance the sound of cymbals came wafting like wisps of smoke along with voices singing a sacred song. The smell of incense rose from a niche that had been carved into a tree. Within this niche a statue of a multi-armed, tri-headed god stood swaddled in clothes of gaudy colors. Children squatted by the side of the road, emptying their diarrheal guts in streams of open sewage. Corrugated tin and cardboard huts stretched as far as the eye could see.

We passed through vegetable markets where thousands offered their wares stacked in pyramids on squares of cloth. The ground was thick with the detritus of the day's business. The pavement was so old in places that it had reverted to dirt. We entered a market lit only with the light of gas lanterns. It felt as if we were walking down a village road. It was strange, evocative of an earlier age. Children swarmed around us. An old man, standing next to the ornately carved stone portal to a temple, silently watched us pass. Looking into his eyes was like looking into the ages. So old were those eyes, so peaceful amidst the city's incredible bustle, that I could imagine them watching that scene for centuries, unmoved by the masses passing them by.

Ed glided seamlessly through the scene. He nodded to people as if he knew them. Occasionally he stopped to ask directions in a language I didn't understand. Then he set out again. Not once did he turn to check on me, to make sure I wasn't lost.

I was thankful that Ed was tall, standing two or three heads above the others. Once, when we were going through an especially crowded market, I fell back half a block. And while the crowd seemed to part for Ed, I had to push to get through. Ed was just a white shock of hair above the rest. I followed it like a beacon. If I'd lost him then, I knew I might never be found; I might never have made it out of those markets.

~

After so many miles and so many impressions that I was wondering which would give out first, my weary legs or my tottering mind, Ed turned at a short alleyway with a tailor's stall on one corner and a sweets stall on the other. On either side of the alley were open bunks built into the stone walls, some of which were occupied by dark skinned young men who eyed us closely as we passed. The alley ended at an open door to an apartment, and as we approached a man appeared at the door as if ready to walk out. He saw Ed and me and his jaw dropped. He ran out.

"Spencer-da," he cried, "is that really you?"

"Hello Bipin," Ed's voice boomed. "*Namaste!*"

A boy of thirteen came to the door, his eyes wide, as if he were beholding an apparition. "Spencer-da," he cried as he jumped across the threshold. Hugging Ed, the boy practically knocked him off his feet.

Then Bipin said to the boy, "Bimal, go tell the others that Spencer-da is here! They will never believe it. Never! Go. Go! Tell them!" Bipin was beaming. The boy scampered inside. His voice rang out, "Spencer-da, Spencer-da!" Soon the entire family came tumbling out the door.

Bipin asked me my name. Then he christened me: Mr. Tom.

"Mr. Tom, how do you like our India?" he asked. I assured him it was too early to tell. Everybody laughed, and he led us inside.

The front room of the apartment was large. It had a red tile floor and two glassless windows crossed with bars to protect against intruders. A couch stood against one wall, and against another were two chairs separated by a small end table. Kicking off our shoes by the door, Ed and I sat on the couch.

Word of Ed's arrival spread with lightning speed through the neighborhood, for soon men in *dhotis* and women dressed in saris streamed in through the door. More came from the apartment's back rooms. It was a dizzying crowd, pulsing with excitement, and it was all I could do to keep the room in focus. Ed bounced two kids on his knees as another climbed onto his shoulders.

A dozen eager-faced people surrounded me and plied me with so many questions that I couldn't answer a single one. "When did you arrive in India?" they asked. "How long did it take?" "Did you see many birds up there?" "How long can you stay?" "Mr. Tom, is this your first time in our India?" "How do you like it?" "Which do you like better, our India or your America?" "How old are you?" "Do you have brothers and sisters?" "Are you married?" "I think you have been to India in a previous lifetime; here, let me look at your palm."

An old, bald-headed man named Rindani came into the room followed by his wife and four children, ranging in age from twenty to thirty years. Three of them were blind and rushed up to Ed to hold onto his hands, just to assure themselves that Spencer-da had actually arrived.

Rindani was dressed in a crisp white *dhoti*, and across his chest was the thin white chord of the Brahmin. "You were lucky to have met Ed Spencer," Rindani said, sitting next to me. "He is a very special man. The gods must have been happy with you. Spencer-da can travel in India like no Indian can. Spencer-da can live with no food or water whatsoever. Spencer-da has walked across the Himalayas and he has crossed the deserts by foot. Spencer-da... Spencer-da... Spencer-da..."

A steady stream of people continued to pour into the room, kicking off their sandals and adding them to the pile by the door. My shoes were buried now beneath a mountain of sandals two feet deep, and the mountain was growing every minute. It was fantastic the number of people that could occupy so small a space. Ed was apparently loved by half of Bombay, and they all pushed to get close to him, pressing their palms together. Some even bowed before him and touched their foreheads to the ground, which clearly made Ed uncomfortable. "Spencer-da, Spencer-da," the name kept ringing out. Ed was laughing, overwhelmed by every familiar face that appeared at the doorway.

Bipin somehow made it through the crowd with a cup of tea. He sat down beside me and handed me the cup. The tea was spiced with cardamom and cinnamon.

"Mr. Tom," Bipin said, "when you are the guest in an Indian home, you are treated like a god visiting from the other world." I was so overwhelmed by it all that I couldn't answer. The man sitting on my other side took my silence as an invitation to start a conversation. "Mr. Tom, Mr. Tom. Tell me, Mr. Tom, how do you like our India?"

Ed still had a toothpick stuck between his teeth. Out of the corner of his eyes he stole a glance at me, a slight smile forming on his lips. Again I had the feeling he was showing me a piece of his kingdom.

Bipin raised his voice above the din and silenced everyone. "Hold on, everyone," he said. "We are not being very good hosts. Mr. Tom, you have just arrived in our country and you must be very tired."

I smiled back, uncomfortable for the attention suddenly shown to me, and he continued.

"Let me introduce you to our family. These are our parents," he said, pointing to a framed portrait of a severe-looking couple that hung above the wide doorway that led farther into the apartment. "They brought us from the state of Gujarat to this place many years ago. They have both passed on.

"This is Arvind. He is the eldest brother, and he is now the head of our household." Arvind, a man of perhaps fifty, stepped forward. He was tall with jet-black hair that was oiled and combed straight back off his forehead. His cheeks and his chest were sunken in and he did not look healthy. "And that woman," Bipin continued, pointing to a well-rounded woman standing shyly by the door to the kitchen, "that is Bhabi, Arvind's wife." She pressed her palms together, inclined her head, and said, "*Namaste.*" I returned her *namaste,* a bit falteringly, and stole a glance at Ed. He gave me a quick wink, and Bipin continued. "Their daughter is Maya," and Maya, perhaps eighteen, with long dark hair and thick glasses said, "*Namaste,* Mr. Tom." "*Namaste,*" I said. Without realizing it, I had tried to give the word an Indian accent, which made everybody laugh.

"My next brother is Indrijit," Bipin continued. It was Indrijit who was sitting next to me on the couch. He was perhaps forty-five and was both shorter and stockier than Arvind. "His wife, Ammu, is next to Bhabi, and their two children are Bimal and Kaitan." The brothers, sitting next to each other on the floor, were thirteen and eleven.

"And I am Bipin." Bipin was perhaps thirty-five and of medium height. His features were more delicate than his brothers', somehow more refined.

The formalities complete, pandemonium again broke out. Bimal and Kaitan sat again on Ed's knees, firing questions at him and pulling at his beard and making him laugh. More people arrived, entire families, who kicked off their sandals, adding them to the mountain at the door. The noise level rose to a roar.

A man named Vyas introduced himself and his wife Kamala and their two girls Krishisha and Nimisha, who were nine and seven years old. Nimisha, the younger of the two, was the most precious child I'd ever seen; with her dark blue sari, almond eyes, and long dark eyelashes, she was a young princess out of a fairy tale.

Vyas was short and stocky. His face was wide and his eyes expressive. "Tell me," he said, "how long have you known our Spencer-da?" But before I could answer, Bimal, Kaitan,

Krishisha, and Nimisha—the whole slew of kids—tried to interrupt. Vyas held them back. "Let Mr. Tom answer my question," he scolded with a smile.

"Not long at all," I replied, "I just met him in Greece."

"I thought you and Spencer went way back. You look like birds of a feather. That's what you say in America, no? 'Birds of a feather?'"

"Yes, that is an expression."

"What was that," Kaitan cut in, "'Birds of a feather?'" Soon all four kids were running around the room teaching everyone their new American phrase.

"Those kids, they make too much noise," Vyas said. Then, leaning forward, his eyes bulging, he said in a hushed tone, "Spencer—he is no ordinary man. He is a *sadhu*. You were fortunate indeed to meet him." By then the kids were back, ready to pick up their next American phrase. "We've known Spencer," Vyas continued, "for a long time—fifteen, maybe twenty years."

"Yes," the kids all chimed in like parrots, "twenty years, maybe more." They rocked their heads back and forth Indian fashion to add credence to their words. Vyas and I laughed at their show, for the oldest among them wasn't much more than half that age.

Just then Bipin announced that dinner was ready and that the others would have to go. "We will have more time to talk later," Vyas said.

All the neighbors left, pausing at the door to put on their sandals.

5

"Come!" Arvind, the eldest brother, said. "Now we will eat. It is important to eat on time. Each evening, we eat at exactly seven-twenty. Regularity is good for the digestion. We are already late tonight because of your coming. Who knows what will happen?" He patted his stomach and looked toward the heavens.

The kitchen floor was laid with a semicircle of mats. Before each mat was a stainless steel dish. Arvind motioned for me to sit. In the open part of the circle sat Bhabi, Arvind's wife, and Ammu, the wife of Indrijit, surrounded by pots of steaming food. The women were making *chapatis*—Indian flat breads—with Ammu rolling the balls of dough into flat disks and handing them to Bhabi, who slapped them onto a slightly concave pan over a fire of hot coals, flipping them occasionally from side to side. When each *chapati* was cooked it puffed up into a ball, which Bhabi then pierced with a pointed stick, letting out a cloud of steam. Adding it to her pile, she took the next flattened ball from Ammu. Their movements were graceful and harmonious, for at the very instant Ammu had completed rolling the dough into a perfect disk, Bhabi held out her hand to receive it, the last *chapati* having just been added to the pile.

Soon Arvind was sitting on the mat to my left; Ed sat on the mat to my right. Beyond him sat Bipin and Indrijit.

"Don't the women and children eat?" I asked.

"It is our custom," Bipin answered, "for the men to eat first. After the men have eaten, then the children eat. And only when they are through do the women eat."

Arvind told me to hand my plate to Bhabi. The women didn't speak English. It came back piled high with rice, curried vegetables, and various chutneys. I waited for the women to serve the others, and even after the others started eating I waited a little longer, taking my cue from them exactly how one was supposed to eat without fork, knife, or spoon.

I reached my hand to my plate and tentatively mixed a little rice in with some vegetables. It was an odd sensation. The curry colored my fingertips yellow. It was difficult for me to bring myself to shovel the food from my dish into my mouth, for I knew I was being watched. Ammu and Bhabi were still making *chapatis*, but they were doing so absentmindedly, their heads bent toward their tasks, but their eyes riveted on me. A silence fell over the room as I scooped some food in my fingers, brought it to my mouth, and deposited it on my tongue with a forward motion of my thumb.

The silence broke, everyone breathed easily again, and Arvind said, "There, that wasn't too hard, was it?"

Before I could form the word *no*, my mouth began to burn as if I had swallowed live coals, and it was all I could do to call out for water. Arvind's smile fell and he called out, *"Pani!"* Some hurried words followed in their strange tongue. Then I heard water being poured behind me. I turned and there was Maya, Kaitan, and Bimal. I hadn't known I had an audience on all sides. Bimal poured water from an earthenware jug into a metal cup.

"Oh, Mr. Tom!" he said, handing me the cup. I drank the water, tears rolling down my cheeks. The burning passed and I began to laugh. "Are you all right, Mr. Tom?"

For desert we each had a ball made of flour, honey, and butter saturated in thick sugar syrup. The syrup dripped down my fingers, across my hand, and down my arm. Ammu handed me a brass water jug and I rinsed my hands over my plate. The others did the same and we made room for the children to eat.

Arvind led me back into the front room. "So, how do you like our Indian food?" he asked as he took a seat beside me on the couch. He sat very upright and leaned toward me.

"It is very good," I answered, "but I'll have to get used to those hot peppers and the curry."

"What?" Arvind gasped. They had hardly used any spices tonight! "Hot peppers are good for you: you'll see once you get used to them. You eat a hot pepper and—ahh!—it cleanses you inside. And very good for the digestion!

"In this house you find the best food in all of Bombay. You eat here and you are fine. You never get sick. Do not worry. But in a restaurant—oh!—you never know what kind of oil they use. Some restaurants use motor oil! It is very cheap, especially used motor oil... Our women use only the finest oil. In a restaurant you don't know if the water is clean. Here the water is always clean. You pour it into a glass and it is clear. You drink it," and he made as if he were doing so, "and— ahh!—it is good for the digestion. Our water is good because it is filtered once, it is filtered twice, it is filtered three times— and the servants never touch it. If the servants touch the water it is no good and we have to throw it away. That is because of this," and he pulled a string from under his shirt. "This means we are Brahmin, the highest caste." He tucked it back under his shirt and continued: "I used go to restaurants or get something from a stand in the streets, but then my stomach would ache. When I came home moaning and holding my stomach the women would get angry with me. Then they'd make me a little rice. Just a little. Nothing more, like this," and he showed me with his hand. "Just plain rice is the best thing for a bad stomach. It aids the digestion. Rice *and* water. He made as if he were drinking another glass. "I'd have some water—very little, just one glassful—and then I'd feel better. And those sweets we had after our meal, we don't eat them only because they taste good. After a meal it is always good to have a sweet. Not too much, just one or two: it takes the hot taste from your mouth. And it is good for the digestion."

I had never met anyone with such a zeal for the elements contributing to good digestion. And it seemed a fortuitous stroke of luck to be sitting with him just then, for as he spoke I could feel small pockets of gas swelling in my stomach into sizable areas of pain. It was difficult, though, to believe his gastronomic philosophy, for he was one of the most unhealthy-looking people I had ever seen. Perhaps this explained his obsession: just as one doesn't think of one's shirt unless it is made of wool and is uncomfortable, so it is with one's stomach; if it is functioning correctly, it stays out of the conversation.

Soon Vyas was back with his wife Kamala and their

children. "Ah, Mr. Tom," Vyas said as he kicked off his sandals at the door, "now we can continue talking." He sat on my left, practically on top of me. On my right, Arvind, ignoring Vyas's presence, continued to talk about the elements that made up a good digestion. Kaitan, Bimal, and Maya, who had rushed through their dinner so not to miss a thing, joined Vyas's wife and children. They all sat cross-legged on the floor by our feet, ready to soak in every word the heads of the two households exchanged with the visiting American, friend of Spencer-da.

"As I was saying," Vyas told me, "we have known Spencer for twenty years. We are all followers of Thakur. Spencer goes back with Thakur a long, long time. Spencer was Thakur's first Western disciple. Even before you were born Spencer was spending every day at Thakur's side. Yes, you were lucky, lucky to find Spencer. Do you believe our steps are guided, Mr. Tom. I do." And he went on and on.

It was good to be distracted from the subject of digestion, for I was now experiencing rather violent rumblings in my nether regions. While talk of Spencer and Thakur streamed into my left ear, talk of digestive maladies and their remedies filled my right. I could be rude to neither, for a small crowd of witnesses was taking in the entire scene. Nimisha started to squirm and Bimal reprimanded her: "Quiet, or you'll have to go. I want to hear what Mr. Tom says."

Jet lag caught up with me, and my eyes glazed over. Luckily, just at that point, Rindani came in leading his daughter Ila. Ila, who was blind, could not see what an earnest discussion I was engaged in, and yelled out, "Tom Uncle, where are you?" Someone pointed her in my direction, and she said, "Tell me, Tom Uncle, where are your parents, and why you are not with them?" It was a question that had obviously been nagging her.

"They are at home in America," I answered. "And why am I not with them?" I asked rhetorically, trying to figure it out myself, "well, I suppose because I'm here in Bombay talking to you. I cannot very well be in two places at once!"

"Oh, Tom Uncle," she said, "you are very funny." She covered her mouth with her hand and tittered.

"Mr. Tom," Bipin said, "would you like *paan?*"

"What's that?" I asked.

"It is a leaf we eat, we wrap tobacco, betel nut, and spices in it."

"It sounds good," I said, not knowing what else to say, "but I don't know about tobacco. It might be hard on my stomach." I turned to Arvind. He rocked his head and patted his stomach, smiling uncertainly.

"Then you can have sweet *paan*," Bipin said. "No tobacco, but candies inside."

Just then Ed walked into the room. He had overheard the conversation.

"What do you think?" I asked him. "How does this stuff work on a Western stomach?"

But before he could answer Arvind cut in: "Do not worry, Mr. Tom, the juice from the *paan* is the best for the digestion. We always take it after taking our meal. Our father," and he pointed to the stern man in the framed portrait over the door, "he took *paan* every day." Arvind patted his stomach. I looked back at Ed.

"When in Bombay..." Ed said, letting his sentence dangle.

Bipin gave some coins to Bimal, instructed him on exactly what he should buy, and Bimal scurried out of the house with his brother Kaitan close behind.

They returned a few minutes later with a small parcel of stitched leaves. At first I took this for my *paan;* I was greatly relieved when they tore open the top and spilled onto the low table half a dozen smaller leaves, each folded ingeniously into a tight little pouch. Bipin examined each one and distributed them, one to Rindani, Arvind, Indrijit, Vyas and one to Spencer. There were two left and he popped one into his mouth. He handed the other to me.

"Here," he said, "put it into your mouth between your

teeth and your cheek. Like this," he said and opened his mouth to show me the soggy wedge, dripping blood-red juice. "Suck on it. Don't chew. Just let it dissolve slowly."

I examined the leaf in my palm and admired again the intricate handiwork that went into its construction. I wondered what lay inside, and I also wondered how I was supposed to fit it in my mouth; it was triangular, about an inch and a half on each side. Too many people were watching me too closely for me not to follow through, so I popped it into my mouth and worked it into place.

"There you are; you did it," Bipin exclaimed.

"What did he do?" asked Ila.

"He put the *paan* in his mouth," he answered.

"Tell me Tom Uncle, how do you like our *paan?*"

I opened my mouth to answer, but the *paan* popped out, and I had to push it with my finger to get it back in place.

Each of us partaking in this rather strange Indian delicacy looked in need of a dentist; cheeks were swollen into tight balls, and whenever one of us opened his mouth to speak, red tobacco juice dripped down his teeth. Every other word was a slurp.

Soon I got the hang of it: I sat on the floor with my back against a wall, spoke to no one, and let the pandemonium unfold around me. There was something primal about sucking on a leaf in Bombay.

~

After some time a palpable shift in mood came over the room. The pandemonium became more concentrated; anticipation grew, especially among the youngsters. Something was clearly about to happen. Ila, the only one of the children with a timepiece, kept careful track of the time. She opened the lid of her watch every thirty seconds, ran her fingers over the hands and Braille numbers, and reported time's progress with precision. The children sat on the floor, facing the wide doorway that led farther into the apartment. The iron-barred windows that opened onto the alley filled with dark faces and bony hands clutching the bars. These were the people that worked in the restaurant whose back door opened onto the alley and who lived in the alley's open bunks. They were Tamils from South India, whose ancestors were the Dravidians, India's original inhabitants. They too were waiting for whatever it was that was about to commence. As the time drew near, Ila called out the time in some strange language, and the adults joined the children sitting in rows on the floor, facing that inner door. Even Bhabi and Ammu came in from the kitchen. The children squirmed with excitement.

Then a hush fell over the crowd. I was in a delicious state of anticipation, ready for anything to jump from out of that inner door: a ritual priest, a dancing girl, a whirling dervish, an elephant, a Bengal tiger; I was ready for anything, for I was chewing *paan* among friends on Matunga Road.

Arvind—the eldest brother, the head of the household—got up and walked toward the front of the room. He paused before a large box next to the door draped with a piece of cloth. Then, as if he were a magician, he tore the cover from the box, and there it was!

I hadn't seen one quite like it in a long, long time—an ancient, oval screened Zenith TV. He turned it on and sat down again. It hummed as the picture came slowly into focus.

"Mr. Tom," Bimal called out, "it's Charlie Chaplin!"
"Yes," Ila said, excitement rippling through her, though she was blind and couldn't see the TV, "it is a movie: *Modern Times!*"

6

I awoke to the ringing of a bell. I thought it was an alarm clock until I remembered where I was: on a thin mattress on the floor at Matunga Road. There were mattresses on either side of me as well. Ed still slept on the mattress to my right. The mattress on my left, where Bipin had slept, was empty. His light cotton sheet lay crumpled at the foot of the bed.

Windblown Clouds   Thomas K. Shor

The previous evening, when all the neighbors had finally gone and it was time to sleep, I realized there wasn't a single bed in any of the rooms. With Arvind and his family, and Indrijit and his family, and Bipin and Ed and me, there were ten of us to sleep that night in an apartment that in the West would house no more than two or three people. Thin folding mattresses, stored in closets until bed time, had transformed the front room into a bedroom for Bipin, Ed, and me; each of the back rooms were made into a bedroom as well, one for each of the two other families.

The bell rang again, accompanied this time by a low, monotone chant. In time, the ringing stopped; the chanting continued. Arvind stepped out from the doorway of what had once been a closet but was now the family shrine. A white cotton cloth was wrapped round his waist. His dark skin offset the Brahmin chord strung over his shoulder. He held a brass water vessel in one hand and a long metal rod whose end was shaped like a spoon in the other. He opened the windows' wooden shutters and unlocked and opened the front door. He dipped the spoon into the water, recited a sacred prayer, and sprinkled water out each of the windows and then out the front door. Then he disappeared back into the closet.

The breeze that flowed in through the open windows brought with it the voices of the Tamil restaurant workers. I sat up. The Tamils were bathing at an open faucet in the alley. The sound of splashing water was punctuated by their strange tongue, which itself sounded like flowing water. Somewhere someone was cooking on an open fire. A temple bell rang in the distance. From the head of the alley came the sound of trucks and buses lumbering by and the trilling of rickshaw and bicycle bells.

Arvind appeared again from the closet, this time with a piece of smoldering incense on a brass tray. Placing the tray on the low table, he bowed to the incense, pressed his palms together, and muttered a final chant. And with that his morning ritual was complete.

"*Namaste,* Mr. Tom," he said, pressing his palms together again.

"*Namaste,*" I returned.

"Did you sleep well, Mr. Tom?"

"Yes, I did."

"Ah, very good." He rocked his head and disappeared into the kitchen.

Ed was now sitting up in bed. "Good morning," he said. "Looks like we're the last ones up." I smiled and yawned.

"*Namaste,* Mr. Tom," Bimal said. He was dressed and ready for school. "I woke up this morning long before the sun," he said, sitting on the edge of my mattress. "I was so excited I could not fall back to sleep. I was afraid I had only dreamed that you and Spencer-da had come. I had to sneak out of bed to see you sleeping here before I knew it had not been a dream. Only then was I able to sleep."

Ammu and Bhabi came through the front room carrying bags to fill in the market. They looked shyly at Ed and me as we sat up in bed. "*Namaste,*" they said as they kicked on their sandals and went out the door. Maya and Kaitan were going back and forth between the kitchen and the bathroom, stealing glances at us. When we finally got up, Maya folded our sheets, tucked them into the mattresses, folded each mattress, and carried all the bedding away. Our bedroom was once again the sitting room.

Bipin came in and told us to sit on the chairs on either side of the low end table. We did as we were told. Then Maya brought us tea and sweet rolls from the market. The tea was hot and sweet and we contented ourselves by sitting quietly and watching the tide of humanity that flowed in and out of the tiny apartment.

In came Ammu and Bhabi, their bags now filled with vegetables, and out went Indrijit on his way to work. In came some classmates of Bimal and Kaitan to meet the Americans they had heard rumored to be in the neighborhood, and out they all went on their way to school, books tucked underneath their arms. In came an elderly servant woman who began to sweep the floor with a short-handled broom. She squatted and swept with long, arching strokes then hopped to another position. Out went Maya to get Ila, whom she had promised to bring over—since Ila was blind and couldn't come on her own. In popped Nimisha and Krishisha on their way to school, begging us to go nowhere before school was out. We promised not to move.

The harmony and peace with which so many people occupied such a small space was wonderful to experience, as was the open exchange between the world inside and outside the apartment. Though the apartment was the private domain of the Dholakia family, the men living on stone bunks not three feet across the narrow alley could gather at the windows when it was time to watch Charlie Chaplin. Neither the Tamils, each of whom had but a few square feet of their own space, nor the family members in the apartment, had any privacy. I saw not one corner of the apartment that had the stamp of any single person's personality.

In the West, so many people living in such close quarters would be forever stepping on each other's toes. The polite veneer would be quickly stripped away, causing tension and irritation. In general, Westerners take up a lot of room, placing the highest premium on personal space. One mark of success, in the eyes of a Westerner, is to have earned a place of retreat, a place one can go when the trials of being in the same room with one's near and dear become too intense.

In contrast, the Indian typically has no place of retreat, and he would consider having one a sign not of strength and success, but of weakness, indicative of the family's failure to live together harmoniously. While the Westerner's identity is derived from his relative autonomy from the family, for the Indian it is just the opposite. That is why it was hard for my hosts to understand how I could be so far from my parents. It would have horrified them to be alone so far from home.

While the Western family is a loose conglomeration of

individuals in which the individual is the highest authority and is more or less free to leave if conditions do not suit his needs, in India the good of the family always comes first, the individuals being mere organs of the greater unit. Indians do not stand apart from one another, but stand with each other as a part of a greater whole. Westerners stand like so many islands, each rising independently out of a vast and endless ocean, while the Indian lives in the center of a vastly interconnected network of circles within circles. For in India the family isn't the final unit, but it too—like the individual within it—is but a part of a greater whole. The Indian says I am a Brahmin, a worshipper of Shiva, a follower of this great teacher, or I am Hindu. It is these bonds that connect family with family in ever-widening spheres. And these bonds are not limited to the present and with those living but with the past and with the forefathers: the Indian is steeped in tradition. For him the new is of less importance than the old. Knowing that the rituals he performs in the morning, the way he bathes, and the way he takes his food are in accordance with laws laid down in the dimmest beginnings add a meaning and nourishment to his life that we who know of no such traditions can hardly imagine.

~

As Bipin left for work at his job at a bank he said to me, "Mr. Tom, I told you yesterday that when you are a guest at an Indian home you are treated like a god. It is up to us to see that all your needs and wishes are fulfilled. This is our custom and it is our duty. And with you and Spencer-da, it is also our pleasure."

"Why is it," I asked Ed after Bipin had left, "that while the other brothers now have families of their own, Bipin has never married? Surely he is a handsome man and would make a fine father."

"I don't know why a marriage wasn't arranged for him when he was younger," Ed answered, "but more recently there was a woman of whom he was rather fond. She was a schoolteacher. I think he would have married her, but he felt it would have placed too much strain on the family. As it is, he sleeps here in the front room. Where would he put a wife and children?"

"Couldn't he and his wife move to their own apartment?" I asked.

"Then this apartment would become too expensive for the other brothers. The brothers all pool their money together. Bipin's salary is higher than either Arvind's or Indrijit's. He is the youngest brother, yet he has excelled professionally. If he pulled out and raised a family somewhere else it would bring hardship on the others, which is something he couldn't do. Since the death of their father ten years ago, all decisions in the family rest on Arvind's shoulders. He is the eldest and tradition prescribes it so. Yet I wouldn't be surprised if behind the scenes it is really Bipin who is the family's prime mover. He would never do anything that was a detriment to the others, even if that means not getting married."

"But that doesn't seem fair," I said. "Couldn't they all move to a larger apartment?"

"It is not as easy as that, just to move. The family came to this apartment when they left Gujarat, their native home. They came when the three brothers were younger than Bimal and Kaitan are now. Their parents lived here and they died here, right in these rooms. The family is indissolubly bound up with these rooms. Too much has happened here for them to up and leave. But you are right. It is unfair to Bipin. He carries a heavy load."

The morning wore on. Maya came back with Ila. Kamala, Vyas' wife, came over. And then came Rindani, the tall bald-headed man. Ed and I remained rooted to our seats and let the world come to us.

The moment we stepped into this little Indian world of Matunga Road we had forfeited our freedom of movement: time was no longer our own. This became clear when Kamala announced to us that she had promised her girls that we would come to their house for dinner. But when Maya caught wind of the plan she stepped in and firmly reestablished her family's sovereignty. "Spencer-da and Mr. Tom are guests of *my* family," she said. "Any arrangements for dining must be cleared through us first." We might indeed be gods visiting from another world, but we were newly arrived gods and we were not to be let out on loan so soon.

"Then why don't they come for lunch?" Kamala suggested. "Krishisha and Nimisha will be home by noon."

"Because," Maya retorted quickly, "their food is already being prepared." And sure enough Ammu and Bhabi were sitting on the kitchen floor chopping vegetables and preparing the fire for *chapatis*.

"Well then," Kamala said, getting a little hot under the collar, "why don't we ask them?" She turned to us. "Spencer-da, Mr. Tom, where do *you* want to take your lunch?"

"It's not fair to ask them," Maya cut in before we could respond. "They don't know."

"What do you mean we don't know?" Ed boomed out in mock severity.

"Spencer-da," Maya said imploringly, "I think they are trying to push you around."

~

After lunch we took a nap. And somehow the day slipped away and it was four o'clock and the kids were all home from school and the three brothers were home from work. The Vyases, Rindani, and Ila came. It was time for prayers, which the Dholakia family hosted every afternoon.

Upon the television, now draped by cloth, Maya propped a picture of Thakur, which she then adorned with a garland of orange and white flowers. Nimisha put a small bowl of candy at the base of the picture. Maya put mats on the floor. Everybody sat, and silence fell over the room.

Bipin sat in front with a harmonium. With one hand he pumped the bellows; with the other he played on the keyboard a melody that circled endlessly and followed a theme that snaked up and down an Oriental scale. It built to a crescendo then faded again.

Vyas sat beside me, his eyes closed, his corpulence twisted into a cross-legged posture, his back straight. He was totally still, absorbing the mood evoked by Bipin's playing.

On my other side sat Nimisha. At seven years old she was trying to emulate the stillness of the adults. She squeezed her eyes shut to prevent herself from looking around, especially at me; but this proved too difficult. Every time our eyes met she squeezed them tighter.

Incense burned on the TV-altar. Its smell, together with the music, transformed the front room of Matunga Road into a place suffused with the ancient holiness of a temple.

The tune that Bipin played on the harmonium faded, and after a brief pause another began, this one at a faster tempo. Bipin's voice rose above the harmonium, and the others joined in. It was a devotional song, evoking sweet yearning. Though I didn't know the language in which they sang, the mood hit me directly in the gut and moved my heart. Rindani—tall, bald, and of great stature—sang with his eyes closed, gently rocking back and forth with the rhythm of the music. His voice came from deep down in his vitals and rang clear and strong above the rest. Nimisha, who was too young to know the lyrics, tried as best she could to sing along. She fumbled for the words, lost them, and picked them up again. I met her eye and she smiled and lost her place completely. The singing ended; the harmonium played the tune one last time.

One clear note rang out so low that I could practically hear the pause between vibrations. It slowly acquired a rhythm of varying intensities as Bipin worked the bellows. Then, all at once, everyone took a deep, chest-expanding breath, which they released as a single breath and launched into a resounding chant. Each verse, powered by a single breath, began with the sound of exhaling air that was then trained into words and accented in an uneven beat; each verse was the same but for the last word, which I could understand, for they were evoking the names of the gods and holy men of all ages and places: Buddha, Christ, Shiva, Mohammed, Vishnu, Ganesh, Yahweh—each was invoked and paid homage to with unanimity and fervor as if they were cast from a single die, issued from a single breath, and made present to show the many means for reaching the single goal.

Despite the violent animosity that has marred relations between Hindus and Muslims since partition—there are, after all, bigots in every land—Hinduism teaches an unequaled tolerance toward other religions; instead of seeing contradiction and feeling conflict with other faiths, Hinduism teaches that there are many paths to the single summit, and that all gods are but the many forms that the one God takes to teach humankind.

I have heard Hindus say on many occasions that Christ was a very great teacher. They don't mean to belittle him by calling him a teacher and placing him beside Ramakrishna, Sankara, Buddha, and the other great souls who have been beacons to humanity; rather, they exalt his name by placing him in such company. Where the Christian and Hindu views diverge is in their feelings on the periodicity of God's manifestations. To Christians, Christ was unique, the one and only son of the one and only God. He performed miracles and had the gift of prophecy, as did the prophets of the Old Testament. But all of this happened long ago, in an age before our own, in a Golden Age of the spirit in which a deeper reality impinged itself upon the everyday. To the Hindu this Golden Age has never passed; the plane of the world continues with the greatest regularity to be intersected by the divine. Hindus are quick to deify, to see in an everyday situation a manifestation of the divine. They are the supreme idealists, seeing everything on the scale of the heroic.

When the songs and prayers were over Nimisha picked up the small dish of candy placed on top of the television and handed out pieces to everyone in the room. I noticed the particular way in which people received this gift, with their right hand cupped in their left. When it was my turn to accept this gift, Arvind explained that it wasn't merely candy I was receiving; it was *prashad,* a gift from the gods. Nimisha stood before me holding the bowl, smiling sweetly as Arvind explained: "While we were singing we were calling forth the presence of the gods and our teacher. All of our energy was concentrating in this bowl of candy. It is now charged with something we cannot see. By taking the candy and eating it, that energy comes into us and we become one with it." I held my hands in the prescribed way, with my left hand cupped beneath my right, and inclined my head slightly as Nimisha placed a few pieces of the sweet-tasting gift of the gods in my palm.

~

That evening after dinner some of us went for a walk down the market street around the corner from Matunga Road. The wide street was flanked with tea houses and stalls that sold rice, grains, and lentils out of sacks that overflowed onto the street, sweet shops, whose counters swarmed with honey bees, and shops that offered saris and *dhotis* and long lengths of printed cloth. Roaming venders of cheap books, hawkers of brightly printed images of the Hindu gods, and venders of herbal remedies all called out their wares. The sidewalks were clogged with women selling produce stacked on sheets upon the ground, their wares lit by oil lanterns. The road itself was bare earth trampled flat by the thousands of feet that struck it every hour. Motor rickshaws, buzzing their horns, pushed through the crowd, as did carts pulled by both horses and men.

This market off Matunga Road which, no matter how deeply one penetrated, always stretched farther than the eye could see, contained more sights and smells and varieties of humanity than one would encounter by crossing the entire United States by foot. I say this without exaggeration. I could walk down that road forever and never cease to find wonder in the barrage on my senses: the intensity of the colors and smells, the variety of people, the clothing they wore, the languages they spoke, the odd vegetables and medicinal remedies they sold, the strange cries they used to announce their wares, the shrines built around ancient trees billowing clouds of incense, the bells over their portals rung by devotees laying wreaths of flowers at the stone gods' feet, the riches of the tropical harvest juxtaposed with the rag-attired begging denizens, whose well-to-do live in cardboard lean-tos and whose unfortunates get chased from the broken sidewalks by others who have staked claim to every inch of Bombay's streets, fighting over the space before a rich man's door, where liveried guards protect their master's riches for pennies, where malnourishment, like a ghost, haunts the perfectly stacked pyramids of jackfruit, mango, and papaya, where open sacks are filled with as many varieties of rice as there are stars in the sky, where there are as many hues, colors, and sizes of lentils as there are gods in the Hindu pantheon, and whose vastness is measured out with brass scoops, where the sacred Brahma cow roams free and though owned by no one has painted horns tipped with brass balls, eats the market's detritus, cleans the gutters, and is shown more respect than the destitute, is given wider berth by screaming rickshaws, whose dung is collected like gold to dry in the sun and be used as fuel to boil the rice.

Despite its vast size and dizzying, monumental array, despite the fact that it stood in the middle of a city of over eight million, the market street at Matunga Road retained the atmosphere of village India. One could feel the weight of the past and know just how very ancient India was. And despite the electric lights and the tangles of electrical wires, despite the high whine of the rickshaws' internal combustion engines, the pace was still that of the human foot and of the bovine hoof, and in reality the cow set the pace. For the animal was still wedded to the human, right there in the middle of Bombay. People communicated from mouth to ear. Many things are closer together in India than they are in the West:

Windblown Clouds

Thomas K. Shor

the animal and the human, the well fed and the hungry, the healthy and the sick, the living and the dead, the sacred and the profane, the human and the divine. For India is inclusive. It is vast and absorbing. Everything is part of the great round. That is why India is such a great spiritual homeland. In India the spiritual is more fully human and the human being is more fully divine. To walk down the market street at Matunga Road was to swim in an atmosphere at once exotic and totally familiar. A shopping mall, though a product of my own culture, makes me feel uneasy and out of place. On Matunga Road I felt as if I was remembering something from a past so old it was ancestral. Something moved in my blood.

We left the market street for a wider avenue and then we crossed a park, which Bipin told me was the largest in all of Bombay. The park, which stretched the length and width of innumerable football fields, hadn't a tree, bush, or bench: nothing that would recommend it as a park to Western eyes. The flat ground was covered with grass overgrazed by the many freely roaming cows. Paths that cut deeply into the ground attested to the multitudes that crossed the park daily. We passed a young girl pasturing a small heard of goats, the bells round their necks tinkling softly. Again the distinctions we in the West have learned to make from birth, such as that between city and country, were blurred. Cows lay on the ground, chewing their cud as the people walking by chewed *paan*. The cows, rather than being another species altogether, seemed almost another caste. And their place in the order of things was rather high, their position privileged in comparison to many people. I've seen many a cow break through a fence, knock over a vegetable stand, or hold up traffic with impunity, while a person doing similar deeds would have faced retribution. Perhaps the cow's place in Hindu society comes closest to that of the wandering holy man who, like the cow, is given alms and wide leeway when it comes to transgressions of the law. But perhaps the cow provides a more temporal service than the holy man does by transforming all manner of roadside debris, from food scraps to paper scraps, into a uniform and useful product: dung.

We ended our walk at the Arabian Sea, where we took off our shoes and waded into the cool water. Across Mahim Bay rose the tall and surprisingly modern buildings of downtown Bombay. Bimal was enthusiastic about the view. He told me that when one walked amidst those tall buildings, everything seemed so modern that one might almost believe he was in London. London was the city of Bimal's dreams, to which he was forever comparing his native city. And but for this one downtown section, Bombay, in his estimation, always came up short.

7

The next day I took a bus to the center of the city with Vyas. I had received a vaccine against cholera and typhoid in Athens before flying out. It was time for the booster. Vyas worked not far from Saint George's Hospital where the World Health Association administered inoculations. He promised to point me in the right direction. The bus was red and it was a double-decker. We sat at the front of the upper deck where we had a good view. On our way into town we passed through Dadar, one of the main markets of Bombay, which dwarfed the market at Matunga Road. From on top of the double-decker, the market's frenzied activity resembled a busy passageway within a beehive, in which one can hardly discern individual bees. All one sees is a blur of color as the workers go one way, the drones another, with packets of pollen under their wings. The cows stood idle like queen bees, large and imposing, demanding respect.

We alighted in downtown Bombay where the buildings, as Bimal had suggested, looked quite modern. But to say you could think you were in London or any other Western city would be stretching the point. For nowhere in the West would you see a modern, glass-fronted building next to a lot in which stood a collection of mud-walled huts whose roofs were made of palm thatch. Nowhere would the alpha and omega of building practices be juxtaposed so closely. And never in London, except perhaps at the Queen Mum's seventy-fifth birthday, or at the coronation of a new king, would you see so many people out on the street.

We entered the vast throng. From every doorway and cranny came the hawkers' cries. "Rupee—rupee—rupee," they called, brashly announcing the currency and not their wares. They sold everything from plastic combs, bracelets, anklets, and icons of gods, to watches, batteries, dried dung, knives, umbrellas, and medicines made from vile-looking dried mushrooms and fungi. The mushroom dealer had a large blanket laid out on the sidewalk upon which he displayed his wares with before-and-after photographs of people with horrible skin diseases and large tumors on their necks. For those who could read, he displayed hand-lettered cards describing the maladies for which his medicines offered miraculous cures. He worked the crowd masterfully, regaling them with such graphic descriptions of scabrous, lesioned, pustular skin that the non-afflicted recoiled, horrified by what they heard, yet too fascinated to leave, while the afflicted pressed closer, holding out coins and bills to exchange for small packets of brown dust.

As we reached the corner at which we were to part, Vyas produced a map of the city on which he had already marked out my route to the hospital and from the hospital to the local train that would take me back to Matunga road. His map was accurate, and before long I was climbing the steps under a large wooden sign that read, "St. George's Hospital for the Sick and Impaired."

I was expecting to find the hospital's corridors clean and white, and in these corridors I expected to see nurses walking snappily in tidy white uniforms and white polished shoes; I expected to see white-smocked doctors holding clipboards with stethoscopes hung round their necks; I expected to find an information desk at which I could ask for the office of the World Health Association. Instead I was met head on with the stench of sickness and disease. It was not the typical hospital smell that we in the West are accustomed to smelling, which, no matter how distasteful it might be, is not actually the smell of disease, but that of disinfectants, soaps, medicines, and healing balms. These are the smells that hide disease; the stench of disease itself is infinitely worse.

The sick were laid out in the front hallway on cots and on bare foam mattresses on the floor. Family members lived in the hospital for the duration of the patient's stay, cooking, suckling their children, sleeping—all right in the open hallways. Children wailed with boredom and fear. The gray walls and ceilings were splotched with dirt and patches of mold, lending the place more the atmosphere of a rundown bus station than a hospital.

I searched the halls for an employee, someone—anyone— to direct me where to go for my inoculations. Wandering the hallways, stepping over patients and their families, I feared getting too close to the sick, for I didn't want to catch whatever it was that was ravaging their guts, eating away at their noses, and blinding their eyes.

Finally I found an office where an old man sat behind a desk. The desk was empty except for an ancient manual typewriter. The man approached the keyboard as if it were a riddle to be deciphered. He stared at it long and hard before raising his hand and punching a single letter with his index finger. Satisfied, he took a sip of tea and considered his next move.

I pressed my palms together. "*Namaste,*" I said. "Do you speak English?"

"Quite certainly," he replied, looking up from his work. "What can I do for you?"

"Could you tell me where to find the office of the World Health Association?" By intoning the name of the World Health Association I felt as if I were surrounding myself with a protective aura that would save me from catching any of the multitudinous infectious agents with which the atmosphere of that place swarmed.

"World Health Association," the man said, with the far-away look of someone trying to remember the name of a long-lost friend. "No, I've never heard of it." He folded his hands on the desk with finality.

"Then could you tell me where I get my cholera shot?"

"Oh, cholera," he said, his face brightening. "Yes, we have cholera here. Many people have it." He was grinning now from ear to ear, triumphant, self-satisfied for answering my question. "If you will excuse me," he then said, "I must finish typing this form before noon." He started again the painstakingly slow process of pecking at his typewriter.

"Please," I implored, "where do I get the shot so I *don't* get cholera. You know, a shot," and I rolled up my sleeve and pretended to give myself an injection.

"Ah, an inoculation," he said. "Why did you not say so? You must go back to the main entrance and go right. You shouldn't have come this way. There are many ill people here. In the future, you should be more careful."

I made a beeline for the front entrance, holding my breath the entire way.

I was then in what appeared to be the administrative wing of the hospital. There were long hallways of solid wood doors with smoked glass windows and nameplates announcing the offices of Dr. R. H. V. Rao, Mr. Bandrath, Mr. Chakravarti, and on and on. Finally I found the door that announced the World Health Association, and I knocked on the door.

"You must sit here," a voice called to me from behind. I turned and saw that there was a long wooden bench against the opposite wall of the hall and a line of people sitting on it. I took my seat at the end and waited. Soon the door opened and three or four people came out with cotton balls pressed against their forearms followed by a man with spectacles who seemed to be in charge. The first four people in line followed the bespectacled man back into the room and the door clicked shut. I moved over on the bench. I was now third in line.

Fifteen minutes passed; the door opened, allowing the others to leave, and my group entered. It was a small windowless office with a desk and a single chair. The desk was piled high with papers and an old typewriter was pushed to one side.

The first man in my group sat in the chair and rolled up his sleeve while the spectacled man picked up a huge syringe filled with a milky solution. He then took the lid off a stainless steel pan and put it on the desk. In the pan was a line of needles imbedded in cotton. He pulled a needle from the cotton and fitted it onto the syringe. He didn't replace the lid as common sense or any understanding of sterile technique would dictate; instead he left the lid on the dirty desk, stood over the pan, and got into an animated discussion with the man awaiting his shot. He was gesturing with the hand that held the syringe and a fine spray of his saliva settled over everything.

I broke into a cool sweat and started calculating my chances of getting hepatitis from a dirty needle against the odds of getting cholera or typhoid without the booster. I knew the full course of shots was only eighty percent effective. I didn't know the numbers with only a single shot. Cholera and typhoid, both diseases of the gut, are often fatal, while hepatitis, a disease of the liver, can leave one with permanent liver damage, but one does survive. Eyeing the door and on the edge of bolting, I knew that if I left without receiving the vaccine, I would live in fear each time I drank a glass of water that might possibly be harboring deadly microbes. At least if I got the shot I could rest assured on that count and wait out the gestation period for hepatitis, knowing my fate was already sealed.

So I stayed. When my turn came I sat in the chair and watched the spectacled man come toward me as if he were an executioner. "I'm here for my typhoid and cholera booster shots," I told the man.

"Oh, yes," he said. "That's why everybody is here. It is all in one shot, called TAB. Come, roll up your sleeve."

I unbuttoned my cuff and slowly pushed up my sleeve up, eyeing the door the whole time. A bead of perspiration dripped down my forehead as I eyed the open pan of needles. A fly flew in circles and landed on the pan's lip.

"My friend," he said to me as I mopped the perspiration from my forehead with my other sleeve, "you look uneasy."

"Yes," I said, "you are right." I thrust my arm to him and said, "Here, do it." The cold needle penetrated my vein as he pressed five mils of the solution into my system. I bolted out of that place as fast as I could, vowing never to find myself in an Indian hospital again.

~

That night Rindani came over and told us stories of Jim Corbitt, the famous stalker of man-eating tigers of the Himalayas, author of such books as *Man-Eaters of the Kumaon*. The light in the room was turned low, and Rindani, with his bald head, bare chest, and simple white cloth wrapped round his waist, set the scene well. We sat in a circle on the floor, soaking in his every word. At one time or another each of us took a fearful glance over his shoulder, expecting a tiger to jump out from the imaginary brush that had sprung up out of our imaginations during the course of his tale.

"Imagine," Rindani said, "that you are living in a little Himalayan village high above the plains. There is not a flat piece of land for hundreds of miles in any direction. High overhead loom the permanently snow-clad peaks, beyond which is Tibet, inaccessible but for a few impossibly steep mountain passes.

"Now imagine thick jungle surrounding your village—jungle harboring the wildest and most treacherous beasts. One day you hear a blood-curdling scream coming from the jungle where a party of women has recently gone to collect firewood. You huddle with the rest of the village by the headman's hut, fearing the worst, not daring to leave the security of the village to investigate. Finally the woodgatherers return out of breath, their clothes torn from their hasty retreat from the jungle. One of their number is missing, and the story they tell confirms the worst fears."

Rindani leaned forward, and the rest of us instinctively followed his lead. For that moment he was the headman, we were his villagers, and we were sitting on the earth before his hut. He continued in a hushed tone: "Between great sobs, one of the women recounts how they had been in the jungle cutting firewood at the base of a cliff when, all of a sudden, out of nowhere, a tiger that was larger than any of them had ever seen pounced on the youngest of the women and carried her off between its jaws. They heard her screams for help as the tiger dragged her into the ravine. And then her screams stopped. There was nothing they could do. They were up against a man-eater. Even the bravest hunter lives in fear of the man-eater, for while hunting the man-eater, the man-eater hunts the hunter, catching his scent on the wind. The man-eater is always lurking, always coming up from behind, ready to pounce.

"This death was only the first of what amounted to forty-seven before word of the killer reached the one man in all of India whose senses are sharper than a tiger's, whose mind can fathom the mind of a beast. That man was the famous hunter, Jim Corbitt. When Corbitt arrived in the mountains he found the people in village after village barricaded in their huts. Fearful of leaving their huts for any reason, they were half-starved. Not a drop of water had passed their lips in days, for springs and wells in the Himalayas are always in the densest thickets where the tiger can best hide. Corbitt heard the sounds of infants with barely enough energy to cry. His heart was moved to act immediately.

"Somehow word of the most recent killing passed from village to village, and Corbitt hastened to the place where this killing occurred. He heard the wailing of a woman who had just lost her husband, and of children who were now fatherless. The killing had occurred the day before. But on the very morning of Corbitt's arrival, they had heard the beast's wail from a ravine below the village. Though night was falling, Corbitt hastened in the direction where the beast had been but hours before. The villagers, emboldened by the great hunter's presence, watched him through cracks in their open doors. The moment he disappeared into the jungle they barricaded themselves again inside.

"Night fell.

"Jim Corbitt had a sixth sense when it came to hunting tigers. An unseen hand would guide his way. No matter how many people a tiger had eaten, he felt no anger toward the tiger; he harbored no hatred in his breast. For Jim Corbitt knew a tiger only took to eating people if it had been hurt and could not pursue its normal diet. Often the tigers he pursued had been shot or had had their legs mangled by snares or had been otherwise hurt by man. Although a tiger prefers not to hunt human beings, if forced, he will. Human beings are easy prey. We can't run fast, nor defend ourselves from all those hundreds of pounds of pouncing cat. Jim Corbitt knew that even with his gun he was helpless unless he knew of the tiger's presence before the tiger pounced. The tiger knew the danger of pursuing man. He knew of man's intelligence. In the jungle the keenness of one's senses determines who is winner in the game of prey and predator. If you lose concentration for a moment, if your mind wanders, you are lost. Jim Corbitt, since his heart was free of hatred for the beast, since he actually pitied the beast he had to kill, possessed a mind free of agitation. He had the calm mind of a man engaged in meditation. And not only was Jim Corbitt a fine marksman, not only were his senses as sharp as the point on a needle: Jim Corbitt could enter the mind of a man-eater, anticipate its next move, and be waiting for it when the beast itself arrived. And this is precisely what Corbitt did when he entered the ravine."

Rindani fell silent. The moment of the hunt was upon us. Shivers were riding spines around our little circle. I gave a furtive glance over my shoulder and saw that the barred windows were filled with the faces of the Tamil restaurant workers. They clutched the bars so tightly that their knuckles were white.

Rindani raised both his arms into a sharp V. "The ravine was like this," he said. "Steep, inaccessible, thickly forested, and filled with boulders the size of this room, behind any of which the man-eater could be crouching, ready. Since the sun was touching the horizon, shadows had long ago cloaked the ravine. The full moon was rising, but it would be hours before its light penetrated the earth's deep fold. The air was still but for the cool air riding down the slope of the ravine into the valley. Corbitt knew his scent was running out ahead of him down the ravine. If the man-eater was still there he surely knew already of Corbitt's presence.

"The hunt was on, that shifting dance of hunted and hunter. Corbitt, the Himalayas' greatest hunter, was himself being hunted in the silence of the night. Although he knew it, the man-eater had no way of knowing what Corbitt knew. The man-eater could move in the jungle soundlessly. He could lurk in any shadow, behind any boulder. They say a tiger can hide behind a single blade of grass. He knew exactly where Corbitt was. Corbitt was in the dark. A cat's sight is superior to that of man. A cat's ears can pick up the sound of man at a half mile. A cat's pads are made for silent transport.

"Since cats don't know that our noses are inferior, they stalk us as if we could smell as they do. So Corbitt knew the cat would come upon him from downwind. Corbitt wedged himself between two boulders, propped his rifle on his knee, and waited. The night was long. Though he had traveled on foot many days to reach this ravine, he could not let his attention flag; he could not allow himself to fall asleep. If he missed his chance, the man-eater would claim another life, and that life might very well be his own.

"He was vigilant till the morning light began to tinge the eastern sky. With the rising of the sun, the wind shifted. Corbitt, sunk as he was between two huge boulders, could not feel the shifting winds. He had no way of knowing that the cat had circled behind him and was waiting and watching him from above, from atop one of the boulders between which he was wedged. As Jim Corbitt stared into the night, vainly looking for the cat's eyes like burning coals to appear in the darkness, he himself was being watched.

"The moment Corbitt moved to get up, something made him turn. The cat was already launched and was in mid-flight. Corbitt raised his rifle just in time to catch the cat in the neck, and he pulled the trigger just as the tiger's claws were digging into his flesh. All at once the life force flowed out of the huge beast, and it was a lifeless sack of flesh and bones that pinned the hunter, Jim Corbitt, to the ground.

"Extricating himself, Jim Corbitt examined the beast. He found an old bullet hole festering in the tiger's front right shoulder. It was a lesser hunter's bad shot that had set this tiger on the road of being a man-eater, had cost forty-eight people their lives, and in the end had cost the tiger his own life. Corbitt felt sorry for the beast. He walked back to the village to announce the news that would release the villagers from their self-imposed imprisonment. News of the man-eater's demise spread instantly through the surrounding villages, and as Corbitt walked out of the mountains he was met by cheering crowds."

8

A few days later, in the afternoon, Ed suggested we take a walk alone along the market street. As soon as we were around the corner Ed said, "You know, these people make it so easy for us that we could stay on here forever and never notice the years that have gone by. This always happens when I come to Bombay. When you start talking of leaving they make up excuses for why you shouldn't go; and they ply you with such delicious food that before you know it you believe them and you're growing fat and lazy and a month has gone by. I once spent two months here when I was only planning one week. I'm beginning to feel that old itch again, that longing for the open road. Perhaps we should leave soon, before it's too late."

I knew exactly what Ed was talking about. For me, India *was* Matunga Road. Our point of arrival had unwittingly become our destination. I had hardly thought of the vast subcontinent on whose edge we had landed. And when I did think of it, and of moving on, it was with so much apprehension that I put the thought out of my mind and hoped we could stay on in the security of Matunga Road forever. I remembered what had happened at the money exchange when we got off the boat in Greece, and I knew we would have to cross that threshold again.

"You're right," I said, "we can't stay here forever. But which way should we go?"

"Doesn't matter much to me," Ed said, "though the south might not be a bad choice. Winter is coming on. It shouldn't be too hot down there. But let's not think too much of destination; each road will be our way and each place we lay our heads will be our destination. Destination is always something to consider with a backward glance; it is simply the place at which you've arrived, the place from which the next morning's walk will begin."

We decided to stay in Bombay one more week, though we deemed it best to wait a day or two before making the announcement to our gracious hosts. When we returned to the apartment another wonderful home-cooked meal was waiting for us, a meal seemingly designed to weaken our resolve and keep us in Bombay forever.

~

That evening the kids were busy doing their homework,

the women were talking quietly in the kitchen, and Indrijit and Arvind were reading in a back room. Bipin was sitting on a chair in the front room looking downcast.

"Why so glum, chum?" Ed asked.

"It is these people at the bank," Bipin answered with a sigh. "The manager at one of our branch offices in the country has taken ill. Now I must go and be manager. I feel honored to be chosen for a position with such authority, but the responsibility is great. It means three extra hours on the train every day. It means I'll have to be out of the house before six o'clock every morning and I won't return till well after the evening prayers and dinner. The women will have to prepare a separate dinner for me. Nobody is happy about it—except the bank. They know I must obey."

I felt bad for Bipin. So much already weighed on his shoulders. I wished I could do something to lighten his load. I wished he could have dropped everything and hit the road with Ed and me. It would have relieved the apprehension that had started growing inside me the moment Ed and I settled on our departure. Bipin's presence would moderate Ed's stark way of travel. I imagined the two of us against Ed, and Ed having to change his ways in the name of prudence. Of course this was pure fantasy.

Bipin was asking Ed for advice and Ed listened. When Bipin had finished, Ed said, "You must always do your duty. I don't care if your duty is to quit the bank or to follow unquestioningly their every command. That matters little— and only you can know. It matters little what you decide, for it isn't what you do, but how you do it: that's what's important. What is important is your level of remembrance. Missing the evening prayers means nothing. Prayers are there to help us remember. They help us to remember God. God is behind all works and he is trying to push through and be realized in our every deed. It doesn't matter whether you realize Him in a cave in the Himalayas or on the road. He is equally present in your bank as He is in the country or on the train in the afternoon after you've missed prayers and dinner. You must practice the presence of God. And remember," Ed concluded, "remember to remember God."

Tears welled in Bipin's eyes. He rocked his head and looked deeply into Ed's eyes. "Thank you, Spencer-da," he said. "Your words reside in my heart. I understand."

We turned in early that night since Bipin had such a long day ahead of him. When we awoke in the morning Bipin was gone, probably already at the bank in the country. At the afternoon prayers his presence was sorely missed; it was literally the first time in years that Bipin had missed prayers. Everybody was sad. And although Indrijit sat in for him on the harmonium, it just wasn't the same.

Bipin returned tired but in a better mood than any of us had expected. "Spencer-da," he said when he sat down, "I told the people at the bank that you and Mr. Tom were visiting, and they told me of a local fruit farmer who has been to America. I sent a messenger to his farm. He sent a note back. He would like to meet you. So one day you and Mr. Tom should come with me to the country and visit his farm."

"Yes," Ed answered, "that would be good. How about tomorrow?"

~

In the morning Bipin shook my shoulder. It was well before sunrise. He was already washed and dressed for work. By the time Ed and I had washed, Bhabi had boiled some tea. We drank the tea quickly and dashed out. Across from the alley's mouth lay the local train station. We jumped on a train heading out of the city.

The city of Bombay sprawled inland in an endless succession of factories, shantytowns, and bazaars. We passed broad salt flats into which flowed the effluence of surrounding factories. In the dark stew, cows were bloated, belly up, ribs exposed to the sun, the bone bleached orange by belching smokestacks.

Then we crossed beyond the city's sprawl. The train

slowed and we passed the first village of reed huts surrounded by green fields. A man dragging a plow behind a water buffalo stopped his work to watch the train pass. A barefoot woman walked gracefully down a dirt path with a large brass urn on her head and a baby on her hip. Bullock carts took the place of cars and trucks. The train stopped now in tiny villages where women got on carrying huge sacks of vegetables, rice, and other fruits of their labor.

We came to the small market town where Bipin's bank was located. All of the women on the train got off, and we got off too. Bipin's bank was just down the road. The bank building was fairly modern, especially when compared to the native construction of mud and bamboo. The bricks and stones gave it the air of stability and permanence that banks around the world are built to exude.

Two clerks, village boys no more than eighteen years old, were waiting by the bank's front door. They pressed their palms together and bowed their heads deeply in deference to the new, temporary replacement bank branch manager. Though I expected Bipin to object to their show of obeisance, he accepted what apparently was due him in his new position. Bipin pulled an impressively large key chain from his pocket and solemnly unlocked the half-dozen locks that secured the door.

Inside, Bipin and the clerks readied the bank for opening, as Ed and I kicked off our sandals by the door and sat on a bench. Opening the vault, Bipin took out trays of notes and piles of coins to fill the money drawers behind the caged tellers' windows. One of the clerks followed his every move, keeping track of everything he did in a huge ledger book. The other clerk changed the wall calendar's date and opened the shutters to a refreshing breeze. When the clock showed that it was exactly eight-thirty, the tellers took their places behind the caged-in teller's windows. Bipin opened the front door for business then sat at the bank manager's desk. He motioned for us to sit on the chairs beside him. As we came over he noticed that we had no shoes on, and he turned bright red. "Spencer-da," he said in a barely audible tone, "why did you take off your shoes. This is not a temple. This is a bank." The tellers had noticed us barefoot, and they were trying not to smile. They probably thought it was the custom of our home country. It embarrassed Bipin; only poor people without shoes went barefoot in a bank. Ed and I went back to the door, put on our sandals, and sat down with Bipin.

"This is a very quiet bank," Bipin said. "Yesterday we only had three customers. When the regular bank manager is here a lot more goes on. He is authorized to approve agricultural loans and mortgages. Since I'm here only temporarily those transactions have been suspended and we have walk-in customers only." His last words trailed off and silence filled the room. The two clerks sat at their posts, vacuously twirling pencils while staring at the walls.

After a long stretch of silence, Ed grew impatient and said, "Since we're not being paid, I don't see why *we* should stare at holes in space. Which way is it to the fruit farm?"

"We'll have to send a messenger first," Bipin said. He called to one of the clerks. Practically running to Bipin's desk, the clerk clicked his heals together then bowed his head, ready to receive Bipin's command. Then he hurried out of the bank and returned a moment later with a barefoot, half-naked man. He was the clerk's brother, and he would be glad to run a message to the farmer. So Bipin wrote out a note, sealed it in an envelope, and the messenger tucked it in the rag wrapped around his waist. Then he ran out of the bank. I stepped out the front door and watched as the man ran full speed down the dusty road.

In India, where there is an overabundance of labor, even the most basic tasks that machines perform in the West are carried out by hand or on foot. This bank was a branch office of one of the largest banks in Bombay. Still, every single function was carried out by hand. When a form had to be filled out in triplicate it was filled out three separate times, the existence of carbon paper being virtually unknown. While in the West each bit of information would be recorded in a computer, here ledger books fulfilled this function. These hardcover books were at least two-feet square and six inches thick. This one bank had enough ledger books to sink an entire armada. They were stacked everywhere, eight and ten feet thick. A back room housed the bank's records. There the stacks began on the floor and ended at the ceiling.

The messenger returned about a half hour later. He was drenched in sweat and out of breath. The farmer's note said we were welcome any time. Since we were Americans, he wanted to know whether we wanted a meal of meat prepared for us. And since his farm was on the edge of town and the sun was getting high in the sky, he also suggested that he send a bullock cart to fetch us.

Ed immediately refused his offer both for a meat meal and a ride in his bullock cart. Bipin agreed that a meal of meat was out of the question, but he wanted Ed to reconsider the offer of a bullock cart. Ed stood firm and said we would walk. Bipin implored Ed to reconsider. Ed refused. He demanded instructions to the farm. Bipin started arguing, saying it was hot and too far to walk, but Ed was adamant. I thought it best to keep out of the fray, though I had never been on a bullock cart and would have enjoyed it. As Bipin and Ed bantered back and forth it became clear to me that more was at issue for Bipin than it merely being too far for us to walk. Everybody knew that Ed was a walker. Bipin was usually so proud of Ed's ability to walk, even across deserts.

So I asked him, "Bipin, despite the fact that the farm is far away, why do you want us to ride? There must be more to it."

"You are quiet right, Mr. Tom," Bipin answered, smiling, relieved that he could more fully explain himself. "You are Americans, guests in our country. If you walk through the town, people will know who you are, that you are guests of the new bank manager. They will wonder why I don't take better care of you. They will also know where you're going. Mr. Sharma, the farmer, is a well-respected man. He is a large landholder and highly educated. He has even been to America, and he speaks English. Because of all this the people look up to him. If they see his guests from America coming on foot, what will they think? And what will Mr. Sharma think of me? He is the bank's largest customer. I will be the one he holds responsible for letting you bring harm to his good name."

Ed was angry now. "Let them think what they will," he said. "I can't stand this small-minded drivel. We will walk."

"Then let me send a note," Bipin said hurriedly, "announcing your arrival on foot." He took a piece of paper, scribbled out a note, and sealed it in an envelope. "I told him you are *sadhus*—holy men—and prefer to walk. I told him you aren't meat eaters and won't be requiring a meal." He handed the note to the messenger, reached into his pocket, and gave him some coins. The messenger ran out the front door.

9

To reach Mr. Sharma's farm we had to pass through the market, which was bustling and busy as any in Bombay, though here everything moved at a far more leisurely pace. Missing was the staccato clamor of the internal combustion engine. Everything was more peaceful and measured, suffused with a gentle rhythm of life.

We passed a school made of thick bamboo poles that held up a thatched roof. It was open on all sides. The children sat cross-legged on the earth facing the teacher, who was drawing Hindi letters on a blackboard. The children copied the letters using rough pieces of chalk on thick slate boards, chanting each letter's name as they wrote it.

We passed women returning from a well with huge brass water vessels on their heads. They trotted smoothly, never spilling a drop.

Windblown Clouds   Thomas K. Shor

At the edge of the town was a bamboo tea stall crowded with men. Someone called to us. It was the clerk's brother, our messenger. He was spending the few coins Bipin had given him. He invited us to tea, and Ed readily accepted. The others made way and we sat next to our messenger on the wooden bench. Big blackened teapots, bellowing with steam, hung low over a smoldering wood fire.

Tea in an Indian tea stall is not like tea in the West. The part of the plant used is not the leaf, but the powder left behind when the leaf has been processed and sold for export. The boiling water is not added to the tea, but a few pinches of tea are added to the water along with copious amounts of sugar and milk. This brew is then boiled over a fire until it is poured off for the customer. Boiling the tea insures the tea's full utilization. And judging by the ratio of tea to sugar, I would guess tea is relatively expensive and sugar cheap. The tea is there largely for color, the sugar for flavor, and the milk for heartiness.

The tea *wallah* squatted by his fire and poured some of the boiling brown liquid into a tall glass. Then he poured it from that glass into another to cool it. He transferred the liquid from one glass to the other gracefully and with great skill, separating the two glasses as he poured, alternately raising then lowering each of his arms. The tan, milky tea looked more elastic than fluid as it moved one way then the other. After a while he tested the tea's temperature with his finger and poured the tea into two clay cups, which he then handed to Ed and me.

Beyond the teahouse the road passed through dry scrubland with hard-baked earth. We could see Mr. Sharma's farm a long way off, and as we passed through the gate of the farm the land turned green. The long, gently curving driveway laced between endless rows of papaya trees. We passed a cart with wooden-spoke wheels being pulled by three thick-muscled men. The sun glistened off their sweating bodies. They stopped at a row of trees and two of them climbed on top of the tank to pump while the third uncoiled a thick black rubber hose and started watering trees. Farther on, women cut bananas from trees and threw them to others who stood below with wicker baskets strapped to their backs. Everyone smiled as we passed, pointing us in the direction of Mr. Sharma's house and staring at us until we were out of sight.

The house was large and sturdily built, its thick stone walls smoothly plastered and newly whitewashed. A wide veranda wrapped round the front and both sides of the building, and a trellis of wide-leafed tropical vines overhung the veranda. In the shade sat a man of late middle age.

"Welcome," he called out in English as we drew near. He rushed out to meet us under the sun's harsh rays. Shaking our hands firmly, he introduced himself. His English was excellent, though spoken with a heavy Indian accent.

Ed introduced himself. Then he turned to me and said, "This is Thomas Shor—eternal student, student of the eternal." I looked askance at Ed. Mr. Sharma looked cautiously first at me and then at Ed. He asked us to sit down. We sat on well-cushioned garden chairs. Mr. Sharma called a servant and asked for a pot of tea. The servant bowed and retreated into the house.

The farm, though in India, had the air of a southern plantation; Mr. Sharma, though Indian, walked and talked and shook hands like a Westerner. It was strange to me how, so quickly after leaving the West, such a simple thing as sitting on a garden chair could seem so alien. The tea came in porcelain china cups on saucers. Milk was in a pitcher and sugar in a little bowl with a spoon of its own.

"They tell me that you have been to America," Ed said.

"This is true," Mr. Sharma said, "but that was long ago, when I was an agricultural student. I participated in an exchange of students between your country and mine. We attended classes at agricultural colleges, lived at some farms, and learned many things that we could bring back and apply here in India. I was working at the time on my Master of Science degree, hoping to go into the agricultural ministry. But then my father died quite suddenly. I came back to take over the family farm, and I've been here ever since."

"How long has your family been here?" I asked.

"Not that long," Mr. Sharma answered. "We are still newcomers."

I looked around and it certainly looked as if they were well established. So I asked him how many years.

"Just over two hundred and fifty," he answered.

"But surely you are kidding," I exclaimed. "There's not a farm in the United States that's been in one family that long. Two hundred and fifty years ago the United States didn't even exist!"

"You are quite right," he answered, "but you must understand that this is India. Our history began over five thousand years ago. The customs and rules by which we conduct our daily lives date back to these early beginnings. From that perspective, two hundred years is nothing. Even five thousand years is nothing to Brahma, our god of creation. Our pundits say Brahma lies on the coils of the cosmic serpent Sesa, who floats upon the great ocean of existence. He lies on the serpent and he dreams. He dreams our world. One day for Brahma is equal to a thousand *Mahayugas,* or great ages, each of which is comprised of four million, three hundred twenty thousand of our years. And his nights are just as long. All recorded history is but a blinking of an eye. This is meant quite literally."

He paused, grinned widely, and continued, "Most of the villagers cannot read or write; therefore history, as we know it, really does not exist for them. In place of history they have legends: stories told around the hearth, at the temple, or in the tea stall. Some stories have been repeated word for word since the writing of the Vedas some three and a half millennia ago; others were first told, perhaps, last Tuesday.

"The sun rises and the sun sets. Between these events is a

day. Much can happen in a day, the basic and invariable unit of time. The days would be strung in an endless, monotonous chain were it not for the change of seasons; hot days follow cool days and the dry days turn moist. Endlessly, the seasons follow one another and cycle round the year: beyond the yearly cycle there is no natural rhythm. Therefore, something that happened five years ago could just as easily have happened five hundred years ago. It is all very much the same.

"That my family has been here over two hundred and fifty years does not make me any more a native of this place than if we had come only ten years ago. We are not natives. Everybody knows it. Our family name is different than the others, as is the color of our skin. Our status may never change—or perhaps it will take another two hundred and fifty years. Who knows? We must wait and see.

"But enough of that," he said, standing up. "Come, I will show you my farm."

He led us off the veranda and into a grove of orange trees that seemed as endless as his work force, whom we saw everywhere hauling water, pruning trees, and picking fruit. Everyone flashed us broad smiles as we passed. I could tell they liked Mr. Sharma immensely. A group of children playing under a tree ran up to him and hung on to him as if he were a favorite uncle. I noticed that some men resting in the shade of a tree eating a snack did not get up when we came. An older man approached Mr. Sharma with a diseased orange and together they discussed possible remedies. Mr. Sharma listened carefully to the man's advice.

The respect shown to Mr. Sharma seemed genuine, heartfelt, and mutual. It clearly went deeper than that determined by social convention, which determines so many relationships in India. At the bank, for instance, the clerks' respect and deference for Bipin had nothing to do with Bipin, nor with the clerks as individuals. Their relative positions on the vast and intricate tree of caste and their relative positions on the work force predetermined their relationships. Bipin hardly knew the clerks; he hadn't had the time to earn their respect, yet they deferred to him at every opportunity. Well before they had met, their relationships were determined in detail. You could almost say they were worked out two thousand years ago. On the other hand, Mr. Sharma and his workers had obviously earned each other's respect.

"Mr. Sharma," I asked, as we passed a group of women packing fruit into crates, "have most of these people been with you a long time?"

"Most of the people you see here," he answered, "have been working at this farm for generations. Some of the families go back almost as far as mine. We provide housing, a good wage, health care, vacations, as well as money for the festivities when there is a marriage. We give them just about everything they need, and, in return, we have a smooth-running and harmonious operation. I also give them responsibility. Most of my workers know some particular aspect of the farm better than I do. I have an overview of the entire operation and my specialty, my area of unique knowledge, is in the business side of farming—finding the best market for the fruits, maintaining the books, buying the equipment and the like. I am also somewhat of an expert in tree propagation—we do quite a bit of grafting here—and I also treat sick trees. But if you ask me how the water-pump works, I haven't a clue. I bought the pump. I know its model number, but that is as far as my knowledge goes. Our old pump ceased working two weeks ago. The new one arrived yesterday. I believe they are installing it today. Come, we will see how they're getting along."

He led us across a field and into a dense grove of bamboo, within which we could hear women's voices raised in song. We came to a clearing ringed with palm and date trees. In the center of the clearing was a well. The well was over twenty feet in diameter and was lined with huge slabs of rock. A continuous wide ramp of stone was laid into the rock. It spiraled down the well's circumference and disappeared beneath the water's surface. This ramp, which countless generations of water bearers had worn smooth, offered access to the water's surface regardless of the water level, no matter whether it was monsoon time or a time of drought.

Women—there must have been a hundred of them—were evenly spaced along this ramp, from the water's edge to the well's rim. They were singing a rhythmic, chant-like song. On the heavy down beat each passed a large brass water vessel up the line. Their song echoed from the water's surface and was amplified by the stone walls. Hands slapping against the vessels provided the beat and the water splashing into the tank provided the instrumental accompaniment. It was an ancient song.

"Before the pump broke two weeks ago," Mr. Sharma said, "we hadn't hauled water like this since about the time I went to America. One pump and two operators replaced all these women. What a shock it was when the pump broke! It has meant more work for everyone. Come, we will see how they are coming along with the new pump."

We walked around the well to a group of men gathered round the back of an old truck. The pump was still on its skid, its wooden case lying in pieces on the ground, though some kids were quickly making off with the wood. Mr. Sharma spoke to one of the men in their native tongue. "They are ready to lower the pump into the well," he told us. "If you would like, we can watch." We said sure, and the men fell into action.

It took eight of the largest men on the farm to carry the pump to the edge of the well. The women at the water's edge stopped filling the vessels, and slowly the last vessels were brought to the well's rim. The women came out of the well. Men began to appear out of the bamboo forest. From somewhere came three long lengths of thick rope. Before long there must have been over two hundred people admiring the new pump.

Then an old man, his once shaved head now growing white stubble, took charge and divided the crowd into three groups. He led each group to a point evenly spaced around the well's perimeter. He tied the three lengths of rope to the pump and walked the loose ends round to the groups, each of which formed itself into a line along the length of the rope. It looked as if they were readying themselves for a tug of war.

The old man barked something in the local tongue and everybody pulled back on the ropes. The eight men lifted the pump and heaved it over the abyss. A breathless moment of free fall followed and I was sure the pump would meet its demise on the well's smooth stone ramp; but as if caught in a huge spider's web, the taught ropes suspended it in mid-air. Slowly they maneuvered the pump over the center of the well. At the old man's command they lowered the pump carefully into the well. Stones fell where the ropes rubbed over the rim. All the while, the old man ran round the well, barking out orders.

When the pump was nearing the water's surface they let two of the lines out and slowly brought the pump to rest on the ramp below the third, about a foot from the water's surface. They lowered a water hose and someone ran down and connected it to the pump. They lifted the pump again over the water and slowly lowered it beneath the surface until it came to rest on the bottom. A young man dove into the water and untied the ropes. Two other people wheeled a gasoline generator from its thatched shelter to the edge of the well. When they'd finished lowering the pump, a boy was employed to play out the electrical chord. Now they plugged the chord into the generator and started it. Soon a gurgling sound came from the end of the thick black hose. It became louder as the water rose in the pipe. The water gushed out, and a cheer resounded throughout the orchards.

As we walked back to Bipin's bank, we shared a bag full of Mr. Sharma's choicest fruits.

10

The rest of our days in Bombay slid by in lazy tropical languor. We sat in the front room at Matunga Road most of the time. Occasionally I went around the corner and walked down the market street, but that was about it. Arvind was always up for a stroll. He liked going deep into the market. Unbeknownst to anyone in his family, Arvind enjoyed smoking cigarettes. The family would have been aghast. In the market you can buy one cigarette at a time. He would often buy a single cigarette and smoke it, looking over his shoulder the entire time.

We had been in Bombay just long enough that we were beginning to be taken for granted. Ed and I were practically fixtures in the Dholakia family's front room. But when we announced that we were planning to leave, it all began again. The apartment was never without a crowd; the pile of sandals by the door never diminished.

When Rindani heard of our impending departure he came over straight away, his bald head flushed with excitement. "How could you!" he demanded. "How can you leave us alone? I was just getting used to you being here!"

When he heard we were heading south he spoke of the South with passion. "In the South you will find the very innermost heart of India," he said pointing a finger heavenward as if to call upon the gods to attest to the truth of his statement. "The South is the oldest part of India. It is where the Dravidians, the original people of India, fled when foreigners invaded from the North. Everybody has invaded us: it started with the Aryans and it went right up through the Moguls and finally the British. But nobody has ever been able to conquer us. India has always been India—and so it will remain. India is too big. India is too old. None of them had a chance, not even the British with their mighty empire. In the end they were all absorbed into India—or else they had to get out."

Rindani spoke with passion of towns we absolutely had to visit, towns famous for this or that event out of India's past. The past Rindani depicted was a rich admixture of history and mythology. The temples he described were sacred to gods I had never heard of. He spoke so vividly that I could see the ornate stone temples rising out of the steamy jungle. I could see the holy men flocking through the temples' gates. The South was the old India, he told us. The South would reveal to us India's very heart, the very innermost and ancient core. "Wonderful things will happen to you there," he said, as if he were divining our future.

Just as he was saying this Vyas came in the door and kicked off his sandals. Arvind came in from the back room. They all picked up on what Rindani was saying. We had the head of every household we knew rocking their heads gravely in unison, all concurring that the wonders of the ancient core of India would surely be revealed to us in the South. Of course, not one of them had ever been to the South. These exuberant images of India's southern heart flowed through their veins by virtue of the simple fact that they were Hindu.

~

"Come," Nimisha said, "come to our house."

It was Saturday, two days before we were to leave. The front room of Matunga road was full of people, people it seemed I had known my entire life.

Krishisha, Nimisha's sister, said, "There are too many people here." Their big brown eyes implored me. I went to the door and stepped into my sandals. The girls were already outside the door waiting for me to follow when Bimal blocked my way.

"Where are you going, Mr. Tom?" Bimal demanded. I looked past him to Nimisha and Krishisha. Their fingers were to their lips.

"I... I'm just going for a walk," I stammered. "I need some fresh air."

He saw through my bluff and yelled at the two little girls

in Marathi, Gujarati, or Hindi—I know not which—to go away and stop trying to steal Mr. Tom.

Two big tears rolled slowly down the cheeks of each girl.

I took my sandals off again, sat on the floor, and planned my escape. Bimal's coarse handling of the girls bothered me, and I was not to be deterred. I waited until Bimal was busy hounding Ed with questions about sports in America. Then I bolted to the door, grabbed my sandals, and put them on outside. I went round the corner to the Vyas' apartment where Krishisha and Nimisha were waiting for me with tea and a sweet. Since their parents were back at the other apartment, we had time to visit alone. Having me alone, all to themselves, was very special for these girls, so I was glad to honor their request to come; and besides, I enjoyed the intrigue, and the opportunity to outsmart Bimal.

When it was time to return to the other apartment, the girls insisted on waiting a few minutes after I left, so Bimal wouldn't know we had all been out together. I asked what would happen if Bimal found out. I even joked with them that I would protect them from the big bad beast. But they didn't find it at all humorous. They saw nothing to laugh about. Bimal was, after all, a boy. And he was thirteen years old. They were girls, only seven and nine years old. I would be leaving in a few days. After that they'd have to answer to Bimal on their own.

Shortly after I returned to the other apartment, a woman came to the door with three young children in tow. All four of them had matted, dirty hair, and their clothing was ripped. On the woman's face was a look of desperation. The children had the frightened look of rabbits caught in a headlight's glare. I had never seen her before, but she was obviously known to Bipin and Arvind and Indrijit. She rushed to Ed, who was sitting on a chair, and stood before him, her children hiding behind her sari. The children looked furtively at Ed, their expressions a mix of both fright and awe. Their mother tried to get them out from behind her sari. Then she spoke sharply to them. Stepping forward, the children kneeled down before Ed and started for his feet, trying to kiss them.

"Hey," Ed gasped, lifting his feet up onto his chair. "What's going on?"

The children were frightened and retreated behind their mother's sari. The poor woman began to tremble.

The room was silent. Everyone stared.

Bipin came close to Ed and spoke softly in English. "She has come from far away," he said. "She wants you to bless her children."

"How do you expect me to bless them?" Ed cried out. "I am just a beggar. I have nothing to give. Please, tell them I am nobody."

Bipin tried to explain, but it just added to the poor woman's confusion. She grabbed her children and ran out of the house before she met with more humiliation.

"What was that all about?" Ed asked, once they were gone.

"She is a follower of Thakur," Bipin answered, "and she heard you were here. She heard also that you are a holy man. Her husband died recently. She only wanted her children blessed so they would meet no misfortune. They are from the country and they traveled all day just to see you. You should not have been so gruff."

"Gruff?" Ed said. "What did she expect me to do, place my hands on their heads and mumble a sacred chant?"

"Ah, Mr. Spencer," Bipin said, "you have spent all this time in India and still you do not understand our ways."

~

On Sunday afternoon all the furniture was taken out of the front room and mats were laid from wall to wall in anticipation of prayers—prayers in honor of our departure the next day. The women bought flowers in the market and strung them into garlands with which they festooned the apartment. Thakur's picture was so bedecked with flowers that one could see only his eyes. The men's *dhotis* were crisp and white. The women were dressed in their finest saris. They went back and forth to the market to buy last minute things for the upcoming feast. As the guests arrived, the pile of sandals by the door grew. Neighbors stuck their heads in just to see what was going on. And still more people came. These people had become my extended Indian family. The thought of leaving them made me sad. I was apprehensive about being alone with Ed, on the road.

The prayers and songs lasted longer than usual. Vyas brought his tablas and accompanied Bipin's harmonium, and some of the women tapped finger cymbals. I had come to know many of the tunes, and I hummed along. At the height of one song, Bimal ran to the shrine room and returned with a sacred conch shell. He stood before the group and blew into it with all his might. The clear and sharp tone pierced our ears with its ecstatic ringing, and swept us up into its frenzied sphere.

Ed leapt up. His eyes were not his own. They burned like coals. They flitted from place to place, as if unable to focus. He danced ecstatically, his arms a blur of movement—like one of those twelve-armed Hindu gods. His feet hardly touched the ground. His legs were springs. His body flew round the room in seeming defiance of gravity. He was pure energy. It channeled through him as water rushes through a ravine. As suddenly as his dance began, it ended. He sat back down. And almost as if nothing had happened, the song faded, another began, and Ed's dance was never mentioned.

After prayers they passed around sweet balls drenched in sugar syrup called *roshigolies*. They were Ed's favorite. Then everyone pressed Ed for some parting words.

Ed gave it some thought before speaking.

"Well," he said, looking a moment into each person's eyes, "Christ, when he parted, Christ said, 'Love ye one another.' I say also love ye one another.

"Love is for life. And life is again for more love. Don't aid and abet death by love. Don't aid and abet weakness, don't compromise it with complex et cetera by your love. That will kill it in the long run. The love has got to be for life—for strength. Only then is it real love.

"In Bangali the word *love* is *baluvashi*. It means 'I live in your good.' That is love.

"Many times people come together, they nurse and feed each other's weaknesses, and pronounce, 'I love you, I love you.'

"This is not love.

"*Love is for life.*"

11

The fine red dust left billowing behind each passing truck was already ground between our teeth; it covered us like a shroud and penetrated our clothes, turning milky red as beads of sweat ran down our necks.

Whoosh—another truck passed. Shielding our faces from the passing cloud, we looked with squinted eyes to see if it would stop: it slowed, but only for a cow that blocked the road. The trucker blared his horn and kept going, which just covered us all the more in the fine red dust as we pushed onward.

Sandwiched between two cinderblock truck mechanic shops was a well, obviously a relic of the time when this place on the outskirts of Bombay was a rural village. Women gathered around it, raising water in wooden buckets. The sun's rays played upon the water's surface. The women's jeweled nose studs sparkled, points of light on their smooth, dark faces. When Ed asked for water, they flashed broad smiles. "*Pani*," he said, and one of the women nimbly drew a bucket. She poured some over our hands while the others stood in a circle around us. We cupped our hands and rinsed our mouths. We lowered our heads for her to wet our hair. To the women's delight, our wet hair and beards dripped onto our shirts. They laughed and clicked their tongues in their strange language. We wet our *gumchas* and wrapped them around our heads. The only other word we exchanged with them was *namaste*, as we inclined our heads and pressed our palms together.

Then we were on the road again, our heads protected from the sun, water still dripping from our beards. We waved down a truck, and it stopped. We ran to the cab, but it was already full of people. They pointed to the back.

As the truck pulled away, long, dark arms reached down and lifted us onto the open flatbed. The truck was full of road workers who were also catching a lift. They were dressed only in loincloths and turbans of red and gold to shield their heads from the sun. Their skin was hard and cracked. The wind was hot and dry and bit the skin. We sat with the others, our backs to the wall of the cab. Ed pulled out some oranges we had brought from Matunga Road. He broke them open and passed the pieces around as the sprawling tentacles of Bombay receded down the long road to India's interior.

~

Our departure from Matunga Road had been long and drawn out. We were barely out of bed when the Vyas's, Rindani and his family, and a few other miscellaneous friends all converged on the apartment. We should have known better than to believe we could make our departure as quiet and sudden as our arrival.

The whole morning Bimal kept saying, "Mr. Tom, you must come back Bombay." Over and over he repeated that sentence. Again and again, his eyes moist, his voice choking: "You must come back Bombay."

Bimal and Kaitan worked on their father until he agreed to let them walk with us toward the edge of the city. Of course Arvind, Bipin, Indrijit, and all the other men wanted to walk with us as well. So the men all decided to be late for work.

They walked with us for an hour, until we reached a bridge where Ed announced we would go on alone. We stood facing our Bombay friends in silence, all of us with moist eyes.

"*Namaste,*" we said with palms pressed together, raised to the third-eye center, above the eyebrows.

We turned and walked away from them. We were halfway across the bridge when Bimal cried out, "Mr. Tom! You *must* come back Bombay!"

I turned. They were still standing where we'd left them. Ed and I crossed the bridge in silence.

On the other side of the bridge a mad confusion of roads came together. Out of that confusion began the Main Trunk Road to the interior, which began in total chaos, a mad swirl of exhaust and blaring horns, trilling rickshaw and bicycle bells, trucks grinding their gears, buses bulging with riders, roofs sagging under the weight of both luggage and people. No known rules of the road applied here. I felt like an ant dodging feet on a busy sidewalk.

Life at Matunga Road had suited me well. Within the Dholakia's home, peace reigned. Every day had had its even measure. Though I had agreed with Ed to leave Bombay, never would it have occurred to me to leave that comfort for this chaos.

Ed mistrusted comfort. Comfort led to complacency. When you're complacent you're more apt to compromise your ideals. Ed believed the world's problems began with people who were comfortable and wanted to stay that way at the expense of others. On the road everything is cut to the bone. Ed had longed for the road. And now that we were on the road, his feet propelled him at a pace I could barely match. He was leaning into his stride, a toothpick stuck between his teeth, his eyes focused, but far away. People either stared at us or ignored us; I couldn't decide which I preferred. The dust ground between our teeth and parched our throats.

We were passing through a district of truck repair shops where grease-covered men in loincloths were lifting engines off of chassis and rummaging through mountains of discarded metal parts. Metal filings covered everything and everyone. At wood-burning forges, men operated hand-worked bellows

Windblown Clouds Thomas K. Shor

to fashion parts out of raw metal.

Everywhere the industrial had overtaken the pastoral. Firing pistons had replaced the four-chambered heart of the bullock. And the city, like an industrial nightmare, had sprawled over outlying villages. Between a truck repair shop littered with the rusted carcasses of industrialization on one side and a low, mud-brick factory billowing foul black smoke on the other was an ancient stone temple. From within its richly carved portal wafted timeless songs of devotion. Within that ancient doorway time's currents ceased. They lapped like waves upon an island's shore. Inside that temple, India was still India. I would have liked to take refuge from the teaming chaos by entering that temple and diving into that timelessness, but that was more alien still than the teaming chaos.

I felt as if I were entering a dark labyrinth. I longed to turn back, to retreat into security; but the only security I now had was Ed Spencer. Ed knew how to navigate the noisy, smoky, billowy, mad streets of India. Without him, I would have perished in a moment. I wouldn't have had a chance.

We passed a man sitting in the dust on the side of the road who was drooling and incontinent, staring into the middle-space of a dimension entirely his own. Fear welled up within me, and I realized I feared I could end up like this man.

I recalled Ed's stories about traveling in India, the stories he'd recounted when we had first met and were still on the boat to Greece. His stories were really parables, occurring in a far-away time and place. I had been sure the guy was enlightened; and though I knew that in these troubled times one must be mad to be wise, it was only the wisdom I saw. Now his stories sounded like those of a madman. How strong I had thought him, how invincible, for being able to follow his will—to the extreme of eating nothing but the leaves of the betel tree. I now realized that if one started out upon a journey as we had, it was probably inevitable that one would end up eating nothing but leaves in the end. Since I was unwilling to go that far, why was I setting out as if I was?

It occurred to me that Ed Spencer might actually be mad. In following Ed, I thought I might somehow gain wisdom. But what would I find by following this obviously disturbed man into India's endless maze? Would I ever find my way out? Would I end up like him? I became submerged in doubt, flooded by endless questions, my feet slogging as if my doubts had turned the hot baked ground to mire as we went farther into the dark labyrinth of Indian chaos.

How strange, I thought, to have as my sole guide a madman. How strange to follow a man dressed in loose cotton pants suspiciously like those worn by the inmates in an asylum.

But Ed was undoubtedly destined for this type of travel. One of the stories he'd told me on the boat to Greece was of his first hitchhiking experience, at age eight. He was at a summer camp in upstate New York, and one day he wandered into the woods and became lost. After some time he stumbled onto a dirt road. By and by a big black car came down the road, and Ed put out his thumb. The car stopped. Two elderly gentlemen were in the car. Ed told the old men he was lost, and he told them the name of the camp. The man driving knew the camp and told him to jump in the car. When they arrived at the camp, the counselors were grateful and relieved to have their charge back, but they were also obviously totally wowed by his deliverers. As the car drove away, Ed asked who the men were. The man driving was Thomas Edison. The other man was George Bernard Shaw. Edison's laboratory was not far away. George Bernard Shaw had been visiting him.

Ed and the road were obviously meant to be together. Even so, he hadn't come to his present way of travel at the beginning. It was only after living in India for decades that he began to travel without a penny in his pocket.

Traveling with Ed was like entering the cave of a holy

man who has been meditating for longer than you've been alive. You meet him. He invites you into his cave. He assumes his crossed-legged posture and then he enters a state of deep meditation. You imitate his posture, but after five minutes you begin to squirm.

That was how I felt.

Traveling was Ed's spiritual practice. I knew I couldn't make it. My feet kept stumbling on rocks, bits of broken, sun-baked brick. I was ready to fall. I wasn't hungry yet, but I anticipated the time when hunger would wrack my frame. Already I felt the weariness of walking through the ninety-five degree heat. Sweat poured down my back. I would have turned back, but that was not possible.

With this being my state of mind only a few hours into the journey, it was difficult for me to imagine how I was going to last. I knew the only way for Ed and me to survive was for me to let go of my fears. But I couldn't change just like that. Ed had first taken to the road when I was three years old. His pilgrimage came after a long and very personal story. For me to overcome the obstacles I would have to surmount, I would have to emulate him. But why should I be like him? I riled against him—all within the first few hours of being on the road, 'in *his* element.' I felt pitiful, weak. I wondered what Ed thought of me. Surely he must hate me, hate me for being so damned slow. Though he was nearing seventy, he could out walk me. Had he not slowed his pace to match mine, he would have left me behind. But he was good about it; he was ever willing to show me consideration.

It was just when I'd lost all sense of why we were trudging down that road that the truck with the road workers in back had stopped for us. We ate oranges with the men, and the wind dried our sweat. The laborers pounded on the cab's hot metal roof at the first town the truck approached. The driver slowed the truck, and the laborers jumped off—all except for one old man.

We cruised now through flat dry country, farmland

interspersed with villages, an occasional town, and always the refuse of industrial civilization. The burnt out hulks of two trucks that had crashed lay rusting where their disfigured cabs had met, in the very center of the road, causing traffic to swerve around them. A vista of low green fields opened out to the far horizon. The fields were separated by lines of trees in whose shade ran enticing dirt paths that beckoned one to set out on foot into an India that hadn't changed in millennia, an India of bullock carts, grass-walled huts, and village temples. Then we'd hit a town, and all the chaos would return, the horns, the smoke, and the masses.

By afternoon we approached the Eastern *Ghat. Ghat* is the Hindi word for *step*. The Eastern *Ghat* is a high step of land separating the subcontinent's coastal plain from the vast Deccan Plateau. The road mounted the *ghat* in a series of sharp switchbacks so poorly constructed that I believed them engineered to weed the road of trucks with balding tires and poor steering.

Instead of being banked, each sharp turn gave way, adding the force of gravity to the truck's forward momentum, the two together conspiring to send the truck—and us— hurling back down to the coastal plain, a prospect that became more frightening as each successfully navigated turn made the lowland villages nestled in the thick jungle look more and more like villages in a diorama. At one turn we were pressed against the driver. At the next, we'd slide across the seat toward the passenger door and the open window and the cliff beyond. Behind each turn lurked a truck that was released at blinding speed the moment the driver started spinning the wheel. With no escape routes, and no shoulders on which to swerve to avoid danger, we had only a steep rock face on one side, and on the other a sheer vertical drop.

When we reached the top of the *ghat* we came upon a squat temple built over the mouth of a cave. Out of the darkened interior loomed the graven image of a multi-colored, multi-armed goddess. Above the cave sat a monkey, contentedly scratching itself. Before the cave's entrance stood an ash-smeared priest shaking the clapper of a huge bell. The driver sounded his horn. Two young boys swathed in dirty rags shot like bats out of the cave. They trotted beside the truck holding out large brass bowls.

An offering to this roadside goddess gave thanks for safe passage, and kept her from demanding live sacrifices in the future. The driver threw them a handful of coins, but he missed the bowls. The boys ferreted around in the dirt like dogs going after morsels of food.

We stopped above the temple that overlooked the steep way we had just climbed. The drop was as great as the Grand Canyon's. But in place of the wall on the other side, the land ranged out over little hills and valleys, like frozen and irregular waves. The hills faded in the hazy distance.

A strong headwind rose up the *ghat*. The air was cool and fresh. It had lost its heaviness. It was an air that made me want to remain on the move, an air that buoys. I felt expanded.

Ed and I now rode on the back of the truck, and the wind rushing through my hair made me feel free. As each deep breath of cool air filled our lungs, we overflowed with the joy of movement.

12

Then the sun was sinking low and we were climbing a sharp, almost barren hill in a landscape Ed said reminded him of Northern California. The truck choked and sputtered; thick, acrid smoke billowed from the exhaust. We slowed almost to a standstill, downshifted, then continued at a pace just faster than the bullock carts through which we weaved. We were entering a large town.

We came upon a tight circle of villagers at the edge of the road. They stood staring at something. As we passed, the circle opened, as if purposely to afford me a view. They were staring at a man lying on the ground. His arms and legs were bent at broken angles, and his torso was bent back upon itself. He lay in a pool of blood. I saw him for only an instant—a flash, a single frame of a movie projected on a screen—but it was enough to tell the story.

A truck had hit the man just moments before. The truck had not stopped; the driver had left him to die. In his absence, there would be no one to answer for the deed, no investigation launched, no blame placed.

Children made up the innermost circle. They squatted beside the man in the dirt. There was no attempt to shield their tender eyes from so gruesome a sight. Blood still flowed from the wounds—I saw it dripping into an ever-growing pool—and no one had placed a sheet over the body. No one averted his eyes. Here, death stood on equal footing with life. Only a moment earlier I had been filled with a feeling of vitality fostered by the freedom of the open road; now I was afforded a glimpse of death. One has moments of feeling overwhelmingly alive and one sees death; seldom are they so closely juxtaposed.

In the center of that town we pounded on the cab's sheet-metal roof. The truck stopped and the driver got out and insisted on shaking hands, Western style, before he restarted the truck and continued on his way. We began walking, and, as usual, Ed led the way. The town was nondescript, yet exotic and strange. I knew we were exactly nowhere. Thousands of towns just like this were spread across the breadth of India. It was so undistinguished a place that I felt lonely, as if the town's lack of distinction stripped me of the attributes that made me who I was.

I tried to reconcile the euphoria I had felt at the top of the *ghat* with my present feelings. Again, my feelings toward Ed shifted with my mood, my first impression of him, that he was some sort of bum, interspersed with my second impression, that he was actually something approaching a saint. Again he had impressed me, his way of travel—the freedom it seemed to impart. On top of the *ghat,* I had experienced some of the bliss that was Ed's object of travel. Yet I hadn't earned it. I could feel bliss only when nothing touched me. The sight of a dead man had brought me back to a state of fear. Yet by all traditional notions, all conventions, both East and West, our journey was improbable—probably mad. Many times people in Bombay had told me that no Indian could travel as Ed Spencer traveled. Who could expect a Westerner, new to the subcontinent, to do so?

And even if I could have quieted my mind and followed Ed peacefully, my body would not have kept up. I was hungry now, and I knew the purchase of food was the first sin in Ed's book. Under other circumstances, the hunger I felt would not have consumed me; but because I couldn't see how to alleviate my hunger, it took on gargantuan proportions. My stomach began to grumble. As we passed restaurants, it seemed everybody in town was eating.

In the absence of food, my mind began to gnaw on certain questions. Why was Ed willing to accept a meal prepared by the women of Matunga Road, but not one prepared by someone in the kitchen of a restaurant? Was it because he didn't believe in the exchange of money? The women of Matunga Road had exchanged the money earned by the men in the family for food in the market. It wasn't as if he was out of money's chain. He was just one step removed. And now *I* had to go hungry. Indeed, how did he expect to get food? Would it simply drop from heaven?

Food became my obsession as hunger overtook me with the hollow howl of an approaching storm. The body craves sustenance. The animal in me called out for nourishment. I needed food, and I was becoming cross with the world. I was tired. Where would we sleep tonight?

Food and shelter—man's two most basic needs. When you're hungry, and you smell food, and it's the food you'll soon be satiating your hunger with—that is a sweet smell. When it's someone else's food and you can't get to it—that's torture.

We had the means to satiate our hunger (or at least *my* hunger, for I doubted whether Ed felt it) anywhere we wanted. We walked by restaurants. We passed carts piled high with bananas, stalls selling tea and packets of biscuits. I smelled food cooking all around me. It was time for all of India to eat. Entire families were sitting down at tables in restaurants and ordering up feasts. We could have ordered up a meal fit for a raja and not missed the money. We could have invited half a village to eat with us.

What can one think of a man whose pace never slackens, and who seems to need no source of nourishment to keep his fires stoked? I thought surely he would fall. Surely he would get hungry. I thought he was putting me on, trying to prove something. Nobody can do without food. When will he put a hand in his pocket, take out some coins, and say, "Hey, lets get some chow?"

I had sometimes suspected that Ed was mad. Now there was no mistaking it, no getting around the fact that someone who was hungry and had money in his pocket and didn't buy a meal was mad. Or maybe because he was mad the signals got crossed, and he didn't feel the grumbling in his stomach.

When you're hungry and you smell food and it's the food you'll soon be satiating your hunger with—that is a sweet smell. When it's someone else's food and you can't get to it—that's torture.

As I followed Ed, his frame still straight, yet leaning forward as if a destination called to him, I realized I had never really been hungry before. Hunger, though physical, has a psychological side as well. True hunger comes when the person whose belly is empty knows he lacks the means of filling it. One grows up hearing about the starving masses in Africa and Asia. One feels sorry for these people, but one doesn't feel their hunger. Even if you fast, you do so by your own choice. You can break your fast at any point. In India, many people go without food. You see hungry people on the streets. You see people racked by malnutrition. But all this is amid an abundance of food. Markets everywhere are overflowing. Restaurants are bustling with customers, and even at the end of the day the pots of food are full. People starve in India not from a lack of food; the people who starve in India starve because they lack the means by which they can acquire the food that is staring them in the face every moment of every day. Surely this must cause madness.

Beggars had approached us, and each of them was certain of what was in fact the truth: certain that our pockets were brimming with rupees. Even the craziest among them would have done the only sane thing: they would have taken a few of those rupees, gone to any one of the innumerable restaurants, sat down, and ordered a meal that would have stopped the stomach from gnawing on itself. They would have stemmed the hunger. If the body is the vehicle of the spirit, why not answer its call? But Ed ignored the call. Ed didn't even seem to hear it.

Ed was, of course, hearing the spirit's call. It all had to do with his ideal. He spoke often of the ideal. "One must follow the Ideal. One must have the power of Will." I readily agreed with him when nothing was on the line, when it was all in the abstract. It was because of his ideals and convictions that I'd decided to follow him. Charlie Parker once said, "If you don't live it, it won't come out of your horn." Many people sound wise. They have the right words. Yet it is not words, but actions, that count.

I had never met anyone like Ed Spencer, someone who obviously lived his convictions. That was impressive. It showed a great power of the will. Yet the moment I felt the least bit threatened I questioned his sanity, I thought him mad. I convinced myself that had we been walking in the West, I would have felt differently. People had warned me to stay strong and well fed in India, so none of the predatory microbes could get the upper hand. I didn't want to open myself to disease. I wanted to keep myself above the fray. I didn't want to end up like the man we'd passed not long ago, a man who had lain upon a heap of old paper that he'd collected, paper he would sell: a man who slept on his filthy paper so no one else would steal it. One of his legs was blown up like a balloon; the toes were but the tiniest knobs protruding from the end of his foot. He had elephantiasis. Nor did I want to end up like the man that had followed us for almost half a mile, a man walking alongside us, a man whose nose and whose fingers on both hands had been eaten away, leaving stubs of infected flesh: a man stricken with leprosy. I didn't even want to become like the healthy men I saw sitting in the tea stalls; I was glad I wasn't condemned to live their lives, at least not forever.

Never before had I felt as strongly the *privilege* of being of European extraction. Being submerged in such a sea of humanity made me aware just how wealthy I really was. And this realization made me feel threatened. It made me afraid. I didn't fear thieves. I feared someone asking me by what right I had so much without even trying—a question I couldn't answer for myself, let alone for others. I feared falling to their level. And it was horrible for me to realize this. It was horrendous to realize that I would have used those notes and coins in my pocket to extricate myself from anything that threatened. I knew the power of money. We passed some old men squatting in the dirt on the side of the road and talking. If any of them got sick, they would probably die. They would be subject to the local doctor. They would go to the local hospital, which, if it were anything like St. George's Hospital for the Sick and Impaired in Bombay (and being in the country it would no doubt be worse), would probably do them in. If I got sick, I would leave posthaste. I would have hired someone to get me to the closest airport and I would have skipped that continent without a backward glance. I would have flown on the first flight to anywhere in the West. My chance of survival was infinitely greater than any of those around me. Also, I was healthy, which was a condition I didn't want to compromise. And staying healthy was closely bound up with staying well fed. Which always brought me back to the pit that was ever growing and demanding to be filled at the center of my existence.

I wasn't used to the heat. I blew my nose and brown mucus came out. My feet were red-gray. They were beginning to look like the feet of a native. I feared slipping. I didn't want to fall. India had embraced me at Matunga Road. There the women had fed me well. At Matunga Road, I had shelter. I had a family that accepted me into their fold. While I had slipped easily into the fold, Ed had always remained a bit outside it. He could probe his teeth with a splinter of wood and watch it all from a distance. I saw now that that stance was well fit to tramping down the road. I knew he strove for freedom. But his kind of freedom was radical. It was literal. It was physical. And it was his trip, not mine. What was I doing following his way?

Finally, I could stand it no longer. We were passing a restaurant whose front was open to the street, and the smell of freshly cooked *chapatis* filled my nostrils. Pots of rice, dhal, and curried vegetables met my eyes. Inside the restaurant's dark interior I could see people consuming huge plates of food. The money burned in my pocket. It felt dirty.

"Hey, Ed," I said.

He stopped and turned. We hadn't spoken in over an hour.

Ed had this crazy quality of walking as if something was drawing him onward. He leaned forward and stretched to meet this force. But if some thought struck him, or if he wanted to point something out, he would stop wherever he was at the moment—in the center of a busy intersection, or in the middle of a moving crowd—and he'd just stand there, as if he had all the time in the world.

He often spoke of the peripatetic philosophers of ancient Greece, for whom walking was an integral part of their philosophic method, who used the changing aspects of the road as the backdrop for their discourses. Ed was, ultimately, heading nowhere. Time was his. We could stop and talk for an hour and lose no time. We'd be no farther from our destination.

Ed turned and his eyes were milky. They were soft. They had the same look a horse's eyes have when you put a mound of sweet hay before him. I could tell Ed had been experiencing bliss.

I cleared my throat. "What do you say about grabbing a bite to eat?" I asked. My words, once they were out, sounded tinny and impertinent, as if we had been driving down an American highway and were coming upon a rest area with full facilities.

Ed thought a moment. He cocked his head, and spoke softly, slowly: "Yes, that's one way of getting a meal. We could do that." His voice wasn't tinged with even a trace of malice. Rather, it was accepting.

We ordered rice and vegetables. I was thirsty so I ordered a *Thumbs-Up,* the ubiquitous Indian version of *Coca-Cola*. They say it is safe to drink. I asked Ed if he wanted one. He too must have been thirsty.

"*Thumbs up*—what's that?" he asked.

I couldn't tell whether he was living so much in his own world that he truly didn't know, or whether he was just trying to make a point. I had been in the country only a few weeks and already I knew what *Thumbs Up* was. The painted signs advertising this drink were everywhere. Even that first night, when we walked from the airport to Matunga Road, I had noticed a hand-painted billboard of a chic woman in a sari smiling coyly at a man dressed in a modish, Western sports jacket, both of them holding bottles prominently displaying an up-turned thumb. Even if one had never drunk *Thumbs Up,* surely one would know what it was. I thought he really must be crazy, living in the twentieth century, yet inhabiting a reality prior to the advent of bottled drinks.

After eating, we continued down the road, and my stomach's satisfied fullness convinced me we had been right to stop. Yet I could sense that for Ed it was a cheapening of the experience, something he was willing to put up with because I wasn't used to being on the road, something akin to stopping for cotton candy with a child at an amusement park.

Now that I had eaten, weariness overtook me. We must have walked over fifteen miles. We had hung on to the backs of trucks without suspension that careened down roads whose pavement only provided firm surroundings for huge potholes. The heat had been tremendous, the sun punishing. I was tired.

Ed waved down a truck, and it stopped. We climbed into the cab. The engine, in most Indian trucks, is right in the center, between where the driver sits and the passengers. A sheet of metal usually covers the engine, a rattling shell that latches down on either side and opens from the center. This truck's engine had no such cover. The engine was naked. The firing pistons were right there, the ganglia of wires and hoses, the gaskets leaking oil, the stench, the corroded exhaust. Long after dark had fallen we reached the next big town.

This town had none of the lights of Bombay at night. Bombay at night was festive. Shops were well lit. Poles holding nexuses of electric wires sported bare light bulbs. On the market street gas lanterns cast circles of light that overlapped and washed into a single glow that encompassed the entire city. This town was dark, and shadows cast at one end of town stretched clear across to the other. The few lights that did glow were feeble. All the lights flickered at the same time. Every shadow hid a mangy dog. Sweet smoke wafted from incense sticks on store counters. Drums beat through the tropical night.

Again I had the feeling that Ed had traveled the whole of India and had been here before. He walked as if he knew where he was going, and I walked beside him now. He was happy, filled with joy. It was late. Surely we'd have to stop for the night. Ed was searching for a place to sleep. He stopped at the mouth of an alley and stood there as if he had always been rooted to that spot.

Windblown Clouds

Thomas K. Shor

He tilted his head and looked at me. He seemed to be asking what I thought, whether this would be a good place to stop for the night. I looked down the alley, but all I saw was the opening to a great darkness. I had never slept on the street before, and I didn't see why I should start now, especially in India, where the streets were dirty and dark and diseased. This alley, like every other alley and street, had a small gully through which thick brown liquid flowed. I couldn't imagine closing my eyes in such a place. When on my feet, with open eyes at midday, the rats that fed off the day's detritus made me shudder. How much more so at night...

That point beyond which I would not go was Ed's destination.

Ed had cast his lot with those who lived on the streets, those recumbent figures wrapped in cloths as if ready for the funeral pyre, whole families lying in groups, the youngest already sleeping, the mother suckling an infant, the father, squatting on his haunches, silently smoking a *bidi,* a rough Indian cigarette. Ragged rickshaw drivers slept hunched over on their rigs. Ed's distrust of riches was instinctual. He distrusted anything that would put anyone a single notch above anyone else. "One shirt, no dough," that was his ideal. That is what his Road Song said: "One shirt, no dough, was Christ's motto. Then do the same, let heaven flow..."

Without uttering a single word, Ed pointed out to me the superiority I felt to these street dwellers.

He was suggesting we join them. Indian streets are as gentle as the cows that roam them, he had once said. His was not a romantic notion; nobody motivated by a romantic notion of solidarity with the poor would sleep on the open street with them. Not in India. Not by choice.

By nature, Ed gravitated to the streets.

I longed for a hotel.

His silent suggestion as to where to lay our heads till morning fell on my deaf ears.

Ed started walking again. He led the way to the train

station. "It's always safe to sleep in an Indian train station," he said. For him, this was like choosing the Ritz over an ordinary hostel.

An Indian train station, at that late hour of night, resembles a Red Cross shelter in a disaster area. Bare bulbs illuminate entire families sleeping on sacks containing the entirety of their earthly possessions. Every inch of space is staked out. One must thread carefully between one person's foot and another's outstretched hand. Vendors boil huge pots of tea on open fires. Children wail. From the office of some petty railway official come the screeching tones of Hindi movie music.

We picked our way through the lobby leading to the first platform. All was dark but for a single lantern hanging from a hook above a tea stall. A circle of men squatted in the dim light, sipping tea. One of them called to us: "Hello, my friends. What is your good country?"

"Our *good* country?" Ed said. "Our country is America, but your country is now our home."

"That is very good," the fellow said, rocking his head as only a Hindu can. "In that case we are brothers and you must let me buy you some tea. It is late. The next train will not arrive for many hours. You have a long wait. Come. Sit."

As they widened their circle to accommodate us and as we took our places squatting on the ground, Ed said, "The only wait we have is for sleep. We're not here for a train but for a good night's rest."

"But my friend," the man said, truly astonished, "it is dirty here. Bad people patrol this station. Thieves and dacoits. They will slit your pockets, and in the morning your money will be gone. You are Americans. There are hotels near this place. I will take you to one. We will wake the guard, and he will let you in. It is okay, he too is my brother."

"You just said we are brothers, no?" Ed said.

"Yes—"

"And you will sleep in the station tonight, won't you?"

"Yes, but—"

"If you can sleep here, surely your brother can, also."

The man quickly changed the subject.

"Where are you going?" he asked.

Ed just laughed.

"What are you looking for?"

"God," Ed answered.

This took the wind out of our friend's sails.

We finished our tea quickly.

Ed turned to me. "Shall we assume the horizontal?" he said.

"Yes, we shall," I said.

We bid our new friends goodnight and stood up.

"To the promenade!" Ed said with a flourish.

We sauntered down the platform as if we were entering the lobby of a fine and expensive hotel. At an unoccupied spot at the end of the platform we swept the dirt away with our *gumchas*. We lay wrapped in our *gumchas* with our head on our packs. Ed fell asleep the moment his head touched his pack. I lay awake for some time. The last thing I heard was a cow meandering lazily down the platform, stopping now and again to eat a piece of paper, then moving on, contented.

13

The next morning we awoke to the ground rumbling beneath us and to the sound of steel wheels clacking over steel tracks. There was a loud blast of steam, a whistle sounded, and a train entered the station, transforming our quiet sleeping place into a chaotic mass of humanity. Rushing to the doors of the slowing train, pressing their belongings before them like ants carrying crumbs in their jaws, people pushed and jostled each other into tight knots at each of the train's doors with the intensity of passengers fleeing a sinking ship, with the desperation of people fleeing a plague, each pressing forward for a seat long ago taken, a seat they hadn't a chance of claiming. They fought for places to stand, but the only places available were those that had been vacated by passengers trying get off the train at the station. The train's windows were barred, so the only way in or out was through the doors at the end of the cars. It was a mess, but somehow the people sorted themselves out.

Tea vendors carrying huge blackened pots walked up and down the length of the train sonorously chanting, "Chie, chie, chi-*eee*." They stopped wherever outstretched hands clutching coins were thrust through the bars of an open window, and they'd filled a clay cup with the thick milky brew, exchange it for a few coins, then move along the platform, resuming their chant.

Traveling as lightly as we were, and sleeping with only our *gumchas* over us, we were instantly awake, on our feet, and ready to go. The transition from undisturbed and deep sleep to full wakefulness was instant. No time to linger lazily in that in-between state of half consciousness; no residue of sleep to be cleared like cobwebs from a dulled mind.

~

When we left the train station that morning we walked into rural India and stepped back in time. We moved in a realm that the internal combustion engine sullied only occasionally. Our rides came not in trucks of rattling steel, but in bullock carts with wooden wheels and wood slat backs and sides of bamboo.

In the country, India's rough edges were rounded, and I found it easier to follow Ed's lead and not worry too much about what might happen to us. Ed's great confidence was born of a tremendous trust. Though reluctant at first to follow suit and stop struggling to stay afloat—reluctant to allow a force as natural as the body's buoyancy in water to uphold me—in the end I had no choice.

The same embrace I had felt at Matunga Road now embraced me again. The same warm smiles greeted us. I knew now something of India's character. Matunga Road had not been unique. The care given to any guest comes from deep in India's heart.

We walked to the south, finding rides on bullock carts, stopping at village wells. Occasionally we came to a larger road and jumped on the back of a truck that brought us to a new landscape. We were in the tropics. Banana and papaya grew wild. We passed through gentle hills of coffee. We crossed a deserted landscape.

One night a young man in a tea stall invited us to a cup of tea. He was a petition writer at the district court. He invited us to his home for a meal and a place to sleep. He lived with his parents, two brothers, and three sisters in a house made of homemade red mud bricks. Its roof was made of thatch and it was in the middle of green fields. They shared with us their simple meal of rice, dhal, and vegetables. Then we slept on the floor next to his brothers and sisters.

In the morning, when we were ready to leave, our host interpreted for his aging parents. "They are asking," he said, looking Ed square in the eye, "that you stay here with us." The boy's mother nodded her head in eager agreement, her soft eyes imploring. "They will build an extra room onto the house. They want you to live here for the rest of your days. We would feed you, and if you got sick we would take care of you. We would do anything, if only you would stay."

Ed regarded the elderly couple gently. He shook his head. "No," he said, raising his pressed palms to his forehead. "We will move on. We cannot stay."

The boy's parents understood. Tears welled up in the old woman's eyes.

When we left, the entire family lined up in front of the house. The sun was just lifting over the trees. The breeze was as gentle as the tender looks that followed us as we threaded through the fields to the road.

One day, as we passed through a hilly region, a Jeep full of geology students from Lucknow stopped for us. They were heading to a mine somewhere in the hinterland. They spoke

Windblown Clouds   Thomas K. Shor

English well. None of them had been in these hills before, so we all looked excitedly about as we crossed each ridge and a new vista of hills and valleys opened before us; all of us except Ed. Only Ed acted as if he had been there before. He sat and stared at the road receding behind the Jeep. The radio was tuned to a station playing local music. Maybe he was listening to that, maybe not. A toothpick was in his mouth and he was ruminating deeply. He was a million miles away.

The man sitting next to Ed tapped him on the shoulder. Ed turned. The man said, "What is the purpose of your travel?"

"The purpose?" Ed said. "Unless we talked longer or you knew me better, you'd not understand."

"But what is the *purpose* of your travel?" The man was not to be deterred.

"Well," Ed said, "I travel for *love*." He intoned the last word with strength in his voice.

"Love?" the young man asked. "Love for *what?*"

"You see," Ed said, turning to me. "I told you he wouldn't understand. As if love has to have an object!"

Shortly after they left us off, the road went through a little valley of gently sloping green fields. We came to a village consisting of a few shops, tea stalls, a State Bank of India, and stone houses ranging up the side of the mountain.

In the center of the village was a spigot that must have been connected to a spring on the mountain, for the water flowed out of it continually into a concrete basin. Ed stopped. I stopped, too. We regarded the spigot for some moments. A child came and put a bucket beneath the flow. He stood regarding us as we regarded the water. Then Ed suggested we bathe. So we put down our belongings. Ed got his soap out of a plastic bag. He took off his shirt. Then he wrapped his *gumcha* over his waist and took off his pants. The boy filled his bucket and lifted it, staring at us the entire time. He walked away with head turned, eyes riveted. Ed put his pants under the flow and rinsed them. Then he rubbed the bar of soap on them. Then he pounded them against the concrete of the water basin. He rinsed them and then did the same to his shirt. I squatted and looked out over the valley. When he was finished he asked if I could find some rocks to lay the clothes on to hasten the drying process. Then he lathered himself and washed. By the time he was finished, a man from a chie shop came with some dirty pans to wash, so I waited. Then I wrapped my midsection with my *gumcha,* took off my pants, and washed them. Then I washed myself.

We loitered while we waited for our clothes to dry. When they were still half wet a low cloud rolled over the valley and a gusty wind raised clouds of dust. Grabbing our clothes, we took refuge in an empty doorway. Then, as the sun peeked out from between the billowy clouds, we put our clothes out on the still-hot pavement, only to gather them again when the clouds of dust reappeared. Ed and I were practicing absolute spontaneity: when dirty, wash, when a storm comes, take refuge.

Ed put on his other pair of pants, which were light white cotton. When his shirt was dry he put that on. My shirt was also dry and I put it on. Ed's pants were still wet, so he hung them over his shoulders, the pant-legs draped over his front. And in such a fashion we headed out through fertile terraced valleys.

The gusting wind had been caused by thunderheads. They were coming our way. Before long it started to rain. The rain was light at first, but soon it became heavy. Ed draped his pants over his head and I put my *gumcha* over my head and draped it over my pack to try to keep its contents dry. We walked through this storm of lightning, rain, and hail for a long time without saying a word.

Then a car came up behind us. Private cars in India were rare, owned only by the rich. It looked like two couples out for a ride, the men in front, the women in back. We tried to wave the car down, but they only looked at us as if we were crazy. This made us laugh.

"Who'd want to pick up a couple of wet rats like us?" Ed asked, still laughing.

"Like something the cat dragged in!" I said. "Like something the cat didn't drag in!"

"They sure looked comfortable, didn't they?"

"Yeah, did you see how those two women were stretched out, taking up the *whole* back seat?"

We were high as kites: on the road and free. The rain and hail only accentuated that fact. When the rain stopped, it left us cold and wet.

Turning a corner, we came upon an open shed whose walls and roof were made of flattened oil tins. Inside the shed, tins were stacked to the rough roof and more empty tins overflowed into a dirt courtyard, across which stood a rough shack. We stopped at the dirt driveway, pockmarked with puddles. Another dark cloud approached. Thunder was already echoing off the mountains. Two little boys stood on the driveway, looking at us as we contemplated shelter.

Rain began to fall again. Ed suggested we see what we could find at the house, so we started up the driveway, the two children running ahead of us to the dirt-floored veranda where two men stood. They had a difficult time figuring out who or what we were. They tried speaking to us, but we knew not a word in the local dialect. One of them moved out a wooden bench and motioned for us to sit.

"Make ourselves at home, why don't we?" Ed said, and he laughed. One of the men went over to the shed and returned a moment later with a brazier full of freshly split wood. He lit a fire. It was a magic moment. We held our wet clothes over the fire. I stretched my legs toward it and steam rose. The elder of the boys, who was about seven, brought out an English schoolbook. I read out loud a few of the short, one-page stories. One of the stories was of Buddha's renunciation. The last sentence read: "He went into the forest and attained enlightenment." Very simple, very direct. Another story was of a boy on a farm, and another was of a class trip into the

Himalayas, to Naini Tal. The children on this trip drank soda; the teacher had tea.

When we were dry, we walked on.

One day we came upon a tea stall built around a huge and ancient tree. The tea wallah was alone with his young daughter. He was oiling her hair and combing it out. They lived in a mud hut beside the fire pit. I had the feeling there was no mother, that it was just the two of them. Everything was immaculately clean. You could feel the deep love between this father and daughter, and you could feel the calm that surrounded them. The quality was extraordinary. I never wanted to leave that place. In a corner was a low table before a shrine. On the table was an open book, and lying on the book was an ancient pair of wire-rimmed glasses. The book was the Bhagvat Gita. The road before the teahouse was quiet and on the other side a river flowed over huge boulders. We lingered there an entire morning.

~

The days tended to meld together during our journey to the South. Since we were headed nowhere, no progress toward a destination marked each day's passage. Traveling as we were, we had to live in the present. Nothing we did today had bearing on what we would do tomorrow. Neither sleeping tonight in a rich man's castle, nor sleeping wrapped in our *gumchas* on the edge of a field had any effect on where we would sleep tomorrow night. You can only eat so much today. Tomorrow you will grow hungry again. It doesn't matter if you wash twice today; tomorrow the sun will make you sweat and the dust will stick to you.

The afternoons were always hot. It was worst when no trees shaded the road. Once we found an open veranda of an abandoned house and there we passed the afternoon, our only activity noting the passage of time by the sun's progress across the sky.

On another hot afternoon, along a stretch of equally exposed road, we kept walking. I became wearied by the

Windblown Clouds Thomas K. Shor

ordeal, but the more wearied I became the more strength I seemed to possess. I understood some of what Ed meant when he spoke of following the ideal. It would be hard to say exactly what the ideal was, but it had something to do with not fearing, with holding firm to the belief that a force would uphold us, and with knowing that only by exposing oneself could this force express itself. Ed had built his life upon this reliance on the unseen. It was upon this that he gained strength. By traveling with Ed I caught a glimpse of the upholding nature of the universe and how it works through other people. I understood why it was practically against his religion to ask for assistance, or to exchange money for the satisfaction of bodily needs. Now I knew why, even though we had money in our pockets, we would be compromising the ideal to spend it. And though I still doubted I could have traveled alone in such a fashion, Ed's strength lent me strength.

Once we walked all day and nothing came our way, not as much as a well at which to wash ourselves or to wet our parched mouths. We had somehow ended up on a dirt road that passed through a huge flat plain. There was scrub and not much else. Without aiming toward a destination, one couldn't help believing that what came one's way was meant to be, that something was drawing one forward. Give up control and cast your lot with a power greater than your own—that was Ed's credo. I would have had a hard time believing in this greater power in the West. But all of India is founded on the fact that the ego is not supreme. I caught a glimpse of how this greater power operates by traveling with Ed.

And we were not the only ones traveling that dirt road in search of the truths hidden at the bottom of the human soul. We passed and were passed by a surprising number of *sadhus* and wandering mendicants. Two of the *sadhus* were particularly wild looking. They carried tridents in one hand and gourd begging bowls in the other, and their faces and chests were smeared with ashes. In the West, one look in their eyes would tell you they were mad. Here, no such categories applied. The way they walked in locked step without exchanging a word gave the impression that they had been walking together for decades. They walked quickly, handily passed us, and disappeared around a bend in the road.

As the day wore on I was increasingly tempted to go to a village and ask for food and water. I even would have paid for it. I would have gladly treated Ed to a feast. But the closer the sun dipped toward the western horizon, and the longer it was that nothing had come our way, the more distant Ed became, the more determined became his step. I knew better now than to think madness had come over him. From the time the sun was at its white-hot height, till it turned red in the western sky, neither of us uttered a word.

Just as the first stars shone in the sky, a glow appeared directly ahead of us on the horizon. The glow grew larger and more pronounced until the full moon appeared pale red and larger than life behind a line of trees. We hadn't seen a tree in miles. We quickened our pace and soon we were walking in blue shadows beneath the trees. Before us was a large village.

The village's main street was lined with shops and stalls. Street vendors were lighting kerosene lanterns. It seemed the entire village was out enjoying an evening stroll.

We were about halfway through the village when a short man dressed with only a cloth wrapped round his waist came up from behind us and tapped Ed on the shoulder.

"How may I be of service?" he asked.

We stopped. Ed turned and took the twig he had been using as a toothpick out of his mouth; he looked at the man and smiled.

"You look hungry. Are you needing food?"

Ed smiled broadly now, but still he didn't speak.

"Very good," the man said. "You are tired too, am I not correct? You will be needing a place to spend the night?"

As if Ed were coming out of a trance, he said, "Yes, that's right, isn't it?"

"Then follow me," the man said.

He led us through the village to the school, which was made of mud and thatch. The courtyard was made of stone. He sat us on a cool stone slab and told us to wait. "I am the village schoolteacher. You will be safe here. I will come back with food."

"I've been led to school yards before," Ed said to me. "It is the only public property in many of these villages, the only place the village itself can put you up. Once a principle of a school asked me if I'd speak to the English class. I was hardly dressed for lecturing. All I had was a *gumcha* wrapped round my waist—those were lean times for me. But I agreed. I told him I would speak to the class, but that my talk would be like my attire: short enough to be interesting, yet long enough to cover the essentials."

Ed pointed over my shoulder. "What have we here?" he said.

About a dozen men, holding long poles tipped with kerosene-soaked rags that emitted equal proportions of both light and oily smoke, were coming in through the school gate. We rose to meet them. Our friend, the schoolteacher, was not amongst them. I noticed a man with a long machete. Instinctively, I took a step back, but the torchbearers had formed a circle around us. They had planted the ends of the long torch poles in the ground. For a moment I felt trapped. But then I looked closer and saw that a ring of smiles encircled us. The musical tones of their South Indian tongue rose above the crackling and sputtering of the torches. They looked at us with the rapt wonder of children who have discovered a new kind if frog on the edge of a pond. It seemed they didn't quite know what to do with us.

Then someone produced a coconut. He handed it to the man with the machete, and with a single, skillfully executed motion, the man chopped the pointed tip cleanly off of the coconut. Stepping forward, he handed the coconut to Ed. Ed drank deeply of the thick, cool milk. Then I drank. It was like nectar. It cooled my parched mouth, wet my throat, and filled me with nourishment. The man with the machete took back the empty nut and cleaved it in two. He sliced two flakes from the outer shell, which we used as scoops. Nothing has ever tasted as delicious to me as the soft, fleshy interior of that coconut.

The delight we took in our meal was easily matched, if not surpassed, by our circle of newfound friends. They stood holding their torches with broad smiles across their faces, commenting in their strange, singsong language, their voices scarcely above a whisper, upon every move either Ed or I made. To them, we had blown in unexpectedly from out of the night. They were obviously speculating on who we were, what we were doing there, and from what strange land we had come. They could tell we'd come from far away—as far, perhaps, as the land across the great ocean from which the British had come. But what did these villagers know of other continents, separated from their own by vast oceans? It was unlikely that any of the men had been much beyond the neighboring villages, or the closest town. They closely watched our every move, as if some gesture would supply a clue, a foothold to an alien world. But the gap was too wide, the distances too great between our two cultures to make understanding of our differences possible. We *did* find common ground though—our shared humanity—and we found it through a medium, a common denominator of expression known the world round: the smile. In the primitive torches' golden glow, an understanding developed between us, expressed simply by smiling. It didn't matter that they didn't know our home country. It was immaterial.

The village teacher came through the gate, carrying two warm banana-leaf parcels containing rice and curried vegetables. We sat on the ground to eat, and the schoolteacher sat with us. When we were through we thanked him for the meal, but he would not hear our thanks.

"You come from far away. It is dark. You were hungry. Should I have let you go without food? It is our pleasure to feed pilgrims. It brings us joy; it brings us merit to show kindness to strangers. We are thankful for the opportunity." The others prodded him to translate our exchange, and when he did they all nodded their agreement. They pressed their palms together and inclined their heads. They were thanking *us* for coming. What more delightful situation for a guest to be in? We were all smiling, like beacons of joy.

Then the schoolteacher continued, "You must tell me: what more can we do for you?"

The very idea that they could do more for us was completely preposterous. If anything, I felt it was our turn to give. If I were a singer, I would have sung them a song. If I'd had a flute, I would have played a happy melody. But we had nothing to offer.

"No," I said. "We were hungry, but now we are full. We have everything we could possibly need or want. Thank you. Thank you again."

He eyed both Ed and me carefully to make sure we weren't merely being polite. Then he stood. "In that case," he said, "we will let you sleep." He motioned for the others to follow him. They passed single file across the courtyard and out the gate. The torches' oily smell hung in the air until a breeze replaced it with the fragrance of flowers.

By the time we lay down and wrapped ourselves in our *gumchas*, figures started appearing in the darkness around us. Slowly they came closer, and we saw that they were children. As I closed my eyes to fall asleep, I knew they were silently watching us.

14

We left the village before the sun had time to show over the horizon. The cocks were just beginning to stir. The village well was untended; not a bucket broke the still water. Nor did the women's soft voices break the silence. The dust of the previous day had settled under the dew. It was the moment before the world awakens. We were alone with the endless road and the trees, the still air and the birds' songs. The peace of the hour entered our hearts and settled there.

Just when the sun was peeking over the horizon and filling the world with long shadows, a bullock cart, driven by a boy of seven or eight, came up behind us. He sat on the back of the huge black beast and directed it with a short stick. The cart was full of straw. He offered us a ride, and we accepted. By the time the sun rose above a line of distant trees, an occasional villager on his way to his fields joined us on the road. Then bicyclists started rattling by. As the morning progressed, the tiny dirt road became a busy thoroughfare.

It soon became apparent that we were not the only ones traveling a long distance by foot down that road. We passed the two *sadhus* of the day before. They were washing themselves in an irrigation ditch. There were others too, entire families who weren't merely going to their field or to a neighboring village. And there were more and more *sadhus*. All were heading in the same direction as we were. We had unwittingly entered a flow of people all heading toward a destination, and as we moved closer to that destination, the ranks of the pilgrims swelled.

By midday, though, the sun drove almost everyone into the shade. Every tree—and there weren't many—sheltered somebody. We were just about the only ones still on the move. The hot sun made me lightheaded. It added to the euphoria that comes from being on the open road. We were both happy, just plainly and simply happy to be on the earth on a long stretch of road.

This was our state of mind when we passed through a small village of a dozen or so palm-thatched mud huts situated around a well. The first hut we came to had a wide overhang, in whose shade sat a dozen or so people. In the

Windblown Clouds

Thomas K. Shor

center was a baby sucking its mother's breast. Older children sat on either side, lethargically staring into space. At their sides and behind them sat older folks and grandparents. It looked like a pose for a family portrait. But no one was really smiling. In fact their faces were expressionless; it was too hot to work in the fields or collect water, so they sat, like everyone else, hoping for a breeze. With what energy they could muster, they shooed flies. It looked as if they had been sitting there for ten thousand years, waiting for something to happen.

And then we appeared. They all saw us at the same time, and in unison smiles flashed across their dark faces. Their smiles were tremulous at first, but quickly turned to expressions of pure mirth at the sight of so strange a pair of sadhus. We smiled back, and within seconds the feelings that flowed between us broke the bounds, and everyone started laughing. We all fell into it, not quite sure why. And because the laughter sprang from no known source, it only became more hilarious the longer it persisted. It was an uproarious, uncontrollable, and sidesplitting laughter. The baby had long ago slipped from its mother's breast and was joyfully gurgling in its mother's lap, which was convulsing with laughter. The old grandpa, pointing his crooked finger at us and slapping his thigh, roared till he was out of breath, took a deep breath, and roared again. The children rolled uncontrollably over each other, tears streaming down their cheeks.

We kept walking. At the next hut, a family sat in the shade of an overhanging roof. They too looked as if they had been waiting years for something to happen. Ed and I were still laughing when they saw us and we set them aflame with our laughter as though we were a spark and they were dry straw.

~

By late afternoon, a mass of pilgrims was walking along the small dirt road and we found ourselves swept along with the tide. Wherever a path crossed a field and met the road more people swelled the ranks. Though still walking without a destination, we could feel ourselves being drawn forward to something as yet unseen.

A town appeared in the distance, over which loomed an ancient stone temple with richly carved towers, darkened by age. We entered the town and moved with the crowd through the winding streets toward the center. The townspeople were adorned in their finest saris—bright red and orange, pink and gold, and the purest white. Even the children were decked out that day.

Everywhere flowers were for sale, huge bouquets and garlands. Flower heads were stacked six feet high. Knots of bright color set aflame women's jet-black hair. Men wore garlands around their bare brown necks. Even the cows had flowers in strings around their horns, or braided into their tails. Doorways were strewn with the brightest colors. People threw huge handfuls of flowers into the air, and the flowers fell to the ground where thousands of bare feet trampled over them. Petals stuck to sweaty flesh. Arms and legs were speckled with color; even the crowns of those with shaved heads were transformed into colorful patchworks.

People pressed forward to enter the mad flow. The crowd became tighter and tighter, and we became submerged in the joyous crowd's single mind. Now we moved as a single body, a myriad of legs, arms, and shoulders. A single life or spirit flowed through us, a frenzied, quivering anticipation. The crowd strained forward toward a culmination, a consummation of what brought us all together.

Streaming down the town's main road, I jumped up to see where we were going, but all I saw was a stream of people—identical in its color, in its density, and in its mad frenzy—heading straight towards us. Where the two streams of people met, I heard screams of agony, and of joy. The heavy beat of drums shook the ground. The soaring notes of flutes hovered in the air. The screams grew louder, babies squealed and wailed. We were all treading that thin line between fear and

Windblown Clouds   Thomas K. Shor

joy.

    Though swept into the frenzy, I still feared I'd stumble and fall, be trodden, and split apart. It was impossible to tell whether we were moving headlong toward our deaths, or to a meeting with God. All that was clear was that we were heading toward dissolution. The drumbeats grew deafeningly loud. With each beat we drew closer, both to our destination and to each other, for it was as if we were single cells passing through a vein, nearing the heart. The valve of the heart would open with a pound, the sound would echo off the inner walls of the pulsating chamber, and we would have arrived, arrived at the center, at the pulsing heart of South India.

    Our stream merged with the other. We had arrived. Carved into the ancient stones of the temple numberless stone gods and goddesses stared down at us, their myriad arms and legs frozen for all time, their faces in attitudes of bliss or despair. There were gods making love with other gods, with men, and with beasts. There were gods dancing in ecstasy, blood dripping from their lips, garlands of skulls hung round their necks. There were gods riding elephants, peacocks, and rats, and other gods with the heads of elephants, monkeys, and beasts unknown to mortal eyes. Every emotion, thought, and feeling of man had been etched into the stones of the tower centuries ago by the hands of men long forgotten—but still they spoke. They mirrored the ecstasy that flowed through the throng, the ecstasy of being on the edge of fear and joy, where everything is exaggerated, where the stream of colors merge with an ocean of light, where each becomes lost not only to his companions, but to himself, and is found again in the identity with the whole of the rainbow, with the ocean, and with the gods on the tower. For now the gods spoke. They waved their arms and flashed their tongues and light came to their eyes. They laughed for all of humanity's happiness and cried for all of humanity's sorrow. They cried for the beggars who lined the way to the temple. They cried for those whose bodies disease had laid waste, whose faces pain had disfigured, who stood by the side of the road with hands outstretched. And they cried for the lepers who ripped open the festering wounds in their eroding limbs and writhed to the ground with pain, who waved their bloody, festering limbs and scratched at their faces to elicit both pity and horror. The crowd showered these leprous beggars with coins. The gods took pity too, and they cried. They cried for the lepers and they cried for those showering coins. They cried for us all and for all the pain and sorrows we'd have to endure. They cried, but they also laughed. They laughed with the babies, who, held tightly in their mother's arms, tried to wriggle free in order to crawl over the top of the crowd and climb the high tower to play with the baby gods. The gods laughed for all the good harvests, the sunny days, the days of ease and prosperity, and of marriage and birth. And they laughed too at the moment of death. For they stood on their tower high above the turmoil and saw that the world was spinning round and round and round again. They saw, as if it were a single moment, the rise and fall of generations; they saw birth and death and birth again, and they laughed over all of it, for it was all part of the endless dance of creation. They laughed over the sick, the poor, the homeless, and the ones racked with leprosy, for that too was life, and all life was one. They laughed over all of it, and they cried too, for all of life is pain and joy, suffering and health, birth and death.

 The crowd lunged forward toward the gaping hole of the tower's gate, which was open wide to receive us. The drums beat on my eardrums. Everyone screamed and groaned and pushed. People pushed me forward, and I had no choice but to push forward the people in front of me. Suddenly, a shower of bananas and oranges were thrown in the air, and I turned to see the fruit hitting the sides of a huge carriage. The carriage's wooden wheels were twenty feet in diameter and the canopy was forty feet off the ground. A god made of wood sat in the carriage's seat. It was wrapped in colorful cloths, its face anointed with oil and ghee. The fruit hit the wooden wheels and the sides of the carriage then fell to the ground. A line of priests with sandalwood paste smeared across their faces and chests held onto long, thick ropes and pulled the god's carriage with all their might. They cried out to the beat of the drum as they pulled the carriage. Ho! Ho! Ho! The wheels creaked, and the carriage moved. A frenzied woman rushed toward the carriage and tried to hurl herself beneath the wheels. Then another and another followed suit. A line of burly attendants lifted them off the ground, holding them back. Forces beyond the women's control had taken hold of them. They bit and screamed and tried repeatedly to throw themselves beneath the wheels.

Now we were before the tower, and it looked as if the tower and all its gods would fall right on top of us. We were close enough to receive the god's tears on our heads, their drools, their drops of blood. A mile of humanity pushed me from behind, and with a pounding of the drum I passed inside.

15

My departure from Ed was sudden. One day, as we sat under a huge tree whose gnarled roots ran along the ground, almost as far as its branches, the subject came up. I knew I had been cramping his style. Traveling for Ed was a solitary affair. I asked him whether he had ever tried traveling with anyone else.

"Yes. One time. He was a young fellow, like yourself, and he was American. But he was a horrible failure."

"What happened?"

"He insisted on traveling with me. He had a lot of ideas in his head. We were in the Himalayas. He came down with hepatitis. I brought him to a hospital. In the end he died.

"You know," he continued after a moment's reflection, "when I left India I gave up my permanent residency. If I'm to stay here longer than my three-month tourist visa, I'd better get started on the paperwork. I'll need a sponsor, someone who will vouch for me. I thought maybe Bipin would do that. I actually should be going back to Bombay. If that won't work, I'll have to go to Bihar. I've friends there. Have you any interest in going back to Bombay?"

I didn't. I wanted to see more of India. I told him so.

"Where would you suggest I go?" I asked. "I'm not so much interested in seeing places as I am meeting people. Do you know anyone I should see? Anyone I could learn from?"

Ed thought a while. He looked at me. I had the feeling he was sizing me up.

"There is one person you should meet," he said finally. "Someone I haven't seen in years. When I was still living at the ashram, a famous Swiss psychologist, Dr. Kurt Fantl, came to study the phenomenon of extra sensory perception. He came to see Thakur, who was renowned for his abilities. Since I was the only Westerner at the ashram at the time, Thakur made me Dr. Fantl's host.

"When Dr. Fantl left Bihar, he went up to Almora in the Kumaoni Himalayas, the area just west of Nepal, to see a lama, scholar of Tibetan Buddhism. I received a telegram from him shortly after he arrived. He said I should come at once to meet this lama. He was quite taken with him. That was my first destination when I was on the road. When I arrived there I was so awed at being in this man's presence that I hardly dared open my mouth the entire time. The lama interpreted my behavior differently, and later he told me he thought I was enlightened the way I kept my silence. While on the road, I went back there regularly to live there with the lama and his wife. I used to go there when the chestnuts were ripe, and I would collect the nuts, hitch a ride on a truck to Delhi, and sell the nuts to a fancy restaurant that used them to make some special desserts. Then I would bring the money back to give to the lama."

"Does this lama speak English?" I asked.

"Fluently. He also speaks Tibetan, Hindi, and, of course,

German, for he is originally from Germany. He spent years traveling in Tibet. Some consider him the leading Western scholar of Tibetan Buddhism alive today."

"What is his name?" I asked, for I had the suspicion that I already knew of him.

"His name is Lama Anagarika Govinda."

Indeed, I had heard of him. He wrote the preface to Professor Evens-Wentz's translation of *The Tibetan Book of the Dead,* which Carl Jung wrote the introduction for. He wrote the celebrated book on his travels in Tibet called *The Way of the White Clouds.* I had read quite extensively in spiritual matters, and these three men—Govinda, Evens-Wentz, and Jung—held the position in my personal pantheon reserved for the immortals; all three had successfully translated the wisdom of the East, had made Eastern Wisdom accessible to the modern West. I knew Jung was dead, and I had suspected Evens-Wentz and Govinda were dead as well. One never expects the immortals to be alive. And never in one's wildest dreams does one expect to meet one.

"Can I just go there?" I asked. "Can one just show up on such a man's doorstep?"

"I'll write all this down," Ed said, "but what you should do is go to Almora and find Mary Opplinger. She is American. She must be nearing seventy now. She is married to the Swiss consul. She lives in a house called Haimavati. It is on the way to Kasar Devi, the hill on which Lama Govinda lives. Govinda's house was built by Evens-Wentz. I've known Mary for years. She's a good friend of Govinda's. Explain who you are and that I sent you, and she will take you there."

Ed wrote down all the pertinent information.

"How do you propose to get there?" Ed asked, handing me the piece of paper.

This was all so sudden, as sudden as our meeting and decision to travel together. I hardly knew what to say. I didn't know what he meant. The tree we sat under was at a crossroads: one road went east and west, the other north and south.

"I must go back to the west," Ed said, indicating the road to the west. "You're heading north. Are you ready to walk on your own?"

"I think I'd rather take public transport," I said, laughing.

We hitched to Bangalore. Ed brought me to the train station. He saw me to the train, and there we said good-bye. We knew we would meet again. But when, neither of us could say.

~

I stared out the window as the train picked through the mad confusion of tracks. The tracks ran parallel, crossed, and branched. At first there were dozens of these tracks running beside the train, but as it chose its way through the maze-like tangle, a set of tracks angled off now and then at a junction whose crossing was announced by an off-beat clank that passed from car to car. I couldn't help feeling the pulse that marked each passing junction strike at my heart, for I was now alone.

Ed was probably just leaving the station. The image of him standing on the platform, his palms pressed together, his eyes holding mine until the train rounded it's first bend, burned in my mind.

I let go of that image, left the window, and went in search of a seat. I had days of travel ahead of me. The aisle of the train was piled with bags, boxes, bundles wrapped in sheets, suitcases, and trunks. There wasn't a single person standing. I took this as a good sign.

The thick metal door of the first compartment I approached was shut, and the shades were drawn over the window. Since I had to start somewhere, I decided to try it. Positioning myself squarely before the compartment, I slid the door open and stuck my head inside. I was met with the sound of over a dozen women gasping in unison. There wasn't a man in sight. The gasps of the women were followed by a rustling sound, like the flutter of a thousand wings, as they whipped the corners of their saris over their faces to protect themselves from my gaze. You would think I had surprised them at their bath. Then they started screaming at me as one woman lunged forward, grabbed the handle, and slid the door shut with a vengeance.

My nose was inches from the glass. And while the shade was still rocking back and forth, I heard them curse me. The latch snapped shut. I took a step back. There was something written above the door, stenciled in three languages. English was at the top: FOR LADIES ONLY.

Cautiously, I moved on. All the other compartments had no doors. Each was an open alcove with wooden benches on either side. A high, shelf-like bunk hung suspended on chains over each bench.

At the first compartment, a toddler stood on his mother's knee, leaning over and grasping firmly to the bars of the window. He seemed delighted by the outskirts of Bangalore moving by so quickly, and expressed his delight with shrieks of excitement. His mother's face was drawn. Tired of holding the energetic boy, she pulled him from the window, and, with cross words, told him to sit still. It was apparent that they had been traveling a long time; the battle was an old one, which neither side could win. The mother wanted the boy to sit still, perhaps like his sister and brother, who sat beside her. Or perhaps she wanted the child to sleep like his two other brothers and a sister, who slept curled like a litter of kittens on one of the benches. The father sat aloof with one of the sleeping children's heads on his lap. Taking long pulls off a cigarette and exhaling the smoke through his nose, he stared blankly at a point on the ceiling as his body swayed gently with the train's motion. By his side, on the piece of bench closest to the hallway, sat an old couple, most probably the grandparents. Together, the elders had less than a square foot to sit on; they looked tired of trying to hold themselves up. Ten of them sat on the bench, which was meant to seat three. The other bench wasn't much better. Nine sat there, but they were all adults. The upper bunks each sat four, and the people sitting on those seats looked the most uncomfortable. They sat cross-legged, backs bent forward, necks bent sideways, their heads hitting the ceiling, going bump, bump, bump as the train moved down the tracks.

The next compartment was worse. The luggage, piled on the floor between the benches, looked at least three feet deep. Since all of the benches were taken, many people were perched on their luggage. A fat man, sitting on a bench, quarreled with a thin man, sitting on his luggage. Their battle appeared to be territorial: three thin men could have easily sat in the space occupied by the one fat one. I pressed onward.

Each compartment I passed had a cast of characters and a story to tell. Unfortunately, in each case, the casting was already complete, the scene already full. So I went on and on and on down the car till I came upon another compartment with doors and shades drawn over the windows. Carefully noting the stenciled letters above the door, I crept quietly past the compartment and rounded another latrine.

The situation was the same in the next car. It was just another dizzying repetition of latrine, ladies' compartment, open compartments—all of them overstuffed from top to bottom, ladies' compartment, latrine, door to the next car. Not one compartment could possibly admit another soul. What was I to do? Tell the old grandparents to move over and split their square foot of bench three ways? I couldn't do it, so I passed from car to car, wondering the whole while why I was the only one without a seat.

Finally, I came to the end of the train. My search had proved fruitless. We were in the country now, and I watched the tracks recede behind the train.

I sensed someone watching me. Turning, I saw an old man squatting on his haunches with his back resting against the door to the latrine. His hands grasped firmly the base of a walking stick, which was planted solidly between his legs, and which he used to steady himself. The walking stick's curved handled loomed high over his head. It rocked gently back and forth, like a solitary sapling swaying in a summer breeze. As I squatted next to him and opened our friendship with a smile, he patted his rear and pointed with his stick toward the front of the train. Go, he was saying, find yourself a seat. I pointed to my eyes, made my fingers walk, and told him I had looked. But he wouldn't take no for an answer: he tapped and tapped and tapped his stick. So I motioned, here is good. He shrugged his shoulders and hummed a little tune.

Soon the train slowed and entered a station. The old man rose to his feet. Holding his walking stick firmly with one hand and steadying himself on the wall with the other, he positioned himself in front of the door. The instant the train stopped, he jumped from the step. Shouts came from outside. Someone threw a bag through the door, which was followed by another and another. Then a mass of hands gripped the doorjambs as people fought to be the first ones on—as if it mattered who was first. What they didn't know was that we'd be vying for floor space now. So I positioned myself in a corner, set my pack before me, and staked out a claim. A seemingly endless procession of people climbed aboard and disappeared down the hall around the corner. I kept expecting the flow to back up and start crowding my space—but it never did. A conductor shut the door from the outside, a whistle blew, and the train rolled out of the station.

I got up and peered around the corner. The hall was fuller now: baskets, bundles, and sacks, but empty of people! They had all found seats. Okay, I thought, the old man was right. I, too, will go and find a seat. Walking quickly to the middle of the car, I turned into a compartment and looked imploringly at the occupants. Fifty-four eyes fell upon me, and I felt naked, the way you'd feel if you jumped from a burning building toward a ring of people holding a net. I was suspended in midair, wondering whether they'd receive me.

Then came the miracle, like the parting of the Red Sea: ten people, crammed onto one of the benches, shifted to the

Windblown Clouds   Thomas K. Shor

side, and, as if by magic, a piece of the bench appeared for me to sit on. And as if that wasn't enough, the piece they gave me was the window seat. I looked down the long line of my new companions and thanked them all. They all made like it was nothing. The man next to me said, "Not to worry, that is how we do it here. That way everybody has a place."

Soon the train stopped at another station and vendors walked slowly up and down the platform to announce their wares. First came the man selling tea from a big blackened teapot. Then came a man with a broad basket on his head: "Mango, mango-mango-mango, mango." Then a shrill, "Peanut, peanut, peanut, peanut." Vendors sold pencils and paper, envelopes and stamps, bracelets and combs, shoes, watches, books, spiced and dried chickpeas, betel leaves and *paan,* bottled fruit drinks, *Thumbs-up* cola, oranges, bananas, papayas, and more. The calls were as rich and varied as an orchestra, and each vendor had a solo as they passed outside my window. There was nothing one could possibly need during a long train ride that wouldn't be pressed against the bars of his window and displayed for his inspection. The scene had the air of a carnival and the excitement at a ball game.

"Hey!" I yelled through the bars at a tea vendor. He stopped his chant, came to the window, and filled an earthen cup. As he handed it to me, I gave him one rupee. I received sixty paise in return. It cost forty paise, about four cents American. Then I stopped a peanut man and handed *him* a rupee. Lifting a simple scale out of the basket that hung around his neck—the scale was but a stick with a tin platter suspended off each end—he put a weight in one dish and filled the other with peanuts until the two dishes were even. Then he made a cone out of a piece of newspaper, poured the peanuts into it, and handed it to me. I had more peanuts than I knew what to do with, so I handed them out to neighbors and made some friends.

The scene outside the window enthralled me so much that it wasn't until we passed out of the station that I noticed we had taken on more passengers. Only a few had room to sit on their belongings; the rest had to stand—for hour after long, hot hour. At each station, crowds ran beside the train as it slowed, and when it stopped they used their bodies as battering rams to press themselves into tighter and tighter spaces. They spilled into our compartment and stood in the space between the benches. Pulling my legs up so they wouldn't be crushed, I sat with my legs pressed against my chest and my head resting on my knees. And so I sat through the afternoon and into the evening.

When seven o'clock arrived, I had to think about getting to one of the doors so I could get off at Jabalpur, where I had to change trains. We were scheduled to arrive at seven-twenty, but since I had no idea if the train was running on time, I decided to inquire. It was a labor just to turn my head, and when I had done so, my neighbor's head was just inches away and I could clearly see each pore on his face.

"Jabalpur?" I said.

He didn't respond. He just stared blankly at the hip of the person standing directly before him, as if he were in a trance. A bead of sweat dislodged from his hair, rolled across his pulsing temple, down his cheek, and came to rest on the side of his jaw. Then it rolled again, stopped a moment on his chin, and dripped onto his lap. The moment it landed, another drip began its long journey down his face.

"Jabalpur?" I said again, this time in a louder voice.

Still he stared blankly.

My arms were clasped around my legs, my fingers interlaced and held in place by the pressure of the bare leg of the man standing in front of me. I worked my fingers loose, dislodged my arm, and gave my neighbor a jab with my elbow. This broke his catatonic state.

"Jabalpur?" I said for the third time.

"Ah, Jabalpur," he said, and he shook his head in agreement, as if I had said it was hot.

I pointed to his wristwatch and repeated again the name

of the station. This time he understood. He shouted something out so all could hear. The word *Jabalpur* echoed around the compartment. Finally the answer came back: he motioned that I should get up.

I stood on the bench, held onto the bunk above me, and surveyed the sea of people and luggage. Without an obvious route to take, I set out with the faith that people would move their hands when they saw my foot coming and squeeze to the side to let me pass. When I got to the mouth of the compartment, I looked back one last time. My place had already been taken. It looked as if I had never been there.

I once read that when the Europeans came to America the land was so densely forested a squirrel could have climbed a tree along the rocky coast of Maine and jumped from branch to branch across the vast continent all the way to the pacific coast, never once setting foot on the ground. I felt like that squirrel of yore as I swung, hung onto whatever I could, jumped over and stepped on bundles and bodies, never once touching the floor of the train as I made my way to the door.

I reached the door just as the train rolled into a station. The sign on the platform said Jabalpur, and I jumped out, fought through the crowd of people trying to push me back on, and felt with great joy the earth beneath my feet.

Locating a water spigot with a stone trough beneath it, I stuck my head into the flow of the water and felt my temperature drop by degrees. I rinsed my mouth, took some large gulps, and the world seemed manageable again. A whistle blew and the train rolled out of the station. I was glad to see it go.

16

Having survived my first day on an Indian train, I had only another three to endure; but I didn't let my thoughts go that far. All I could think about was the night to come and whether or not it would be possible to reserve a berth. A stairway led to an elevated walkway that brought me to the station lobby, a vast and tumultuous sea of people contained within four walls. Against the back wall a contentious knot of people, each of whom believed his turn was next, stood in line before fourteen ticket windows. I harbored no such illusion concerning my turn, so I wandered off in search of I knew not what—perhaps a man wearing a hat with RESERVATIONS CLERK written across its front. Anyway, I had a few hours to kill.

The station's high ceiling and bare walls echoed thousands of voices speaking a myriad of different languages. The government in Delhi had long searched for a single language that would unify the country. They had tried to promote both Hindi and English, but neither had worked. Hindi, a northern language, resembles the southern, Dravidian languages no more than it resembles English. To those in the South, the Hindi-speaking lands are as distant, perhaps, as Inner Mongolia is from Washington DC. For in India one can't reckon distances using a map. A map would show Jabalpur as a thousand miles from Delhi. Yet how many lands would one have to cross to get there? Indians populate space with a kaleidoscopic array of cultures: so one passes not only through mere geographic regions, but regions of thought and spirit as well. One's neighbor's apartment may lie on the other side of a flimsy wall, yet how distant may his thoughts and beliefs be? A southern villager who is a direct descendant from the original Dravidian inhabitants of India would be far removed from his neighbor, a descendant of northern Muslim Moguls. Continents often dwell within a single wall.

And how is such a gap bridged? If language is the way—as the government in Delhi seems to believe—then perhaps the national language of India is the reflected voices of thousands echoing off train station walls; for it is there that the races mix and their words commingle.

I must have looked lost, for a man approached me, and in thickly accented English asked if I was in need of assistance.

He looked both prosperous and preposterous, dressed in a business suit, tie, and plastic sandals. He clutched a plastic briefcase.

"Assistance?" I said. "Why, yes. I'd like to reserve a berth on a train I'm to catch in a few hours; but I don't know if this is possible, or how to go about it."

"It is not easy," he told me gravely. "But you are talking to the right man. I am in the employ of the railroad. What is the train in question?"

"The ten-fifteen bound for Delhi. I'm going as far as Hyderabad."

"Follow me," he said. "We'll see what we can do. This is not my home station, you see. I too am far from home. I am on the return from an official railway business meeting, but, unfortunately, I must stay at this station for some time. It is all because of some scoundrels. They came while I was sleeping on the train and took my luggage. They took my money, too. But they didn't take this," he said proudly, patting his plastic briefcase. "It contains official documents. I was holding it on my lap."

I gave him a sympathetic nod and hoped he wasn't buttering me up for a handout. In a reflective tone, he continued: "There are many useless fellows out there. They will rob your pocket and cheat your mind. It is because of them that I quit my job as an engineer and became an official. I could take it no longer. I thought a job behind a desk would be safer. But now I am not so sure."

"You had problems when you were an engineer?"

"Problems! More than my share! You see this gray hair? That comes from being held up by dacoits. That comes from just recalling what has happened to me. That comes from nightmares that I am an engineer again, and that they are stopping my train. Being an engineer of a train is like being the captain of a ship. You are responsible for your passengers' well being. It is a great responsibility, one I took extremely seriously.

Windblown Clouds

Thomas K. Shor

"The first time dacoits robbed my train, they moved the rusted hulk of a truck onto the track. It was at night, and by the time the light from my engine struck the truck it was too late; I could not stop in time. I plowed right into it, horrified; I thought the truck was occupied. The moment I jumped from the train to see, I knew I had landed in a trap. From out of the bushes came scores of people, men, women, and children, all with huge sticks and knives. In India, there is a separate cast for every occupation; even the bandits have their own caste. They take their children along so they can learn their people's trade. Despite all that they steal, the dacoits of Bihar—for that is where I was always robbed—are desperately poor. They had but one gun, and that gun they held to my head. While others worked their way through the train, relieving my passengers of their jewelry, watches, and cash money, I had to feel the cool metal of the gun's barrel on my temple and watch the thieves strip my engine of all the brass and copper. Just imagine! They tore the engine apart for the scrap metal! That is the condition of my country. Having been relieved of all the brass and copper fittings, how was I to move the train? We had to wait until another train came along. Train robberies were so common in this area that it didn't even reach the newspapers. My head was nearly blown apart by a bullet, and the police never asked me to describe my assailants. We have a very big problem with corruption in this country.

"The second time my train was attacked by dacoits it was also in Bihar. This time they attacked the train on horseback, just like in American movies about the old west. They came up from behind, rode like the wind, and jumped onto the train. All of a sudden they invaded the engine room from both sides. Again they robbed the passengers at knifepoint. And again they had only one gun, which again they pointed at my head. This time they held it against the back of my skull, right here at the base, where the soft spot is."

The man was sweating now, recalling these horrible

Windblown Clouds Thomas K. Shor

events.

"The only good thing I can say about this second robbery was that since they were on horseback, they couldn't strip the engine for scrap. And since they hadn't stopped the train by making me ram into a rusted truck, once they mounted their horses again and disappeared into the scrub, we could move on to the next station.

"The third time my train was robbed it was an inside job. The dacoits posed as passengers. They got on at one station and sat in different cars. Then on cue they started robbing the passengers. I didn't even know about it until one of them pulled the emergency chord and they all jumped off and disappeared into the scrub. It was nighttime and there was nothing we could do. The good thing about that time was that I didn't have a gun to my head and I didn't even know the train was being robbed until it was all over. The bad thing was that one of my conductors got hit over the head with a stick when he tried to resist. He suffered no permanent damage, but all the same I felt horribly responsible."

We arrived at a door with a plaque mounted on it that read, RAILWAY EMPLOYEES ONLY. He pushed open the door and motioned for me to follow. Desks and chairs were strewn in a perplexing disarray as a dozen men, clustered around one desk, argued and pecked at each other like vultures over a kill. They were fighting over numbers and figures, dates and names written in thirty-pound ledger books that looked like old Bibles. These ledger books were everywhere, piled four feet deep on chairs, desks, and on the floor. At least a dozen people carried huge stacks of these books from one pile to another. It appeared that there were two classes of people who populated this hidden realm behind the ticket windows: those who wrote in and argued over the ledger books and those who ported them from place to place. Two of the porters, each piled so high with ledgers that they couldn't see over the tops, collided directly in front of me, spilling their loads into a single, homogeneous pile. A raging war of words ensued. It almost came to blows, but at the critical moment the two porters stopped; their verbal ammunition suddenly spent. As they gathered the books back into their arms to complete their separate journeys, I noticed that as they pulled the books from the pile they paid not the slightest attention to whose books they gathered; I could just imagine the arguments that would ripple from this event.

 The ex-engineer led me through the maze of desks to the back side of one of the ticket windows. The press of people on the other side was so intense that the first person in line was practically squeezed through the spaces between the bars. The former engineer, Mr. Das, introduced himself to the ticket seller, who then slid a board down over the window, practically taking off the hands of the poor man who was just about to receive a ticket. He had probably been working his way to the front for hours, and he started to yell. Others yelled with him and innumerable fists pounded the board, which would have spilt if it weren't thick and well suited to its purpose. The ticket seller appeared not to notice the board rattling and shaking, for he calmly discussed my request with Mr. Das. Choosing a ledger book from a pile on the floor by his feet, the ticket seller wrote down my name then took my ticket and wrote a car number and berth number on it. He wanted three rupees for his trouble, which I gladly paid.

 I still had hours to kill, so Mr. Das and I wandered up and down the various platforms. We were walking along when a train pulled into the station at a crawl. It was a freight train. About half of the cars were sealed and half had their sliding doors open. Inside the open cars were cattle. The train slowed to a halt and we walked over to one of the cattle cars. The inside of the car was padded with clean straw, and lying on the straw were beautiful, strong cows. I don't know what breed they were, but their fur was milky white and their horns curved gracefully. They were magnificent beasts.

 A boy of twelve or thirteen was in the car with them. Most people in India speak a handful of languages and Mr. Das found a language he and the boy spoke in common.

"He is coming from the Punjab," Mr. Das explained.

"How long has he been on this train?" I asked.

Mr. Das asked the boy. "The boy is not certain," he replied, "but he thinks they have been traveling over three weeks."

If the speed at which they came into the station was any indication, I believed it.

"Where is he going?"

"They are delivering these cows to Calcutta. That is over fifteen hundred miles from here. It will take him another month at least."

I asked him why it took so long.

"Freight moves slowly in India," he said. "If a passenger train comes along the tracks, they must move this train onto a side track to let the other pass. If another train will be coming along in five hours, they may just leave the freight train where it is until there is a big enough break to get it to the next side track. Freight trains are heavy. To move them you need more than one engine. Sometimes they take away one of the engines for another train. Then they may sit for days or a week at a time. This boy belongs to a Punjabi caste that has been transporting cattle since the time of the Vedas. Since the beginning, they have been driving cattle on foot. Now they use the rails. Even with all these delays, they can still move cattle farther than they could before, and in less time than they ever could have imagined."

The platform was alive with these Punjabi cattle herders. They hauled buckets of water and sacks of grain and armloads of straw onto the train. They were even selling cow dung to locals, who would make it into patties and dry it in the sun for fuel. After a while the platform smelled like a farm.

Mr. Das was a good companion. He told me many stories, which was good, considering my wait was long.

When my train finally arrived, it entered the station on

Windblown Clouds
Thomas K. Shor

the wrong track. Running so not to miss it, I jumped on just as the train started out of the station. It was already so desperately full of people that I could hardly push my way in through the door. For each person that occupied a seat, there must have been a dozen or more who had staked out claims on the floor. I had to find the car in which my berth was reserved. Each car was numbered. The numbers were written on the outside of the cars just beside the doors. The numbers were not consecutive. So I worked my way down the train leaning out the doors into the rushing tropical night. When I found my car and located the compartment in which my berth was located, I was faced with yet another dilemma: over twenty people occupied the compartment. It was then that it dawned on me that I hadn't seen a single person lying in a berth.

By pointing out that I had a reservation in that compartment, I was able to secure a place on one of the benches, a tiny space, enough room for exactly one half of one buttock. At least it was enough to keep me off the floor, where I would be stepped on by vendors and beggars and those rushing for the toilet.

Minutes flowed like molasses; hours moved glacially. The train slowly threaded its way north.

When my ass was thoroughly tired of being bisected by the bench's sharp edge, I asked one of my neighbor's exactly where my berth was located. Examining the number, he pointed to one of the high shelves, which was occupied by four huge burlap sacks. I found out to whom the sacks belonged—a man standing by the compartment entrance—and after convincing him that as the holder of a reservation I had a legitimate claim to a place on the bench, I made a deal with him to clear the shelf in exchange for my few square inches on the bench. And thus I secured my berth and was out of the fray. I couldn't sit up—there wasn't room—but I could stretch out, and like a bird on a high branch, watch without being seen. The chaos that overtook the train at every station, the constant disputes over territory, the necessity to at least react to the venders' long pitches—all of these things and more were no longer my concern. I could watch it all as if it were on a stage. I couldn't see out the window from my perch, so the world was reduced to my compartment and the tiny slice of the passageway opposite. There I spent the next twenty hours.

In the middle of the night I awoke and looked over the edge of my bunk to see a group of men sitting on the edge of the benches below me. One of the men was reciting a poem in some Indian tongue as the others leaned forward expectantly. When the man reached the refrain of the song the others joined in and recited it in chorus, laughing and patting each other on the back. Then, so not to miss a single word of the next verse, they all leaned forward again. And thus we clacked down the endless parallel tracks in the Indian night. I fell asleep listening to them, and when I awoke they were still at it. We could have been gathered around a village fire. The intimacy of the night and the endless tracks had a timeless quality.

One of the men noticed me watching from my perch. I gestured with my hand: What is this? "Ramayana," came the reply. "Ramayana-Ramayana!" someone else concurred. They were reciting India's ancient epic, the story of prince Rama and his wife Sita and her abduction by the evil Ravena, king of Lanka. People have recounted this story in villages and towns from India to Indonesia for millennia.

~

I had to change trains the following afternoon, a day and a half into my journey north. Those still on the train when I left it I imagine still to this day on that train, for every Indian train is a world unto itself—at once a market, bazaar, dormitory, village, outhouse, and stage. It is an epic of infinite duration. Traveling with a cast of thousands in a few cramped square feet, your attention becomes focused close at hand as time leaks slowly by, like something held tightly in a miser's hand. The intensity of the immediate is so great that life outside your moving sphere, even your own life before boarding the train, seems but a flimsy abstraction, nothing but a dream of sweet comfort.

~

My next train was late. At two in the morning, working my way to the middle of the car, I stepped over hundreds of sleeping people. There wasn't even a space for me to sit on the floor. The largest place I could find would accommodate only my two feet. It was at the doorway to a compartment, and by keeping my tiny pack on my back I could lean on the edge of the doorway. I wondered whether it was possible to sleep standing up and hoped I wouldn't fall over sometime during the night. It was a miserable situation and I was dead tired.

As I settled into my spot, a man lying in one of the high shelves caught me in his gaze. There was something haunting about his eyes, yet infinitely rounded and human. He collected his possessions together, jumped down, and silently motioned to me to take his place. This was an unprecedented stroke of fortune. I was under no illusion that he was doing me a favor. Figuring his station must be next, knowing it took time to pick one's way to the exits, I was not surprised when he brushed my thanks aside.

I awoke from a deep sleep to find the compartment bathed in clear sunlight. I had slept right into the morning, and I must have slept through a lot, for half the people in the compartment were gone. I had been dreaming of home. The atmosphere was still with me. I felt a pang of loneliness. Being in such an exotic place made me long for home. I felt like an exile.

I ducked my head down to see out the window. We were entering a city, and I could see the shantytowns that often line the tracks in India. As the train slowed for a station, a man standing by the doorway to the compartment started getting ready to leave. It was then that I realized it was the man who had given me his berth the night before. I jumped down from *his* berth. I couldn't let his sacrifice go unnoticed.

"Thank you," I said, not even sure if he spoke English.

"It was nothing," he said. "We all have to sleep."

I noticed a chain around his neck. It held a silver pendant composed of two triangles interlaced, one pointing up, the other, down. In India, many temples and doorways are adorned with swastikas. They are an ancient Hindu symbol for good luck. The Nazis appropriated the symbol and even the name, which is Sanskrit. I had never seen the *Magen David*, the Star of David, in India before.

"Are you Jewish?" I asked.

"Yes," he said, picking up his bag.

The train had entered the station and was stopping.

"I am too," I said.

"Yes?"

"I didn't know there were any Jews in India."

"There used to be more," he said softly. "I am a member of the last family. There are only a few of us left."

His soft brown eyes, which held in their depths the suffering of an entire race, the accumulated pain of exile, seized me and held me a moment in their grip.

The train had stopped now.

"Shalom," he said, and with that he stepped over the sleeping bodies on the floor and left the train.

17

Two days and four trains later I arrived. Or so I thought. My destination was Varanasi. That is what was stamped on my ticket. Yet at the last minute a conductor pushed me through the door at a place called Mogul Sarai. I had shown him my ticket and tried to argue but he spoke no English and it was no use. He bodily expelled me from the train and there I was, on a deserted platform at three-thirty in the morning.

Silence hung over the platform, a silence made all the more eerie by the presence of dozens of figures sleeping under dirty cotton sheets. I picked my way through these sleeping people and crossed the tracks to a staircase that led to the station house.

Or so I thought. The stairs actually led directly onto a road that was lined with shops and more sleeping people, entire families huddled together under blankets, and still others lying on stoops and steps. All the shops were boarded up—though whether for the night or permanently I couldn't tell. The air was thick with smog. All edges were blurred.

Since I hadn't any idea where I was, nor what I was doing on this road, I decided to climb back up the stairs to the platform. But just as I turned, a dog came at me from out of nowhere. It howled at me as if it had just been beaten, and it growled and showed its yellowed teeth. The dog was missing an eye and a leg, and its skin hung limply over its ribs. Its one eye was glassed over with the look of death. The hair on its neck, what there was of it, was bristling. I had never seen such a creature. One bite from that dog would surely send me directly to a funeral pyre on the banks of the Ganges. The dog encircled me, fearful yet crazed, slowly closing in. I froze.

Someone groaned—a man who had been sleeping on the back of a bicycle rickshaw. Pulling his head out from under a sheet, he jumped down and came to my rescue. He kicked the dog in the ribs with his bare foot. I heard the dog's ribs crack. Yelping, the dog ran whining down the road and fell into a gutter.

The silence that followed was stunning. I faced my rescuer and was sure he had just saved my life. I couldn't speak, even to thank him.

"Rickshaw?" he asked. There was such hope in his voice, such an imploring look in his eyes, as if the fare would save his life. The man was thin as a rail, his bones pushing through his skin. He stood before me in nothing but an old *longhi* wrapped round his waist.

I hesitated a moment, hardly knowing where I was, much less where I might go on a rickshaw. With trepidation, with a question in my voice, I said, "Varanasi?"

"Ha!" he said, shaking his head, "Varanasi, Varanasi." He held out nine fingers. "Rupees," he said.

I agreed and he led me to his rickshaw. His sleeping sheet was still on the rickshaw's bench, and he collected it, used it to sweep off the bench, and bade me to sit. Then he wrapped the sheet over him like a shawl, tucked the ends up so they wouldn't become caught in the chain, and mounted his vehicle. Pedaling came hard for him at first. He had to stand and put all his weight into it, first on one pedal then the other. Finally, he picked up enough momentum to sit and pedal with only the force of his legs.

We rode through deserted, silent streets, passing recumbent figures under brown and gray sheets. It felt like the land of the dead. The clammy air and the silence of eternal repose absorbed the chain's squeaks and the driver's heavy, pained breaths.

Riding to the edge of the town, we continued on a long and straight road that went for mile after mile through vast tracts of nothing. No trees, no shops, no people: just an unbroken circle of darkness without a landmark to distinguish the distance traversed. I dozed, jostled, held onto the metal hoops of the awning, dozed again, and awoke always to the same darkness.

We reached the outskirts of a city, and even in the dead of night I knew we were entering the holiest of all the holy cities in India. The air hummed as it does when you walk by an electrical generating station. There was no mistaking that people had been occupying this city since a thousand years before Christ walked the earth. This was the energy that had worked like a magnet on the millions of pilgrims who had been flocking to the city for millennia. The power of the place had sent its tentacles to the farthest reaches of Hindustan and, like iron filings, had drawn the pilgrim's into its field of energy. I knew that I was but one of thousands who would come to the city that day.

When we reached a place where many roads crossed, the squeaking chain grew silent and we glided to a halt. The driver sat a moment to catch his breath, then we both stood, he on legs weary from miles of pedaling, me on legs feeling the accumulated exhaustion of four days of ceaseless travel. I reached into my pocket to pay him, but he stopped me.

"Hotel?" he asked.

"Yes," I said.

He pedaled down a side street to a high metal gate in front of an old stone building. A tin sign fastened to the gate said: Lodging. He banged his fist on the sign. Nobody came. He yelled, but still no one came. So he gathered a handful of stones and threw them at the open door. His aim was good. Moments later, a man, still half asleep, came stumbling out of the hotel, rubbing his head where a stone had hit him. He exchanged some rather sharp words with the driver; then, turning to me, he said in English, "You want a place to sleep?"

"Yes," I said.

"Ten rupees a night," he said. I agreed, and he went for the key to open the gate. As I reached into my pocket to pay the rickshaw driver, he put up nine fingers again. The first bill I pulled out was a fifty-rupee note, and I handed it to him. He had, after all, saved me from a crazed and probably rabid dog, carried me on the back of his rickshaw for two hours, and now had found me a place to sleep. I knew that I was probably giving him a week's wages, but I didn't care. He patted his *longhi* to show that he had no pockets and no change and he tried to press the bill back into my hand. I pulled my hand away and motioned that he should keep it. A broad smile crossed his face as a weight lifted from his shoulders; he stood straighter now, and in English he thanked me repeatedly. The man came back with the key and opened the gate.

Stepping over a sleeping roll, I followed him through the tiny lobby, down a short hallway, and up a staircase. The narrow stairs gave slightly under the weight of my body with a squeak. The sloping ceiling over the stairs was low, as if designed for an earlier race of people whose height never exceeded four feet. We stopped on the third floor and walked down a long, musty hall, at the end of which he pushed open a door and flicked on a light. The bulb, dangling from the ceiling on two bare copper wires, was feeble, probably not exceeding fifteen watts. The corners of the tiny room were obscured in darkness. But perhaps it was better this way. The walls were spotted with squashed bedbugs; the corners were best left unexplored. The room contained a bed, chair, and window.

I dropped my pack on the floor and fell back on the bed. Through the open window the sun began to tinge the sky. I fell into sleep like a leaf falling into a dark, still pool until I reached a place where not the slightest ripple from the surface could disturb me. I was in the place where consciousness brings the body when the body is in need of rejuvenation. It is there that a wellspring of life gushes forth; and it is there that I went like a taproot searching through the living topsoil and subsoil, past the inert gravel and shale, to solid bedrock where the veins of water flow. Then, like a diver rising to the surface, I reentered the living regions of my mind. As my body lay sleeping, I went on a journey under the guidance of the rickshaw driver, whose legs were now strong.

During an endless night he pedaled me through vast cities of temples whose population consisted solely of ash-smeared priests and rag-torn pilgrims. We crossed wide, swirling rivers known only by their ancient names. Then we followed one to its source. Where the valley rose to snow-capped peaks we abandoned the rickshaw. He walked ahead of me and we went high into the mountains.

Then I stood alone at the top of a ridge. The sun rose over the horizon and illuminated a high chain of peaks. A voice rang out. "Kasar Devi," it said, and I awoke, my ears still ringing with the name of the mountain on which Lama Govinda lived.

The sky had but a hint of light to it, the same half-light as when I had gone to sleep, and I wondered whether I had slept at all, if it was morning, or if I had slept the entire day. I went down to the lobby to find out.

The man who had shown me my room now sat at the desk. I asked him the time of day and he told me it was evening. Registering in the book, I paid, and stepped outside.

The streets, which had been so quiet in the early morning, were now coursing with traffic. Everywhere shops were open for business; the sidewalks were jammed with people. I pressed through the crowd until I came to a restaurant advertising vegetarian meals. I sought sanctuary in the restaurant's quiet interior.

This was the type of restaurant in which you buy a ticket at the door, sit at a long rough-planked table, and are served an all-you-can-eat meal by a dozen men roaming the huge restaurant with buckets of rice, dhal, vegetables, and chutneys. There is even a man, usually an old man, whose job it is to serve salt from a small bucket with a long spoon. The first man takes your ticket and places before you a banana leaf, which serves as a plate. Then comes a man with a bucket of rice, followed by another man holding a bucket of dhal. Afterward the vegetable and chutney men follow. After you are served, they continue to roam the floor, filling plates until you fold your banana leaf in half to signal that you are finished.

As I sat at a table, a tall and rather lanky man came into the restaurant. His fair skin, shorts, and T-shirt announced that he was a Westerner, and I realized how strangely exotic he looked in a land of *gumchas, longhies,* and *dhotis.* It was then that I realized how much I too must have stood out. I hadn't seen a Westerner, other than Ed, since my arrival in India.

He came over to my table. "Mind if I join you?" he asked. His accent was British.

"No," I said. "Please do."

Lifting his leg over the bench, he sat down across from

me. I noticed he wore heavy hiking boots. They were old and well worn.

Stretching his hand across the table, he shook my hand. "The name is Stephen," he said, "Stephen Johnson."

"You're from England, aren't you?"

"Cornwall," he said. "Although I don't know if it's really my home anymore. I've been away so long I doubt I'd still recognize the place."

"How long have you been traveling?" I asked.

"Ever since I was eighteen. I'm thirty-five now."

As our leaf-plates were placed before us, he began to recount his journeys. The water man came and went, the rice, vegetable, chutney, and salt men all came and went. We ate. The vegetable man came back, and we ate some more. Finally, we sat with the banana leaves folded in half before us as he told me of his travels in North Africa, Ecuador, Japan, Tahiti, Madagascar, Taiwan, Alberta, Fiji, Bulgaria, Iran, Iceland, Israel, Peru, and Algeria. He had been up the Amazon and down the Nile, through the Sahara and over the Andes, around the Cape of Good Hope and in the middle of military takeovers and crooked regimes of every description. His monologue was dizzying and dazzling, fantastic and farcical, and when he was through we were both left speechless and utterly exhausted.

So we got up and stepped into the equally dizzying rush of the street. "Where are you off to now?" he asked.

"Don't know," I said. "I've only just arrived."

"Been to the river yet?"

"No. Do you know the way?"

"Sure," he said. "I've been here over a month. I spend a lot of time down there."

So we went in the direction of the Ganges. A band of orange-robed *sadhus,* their hair thick and matted with dung, sang and banged on drums. As we walked across a huge thronging square, Stephen yelled over the din of the crowd, "Thirsty?"

"Thirsty for what?" I yelled back.

"*Bhang*," he said. "Have you ever tried it?"

"No."

"Come, I'll buy you a glass," and he pushed through the crowd to the edge of the square where a man sitting cross-legged on a high platform, his eyes looking out over the sea of people, presided over a stall. Dozens of bottles of colored liquid—bright reds and pinks, blues and browns—surrounded him. His oiled hair was combed straight back off his forehead and his eyes were large, too large for his head, hidden behind thick, drooping eyelids.

"*Bhang*," Steven yelled up to him. "Two *bhang*."

The man turned his head slowly. A few moments passed before his eyes focused on Stephen. It seemed to take even longer for his mind to focus. Then, suddenly, everything seemed to register, and he flew into action, propping a large glass between his feet, pouring into it drams of green and drams of red, a little pink, and a lot of brown. As one hand poured, the other dipped into small boxes, adding a pinch of dry powder or a few black flakes into the concoction. Pausing for a moment, he let his eyes wander again over the crowd. Then, placing his palm over the end of the glass, he shook it, and poured the potion into two smaller glasses. He recited a short verse as he lowered the glasses into our outstretched hands.

The glass was warm, as if the mixing of ingredients had produced a chemical reaction. I sniffed; but nothing much, just a slightly fruity smell. So I took a cautious sip. It was delicious—a blend of fruit juices mixed by a master of the trade. By the time I had drained my glass I believed that in India even the fruit juice man has his own god. When we were through we held our empty glasses up for him to take, but he was lost to us again, staring over the sea of people, his eyes behind heavy lids. Placing the glasses by his feet, along with a few rupees, we continued toward the Ganges.

18

Stephen led me to the edge of the bustling marketplace where the narrow, maze-like alleys of old Varanasi began. As if the great River of Time itself had channeled through the alleys, flowing uninterruptedly since the very beginning of time, I felt the press of untold centuries. The *sadhu's* dressed in rags—how did they differ from their predecessors who'd trod the same alleys two thousand years earlier? Wasn't their quest fundamentally the same? Here, where the River of Time and the River of Humanity flowed as one, my mind was drawn to the essentials. Only inessentials change in the course of time. Here all hopes, fears, and aspirations are but a thin film. As we journeyed deeper into the alleys, I felt that film wash away. What was a single life when held against the measure of these ancient alleys?

The alleys suddenly ended and we were faced with a huge, open dark space. I had to adjust to the sudden shift of perspective. I did so slowly, as had the *bhang* seller when called away from his dreamy contemplation to focus on a request. In fact, my eyes felt as droopy as the bhang seller's; something inside me seemed at a heightened state of awareness. Yet my body felt sluggish, slow to respond to what my senses brought in.

For a moment I thought the rushing water of the Ganges was actually blood rushing to my head. But we had indeed arrived at the *ghats*, the high stone steps that led down to the Ganges. Jumping down the steps, I realized just how colossal they were, like steps suited for a giant or a god. At the bottom, the river flowed swiftly. Stooping down, I felt the dark, cool water flow between my fingers.

It is said that the waters of the Ganges have their source in Lake Manasarovar, at the base of Mount Meru, high in the Himalayas. In Hindu cosmology, Mount Meru stands at the center of the world and its peak is so high that it pierces the realm of the gods, the Celestial Sphere. When it came time for the Ganges to flow, Shiva offered to break the fall of the celestial waters so they could flow gently into the lake and gently feed the source of the Ganges. Without Shiva to break the fall, the waters would have sundered the earth with its force. So Shiva went to the peak of Mount Meru and commanded the waters to flow. The waters, gathering all their strength to smash Shiva to pieces, crashed down from Heaven with terrorizing force. But Shiva was unabashed. He caught the water in his long and matted hair and made it flow round and round his labyrinthine curls for ages on end. Then, for the mercy of people on earth, who needed the life-giving and sacred water, he allowed it to fill the river's banks, from the Himalayas all the way to the Bay of Bengal.

Up river, the foggy air glowed red from the funeral pyres for which the city is famous. Hindus believe that one way to be released from the chain of rebirth, which is the goal of the Hindu religion, is to have your body burned in Varanasi and the ashes thrown into the Ganges. Because of this, when their time draws near, people come to Varanasi from all over India. The city is full of people at death's door.

We walked toward the fires' glow, jumping carefully over wide gaps between sets of *ghats*, which were deep enough to break a leg in, and flowed with the city's open and vile sewage. Everywhere diseased and grief-stricken people lay near the river. One old man looked longingly at it, apparently contemplating his end. Down by the river, people sold wood for the pyres, but wood was expensive. Not everyone could afford it. Those without sufficient funds stayed close to the river to throw themselves into it with their last dying breath.

I was yet to see Varanasi during the day and couldn't help but wonder if the sun ever shone over her rooftops, or whether the city existed in one long and perpetual night.

We arrived at a stone platform. Beneath it, fire consumed a neatly stacked pile of wood. The smoke, rising in a thick column, became caught in the shifting wind and enveloped us. The smell was slightly sweet. If I hadn't known what it was, it would not have seemed unpleasant.

Though I knew the purpose of the fire and the origin of the strange smell, it was still a shock to see the fire attendant poking at a leg that had twisted and fallen to the ground. As he flung it back into the fire, my senses stood wide open. It was the first time I had ever seen a dead body.

Stephen put his mouth to my ear. "Do you feel it yet?" he whispered.

"Feel what?" I asked. I felt nothing but my head swimming in a cloud.

A hunk of flesh fell from a bone, and the fire flared.

"The *bhang*," he said. "Can you feel it?"

"What are you talking about?"

"You know what *bhang* is—don't you?"

I turned and stared at him blankly.

"It is made of marijuana," he said, "like hashish. Do you feel it?"

Of course I felt it, but how could I distinguish the affects of the *bhang* from that of seeing burning flesh? What was I supposed to feel while watching a pack of mangy dogs fight over the contents of a half-burned skull?

An old man, naked, his skin sagging from his bones, appeared from the river's edge. Dripping with water, he sat down in a pile of ashes still glowing with embers. Then he lay down in the ashes and rolled until he was entirely coated. He stood up, the very color of death, and dragged himself to a cow lying on a pile of filth. I thought maybe the cow was dead. Sitting beside the cow, he put his head on the cow's belly and started to cry. No one paid him any mind.

Half a dozen muscular men began unloading huge logs from a barge and stacking them on the site of a previous fire. The barge, listing heavily in the river's swift and powerful flow, was lashed to the side of a partially submerged, ornately carved temple, which itself leaned heavily to one side. The river eddied around this temple, flowing in the stone-framed windows and out the open door. I couldn't imagine how that temple got there. Behind us, ancient temples towered in the darkness, their richly carved stone darkened with age and glistening as if their entire surface had been anointed with *ghee*. Then I heard a low "Hari-Ram, Hari-Ram." Turning, I saw two priests shouldering a stretcher on which a body was wrapped in white cloth. They went straight to the newly stacked pile of wood and placed the body on top. More logs were put over the body. A young man, no doubt the dead man's first-born son, had come behind the priests. He circled the pyre with a burning faggot then set the pyre ablaze. The white cloth burst into flame. Skin bubbled. Fat dripped. The fire flared.

I looked back to see the man still crying with his head on the cow's belly; the dogs still fought over the skull; a fire attendant stuck a leg back into the coals; I saw more wood being unloaded for another pyre.

"Stephen," I said. "I've got to go."

His face was pale. He readily agreed.

We walked up the *ghat* and skirted the front of a temple in search of an alley that would lead us away from the river. But first we came to a small courtyard occupied by circles of women sitting cross-legged on the ground. Wrapped in sheets covering their entire bodies, including their faces, the women chanted the names of God while rocking rhythmically to their chant. These women were widows and would spend the rest of their lives in this courtyard, or begging on the streets, until their turn came to be burned on the pyres, to be rejoined with their husbands. Before the British came to India, women threw themselves onto their husband's pyres and went as one into the other world. Now, they lived as casteless beggars, repeating the names of God until He took them away.

We passed through a low stone arch and entered a maze of dark alleys. It was good to be away from the river. Then I heard that chant again, soft at first, then growing louder: "Hari-Ram, Hari-Ram, Hari-Ram." From around a corner, priests appeared shouldering another corpse. Flattening myself against the wall, I allowed them to pass. The stretcher squeezed by at eye level, leaving behind the stench of death.

Two men played chess by the light of a low kerosene lantern on the other side of the alley. One of the men reached across the board, and with a quick movement of his queen took off his opponent's king. The winner laughed, the loser sighed, and they set up the board for another game.

~

The transition from the ancient, narrow alleys to the broad streets of modern Varanasi—boisterous with clanging bells and honking horns, and noxious with billowing exhaust—was as sudden and intense as stepping from the darkness of a cave into bright sunshine.

We were barely a hundred feet into the crowded street when the banging of drums and the lowing of horns announced a procession that sent rickshaws swerving out of the way for its passing. A vanguard of men—each holding florescent tubes of green and blue light powered by small car batteries strapped to their backs—parted the crowd. Half a dozen drummers followed. Then a line of men blowing into six-foot-long straight brass horns emerged, waving the instruments toward the heavens, blasting the air with a single, shrill note. A brass band came next, complete with tubas, clarinets, and bugles, as well as homemade instruments made of long lengths of twisted tubing. The overall effect was that of a drunken military band playing Dixieland.

Rows of women appeared next, clad in fabulous costumes. They wore hand-woven saris of the finest silk, their noses and ears adorned with rubies, sapphires, and diamonds, and their ankles and wrists adorned with gold and silver. They walked majestically, heads held high, paying not the slightest attention to the gawking crowd. Then came dozens of men, each dressed in baggy silk trousers, wide, intricately embroidered tunics, and swords in ornamental sheaths. Voluminous turbans covered their heads, each with a huge, multi-faceted gem woven into the folds above their eyes.

Next, a loud trumpet announced the presence of an elephant, its long white tusks tipped in brass, its ears painted green and white. Upon its back, on richly carved, wooden pillars, sat an awning of paisley design. Draped over the elephant's back was a thick rug with jewels woven into its silk with threads of gold. Upon this rug was a single silk cushion, and upon the cushion sat a boy of twelve, dressed in splendor. It was for him that this strange and fantastic assemblage worked its way through the ancient city; for this was his wedding night, and he was being brought to his fiancée's house where the ceremony would be performed. On the elephant's tail hung a bell that rang in rhythm with the elephant's weighty steps. The procession ended with a single drummer steadily beating a large bass drum, followed by another double line of green and blue florescent lights electrifying the air.

Stephen brought me back to the restaurant so I could take my bearings and find my hotel. We parted with a handshake, and I thanked him for an extraordinary evening. "Perhaps we will meet again," he said, "and who knows where it might be? Maybe on the Amazon, or in the Caucasus..."

"Yes, perhaps," I said.

That was the last I ever saw of Stephen Johnson.

19

Next morning I planted my elbows on the windowsill, leaned out the open window, and felt the warm sunshine strike my sleep-wrinkled face. Varanasi was no longer the dark and shadowy place it had been. Light streamed down now from an open sky, and the jumbled patchwork of neighboring roof tops stood out sharp and clear. Brightly colored saris, draped over sides of buildings to dry in the sun, fluttered in the soft breeze. They waved like long strands of exotic kelp in a sea of light. Monkeys stood poised at the edges of the rooftops, considering the flow of people in the alleys far below. They jumped the dizzying spans and moved in packs across the city.

To see whether the Ganges was as encompassing of life by day as it was of death by night, I decided to walk to the Ganges. Taking a road that sloped down to the river, I quickly reached the edge of the old town. The alleys teamed with life. Children playing tag ran into me. Old men sat on stoops exchanging morning gossip. Shops and stalls were open, and vegetables overflowed their crates. Women everywhere, their arms over-laden with bags, pushed through the crowd. Caldrons of boiling oils set over charcoal fires sent wisps of enticing steam into the air as cooks extracted sweetmeats with wire-mesh spoons to set them upon racks to cool.

The alleys twisted and turned. At every new branching, I chose the alley that sloped toward the river until I found an alley that ended at the top of the *ghats*. There, an ancient gnarled tree stood almost as wide as it was high. I stood beneath the tree, leaning on its rough bark, my feet upon its tangled roots, and watched in silence.

Directly before me, three old men sat under a woven reed parasol reading ancient scriptures aloud. According to Hindu tradition, and to people all over India, these men were among the blessed, able to spend their twilight years by the Ganges in Varanasi. They were considered as lucky as those in America who retire to Florida with money. Their duties in the world complete, they were now bound only to Brahma, the Absolute, the principle that underlies all of existence. They exuded a deep and abiding peace that is often lacking in their American counterparts. Eventually, each of these three men would be called away, not to a job, or to their families, but to the Absolute itself, for they were following the holy path first marked out by the ancient sages, the path of the Many back to the One. The old men's even and measured recitation of the scriptures was as low and constant as the river's murmur.

Women washed clothes at the water's edge. The slapping

of wet cloth on smooth stone entranced me, the arc of water as the women swung the wet cloth over their heads, the sun glinting off every wet surface, the women's profiles against the moving water.

Bands of children ran nimbly as monkeys up and down the *ghats*, flying colorful paper kites. The wind shifted, causing the kites to tumble earthward like tiny fragments of a broken rainbow. Then the bits of color rose again, this time over the river. The children let the strings back out again, and the kites grew smaller and smaller.

A young woman passed where I stood. She went down to the bank of the river as her forbears had done for thousands of years. Stepping into the brown, murky water to her thighs, she bent forward, squatted, and submerged herself in the river's flow. Then she shot back up, splashing those around her. She stood with the water swirling around her legs, the sari sticking to her skin, her body's soft lines silhouetted against the sparkling water—and she intoned a prayer.

Up and down the entire length of the *ghats*, others washed and prayed. Though some came to the river together, each greeted the river alone. Communion was between each soul and the soul of the river.

As I turned to leave, my eye was caught by a stone god with multiple arms lying on top of an intricate lacework of roots. Then I saw another stone god, it too with multiple arms, though the roots had grown over them. Closer scrutiny revealed more gods buried within the layers of the roots' growth. The roots were like a natural and long-running clock, marking the passage of time, obscuring the past beneath the surface of the present.

~

That afternoon I went in search of one of Lama Govinda's books. If I were to meet this man, I thought it better if I knew something of his work beforehand. I started out at a small bookstall on one of the major roads. It was mainly full of paperback books in Hindi with brightly colored covers.

Windblown Clouds

Thomas K. Shor

Beautiful Indian princesses, held in the arms of muscular, angular-faced Don Juans, multi-storied urban apartment buildings in the background, graced many covers. These were the Indian equivalent of Harlequins. I asked the proprietor if he sold books in English, and he displayed a dozen or so on the counter before me. The only difference between these and the others was the language in which they were written. Thinking that he might know of other bookstores, I tried to explain what I was looking for.

"Books by Lama Govinda," I said. "About Tibetan religion and mysticism."

He stared blankly at me and held up one of the English books. "You want?" he asked. "Only two rupees."

I thanked him, but declined. This he took as an invitation to convince me of the book's merit.

"This is a book of love," he said, holding the book up for me to examine. "The love between Kamala, the beautiful daughter of a rich merchant in the city, and Brij, a poor village peasant's son. They meet and fall for each other at a temple during one of the holy days. The father of Kamala sees what is going on and tries to drive the boy away, but the father of Brij comes and the two fathers begin to fight. The police come and take them away to jail, where they are forced to live in the same cell. While they are away, the mother of Brij goes to the other's house in the city and sets it aflame, for without her husband at home in the village they cannot harvest the rice, and the family will starve. Meanwhile, the young couple meet in secret, and a baby is conceived—a baby who is destined to be a ruler of men. Just as the mystic lotus that rests on the beautiful surface of the waters has its roots in the dark mud, so too does this ruler of men come from families caught in the mud delusion. When the baby is born, it is missing an arm—"

"Please!" I implored. "Stop!"

"The plot does not suit you?" he asked. "Perhaps this one will be more to your liking: it is about a movie star who gets in with some scoundrels and becomes addicted to opium..."

"I have come," I said, "in search of a book by Lama Govinda. If you have none by him, I will have to go."

The man was unable to comprehend that someone could be looking for a book by a particular author. Usually the cover was enough to sell a book. With his more difficult customers, his sales pitch did the trick.

Finally, I was able to extract from him directions to another bookstore. Though that bookstore proved only slightly larger than his, the people there were able to direct me to an even larger one. I was thus led from bookstore to bookstore throughout the city of Varanasi.

Finally I walked into a store that was decidedly larger than the rest. Along the back wall was an entire rack of Penguin Classics. I asked—for what seemed like the hundredth time that day—for books by Lama Govinda. The man led me to a stack in the back of the store, pulled a book from the shelf, and left me to examine it. It was Govinda's *Foundations of Tibetan Mysticism*. What a feeling to finally hold this book in my hands after so long a search! It was a weighty book, one to study carefully. The sections of the book were entitled, 'The Path of Universality,' 'The Path of Unification and Inner Equality,' 'The Path of Creative Vision,' and 'The Path of Integration.' I decided to hold up in Varanasi until I finished a careful study of the book. Only after I had read it would I go into the mountains in search of the man himself. Then I looked inside the front cover for the price. The book was printed in the United States, and I expected the price to be high. But nothing prepared me for the figure I saw: two hundred twenty-seven rupees. That was what I would spend during a few weeks of staying at hotels and eating in restaurants. It was probably a month's wage for a laborer supporting not only himself, but his family as well. How could I possibly spend that much on a book? How could I buy the book and then walk out and face the people on the street? I converted the price to dollars, but that didn't help. Twenty-three dollars. I'd easily spend that much on a book in the West, especially one I had spent so long looking for. But here in India, dollar equivalents didn't count. Ten rupees might equal a dollar, but that was on paper only.

So I put the book back and walked out of the shop, determined to go directly to Almora to see Govinda. I gathered my bag from the hotel and went to the train station. I asked at the information booth how to get to Almora. The man at the station was very helpful. He said what the clichéd old farmer in the back woods of Vermont might tell a stranger: "You can't get there from here." Actually, he said I could get there, but it would be through an extremely circuitous route involving many trains and buses. He suggested I go to Delhi and ask there. He thought from Delhi there would be a direct bus. I jumped on the next train to Delhi.

20

The next afternoon the train crossed a bridge over a wide river. Everyone in the compartment pointed out the window and stared. They were looking at the marble domed roof of a building that, even though obscured by the bridge's abutments and by buildings that periodically hid the dome from view, was clearly of uncommon beauty. I asked someone what building it was. It was the Taj Mahal. The river was the Jamuna and the city we were entering was Agra. When the train entered the station, I jumped off. I couldn't possibly pass up a chance to visit the Taj Mahal.

The train station in Agra was yet another teaming confusion. The moment I set foot on the platform, a quick-talking, well-dressed man with a notebook under his arm accosted me.

"You will come to my hotel," he said without a tinge of a question in his voice.

"No!" I quickened my pace to shake him off, as if he were a stray dog. But he was a persistent fellow.

"My friend, why do you walk so fast? I tell you, I have a good hotel—only thirty rupees a night—near the Taj! It is clean. Only Westerners stay there. Hey! Slow down. Listen! Listen to what a German boy wrote." He opened the notebook and read aloud as he trotted beside me. "'I stayed at Mr. Sharma's hotel for five days and it was very clean. He helped me shop for jewels and he brought me tea every morning...'"

Taking advantage of the fact that he was reading rather than looking where he was going, I headed for the center of a dense crowd and aimed him right into a group of young women, whom he banged into, nearly knocking a few of them over. Slipping through the crowd, I left him with a lot of explaining to do. Indian women are not to be touched; he'd have to wag his tongue quicker than he had moved his legs to get out of it with any grace. As I looked back, a group of men had encircled him; he was gesturing in my direction. Our eyes met. I waved, ducked, and moved quickly away.

In the train station lobby I acquired many more such human shadows. "Hotel, hotel; rickshaw, rickshaw." Newly arrived Westerners were being hauled in like fish and led away. I determined to have nothing to do with it. I thought of Ed, and of how long ago it seemed I was with him.

Outside the station, more rickshaw drivers accosted me; they surrounded me like gnats on a summer's day. Since they would hound me until I let one of them lead me out of the throng, I finally gave in and allowed myself to be brought to a rickshaw.

On the way into the center of the city, I saw what I never would have believed existed in India: middle-aged, well-to-do Western tourists gliding by in the air-conditioned comfort of luxury buses, pressing their cameras against the window, clicking shots and advancing film all the way from their luxury hotels to the Taj Mahal and back. Tourist shops everywhere sold souvenirs and gems.

Tourism was this town's industry. The Taj was the magnet attracting thousands, and the shops, hotels, buses and rickshaws were there to bleed the tourists of their foreign exchange. Clearly, all dealings would be tainted by money. I vowed to stay as short a time as possible.

The rickshaw driver brought me to a hotel. After I paid him, he insisted on taking me inside to the office. He waited until I had signed in. Then the manager slipped him some coins for his catch. I was truly caught and paid for in the market.

After settling, I went down to the office to see if I could get a cup of tea. The manager offered to have one brought to me on the roof, where, he said, there was a bit of a breeze.

As I climbed the stairs—which were cleaner and more solidly built than the stairs in the hotel in Varanasi, this hotel having been built to suit the sensibilities of Western tourists—I heard French, English and German from behind closed doors. I thought again of Ed. "Oh, Ed," I said aloud. What would he have thought?

I reached the top of the stairs, turned a corner around an exhaust fan duct, and saw two women sitting at a long table. One had short dark hair and was reading a book; the other woman's hair was shoulder length and blond, and she was staring over the rooftops.

As I approached, the woman reading set her book down on her lap and asked the blond-haired woman, "In English, what is the difference between the words *prediction* and *prophecy?*" Her accent was German.

The other ran her fingers through her hair to smooth out the tangles and said, "Both prediction and prophecy foretell something in the future, but when you predict you do so by logic."

"That's right," I said, taking a seat beside her. "Prophecy has a more religious meaning."

"Mystical," she interjected.

"Yes, mystical," I said. "Only the gods can make prophecies; unless, that is, one's mind is deeply tuned. Only then can one see around the corner and say what the future will bring. You must be inspired to make a prophecy."

"Because," she said, brushing her hair again from her face and continuing my train of thought perfectly, "inspire means to breathe into, to *in*-spire. And spire, which means breath, is also a word for *spirit*. So it is the inflowing of spirit. Just as expire is the out-flowing of spirit, or death."

"It's funny," I said, "but the words for *breath* and *air* often have spiritual origins. In Greece one of the first words I learned was the word for *wind* or *storm, anemos,* which is close to our word *animate. Anemos* comes from *anima,* the word for both *breath* and *soul.*

We looked back to the German woman, for whom we were defining the two terms. She had been following our conversation as one would follow a Ping-Pong ball being volleyed across a table. She looked completely bewildered. We couldn't help laughing.

"Let me give you an example," I said. "I predict that a man will come around that air duct with a cup of tea."

On cue a man appeared. He set a cup of tea before me without a word and walked away. Both of my companions stared at me as if I were a wizard. I took a sip. "That was a prediction," I continued, "because I ordered a cup downstairs and knew it was time for it to come. It would have been a prophecy if I hadn't ordered the cup and had no logical reason for thinking a cup of tea would be on its way. Do you understand?"

"Yes, I think so," the German woman said. She went back to her book.

"She probably won't be asking us the meaning of too many words in the future," I said.

"She'd be crazy if she did." Then we both laughed.

Something seemed familiar about this woman, as if I knew her from somewhere. It wasn't only the way she looked, her face and her hair, but also her gestures, and even her voice. I wanted to ask her where she was from, but I hated those questions travelers are always putting to each other.

She broke the silence. "Hate to ask you a question you're probably tired of answering," she said, "but you're from the States, aren't you?"

"Yes. Originally Boston. Though I've been living in Vermont. And you?"

"I'm from northern California, though I'm going to college now in the Southern part of the state."

"What are you doing in India?" I asked.

"I've just spent four months in Sri Lanka with a group from school. I'm seeing a bit of India before flying back for the spring semester. I've been in Delhi a week. I'm here on a short side-trip."

"You're here to see the Taj?" I asked.

"Of course. Why else would someone come to Agra?"

"Yes, I suppose so," I said.

The mind of the tourist is amazing, I thought to myself: to come to a town for one building only, as if the rest of the town and its present inhabitants didn't exist. But then again I too had jumped off the train in Agra because of that one building, the Taj Mahal, which was surrounded by the most intense tourist industry in India. I had to accept it.

"I haven't yet seen the Taj, except for a fleeting glimpse from the train," I said. "Is it worth the trip?"

"Of course," she said, eyeing me as if I were an oddball. "You can see it for yourself. It's right over there."

Above the angular and sooty rooftops, about a half-mile distant, loomed the soft white dome of the Taj Mahal. It looked almost transparent, buoyant, as if made not of marble but of thin nylon filled with hot air.

As I turned back toward the woman, she was looking not at the Taj, but at me. She turned away when I noticed this. Then she turned back and looked me in the eye.

"Beautiful, isn't it?" she said.

I nodded. Her eyes were sharp and clear. I smiled.

We were both silent a moment as we stared at the Taj's dome. "It's actually a mausoleum, isn't it?" I asked.

"Yes, though in reality it's a monument not to death, but to love, the love between a man and a woman—a love that transcends death."

"How's that?"

"Do you know the story behind the Taj?"

"No, not really."

"It was built by Emperor Shah Jahan for his favorite wife, Mumtaz Mahal, who died giving birth to their fourteenth child. Their love was so intense that he couldn't bear the thought of its end. So he lived on through their love in the design and building of the Taj Mahal. It took seventeen years to complete. It is a mausoleum—but just look at it, even from here you can see there's nothing of death about it. It is a pure expression of beauty. And what's beauty when translated to human feeling and emotion but love?"

"Is he entombed there as well?"

"Yes, though he didn't want to be."

"What do you mean?"

"When the Shah Jahan finished the Taj Mahal he was even more obsessed. He wanted to build an exact copy of it, though this time in pure black marble, directly across the Yamuna River. This was to be his tomb, and it was to be linked to the white Taj by a bridge. But by this time his son, Aurangzeb, was in power. For his wife's tomb, the Shah Jahan had sent for stone workers from as far away as Italy and France. Over twenty thousand people had been employed. The son was afraid that the raising of the Black Taj would spell the destruction of the kingdom. One can't, after all, spend all the country's resources on monuments. So Aurangzeb imprisoned his father in the Red Fort, where he had a sumptuous apartment with wide windows overlooking the river where his love lay entombed beneath the beautiful white marble dome. He was well taken care of there until he died and was entombed next to her in a crypt beneath the mausoleum's central room. There they lay side by side to this day."

"Incredible, isn't it?" I said.

"Yes, but that's the power of love."

Then we were silent.

"You haven't told me where you are headed," she finally said.

"Delhi."

"When?"

"Well," I said, "I suppose I'll spend tomorrow exploring the Taj. I'll probably leave the day after."

"I'm also going the day after tomorrow. We should go together, don't you think?"

"Sounds good to me," I said.

"There is a train every morning at nine o'clock. We should be ready to leave here at eight. That will give us plenty of time."

"I'll be ready," I said.

She pushed her chair back and stood up. "I've a paper that has to be done by the time I get back to the States. I'd better keep working on it. And remember, eight o'clock the morning after next."

She started walking away. "Hey!" I called after her. "What's your name?"

"Yvonne."

I told her my name.

"See you," she said, and she disappeared around the air duct.

21

Next morning I awoke at dawn to the sound of an imam's plaintive cries from a nearby mosque. He was calling Muslims to the first of their five daily prayers. His call sounded like a lament, a solitary aged voice expressing separation and longing for a god that was far away.

I dressed quickly and walked through the dark streets toward the Taj. Not a soul stirred. The narrow streets echoed with the sad strains of Arabic prayers. The imam made many a single syllable rise and fall through the entire scale. The music grew louder until I came to the mosque, which had a huge megaphone mounted on the roof. I had assumed I was listening to a recording. But when I passed beneath the megaphone it became clear that what I was listening to was live: the plaintive song stopped in the middle of a note, the old man raised a great ball of phlegm from deep in his throat with a horrific gurgling sound that echoed throughout the old quarter of Agra; then he spat onto the floor. It landed with the sound of a wet rag hurled to the ground.

    A young American couple stood waiting by the main gate of the Taj, which was closed. They told me we'd have to wait until the sun actually came over the horizon to be allowed inside. So we waited until a guard walked across the wide courtyard holding an outsized key in his hand, which he used to unlock the gate. We walked, just the four of us, through the outer courtyard toward a high arched gateway.

    We were now on top of a high flight of steps that overlooked beautifully manicured lawns and flowerbeds with interlocking stone walkways set in geometric designs. A long and still reflecting pool was bordered by cypress, beyond which the Taj stood on its high, solid marble platform, set apart, as if in a time of its own. The sun was just coming over the horizon, its first rays turning the eastern half of the rounded dome and the two eastern minarets pink. The western half of the building was still draped in shadow. But even in darkness, the Taj Mahal was lustrous.

    In light or shadow the building stood perfected—each line, shape, and volume resonating to the same harmonious proportions. If music, this would be Mozart. It was as total a harmony as found in nature. Its beauty rivaled that revealed in a flower's spiraling stamens and numbered petals. The wonder of the Taj, and its origin, lies within the heart and mind of man. The impetus behind the construction of the Taj was the love of one man for one woman; it was the yearning for a love that would transcend death.

The sheer size of the monument, the vastness, both defied and deified everything in nature. I felt as if I could raise my arm and stretch it across the long reflecting pool. I fancied I could place my pinkie under a corner of the building, and with a simple flick of a finger send it catapulting into the sky.

I followed the couple down the stairs, along the side of the reflecting pool, and to the base of the Taj's high marble platform. Removing our shoes, we climbed the steps, which felt cool beneath our feet. Then we stood dwarfed before the gaping arched entrance. Every surface was set with inlayed stones of flowers, geometrical patterns, and lines from the Koran. Passing inside, we went directly into the central chamber. The dome curved graciously, high overhead. In the center of the room was a trelliswork screen of white marble. Past the screen the tombs lay side by side. A white-haired man was bent over the tomb of the Shah Jahan, lovingly rubbing the jewel inlayed Arabic letters with a soft cloth. The only sound was of the cloth being rubbed over the smooth stone, and the only light was the newborn sun reflecting off the white marble and filtering through the latticework screen. Everything was soft and malleable.

The couple walked to the far side of the tomb, and the woman stepped back and looked up as if expecting something to fly down from the dome. Then the man opened his mouth and let out a single, long, clear note. The sound echoed back from the pinnacle of the dome with such purity and force as to make one believe the Taj itself was answering his call. The sound echoed off the walls and chambers and returned to our ears at the very center, undiminished from its long journey. It resounded from the mathematically perfectly proportioned walls like an image reflected endlessly in opposing mirrors. Great sonorous corridors carried pulses of sound to our ears in rising and diminishing waves—waves that crashed down from all sides and made our ears feel the three-dimensionality of the enclosed space. The inert stone was made to sing; space was brought to life. Slowly, the stony silence won precedence over the sound. Just when it seemed that all was still, one last reverberating note struck our ears, a distant, soft note that had been echoing in some far-off, hidden chamber.

Then silence reigned again. The old man, still stooped over the tomb with the rag in his hand, stopped his polishing. Motionless, he stared into the vaulted space. The tomb, his face, the pure white marble—everything—was bathed in the newly risen sun's pink glow. The light, like the pulsing sound, was not perceived directly from its source, but it too was caught in the endless reflections that seemed now to be the hallmark of the Taj Mahal. For wasn't the Taj Mahal itself but an image of some greater perfection?

The silence was shattered again by the man's booming voice. He sang a few variously pitched notes of different durations to test the echoes. Then he dove into a deep and moving Gregorian chant that was echoed back as if by a thousand separate singers of some heavenly choir. He adjusted his tempo till the echoed voices fell in line and not a single sound was out of sync. Falling silent, he listened to his multi-voiced creation, then he added a lower-pitched chorus where needed. He played with the echoes as a child toys with waves on a beach.

The old man stood. His rag lay at the foot of the tomb, his head cocked to one side, and with one hand raised he pointed up, to where the invisible chorus sang. Delight shone in his eyes. The singer stood rapt in his song, eyes closed. And I stepped silently back and began exploring the other chambers, which numbered four and surrounded the central chamber in each of the cardinal directions. As I wandered round and round, the Gregorian chant continued to fill my ears with ever-new combinations of echoing sound.

Finally, I stepped outside. Circling round to the back of the Taj, I sat upon the wide marble railing overlooking the *Yamuna*. Upriver, where the flow disappeared around a bend, stood the Red Fort, the imposing sandstone fortress where the

Shah Jahan was held prisoner in a riverside apartment with a view of his beautiful creation. Across the river—where the pure black Taj was to stand—the ground was barren except a few old trees and clumps of swamp grass. An old woman watered her buffalo as a few others bathed in the slowly moving water.

I went round to the front of the building and saw the first busloads of tourists scrambling alongside the reflecting pool and lumbering up the steps. With tour guides at their lead, they learned all the pertinent dates and personages in French, English, German, and Japanese. The moment the first group entered the front chamber, the singing suddenly stopped. The magic spell had been broken, and the Taj now rang with the sound of hundreds of discordant, disjointed voices. The sun was higher now and that special pink sheen that had shrouded the Taj and had penetrated so softly the inner chamber was gone. The American couple passed through the front portal, and we exchanged a knowing look. Only we knew that the Taj had been awakened that morning and made to sing.

~

I spent the rest of that morning wandering around Agra and wishing I were elsewhere. The press of the tourist trade was so intense that I couldn't walk down a street without being constantly hounded by merchants trying to lure me into their shops to buy jewels or trinkets. Rickshaw drivers followed me like shadows, and I couldn't shake them. Finally, I went back to the hotel; but even there a man was selling precious stones as another sold scents and perfumes. I went up to my room and came down only to eat dinner.

22

Next morning at eight o'clock, my little pack on my back, I waited by the front door of the hotel. Yvonne came and we stepped outside. Our packs were signals for the rickshaws to swarm. In a flash we were surrounded. "Cantonment train station," I yelled out, and the figures started flying. They started at thirty rupees, but the competition was so great that without either of us saying a word the price was reduced to twenty. Yvonne was ready to climb aboard at that price, but I held her arm. "Eight rupees," I said to the rickshaw driver directly before us, and he jumped at the offer. It was still a handsome price. We sat together on the narrow bench, and as we pulled away another bewildered Westerner appeared at the hotel door with a pack on his back. They descended upon him and he could walk no farther.

We reached the train station, and as we made our way to the ticket window we were accosted repeatedly. "Hotel, come to my hotel," they screamed in our ears. I had to restrain myself from growing violent. We bought tickets and went to the platform to wait. As we descended the stairs from the overhead pedestrian walk, Yvonne recognized some people up the track. "Oh, look," she said. "I can't believe it," and she ran ahead. When I caught up she introduced us: "Sally, Dave, this is a new friend of mine." She told them my name. Then turning to me she said, "I ran into them in south India on my way from Sri Lanka. I was traveling with a friend from school, and she and Sally are old friends from the States. Isn't this a funny coincidence?"

"It certainly is," I said, "because I've met them before as well." Then turning to Dave I said, "I never got a chance to thank you for your beautiful voice yesterday morning. You really made the Taj sing!"

"Thank you," he said. "I wasn't sure whether you liked it or whether you would have preferred silence."

"No, no, not at all," I told him. "It was beautiful."

Yvonne and Sally were catching up on the news since they'd last met, and Dave and I continued talking.

"You must be a professional singer," I said.

"Yes, I've studied singing for years, though it isn't my profession. I am a film maker."

"Commercial films?"

"No, documentaries, mainly for public TV."

"Is that why you are here in India?" I asked.

"This is pure pleasure, though I can't turn off my film-making eye. I've come up with a few ideas and I've been keeping notes. I'll try them out on some producers when I get back home."

"I'd love to hear what you've come up with," I said, but just then the train pulled into the station. The four of us ran down the platform and jumped onto a car. It was full, but the people on the train were kind and made room for two of us. We let the women take the seats, and Dave and I climbed onto the top bunk a few compartments down. It was hot there with our heads bent sideways so not to hit against the roof, which was already hot from the sun, but we had plenty of room. We sat cross-legged, held on so we wouldn't be thrown to the floor, and talked of everything from film ideas to restaurants we both knew in Cambridge. Every few stops either Yvonne or Sally would appear with cups of tea or some fruit to keep us going, and the time passed quickly.

~

The New Delhi train station at four o'clock in the afternoon was a mess. Somewhere in the confusion Yvonne and I lost Sally and Dave. Only by hanging onto each other did we make it to the wide street in front of the station.

"Where should we stay?" I asked as we faced a multitude of taxis, rickshaws, and buses.

"The place I stayed before was great," she answered. "That is, if you don't mind a dormitory. It's cheap."

We crossed the street and climbed onto a cart behind a team of horses. When the cart was full of passengers the driver flicked the reins and we made our way slowly away from the station.

"Where exactly are we going?" I asked.

"To Connaught Place," she answered. "It's the central hub of New Delhi. I've one stop to make there before we go on to the hotel."

"Do you know where the American Express is?" I asked. "I'm expecting mail there."

"That's exactly where we're going," she said.

I had to laugh. "How'd you know that's where I wanted to go?"

"Ah," she said, tapping her fingers to her chest, "a woman's intuition."

Our horse cart ride was short. We got off, paid two rupees each, and rounded the corner to Connaught Place, which was composed of a large circle of buildings built around a spacious park with tree-lined paths. Everything was neat and trim. The buildings were modern and housed the major branches of banks, both Indian and foreign, and a multitude of shops displaying fine jewelry and clothing for exorbitant prices. Horses, goats, and cows were banned from Connaught Place, making it probably the only place in all of India reserved solely for human beings.

Coming upon a building with the familiar American Express logo on the window, we climbed the stairs and entered the air-conditioned comfort of an office that could have been dismantled in New York and re-assembled in India. It was perfect down to the wall-to-wall carpet. Music played through speakers in the ceiling. I bathed a moment in the atmosphere of the place. It was almost reassuring. But then a wave of sadness came over me. I realized just how far from home I was.

Yvonne was looking around wistfully. Her eyes, usually light and gay, now clouded over and became dark.

"Makes you kind of sad, doesn't it?" I said.

"How's that?"

"Well, to realize how far from home we really are."

"What makes *me* sad," she said, "is to see what I'm going back to. I'll be surrounded by all of this in less than three days." She paused then said, "Come, let's get our mail."

We waited in line with other itinerant Americans. The

suspense of being so close to my mail yet having to wait was excruciating. I hadn't heard anything from home since Athens, and that seemed like years ago. What if I had no mail? What if there was a telegram? What if someone had taken ill or died?

"I'm glad you're here," I said to Yvonne, "just in case..." She understood and didn't make me explain.

By the time I got to the front of the line my palms were so sweaty that my passport was moist. I opened it to where my name was printed below my picture and handed it through the window. The mail clerk glanced at my face, read the name, and slapped the passport back through the window. He flipped through the S's and came up with a small wad of letters held together with a rubber band. I thanked him profusely, but he only shrugged and beckoned Yvonne, who was next in line, to show her passport.

I broke the rubber band and flipped quickly through the mail. There were no black-bordered telegrams, so I figured all was well. There was a letter from Ed, postmarked Bombay, and that was the first I opened. He said that his quest for a permanent resident's visa was proving more difficult than he'd imagined, and that he was setting out for Bihar to see if the officials were easier to deal with there. Bipin and the family sent their best, and in a postscript he told me of how after he had left me on the train platform in Bangalore he had hitched out of the city and found himself in a small village. An old man offered him fresh buffalo milk, and when he was through the old man told Ed he could stay. "And he didn't mean spend the night," Ed wrote. "He meant I should stay—forever!"

"Good news?" Yvonne asked.

"Yes, very good news. It's always good to hear from an old friend and know that he hasn't changed. How about you?"

"Just a letter from my mom. Says she'll be at the airport to meet me."

"Stop looking so sad," I said. "You've still got a few days.

Make the best of them."

"You're right. I will. I promise not to frown again."

Out on the street again and walking around Connaught Place, I carefully studied each of the other envelopes and put them in the order in which I'd open them. Mail was a rare delicacy to be appreciated all the more by long hours of anticipation. They were to be doled out one at a time like fine Swiss chocolate. Turning at the Government of India Tourist Office, we found the hotel.

Yvonne led me up a steep flight of stairs that had been built onto the outside of the building. At the very top we entered a room not much bigger than a closet. Behind a counter sat a young Indian man. He was fiddling with a radio, trying, without much luck, to coax a station out of the background hiss. Color posters of the jungles of south India and the sculpted towers of temples were pinned to the wall behind him. Finally he looked up.

"Do you have room for two?" Yvonne asked.

"We'll see what we can do," he said. Opening a ledger book, he stroked his thick mustache. "We have two beds in the dormitory. How's that?"

We said it would be fine, and he led us through a back doorway and across an open space. It took me a moment to realize that we were on the roof. There was a little kitchen too, a corrugated metal hut before which a tree grew out of a huge metal drum. Western travelers and a few young Indians sat at tables. Everyone seemed to be involved in a friendly discussion.

The man led us across the roof to the dormitory, where we were shown two vacant beds with blankets folded at the foot. We tossed our packs onto the beds.

"These roofs are all connected," Yvonne said. "I know a great place. Come. Let's get some tea. We can see the sun set over the city."

Together we went to the kitchen hut. There a man poured us two big mugs of tea. Yvonne handed her mug to me. "This is practically a desert climate, you know. The minute the sun goes down it gets cold. I'll get the blankets."

Soon she was back with the blankets and she led the way to an adjacent roof. Yvonne wrapped herself in a blanket; I did the same. We sipped our tea and watched darkness descend over the city. Monkeys, silhouetted against the dark sky, clambered across distant rooftops.

"So," Yvonne said, "I've told you where I'm heading, but you still haven't told me where you are going."

"I'm heading north," I said, "into the Himalayas."

"Where?"

"To a place called Almora. There's someone I'm to visit there."

"Who?"

"He's a friend of the man I came to India with. He's a Buddhist Lama, though he was born in Germany."

"What's his name?"

"Lama Govinda."

"You're kidding," she said. "Lama *Anagarika* Govinda?"

"Yes, but how do you know of him?"

"I told you I was in Delhi a few days ago, right?"

I nodded.

"Well, there was this fellow I met who had been studying Tibetan Buddhism. I was interested and asked him what would be a good book for me to read. He mentioned Govinda and a book called *Foundations of Buddhist Mystics,* something like that."

"*Foundations of Tibetan Mysticism,*" I corrected. "I know it, because just the other—"

"So," she interrupted, "I went to find the book. I spent hours searching through bookstores and finally I found it. But the price! I couldn't believe it; they wanted two hundred twenty-five rupees. I couldn't bring myself to spend that kind of money."

"In Varanasi they wanted two hundred twenty-seven rupees," I said. "You're right, that *is* too much."

She stared at me, uncomprehending. "What are you saying?"

"I'm saying that I had the exact same experience, though in Varanasi. I went to bookstore after bookstore—"

"Did you see all those horrible Indian mass-market books?"

"You mean the ones with the gaudy covers?"

"They're terrible, aren't they?" she said with a laugh.

"Do you ever get the feeling—"

"What, that more goes on than meets the eye?" she said.

"Yes."

"Sometimes there's no other conclusion."

"You're right," I said. Then after a pause: "Tell me, what day was it that you looked for Govinda's book?"

"Let me see," she said, thinking back. "It was the day before I met you. I took the train to Agra that night."

"Same day," I said.

"What?"

"I said that we were looking for the same book on the same day."

"How strange," she said.

A gust of cold air rode up the side of the building and made us shiver. Yvonne pulled her blanket up over her head as if it were a hood. Again I had that feeling that even before we met we had known each other. This seemed totally natural, despite its strange logic. And then, as if completing my unvoiced thought, she said, "After all, we did meet discussing the difference between prediction and prophecy."

We sat on the rooftop wrapped in our blankets looking out over the lights of the city late into the night. And as we talked we discovered that our immediate pasts were strewn with unlikely coincidences. At first I was amazed at the concordance of our experience; but in the end I was left with a deep sense of awe. The awe wasn't directed at her particularly, or at me; something very mysterious was happening and it was before that mystery I stood in awe. Our refrain became, "Isn't that a funny coincidence!"

23

Next morning I awoke entirely happy. Yvonne was just waking up. She knew of a restaurant nearby that sold omelets and toast and coffee—rare delicacies in a land so far from home.

We parted ways at the restaurant. Yvonne went to the library at the American Cultural Center to work on her paper, and I went to the Government of India Tourist Office to see about getting to Almora. We decided we'd meet back at the hotel at midday to have lunch.

The Tourist Office was one large, high-ceilinged room comprising half the ground floor of a large office building. In the picture window were huge color posters, each with the Tourist Office's official logo, *The Right Place,* written in bold letters across the top. On the plate-glass door was a round sticker with those same words written around the edge. There was a blue dot in the center. I pushed on the dot and went inside.

Half a dozen middle-aged Western tourists sat examining maps and brochures in a lounge area with cushioned chairs and sofas. I waited in line, and when my turn came I sat across from a clerk dressed in Western clothes.

"What may I do for you?" he asked. He must have been educated in an English school, for his accent was decidedly British.

"I would like to know the easiest way of getting to Almora," I said.

"Ah, yes," he said. "Very good. Let me see," and he placed a schedule on his desk and ran his finger down a column of destinations. "Ah, here we are: Almora," he said. "There are buses direct from the station in Old Delhi every morning—seven days a week—leaving at six-thirty. It takes about thirteen hours—depending on the weather—so you should arrive at about seven-thirty in the evening. The cost is twenty-nine rupees. Let me show you where the station is." He produced a map of Delhi and drew a circle around the station. He pushed it across the desk to me and smiled.

"Now, you'll be needing a place to stay, will you not?" he said, pulling another sheet from the file.

"No," I said, stopping him. "That won't be necessary."

He left the sheet dangling out of the file, folded his hands on the desk before him, and said, "Then where, if I may ask, will you stay?"

"Actually," I said hesitatingly, "I am going to Almora to meet someone. A man named Lama Govinda."

At the mention of Govinda, the man's eyes opened wide. A chill ran menacingly up my spine. Even before he opened his mouth I knew what he was going to say.

"I know Govinda," he said.

I stared dumbly at him, unable to control my thoughts enough to speak. He continued: "I went to Almora some years ago to meet him. He is a most extraordinary man. He lives in a hermitage on a hill outside the town."

"Yes," I said. "I know. The place is called Kasar Devi. "Actually," I said after a moment, "I'll probably not be staying with Govinda at first. There's a woman there, an American woman, who'll take me to him."

"And who, may I ask, is that?"

"Mary Opplinger."

"*Mary Opplinger!*" he yelled in amazement, making all the heads in the place turn. He leaned across his desk and said in a loud whisper, "I know her too." All eyes were riveted on us. He sat back up and stared at me. "This is *most* extraordinary," he said, wiping a bead of perspiration from his brow. Then he leaned forward again and continued in a hushed tone, "You certainly have a remarkable journey ahead of you. Mary is a deeply spiritual woman. But tell me, do you know how to find her?"

"I have the name of her house written down," I said.

"Haimavati?"

"Yes, that sounds right."

"Let me draw you a map," he said. "Otherwise you may never find it. She lives outside the town on the way to Kasar Devi, but back in the woods." He took a scrap of paper and placed it on the desk before him. He looked at me, shook his head in amazement, and circled the landmarks to help identify the road to Kasar Devi. He explained where to find the path leading to Mary's house. He handed me the map.

"I've worked behind this desk for almost fifteen years," he said. "I see hundreds of people each day, and untold thousands every year, but nothing like this has ever happened to me. Never. India is a vast country. Almora is far away. It is a tiny and remote place. It is the only place I've been to in the Himalayas. Govinda hardly sees anyone. Mary Opplinger is one of the most remarkable people I've ever met. How is it that you are heading to see the two people I know in all the Himalayas? This is truly extraordinary."

~

As I stepped back outside my feet hardly touched the pavement. This last 'coincidence,' like the final straw that breaks the camel's back, had blown all the stops in my mind and I was flying, held aloft by wings of certainty. Joy and wonder rippled through me and overflowed all bounds. The dichotomies of inside and outside, of me and you, no longer applied. I realized that like pieces of a jigsaw puzzle, which are meaningless when considered separately, we gain meaning only when we can see ourselves as part of the greater picture.

I wandered aimlessly through the busy bazaar, my mind floating buoyantly in a sea of wonder. Suddenly a turbaned man swirled out of the crowd and stood before me. I had no choice but to stop. "I want to read your fortune," he said, staring deeply into my eyes. I tried to brush him aside. On the roads of India, other soothsayers, many of who were cheats and con artists, had approached me.

"No," I said. "Go away." But he was not to be shaken so easily.

"I am *yoga* man, I am *yoga* man," he said. "I have come to read your fortune. I want no money."

He took from under his robe an old and soiled photograph and pressed it into my palm.

"Look," he said. "This is my teacher and this is his ashram." An old man sat naked in the lotus position on a platform before a reed and mud hut in a clearing cut out of the jungle. Half a dozen men standing in loincloths and staring at the camera flanked him on either side. "That is me," he said, pointing at a man to the right of the teacher. I looked closely at the figure then studied the man's face. It was indeed he in the picture.

But so what? I tried again to push him away.

"I don't have time," I said. "I must go."

But he held onto my arm. "I am *yoga* man," he said yet again. "I want no money." Then after a moment: "If you need proof of my powers, I will give you proof. If you still want to go after, you may go on your way." He took out a little notebook from under his robe and tore out a page. He scribbled something on it, crumpled it into a ball, and placed it in my hand. I made a fist tightly over the ball and he said, "Look. Look here," and he tapped the point between his eyes. "Look deeply and pick a color." I stole a glance to my clenched fist. "No," he said. "Not there. Look here and concentrate." He tapped again the point between his eyes and held me firmly in his gaze.

"Purple," I said. He motioned that I should open my fist and look at the paper. Written hastily across it was the word *purple*.

He tore out another sheet, wrote something on it, crumpled it up, and put it again in my open palm. I closed my fist over it. I was watching him very carefully to discover his trick.

"Pick a flower," he said. My eyes fastened again on his

brow.

"Chrysanthemum," I said, figuring he couldn't have guessed that too easily.

I opened the paper. *Chrysanthemum* was scrawled across it. I studied the paper carefully, but it looked and felt like normal paper.

It could have been luck, I thought to myself, trying to be rational. But what is luck? What is chance? Hadn't I learned anything during the last few days?

"One more time," I said, "and then I am yours." Again he tore a piece of paper from his book. Again he scribbled something on it. Again he crumpled it and I held it in my clenched fist. I held it so tightly that my fingernails bit into my palm. My fingers turned white.

"What is your mother's name?" he asked.

I stammered a bit and choked.

"Vivian," I said at last.

I opened the paper and a surge of blood rushed to my head. My extremities tingled from a shot of adrenaline. He had been right again, and again I was caught in his hypnotic gaze.

"Who *are* you?" I said, almost in a whisper.

"I am *yoga* man," he said. "I have come from the jungle."

I followed the turbaned man to a space between stalls where a plank was set across two stones. We sat and he examined closely the palm of my right hand. He ran his fingers slowly over the lines and thought long and carefully over what he saw. Then he looked up and focused closely on my face. Ripples ran up and down my spine.

He spoke with the deliberation of one in a trance. "You will go north to the mountains now," he said. "There are mountains on this earth and there are mountains in our souls. You will go to the mountains, not only the mountains that are on a map, but you will also go to the mountains within you. There are peaks there, where the air is clear, and you will see farther than you have ever seen. Maybe you will never see so clearly again."

He stopped abruptly.

His countenance suddenly changed. I was suddenly staring into a different face. He made pronouncements, as if trying again to give me proof of his powers. He rattled out facts about my life as if he were a machine reading from a list.

"You have two sisters and one brother, all older," he said. "You all lived together near a big city on the coast. But then you moved. You went to mountains. You have lived in mountains longer than you think."

He stopped again.

He reached into his robe and produced a small black and orange shiny object. He pressed it into my right hand and closed my fingers over it. His large hands enclosed my fist. "Keep this with you at all times," he said. "It will bring you good luck."

"I will," I said, my voice choking. He released my hand and I examined the gift. Flat and black, it was a glass bead layered by yet another piece of glass, orange and slightly smaller, embossed with an image of Hanuman the monkey-headed god.

He told me to put the bead away and I lowered it carefully into my pocket. Then he held both of my hands and examined the lines on each of my palms. He released my hands and said, "You will be meeting a woman. She is slight. Blond hair to here," and he tapped his shoulder. Then placing his flattened hand over his heart he said, "She has a very good heart."

My ears pounded with the deafening sound of surging blood. "I—I've met her," I blurted out. "How do you know all this?" My mind raced through possible explanations, trying to grab onto straws of rationality before the flood of the miraculous.

"I know this because I am yoga man," he said calmly. "Nothing is outside the reach of mind."

"I've met her," I repeated. "You've described her perfectly.

Her heart *is* good!"

"Give her this," he said, pressing another black and orange bead into my hand. "Give her this and she will give you a ring."

I fidgeted nervously with this second Hanuman bead, and he said, "We are through now. You must go."

I hesitated a moment. There was more I wanted to know. There were a thousand questions I'd have asked him but he raised his arm and shooed me away. I pressed my palms together and inclined my head.

"Go," he said, and I walked quickly away.

~

I asked directions, found Connaught Place, took my bearings, and made my way quickly to the hotel. I had lost all track of time, and I was sure I was late. Yvonne was sitting at a table, taking a last sip from a cup of tea.

"I thought you got lost," she said when I took a seat beside her.

"Not lost," I said, "but maybe I was found. I don't really know. You could say I was detained."

"You look as if you were retained by a ghost," she said with a chuckle. "Are you all right?"

"It wasn't a ghost, though perhaps it was an apparition. I've just had the strangest morning of my life.

"Well, are you going to tell me what happened?" she said.

"Hungry?" I asked.

"Famished."

"Let's go," I said. "I'll tell you over lunch. It is a long story."

We went to the same restaurant where we'd had breakfast, and there at the same table at which we had eaten breakfast sat Sally and Dave.

"What a funny coincidence," Yvonne said, putting her hand on Sally's shoulder from behind. She glanced quickly at me with a twinkle in her eye then looked back at Sally who almost choked on the food in her mouth.

"You again," Sally said. "We've *got* to stop meeting like this."

"We'd sit with you," Yvonne said, "but I've got a story to hear. I'm sure we'll catch you later."

"No doubt," said Dave, and we all laughed and shook our heads.

We sat at a table in the back where it was quiet. A waiter came. We ordered, and we sat alone and in silence.

"Well," Yvonne said after a moment, "I spent the morning at the library writing a paper. It was kind of dull but I got a lot done. How 'bout you?" She smiled coyly.

I took a deep breath and launched into the story of all that had happened at the Tourist Office. I had been imbued with her presence and spirit and I couldn't help thinking that the magic I encountered was hers as well.

"He really knew Mary as well?" she said. "That's incredible."

"It sure was," I said. "You should have seen the way he stared at me. He practically fell off his seat!"

"Then it really was an incredible morning you had," she said. "Far more interesting than mine."

"But that's only the beginning," I said. "Then a turbaned man appeared out of the crowd in the middle of a mad bazaar and he knew everything about my life. He even knew my mother's name!" I described to her, again in great detail, all that had happened. I even showed her the bead he had given me. But I stopped short of telling her what he said about her except to say that he had mentioned her and said she had a good heart. I also said that according to his prophecy she'd be giving me a ring. I didn't give her the bead. I didn't want to be too abrupt. I was in the uncomfortable position of knowing her yet not knowing her. And besides, prophecy is a strange business: one can easily get burned.

Then our food came, and I broached the subject of the future. "When do you leave for the West?" I asked.

"Morning after next," she said. "My flight leaves at six-thirty. I'll go to the airport tomorrow evening and spend the night there so I'll be sure to make it."

"Isn't it strange," I said, "that we should meet just now when our paths go in such different directions?"

"I've thought of that," she said. "But I know it is not my destiny to go with you to Almora. Not now anyway." She stood up abruptly. "Come," she said. "I'll pay the bill."

24

We decided to spend the afternoon in the bazaars of Old Delhi. Yvonne wanted to buy presents for her family. As we sat on the bus I could already feel a distance beginning to grow between us. I realized we were as two burning comets crossing paths in the immensity of space. We had illuminated each other momentarily with our burning brightness, but now each of our pasts' momentum was propelling us forward on different trajectories. I was again being called up a mountain and Yvonne was called home by what she termed her 'duties.' Our paths were pulling us apart, but were they really orbits? Did we circle a single star? Would our paths cross again, and perhaps run side by side? The questions burned in my heart. I had no choice but to dwell in the certainty that had enveloped me time and again in the last days. I had learned that there were no mistakes. There couldn't be, unless the grand architect of the universe was a practical joker. I laughed out loud at the thought.

"What's so funny?" Yvonne asked.

"Just a thought," I said. "Nothing really."

"Oh, look," Yvonne called out. "There's the Jami Masjid. We're here!"

The bus slowed at an intersection and we jumped off as the bus barreled away, leaving a line of blue smoke behind.

The Jami Masjid—the main mosque of Old Delhi—stood on a wide stone platform that led to the main entrance where dozens of people sold religious trinkets and clothing. The

Windblown Clouds

Thomas K. Shor

hawkers announced their wares, but they did so sluggishly, half-heartily, for the sun, at its zenith, beat down menacingly out of the white-hot sky. Heat waves rippled everywhere and made the mosque's high stone minarets waver and shift like a desert mirage.

As we made our way across the infernal causeway the heat of the stone penetrated the soles of our shoes and burned our feet. We walked quickly, taking short, pecking steps as one would when crossing a tropical beach. We came upon a boy of seven, squatting on the ground with a small wooden box before him. He was obviously the only one with any sense, for he sat with an umbrella propped between his feet. I grabbed Yvonne's arm and veered her over to the boy, and we squatted on our haunches beneath the umbrella's protection.

"Hallo," the boy said, donning a broad smile. His white teeth gleamed out of a sea of dark skin. His cheeks were high and his nose, though still padded with baby fat, was strong and angular. His clothes were but rags, yet they were clean, and his eyes shone with dignity and self-assurance. He looked sculpted, like a Greek statue of the Divine Child.

"Isn't he something?" Yvonne said, enraptured with the boy.

"Hallo," he said again, and he reached out and felt Yvonne's smooth blond hair. His action was unsullied by an impure thought; he had never felt blond hair before and it was as natural to him as reaching out to touch the hem of his mother's sari.

The box before him was filled with dozens of smooth, pearl-white disks that looked like shells, each a half-inch in diameter. Picking one up, I felt the soft roundness of one side and the flatness of the other. On the flat side, a line that originated on the circumference spiraled slowly to the center, arching round till the spiral became so tight that it terminated in a dot. I knew that the inanimate world could produce spirals—like the whirlpools created in air and water—but I also knew that these physical spirals were never static. I was looking at a static spiral, so I knew I was looking at a piece of something that was once living. Perhaps it was the tip of a conch shell, which are cut off so they can be blown into like a horn in the sacred rituals. I couldn't really tell what it was, but the spiral fascinated me and it felt just right between my fingers. So I decided to buy it.

"How much?" I asked.

"*Ek* Rupee," he said in his soft voice, holding up one finger.

I fished a one-rupee note from my pocket, gave it to him, and we stood up.

"Hallo," he said again, smiling his bright, toothy smile.

"*Namaste*," we said, and hurried away across the burning flagstones.

A moment later someone tugged at my sleeve. It was the boy. He held the note I had given him and pointed out its ragged and torn edges. Indian currency decays quickly, and once a note is torn it seems to lose all value. Even the banks won't take them. People are always trying to pass these notes onto you. The rule is that if you tear it, it's yours and it is worth only the paper it is written on; that is, unless you can pass it on to some unsuspecting person. I had to make good my bargain, so I handed him a rupee coin. Taking the coin, the boy spun on his heals to run, but Yvonne grabbed him, gently, yet firmly, by the arm. He was surprised by her sudden lunge and he tried to squirm away. "Give it here," she said, holding out her hand. Reluctantly, he handed her the tattered bill and Yvonne loosened her grip. His priceless boyish smile came again to his face, though this time tinged with mischief. "Hallo," he said again and darted away.

When we reached the front of the mosque we skirted to the right, went down a short flight of stairs, and entered the winding alleys of the Bazaar. They were as narrow, labyrinthine, and probably as old as those in Varanasi, but far more extensive. They went for mile after crooked, convoluted mile into deeper and ever deeper realms of merchandise.

Windblown Clouds

Thomas K. Shor

Along the first alley were shops selling old wooden sculptures of gods and demons, probably pilfered from ancient temples. The grotesque and sublime forms stared at us out of grungy windows, eyes bulging, myriad arms frozen for all time clutching scepters and thunderbolts, dwarfs and human hearts. They stood at this entrance to the bazaar as gargoyles crouch at the portals of Catholic churches.

Loitering outside one shop, we made faces at the gods through dirty, spider-web-encrusted windows when suddenly one of the wrinkled and cracked faces moved. It was an old man, and he beckoned us to come inside. We ducked through the low doorway into a silent, dark, and musty realm. It took some moments for our eyes to adjust, and when they did all we could see were gods, hundreds of them, some as high as the ceiling, looming, looking ready to topple over with open, blood-smeared mouths; others were so tall that they lay on the floor covered over with deities of lesser size but equal ferocity. It was a wondrous room of indeterminate size, for though a door stood open behind us, along with a large window, no other walls were visible beyond the plethora of the thousand forms of the Hindu's one god, giving the illusion that this realm went on forever.

Our guide appeared from behind a huge statue of Ganesh, the elephant-headed god of wisdom and luck. On closer inspection, my original impression of him from through the window held: he was just another sculpted being among the many. His back was crooked and bent with age, probably from a lifetime of moving and arranging the multitudinous statues, and his legs were bowed almost to the point of being unable to support his crooked frame. And his face: it had curiously taken on the appearance of deeply grained wood; his features seemed chiseled, perhaps by an artist new to the trade. Like a married couple that increasingly resembles one another over the years, this man and his sculptures looked hewn from the same material. Fortunately, he had taken on the likeness of a benign god, and he greeted us warmly.

Windblown Clouds

Thomas K. Shor

He showed us around, pointing out his finest pieces, and then led us to a door. It creaked open on its ancient metal hinges, and he disappeared into a shaft of darkness. Beyond, a narrow wooden stairwell ascended at a frightful grade to a feeble and nebulous area of light. My feet groped for the stairs, which were wooden and groaned and creaked their protestations under each footfall. Progress was slow behind this bent and gnarled tree of a man.

The dull area of light grew in size but not intensity until we reached the end of our climb and stepped into a low garret whose single tiny window was on level with the four-and-a-half-foot high broad-beamed ceiling. A single shaft of sharp sunlight flowed in through the tiny window and illuminated the fierce frozen face of a wooden god. As my eyes adjusted to the diminished light, I saw every fear, every pain, every joy, and every ecstasy that humankind has ever experienced. Gods danced the dance of creation right next to gods that were dancing the world's destruction. They all looked so lifelike—despite their thousand-armed, three-eyed depictions—that I kept expecting, with a quick turn of my head, to catch one in movement. The only one who looked fully at rest was a Buddha that sat in a scarcely visible corner, clothed in silence. With one hand he lightly touched the ground and called the earth and all the beings that inhabit it to bear witness to his feat—that of reaching supreme enlightenment and blissful silence amidst the alternations of fear and hope, joy and pain in the world. His other hand was raised, palm out, in the gesture that says, 'fear not.' Nowhere could the immensity of his achievement be more powerfully depicted than amidst these innumerable forms. He alone stood unmoved and unmoving, a still, hollow hub at the center of a gyrating wheel.

When we stepped back onto the street our eyes smarted in the bright sun. I looked back at the shop's soiled window and there stood our guide, still in the world of the gods, graven-faced, deeply grained, and seemingly frozen for all time.

Windblown Clouds

Thomas K. Shor

That part of the bazaar, comprised exclusively of shops selling old statues, ended abruptly where shops selling colorful ribbons began. Suddenly, spools and rolls and samples of ribbon of various widths and colors were fluttering and waving out shop doors and filling shop windows. Everywhere women haggled for the patterns and colors they wanted, at a price they considered fair. Every other Indian market area that I'd ever seen had had the occasional shop selling such colorful ribbons, but here we walked for the longest time, encountering nothing but these specialty shops.

Then we passed into the world of bangles—of gold, and silver and plastic—which stretched as far as the eye could see. Bangles turned to nose studs, rings, and then watches. Yvonne wanted a scarf to give her father, but we seemed to have strayed from the area with any kind of material, so we backtracked, trying to find again the sari borders; but the further we retreated, the further we seemed to stray from our objective. In fact, we had lost all sense of direction. Eventually, we found ourselves in the fruit market. Then, fruit gave way to grains, and finally to spices. Pungent odors of strong herbs wafted through the air. I closed my eyes and imagined myself in a thick jungle after an afternoon rain.

Down a narrow alley we saw tailors, hundreds of them, each sitting at a tiny stall on a hard plank floor before hand-treadle sewing machines. The rat-a-tat-tat of the machines surrounded us as the tailors turned miles and miles of material into shirts and pants and coats. We followed the line of tailor shops, presuming that the shops selling woven material couldn't be far off. If we were right, then scarves were probably available nearby as well. Our reasoning proved sound; before long, colorful cloths were displayed for inspection. Then we found just what we were looking for: after an area of ready-made garments, there was a short alley where merchants sold scarves. Yvonne bought a brown scarf embroidered with a design of vines.

We wandered aimlessly for the rest of the afternoon until

the deep red glow of the setting sun convinced us we'd better find our way out. We were now in hardware—screws and nails to be exact. Behind us were hammers, saws, and chisels, and before us God-only-knew-what. When we reached stalls selling iron piping, I knew we couldn't be far from a road: they had to get the pipes there somehow. So we delved deeply into the miasma of iron piping, and at length we came upon a chaotic road. We hailed a horse cart, which brought us back to Connaught Place.

~

Next evening I walked Yvonne to the travel agent from which the airport bus was to leave. On the way we talked of trivialities, of flight times and time zones. "Just think," I said, "at six-thirty tomorrow morning, the moment your plane takes off for the West, my bus will be starting its engine, and I'll be on my way to the Himalayas."

She reached into her pocket. "Here," she said, "this is for the prophecy." It was a simple ring of three strands, different metals braided around each other. She placed it on my finger. It fit perfectly. It was then that I decided to give her the bead. "The fortune teller asked me to give you this," I said. "He said it brings luck."

The travel agency was full of Westerners waiting for the first leg of their journey home to commence. "I guess this is it," she said outside the door. We hugged one another goodbye. She turned and walked toward the crowd of travelers.

25

At four-thirty the next morning a nudge on my shoulder awakened me from a deep, dreamless sleep. "It's time," the hotel's night watchman informed me. "It is the time you wanted to wake up." I turned over. Yvonne's bed was empty. She too must be awakening, I thought to myself, readying herself for a long journey to the West, a journey back to familiar ground. My journey, on the other hand, would take me north, to something entirely new. Hundreds of miles of flat and unbroken plains surrounded me. But my day would not end where it began; it would end at the foot of the highest mountains in the world! That thought quickened my pulse, and I was on my feet at once.

As I hit the pavement, the sky was still rich and dark as India ink. The stars faded as the sky lightened and the sun rose over Burma: a continent ready to stir. At the corner, the Tourist Office was locked up tight. Himalayan peaks loomed silently from plate-glass window posters. I peered in through the space between posters and saw the desk where the 'coincidence' had taken place. I patted my breast pocket to feel the map the man had given to me that led to Mary Opplinger's house. The pocket was buttoned, the map, secure.

I turned the corner and walked toward Connaught Place, my ears alert for the sound of a motor rickshaw, my eyes searching for a single bobbing headlight. The street was silent.

Just as I reached Connaught Place, a motor rickshaw pulled up from behind. Ten rupees to the Old Delhi bus station. Riding in the back, I watched the city slowly come to life.

By the time we reached Old Delhi and passed the Jami Masjid Mosque, the sun was just about to rise. Over the engine's drone, plaintive songs in Arabic found my ear. I reached into my pants pocket and pulled out the spiral shell. It felt good in my hand, as if endowed with some unknown power. I placed it in the center of my palm and closed my fingers over it.

At the main entrance of the Old Delhi bus station, confusion reigned: rickshaws dodging buses like minnows before sharks; families everywhere were migrating, pots strapped to their backs and bags and boxes tied shut with jute twine.

Inside the station, thick shutters covered the ticket window for Almora. I banged on the shutters with my fist

Windblown Clouds Thomas K. Shor

until I heard someone grumble inside. Then a man opened the window, sleep still in his eyes. I had but a half hour until the bus's departure. I bought a ticket and ran across the wide lobby and down a flight of stairs. I found the bus and sat by a window, my pack at my feet.

The driver closed the door and started the engine. As a man in a filthy turban guided the bus into the stream of traffic, a spec of light flashing in the sky attracted my attention. The newly risen sun was glinting off the wingtip of a low-flying jet; and as the jet gained altitude and soared westward, I thought of Yvonne. Our paths had first crossed, then run parallel. Now they branched, separated each hour by hundreds of miles, by continents, and by oceans, perhaps never to cross again.

~

For hours the bus forged north and east across the vast North Indian Plain—first through barren, tortured desert, and then through lush fields of sugarcane and banana trees. We traversed a region of rice paddies and passed bullock carts laden with produce and bound for market. We crossed the wide Ganges on a long, low bridge, and now and again we stopped at the edge of a dusty town, where makeshift restaurants in tin shacks dished out watery dhal for next to nothing.

By four o'clock we approached the foothills of the Himalayas. The road here was a narrow swath cut through a sea of low trees. The mountains loomed ahead—abrupt, steep, carpeted in thick jungle. Like the roots of an ancient tree that run along the ground before delving beneath the surface, tongues of mountain overshadowed the plains. Nestled between two such spurs lay the town of Haldwani.

North of Haldwani the road followed the course of a quickly moving river. Although we hadn't yet left the plain, two spurs of mountain reached down like great fingers on either side of us. Where the two spurs met, the river frothed and jumped over boulders. Then the front of the bus angled toward the heavens, and I was pressed back into my seat as we began our ascent.

From the moment I first saw them, it was clear to me that the Himalayas were immense. While Mount Pantokrator, in Greece, might be a high mountain shrouded in mystery, it always remained a solitary peak, one that could be scaled from any angle. It was a great mountain, both conspicuous for its height and its bareness above lush lowlands. It was a mountain that could be scaled and crossed over. But the Himalayas presented a mystery far greater. Each ridge we crossed dwarfed Pantokrator—and these were only the foothills! The Himalayas themselves, the central chain of jagged, icy peaks, pierced the very sky and separated the Indian subcontinent from Tibet, a land itself shrouded in mystery.

Landscape affects philosophy. The Himalayas are vast. They are the largest single terrestrial feature on the planet. And just as we cannot look directly at the brightest light nature presents to our eyes, the sun, without going blind, so human understanding cannot encompass the Himalayan vastness. This is why the philosophies of the cultures that have arisen in the shadow of these mountains stress the mystery that no amount of human understanding can fathom. Perhaps this is why Indians and Tibetans don't scale the peaks they consider sacred, but circumambulate them instead. It is only Westerners who have thought it both necessary and noble to plant their flags at the pinnacles of the most notable peaks. While the Easterner contemplates the unknowable, the Westerner dispels and conquers. He reaches the perilous peak, plants there his nation's flag, and has his fellow climber take his picture. Into the lonely and icy stratosphere he screams, "I, I, I! I have done it! I am the first!" Meanwhile the Easterner slowly circles, lost in prayer and contemplation: "Not me, not me, not me," he says. "Who am I next to your immensity?"

Windblown Clouds

Thomas K. Shor

~

We climbed the sides of wooded mountains, crossed stony ridges, and plunged into valleys cradling wild mountain streams, but always we gained altitude, rising toward the higher mountains, the air cooler with every mile. Just when the sun was setting, the clouds closed in and it started to snow. And even in the darkness I could feel the land's sharp edges, the sloping mountains and steep valleys. The air smelled of trees. It had a cold, sharp edge.

A half hour later we reached the outskirts of Almora. It was a good-size town of stone and wood houses built over a series of low hills. The road narrowed and twisted toward the center of the town, where the road widened again at the main market. There we stopped. Stout men dressed in clothes made of burlap sacks, each with a rope over his shoulder, clamored around the bus. They practically clawed over each other for the attention of passengers in need of porters. They were muscular men, yet lean. And not one of them had shoes. The soles of their feet were thick-skinned and leathery; they left broad imprints in the newly fallen snow.

I stepped beyond the circle of clamor and stood under a street lamp. The wind blew the snow sideways through the lamplight. The snow was sticking to the ground and was beginning to accumulate. Children ran, open-mouthed, to catch the huge wet snowflakes on their tongues. Even the adults seemed delighted by the coat of white adorning their town. Apparently, snow was rare in Almora.

I opened the map, took my bearings, and started walking toward Haimavati—Mary Opplinger's house. The road followed the crest of a ridge connecting a series of hills on whose slopes the town sprawled. The snow muffled the few lights along the road, rendering them but feeble circles visible only at close range. Occasionally, the sound of footsteps crunching through the freshly fallen snow announced the presence of someone walking toward the town. When the footsteps grew louder, and the figure emerged out of the darkness, we'd exchange a friendly *namaste*.

After about two miles, just as the map indicated, I passed an army barracks on the right then entered another market, at the end of which the road turned to dirt and forked. I took the right fork, which mounted a steep incline. Then I came upon a large house on the left. The house was brightly lit with kerosene lanterns. Colorful banners hung from the balcony. Children played in the snow. From the slant of their eyes and their round, open faces I knew they were Tibetans. Their clothes were of hand-spun wool and dyed with bright colors, which contrasted with the sullen grays and browns of their Indian neighbors' clothes.

As the lights of the house faded behind me, it became apparent that this was the last house in town. The dirt road threaded now through a dark forest. Hunching against the wind and snow, I lit a match to consult my map. Apparently a path would mount an embankment to the right when the road made its first sharp left turn. This would be the path to Haimavati. The match sizzled in the wet snow and went out. I was hoping now no footsteps drew near out of the darkness.

I groped along the mountain road, wondering now whether it might not be wiser to turn back and find Haimavati in daylight. But I was cold and wet, and Mary Opplinger's house couldn't be far. The town of Almora was miles away. Now, above all else, I sought shelter.

I came upon a sharp turn. An embankment rose to the right. I searched for a path, but the darkness was profound. I lit a match, but the windswept snow immediately blew it out. Then something happened that I considered a minor miracle: there was a break in the swiftly moving cloud and through the break shone a few bright stars and a half moon. Though the moon was streaked with falling snow, it cast enough light that I could see a path cut into the embankment. I ran up the path and reached the top just as the clouds closed again, encircling me in darkness.

What happened next proved I still had no sense of the

Windblown Clouds Thomas K. Shor

Himalayas; for having just mounted so steep an embankment, I never would have imagined that the land could drop off so precipitously on the other side. But drop off it did. I took a step forward, my foot came out from under me, and I started sliding on my back down a slope every bit as steep as the slope I had just climbed. The trunks of huge pine trees whizzed by me until I came to a stop at the bottom of what seemed like a ravine. I stood and shook the snow from my clothes. It was so dark I couldn't even see the mark my sliding body had made in the snow. I turned around, turned again, and became disoriented.

Rindani's bald head bathed in the low light of a late Bombay evening suddenly appeared before my mind's eye, and I remembered with a shudder his story of Jim Corbitt and the man-eating tigers. Hadn't Ed told me once of a man-eater terrorizing these hills? Yes, he had—and unfortunately I remembered. Its first victim was a young girl who walked out of her house one morning and was pounced upon by a tiger who had been crouching on a roof.

A floundering, thrashing swimmer can attract sharks from miles away; I figured the same was true of fearful thoughts in a sea of trees where tigers were concerned. So I checked my thoughts and tried not to let fear wreak havoc upon my sense of direction.

Circling slowly, scanning the darkness for clues, I saw a faint glow through the trees. I walked toward the glow and it resolved into separate points of light. They were the lights from a house, a big house, Victorian in style, obviously built by the British. A servant stood outside the kitchen door scouring a pan with raw earth and dumping the dirty water onto the snow.

"*Namaste*," I called when I was still some distance away. "Do you speak English?"

"I most certainly do," he said, searching for me in the darkness. "Come closer so I can see you."

I emerged into the light. "Is this Haimavati, the home of

Mary Opplinger?"

"No, it is not," he said. "You must have taken the wrong path from the road. Mary's house is through the woods in that direction," and he pointed into the darkness over my shoulder.

He explained that I could either follow the driveway back to the road, or take a shortcut through the woods, which he assured me would be hard to miss even in the darkness. I decided upon the longer route. I was just about to leave when I inquired, "Who, may I ask, lives in this house?"

"David McKay lives here. He is from Australia. Would you like to meet him?"

Though it was late I said yes. The servant led me into the kitchen. I gave him my name. "Wait here," he said. "I will announce you."

Softly knocking on a high wooden door, he opened it and passed silently inside. A moment later he opened the door, and in a formal, almost solemn voice, said, "You may enter now."

For some reason my heart was beating wildly as I passed through that high doorway. I walked inside, the door clicked shut behind me, and the servant was gone.

The room was large and had a high ceiling. It was paneled in wood. Beneath a handsome hand-carved wooden mantelpiece a fire roared in a fireplace. The room was furnished with fine oak tables and overstuffed chairs straight out of a Victorian drawing room. In the alcove of a wide bay window across from the fireplace was a large sofa. Sitting directly at the sofa's center sat David McKay. Like a king on his throne, or a lion in his lair, he looked regal, his long, silver-gray mane falling upon his shoulders, and his beard—full and snowy-white—completely covering his chest. His stomach, protruding beneath the beard, was ample. He rather closely resembled Father Christmas.

He made no move to get up to greet me, and he didn't say a word. He just stared at me, his coal-black eyes glowing intensely. I felt I'd found my wild cat in the woods. Like an actor pushed onto the stage before his cue, I stood frozen.

I pointed vaguely outside. "I was looking for Mary Opplinger's house. I became lost in the woods. I saw the lights." The words were difficult to form; they choked in my throat.

"Yes, Purum told me," he said, loosening his gaze. His face softened and he said, "Please, sit down."

He indicated a chair facing the sofa, and I sat on the edge with my feet beneath me, feeling rather like a new student on the first day of school.

"It is okay you weren't able to find Mary's house, for you would have found it locked up tight. Mary has gone to the plains, and she won't be back for a couple of months. Are you a friend of hers?"

"Actually not," I said. "She is a friend of a friend. I was hoping she could introduce me to Lama Govinda."

"Lama Govinda!" the old man exclaimed. "Seems like you've run out of luck. Govinda's gone. He came down with Parkinson's disease and left over a year ago. I'm afraid he'll never come back to Almora."

The earth opened beneath me and hurled me headlong into a vast and endless chasm. My mind reeled. So much had drawn me forward, and I had come with so much anticipation. Luck was flashing for me, all the signs were pointing, pointing toward *this* place, toward these hills in the Himalayas. Suddenly, nothing made sense; and the moment it stopped making sense, I started to laugh. I couldn't help myself. The laughter just rose up from inside me. This was the biggest joke ever played on me. The old man stared at me as if I'd suddenly gone mad, as if some strange specimen of humanity had just washed up on his shore.

"I'm sorry," I said. "It's just that I was expecting—"

"Yes," he said, shifting his ample frame forward on the sofa, "you came full of expectations. And now those expectations have proved false."

"I suppose that's true."

"Perhaps you felt something drawing you to this place?"
"Yes." But how did he know this?
"And now you are wondering what you are doing here?"
"Yes, that's right."
"Govinda was like a magnet...for certain people."
"You knew him?"
"Certainly. I studied with him for twenty years. It was also because of him I came to Almora."
"Are you a Buddhist?"
"That's what others might say, though really I've just been searching... Of course I appreciate the Buddha's philosophy...for its purity. But no philosophy—no matter how pure—will impart true wisdom. Wisdom is found here," and he tapped his rounded chest with the tips of his stout fingers. "You must uncover wisdom within yourself by peeling away layers—like the skins on an onion—until you find the sparkling crystal that lies at the center. That's why the Northern school of Buddhism—as practiced by the Tibetans—is called the *Vajrayana*. *Vajra* means diamond and *yana* means vehicle. It is the Diamond Vehicle. I have been a student of the *Vajrayana* ever since I left Australia almost twenty years ago. Having studied their scriptures and practiced their meditations, having even been ordained as a lama—or teacher—I still don't consider myself a Buddhist per se. I think Buddha would have preferred it this way. If you remember, the Buddha's last words to his disciples before he died were: 'Work out your *own* salvation with diligence.' It can probably be found just as easily within the teachings of Christ or within the Hindu doctrines. Here, I'll show you."

Lifting his ample frame with difficulty and striding across the room with the same intensity with which he spoke, he went to the fireplace. On the mantle-piece was a brass sculpture. He picked it up and came back to the sofa, placing it in my hands before sitting down. "Do you recognize this?" he asked.

"Yes, it's the Hindu's elephant-headed god, Ganesh, isn't

it?"

"You are correct," he said, leaning forward, "but do you know *who* Ganesh is?"

I shook my head, and he continued:

"Ganesh is the god of wisdom, the one who unites the macrocosm and the microcosm. He is known as the Destroyer of Obstacles. He has the power to destroy obstacles to understanding. Yet he does not always give his understanding freely; he guards his wisdom.

"Look," he said, pointing to the elephant's tusks, "one of the tusks is broken; the other is still whole. In fact it is quite sharp." He pricked his finger on the end of the unbroken tusk. "These two tusks symbolize the two approaches to wisdom: if you approach wisdom the wrong way, you find yourself impaled on the end of a rather long and sharp tusk. It is a dangerous business, because Ganesh guards his secret well. But if you approach Wisdom correctly, on the side with the broken tusk, there are no dangers, the obstacles fall away, and he reveals his secret. More often than not, people choose the wrong side of approach. They get jabbed a few times, then run to some doctrine or religion for solace.

"I have something else to show you," he said. He crossed the room again and opened the door to a closet and took from it a leather bag. Then he came back and sat down.

He leaned forward, and I leaned forward too. The leather bag was pulled shut with a thong. On the end of the thong was a glass bead. He held it between his fingers. It was orange and black. Pointing to the image embossed in the orange glass, he said, "This is Hanuman, the monkey-headed god."

I reached into my pocket and took out the bead the psychic yogi in Delhi had given me. I held it next to his. They were identical.

The hand in which he held the bead began to tremble, and I felt his eyes fall upon me like flames of fire. He locked me in his gaze, his face not a foot away from mine.

"Where did you get this?" he asked, his voice quivering with emotion.

"From a psychic man in Delhi," I said. "He swirled out of a crowd one day and seemed to know everything about my life."

"What did he look like?"

I described him.

"Where did you see him?"

I described the bazaar.

"This is *extraordinary*," he said, his eyes still locked on mine. My eyes too felt like burning embers. Fire met fire in the space between us, and it felt as though we'd be consumed.

"I got this one from that very same man," he said. Then he reconsidered: "Actually, I got it from that man's father many, many years ago. From the man you saw I got this," and he turned the bead over. Glued to the back was a small white shell. On the shell's flat surface was etched a spiral.

I reached into my pocket, held out my closed fist, opened it slowly without saying a word, and revealed my shell—it was identical to his.

Had I been sleeping I would have dreamed I had left my body, for a wave of detachment washed over me, accompanied by a flood of joy that swept away the last speck of doubt dwelling in my heart. Now I resided in certainty. Blake once said, 'If the sun had but a doubt, it would immediately go out.' I knew that radiance. David couldn't speak. India tells you a thousand times that inner and outer are but aspects of the same thing, that individuals are not separate, that they are one, that we are all one. India was being practical, India was *showing* me, and I loved her for it. If ever I've thought there was a higher intelligence directing our steps, it was at that moment.

The latch to the kitchen door clicked, the metallic sound echoing off the drawing room's walls startling us both. We turned and the servant Purum flung the door wide open and came bounding in followed by three other young Indian men, the last of whom was holding a large wooden drum that he banged once with his open palm, filling the room with its low reverberations.

The man with the drum ran to the center of the room, stopped, sat cross-legged on the floor, and sounded a perfect roll with his index fingers. Then he launched into a deep rhythm alternating flattened palm, fingers, and fist. The others danced in a circle around him, singing a chorus that became louder as their circle became tighter and tighter. When they were practically treading upon the drummer, the circle broke open and the rhythm changed into a deeper, more primitive beat. The men, each acting out a separate part, whirled around the room. In Hindi movies people are always breaking into song—much as they did in 1940s Hollywood musicals—but this was different. These young men were not acting: they were performing a ritual.

David leaned over. "Look at their glazed eyes," he said. "They are no longer with us. They've gone into trance." The pulse of the drum had entered their every muscle and dictated their movements as they danced round the room. Their eyes focused straight ahead as if taking in a scene beyond the confines of the room, a scene out of myth where the forces of good are pitted against the forces of evil. For that is all I could make out: one of the dancers was the embodiment of the good and light while another was the very image of evil. The third, seemingly a human, was in the middle, as if the conflicting forces were fighting over his body and soul.

David leaned over again. "It is the final scene from the great Hindu epic the Ramayana," he said. "Sita, the wife of the hero Ram, has been captured by the evil king of Ceylon. Hanuman, the monkey god—the same as on our beads—and his army of monkeys are fighting for her release." Just as he said this, the evil one, the man depicting the wicked king of Ceylon, fell to the floor screaming in a shrill, inhuman voice, his body writhing with convulsions. The drummer stopped and they all ran and held this man's limbs and tried to calm him. Slowly he came back, though he looked bewildered at first, as if he had forgotten where he was. He stood up, they each took their places, and to the drum's deep rhythm they resumed where they'd left off, each passing quickly back into trance.

"Isn't it amazing how easily these boys pass into trance?" David said. "We from the West, we could never do it. The separation between the conscious mind and the underlying forces, that veil which is so strong and thick to us, is for them but a thin sheet of tissue. A few beats of a drum, an immortal mythic theme, and they're gone."

We watched as the forces of Hanuman defeated the wicked king and spirited the lovely Sita away. Sita and Ram disappeared into the kitchen, leaving the king in a heap on the floor, and the drummer beating a rhythm at once of death and defeat, and of triumph and joy. The drummer stopped, the king stood, and they both walked out of the room, closing the door behind them.

David yawned. "I'm an old man," he said, "and I need my sleep. I have plenty of room. It is too late now for you to return to Almora. Why don't you sleep here? In the morning we can talk more and explore what it was that brought you here."

"That would be wonderful," I said.

"I'll get my servant Purum to show you to your room."

Before David could call him, the door to the kitchen opened and Purum entered.

"Purum, show this young man to the guest room."

David stood.

I stood.

"Extraordinary evening," he said.

"Good night," I said. "And thank you."

26

I awoke late. Purum told me David was seeing someone else. I would have to wait. I stepped outside. Except for the deepest pockets sheltered from the sun, the snow had already melted. Crossing the lawn, I sat on a thick stone wall. Below, the landing dropped off in a series of terraces to a river snaking along the bottom of a valley. On the other side the land rose to a ridge of mountains beyond which rose another ridge backed by yet another until the icy peaks drew a ragged horizon across the sky. Plumes of snow blown by high winds waved like flags off the high peaks. An eagle rose on a thermal wind from the valley below, spiraling on the convection until it was at eye level. It paused, soaring yet stationary, superimposed upon the distant peaks. Then it tucked its wings and flew over my head. I heard its wings cut the air and felt the breeze of its passing.

Purum called from the kitchen door that David was ready to see me. I waited in the kitchen while Purum went through the door to the drawing room to announce me. This was done as solemnly as at the court of a king. The door opened, Purum motioned for me to enter then left, shutting the door silently behind him.

David was sitting exactly where he'd sat the night before, at the center of the sofa beneath the bay window. In the chair where I had sat a Tibetan man now sat dressed in a burgundy robe. A large, silver earring hung almost to his shoulder, elongating the lobe of his right ear, and in his right hand he held a string of beads like a rosary that Tibetans call a *maller*. Repeating a chant beneath his breath, working the beads between his thumb and forefinger, he smiled broadly at me when I entered. Though he wasn't yet old, his face was deeply lined. A few wispy hairs grew from his chin, creating not more than a ghost of a beard.

David stood, and then the Tibetan stood. "This is Lama Kunsang Rigdzin," David said. "Though you can just call him Lama. He is the lama whom Govinda left the house and land at Kasar Devi to, just as Professor Evans-Wentz gave it to Govinda when he left. He lives there now with his wife and their six children. A few monks from Ladakh are there for the winter to help with the animals. They are on loan from a Ladakhi monastery. I told him of our extraordinary coincidences with the beads and shells. I thought perhaps you two should meet."

Lama stopped chanting, and with the beads still wrapped round his fingers he pressed his palms together in greeting. Then he resumed his chant, which flowed effortlessly from his lips. It was as natural as the sound of water rushing over stones.

We studied each other closely. His robe, draped gracefully over his shoulder, ended with long, flowing folds at his calves. The robe was not new. It was patched and there was on it a splotch of dried cow manure. His clothes were at once those of a shaman-priest and those of a farmer. His calm presence put me instantly at ease.

We all sat down. Lama spoke to David in Hindi, and David spoke to me in English: "Lama wants to know what old friend of Govinda's it was that sent you here."

"It was an elderly man," I said. "An American. His name is Ed Spencer."

At mention of the name, Lama's eyes brightened. He spoke quickly to David in Hindi. "He remembers your friend well," David said. "Your friend used to come here years ago, when this lama was younger than you are now. Apparently, he liked your friend very much."

I told them of Ed and my journey south from Bombay. Lama could understand more English than he could speak.

When I was through David interpreted again for Lama: "He says that your friend Spencer was always a great walker."

This made Lama laugh, remembering Ed Spencer and how he used to walk. Then Lama looked at me and just smiled for the longest time. He spoke again to David in Hindi.

"Lama is asking whether you would like to go with him to Kasar Devi. You could stay there, if you like. He is giving you an open invitation."

A half hour later I walked with Lama Kunsang Rigdzin to Kasar Devi.

~

It was one of those crisp, fall-like days when white billowy clouds dance like puffs of steam from horizon to horizon— three dimensional, filled with light and movement. The mountain sky seemed somehow close, as if within reach. And the sun was sharp. It clearly marked distant things and made them seem near; everything stood out in relief.

From David's house we went back to the dirt road and followed it along the crest of the ridge toward Kasar Devi, some five miles away. We passed villagers with bundles of sticks lashed to their backs on their way to the market in Almora. Men, women, and children all labored under these loads that exceeded three feet in diameter. I wondered at the smiles they donned while their backs were bent almost parallel with the ground, as sweat dripped from their bodies. Within thick pine forests, bands of monkeys called to one another, and occasionally an odd breeze brought the sound of a distant drum.

When we reached Kasar Devi, a wooded hill that rose like a bump at the end of the ridge, we left the road for a path that mounted the hill then descended through a heavily wooded slope and brought us to a spectacular outcropping of rock, below which opened a clear view of the snow-clad peaks on the border with Tibet. A huge pole had been stuck in the ground there and secured with stones. It towered thirty feet overhead. Ropes attached to the top were tied to trees to steady the pole. Attached to the ropes and to the pole were hundreds of Tibetan prayer flags, which fluttered in the cool breeze that rose from the valley. The flags were made from squares of coarse cotton that had been stamped with an inscribed wooden block. In the center of each flag a guardian deity held a flaming sword. It was surrounded by the deity's mantra, written repeatedly in Tibetan script. Tibetans place these flags on and around their homes for protection from malevolent forces. When the flags flutter their prayers are carried upon the wind.

Below the outcropping, the path brought us to the rear of Lama's wooden, single-story house. Walking round to the front, we came upon a beautiful, peaceful scene: Sonam, Lama's wife, their children, and the two Ladakhi monks sitting on the front lawn, a plateau of land ringed by mountains. It was a timeless scene. Everyone was busy at something, be it fanning the fire, cutting vegetables, reading from the sacred texts, or playing. An unhurried air hung over them, as if time were no longer measured by the moving hands of a clock, but by the wide arc of the sun. The sun was high in the sky, and time was plentiful.

Lama introduced me to his wife Sonam, a solidly built woman who radiated both maternal warmth and great strength. She stood with her feet planted solidly apart, as if she were a tree with broad roots. Her husband, both shorter and bonier than she, looked like a sapling beside her. Her long dress was made of coarse, homespun material in rich primary colors. Her jet-black hair was braided into a single pigtail that fell to the small of her back. And braided into her hair were pieces of brightly colored yarn. It looked like a braided rainbow.

The children thronged around me, and in a tight knot of rapidly spoken Tibetan we all moved to the center of the lawn where the two monks had remained seated. Lama introduced me to them. The moment I sat, one of the children started climbing on my back, wanting to go for a ride.

Sonam brought me a cup of tea from a pot hanging over a smoldering fire. It was Tibetan tea, made with butter and salt. I liked it; it was a thick and hearty brew.

I watched the older of the two Ladakhi monks sitting wrapped in his red-gold robe with his back against a tree, reading from an old, unbound Tibetan book whose characters were hand written on hand-made paper. His smile was almost like a child's smile, though practically toothless, and his robe was tattered and patched many times over. His boots were much the same; his head was shaved, but the hair was growing back, gray on the sides and thin on top. On his chin grew a few solitary long strands of hair.

In one hand he held a *maller* and with the other he followed the words as he read them on the page. When he reached the end of a page, he flipped the page over slowly and added it to the pile before him. His eyes sparkled as he read. When he reached the end of a section, he smiled to himself, glowing with inward contentment. Then he moved a little to make his position more comfortable and, slowly, as if he were devouring each character with relish, he followed his finger again, word by word, line by line, page by page. I could feel the single-pointed concentration he brought to his task. It was a rare treat to watch him.

Then a little brown puppy and a black kitten strayed into the scene. They frolicked about, the puppy chasing the cat, and the cat mounting the puppy's back, digging in its claws for a ride. They rolled over each other, becoming a single blur of tumbling fur, then started again with a yelp, a snarl, and a dart of movement. They, too, were seizing the moment.

Then the frolicking pair fell upon the monk's pile of carefully placed pages. I watched him closely. Not one iota of anger entered his being. He picked the two up, said some stern words to them in Tibetan, and sent them on their way. Looking up, he caught my gaze. He then continued to read.

After a while Sonam and Lama sat down next to me. "Good you staying," Sonam said. She patted the earth. "Good staying, good." Lama, too, patted the earth as if it were a big beast to be thanked for all of our existences, and he burst out laughing. We all laughed then, even the old monk.

"Come," Sonam said. "Room showing." I stood and followed her down the hill. We passed a little fenced barnyard on the right where about a dozen cows lay contentedly chewing their cud.

"Milk?" I asked, pointing at them.

"Ah," she said, "morning coming, evening coming, milk getting. Sticks getting, fire making, water putting, tea putting, butter putting, salt putting, milk putting—tea drinking!" Her English, though not the Queen's own, was descriptive and to the point.

About fifty yards below the house we came to an unfinished building of bare concrete and reinforcing rods. Sonam brought me first to the front door, which was a large, gaping hole, stitched over with woven saplings in whose center was a door fashioned out of flattened oil tins nailed to a wooden frame. She had to lift the door on its coarse hinges to open it. Inside was a single square room, perhaps thirty feet on each side, with a fifteen-foot ceiling, except in the center, which was raised another six feet into a square clearstory. A puddle on the floor attested to the fact that only two sides of the clearstory were glassed in, the other two being open to the elements. The interior walls, like the external walls, were bare concrete.

"Temple building," Sonam said, leading me to a large box draped in silk along the far wall. There was a soft velvet cushion on the box. "His Holiness coming," Sonam said. "His Holiness sitting. All Tibetans coming." She swept her arm all around to show that they'd come from all directions. Then she reached up and showed me a picture that was propped up on the pillow. "His Holiness," she said. He was a surprisingly young man to be the leader of their sect, perhaps thirty or thirty-five. But even in the photograph it was clear there was something extraordinary about the man. His features were round, his skin smooth, yet his eyes shone with the wisdom of an old man. She carefully placed the picture back on the throne, and we went back outside. She lifted the door again on its loose hinges to shut it.

In the front left corner of the building was an extra little wing not more than ten feet long. There were windows, three tiers high. A door led to the bottom room and an external staircase led to the second and third. Sonam pointed to the top room. "One monk sleeping," she said. Then to the middle room: "One monk sleeping." She pointed to the bottom room: "You sleeping!" She pushed the door open. It was a small room, perhaps eight by ten. The ceiling sloped to the left under where the staircase rose outside. The room's one window was large—eight crosshatched panes—and it faced east to let in the morning sun. The doorway faced south, so once the sun was higher in the sky I could leave it open and let its rays heat the room. The furniture consisted of a chair—broken and beyond repair—a low table, and a bed. The bed was fashioned from wooden planks, and on it were two square mattresses covered with blue material that was ripped in several places, exposing the straw stuffing within. On the windowsill were a kerosene lantern and some broken candles.

"Room good—you liking?" Sonam asked.

"Yes," I replied, "it is very good," and it was: it had morning sun, afternoon sun, and a kerosene lantern to see at night; the table was low enough that I could write on it when I sat on the edge of the bed. I had found my place in the mountains.

27

The only sound was of the torrent of water thundering from the gorge. Every afternoon for weeks it had rained. The water outstripped the narrow rocky ravine and swirled wildly around the trunks of small trees that held on as if for dear life with webs of roots like tiny, clutching fingers. The water plunged over the falls, struck into a deep pool and came up frothing—a caldron brewed by the elements. Bubbles floated to the edges of the pool as the current careened downstream, eddying around boulders and leaping over tiny dams of fallen saplings. The mist rising from the pool in thick, wispy strands merged with the thick fog that blanked the valleys in the pre-dawn morning.

Rising from where I had been squatting by the stream, I

Windblown Clouds

Thomas K. Shor

felt my beard; it was filled with tiny globules of water like those that form on the blades of grass. What was it that Yeats had once said? I tried to remember. The blades of grass, that was it: "The sap would die out of the blades of grass had they a doubt. They understand it all, being the fingers of God's certainty."

High overhead the canopy of leaves dripped huge drops onto the forest floor. The leaves' pale undersides merged with the fog. Above the white blanket of fog, the sky grew lighter; it was time to climb out of the valley and onto the hill.

The fog dampened the water's thunder as I climbed through the forest. The occasional bird fluttered onto a bush before me, chirped, and flew away. The higher I climbed the steeper it became. Where the outcroppings of rock began I stopped for a breath and looked up again. Here, the trees were sparser and stunted. The sky above was undulating, now lighter, now darker, now white as snow, now betraying a hint of blue.

The way was harder now and I had to make detours around steep rock faces and use my hands to hoist myself onto boulders. I came to the surface of the sea of fog and climbed clear of it. The biggest stars still shone brightly in the sky. I went to the peak and sat in my usual place.

The hill's peak was like an island—one of hundreds, some big, some small, some round, and some long and jagged like the spine of a dragon—rising out of the milky sea of fog. But for a splash of pink growing slowly to the east, the sky was a clear and delicate blue, like a deep mountain pool. Devoid of thought, I sat as motionless and silent as a stone. The sky's vastness pulsed between my temples. My body felt firm as bedrock. My skin and its warm, protective layers of clothing were soft and downy as the blanket of fog that clothed the valleys. To the north, the snowy peaks loomed silent, their slopes deep blue, the color of hardened, glacial ice clothed in night. The moment was pregnant, poised, full of anticipation; it was the instant before the start of a symphony.

Windblown Clouds

Thomas K. Shor

Then the first note sounded: the snow on the very tip of the highest mountain to the north, Nanda Devi, glowed pink from the first rays of the sun. Above the sea of soft, muted colors and below the lightly tinted azure sky, this point of light rang out so clearly that I could practically hear it. Then, slowly, as the earth turned to meet the sun, the point grew, following the snowy slopes of reasoned proportion. Now other peaks sounded with tongues of color, and in a single flood the blue snowfields were transformed and set aflame.

It took a full twenty minutes for the earth to turn enough for the sun to rise where I sat, and when it did I felt my body flush with life. I breathed deeply, and as I exhaled I felt my heart would burst with joy. If any sound could fill such immensity it could only be that of a clear, well-forged bell. Though I had risen to greet the sun every morning for months now, each morning was the first morning in all of creation. Each day started fresh, on the same clear note, the first rays of the sun erasing all residue from the past. Had the sun but a single doubt it, too, would be extinguished. I knew this now with certainty.

~

I descended the other side of the hill to the dirt road, which I followed. Out of the fog the teahouse appeared that I often visited in the mornings. It was a low stone structure with a wooden shingled roof nestled in a little rocky fold on the side of the mountain. As I turned down the short, well-trod path, the door to the teahouse swung open and the proprietor stepped outside. He was a short, thin man with a kind face. I often found him playing with his two children, teaching them how to play a new game or how best to fan the fire to heat a pot of tea. Though we hadn't a language in common we had become friends.

"Namaste," I called. He was just buttoning his shirt and I startled him. I stopped, realizing I had caught him a bit early. But he waved me over and indicated I should enter the hut. Following me inside with a load of sticks, he started a fire in the fire pit in the center of the room. The room filled with thick smoke. The open door was the smoke's only line of escape. I squatted close to the fire and slowly felt its heat. He put an old and dented kettle blackened with carbon and age on the fire to boil. The room began to warm. A sheet hanging from the sooty rafters partitioned the hut in two. From behind the partition I heard a yawn. His wife was now awake. She appeared with another yawn a few moments later, her face still wrinkled from sleep. She lifted a wide-mouthed woven basket, overturned on the dirt floor, and set loose a handful of chickens in a flurry of wings and clucking and flying feathers. Waving her arms and hooting, she sent them outside. Then she untied a goat, which had been tethered in a corner and, holding its lead, led it outside, though it clearly wanted to stay in the warmth. Two giggling voices revealed the children's head stuck beneath the partition. They were still lying on their straw mats. With a single command from their father they were up and dressed. They came and huddled beside me at the fire. Soon the tea was ready and the father and I each drank two cups in rapid succession. I paid, bid them all a good morning, and stepped out into the fog.

   The road back to Kasar Devi ran along the crest of a ridge separating two valleys. The valley to the left was higher than the other and it was first to catch the sun's rays. The sun heated the fog in this valley, causing it to rise to where a breeze pressed it against the ridge. At a notch in the ridge the fog flowed over the road and tumbled into the deeper valley like a billowy-white waterfall.

   By the time I arrived back at Kasar Devi most of the fog had burned off or had collected in the deepest valleys. I imagined it flowing down the river valleys and spilling onto the plains.

   Pima, Lama and Sonam's twelve-year-old daughter, was sitting in the sun with her back to the door of my room with Childen, Lama and Sonam's youngest child, wrapped in a blanket and strapped to her back. "Good morning," Pima called out when she saw me. Pima had learned English in school and spoke it better than anyone in the family, even though she had quit school more than a year earlier. She had been the only Tibetan in her school, and the jeering that children are wont to give others who are different from them had proved too much for her. She had begun skipping school to avoid being taunted until Lama and Sonam told her she didn't have to go. This was a shame, for even though Lama attempted to teach her at home, her lessons were usually preempted by more immediate and pressing duties. She was a bright and lively girl and I always felt sad that her education had been nipped in the bud.

I returned her greeting and made a funny face in an attempt to make Childen laugh. But Childen was always pensive despite her tender age. She wore a permanent frown and brooded all the time. She just stared back at me and scowled.

"How about you?" I said to Pima. "Will you laugh?" I made my face again and she giggled. But Pima always seemed happy. She and her sister were antithesis, like the masks that hang over the door to a theater.

Pima asked me if I was hungry. "I sure am," I said. "I've been out walking for hours. All I've had is a cup of tea."

She held onto the sleeve of my jacket. "Can I cook?"

"Sure," I said, and a gleeful look came across her face. Sometimes I ate with the family, but because I came back from my walks at odd hours I usually cooked for myself in the morning in a mud cooking hut next to the temple. Pima was often waiting for me, and if I said I wanted to cook for myself she'd take on the countenance of her sister and I'd have two frowning kids on my hands. Usually I'd give in.

While Pima started the fire in the cooking hut I went to fetch the food from my room. I had rice, flour, carrots, potatoes, and cauliflower—a pretty good hold, for I had just taken a food run to Almora. When I reached the cooking hut the fire was already roaring and a pot of water for rice was heating. Pima insisted on having no supervision while she cooked, so she kicked me out and I went back to my room.

The room in the corner of the temple building had become a haven for me. It was a point of rest and solitude, a place for meditation and study. The room was suffused with the sound of deep-throated, Tibetan chant; for the younger of the two Ladakhi monks lived in the room directly above mine and spent his days chanting. He was chanting the entire text of the Prajnaparamita, one of the Tibetan Buddhist scriptures. He had been chanting from this book from dawn until dusk for months, stopping only for meals and tea. If I noticed his window was open I'd open mine so the sound could flow freely into my room. The sound of his chant was soothing to the ear and calming to the spirit.

Before long Pima was standing in my doorway. "Food ready," she said. Childen, still strapped to her back, looked around the room, her face still set in a pout. I jumped up from where I'd been bent over a book and followed her out. The sun was high now and it beat down strongly out of a crystal-clear sky. Usually, by this time of day, the clouds built toward the afternoon rains. The sun usually appeared for only a few hours after the morning fog had lifted.

"Pima," I said, "where are the clouds?"

"There are no clouds coming," she said matter-of-factly.

"How do you know?"

"Because Daddy said so. He woke up this morning and said spring is coming. It is almost Lusar."

"Lusar," I asked, "what's that?"

"Tibetan New Year. Big celebration. Day after tomorrow. Tibetans coming from all around."

We sat on the ground outside the cooking hut. I dished out a plate of rice and vegetables for Pima and Childen then one for myself. Pima let Childen out of the blanket-pouch on her back and sat her on her lap. We all ate using our hands, scooping the food with chapatis. I went to wash the dishes, but the water barrel was empty, so I took the two buckets and went to the spring.

The spring was set in a moist fold in the hill about ten minutes' walk away. Though this was quite a distance to go for water it was one of the chores I enjoyed the most. As I walked through the woods on the well-trod path I often reflected upon an old Zen saying I had read in one of the books Govinda had left behind at the house. It was underlined and I used to wonder whether he, too, thought of it on his way to the spring. "Before enlightenment," the saying goes, "you gather wood and carry water; and after enlightenment you gather wood and carry water." It was a simple enough saying and I probably would have passed it right by if Govinda's had not marked it on the page.

The spring, nestled in a moist fold on the hill's back side, was so densely green that the sun never penetrated it. Water dripped from moss-covered stones. Flowers, seen nowhere else, bloomed there, and birds chirped beneath every bush. The spring, a stone-lined cistern built right into the side of the hill, was in the center of this dark precinct. The opening was just large enough for a bucket. Once I stuck my head in the opening. The water rippled back under the hill for four or five feet before disappearing into darkness. I could hear water trickling into the cistern and echoing off the walls with an almost metallic ping that gave the illusion that this spring went on to the very center of the hill.

I used a metal can attached to a string to raise water from the spring. If I gave the string a quick flick just above the surface of the water, the can plunged in and came up full. There were eight cans to a bucket and two buckets to a load. So I'd repeat my motions over and over—lowering the can, giving it a flick, hoisting it full and dripping, then pouring the crystal-clear water into the bucket. When the buckets were full I hoisted one last can to wet my mouth. Then I put the can back on the rim of the spring, lifted the buckets and climbed out of the ravine and into the forest. I stopped once to rest my arms then finished my journey in a single go. This day the barrel was empty and it took five or six such trips to the spring to fill it.

When I was through, Pima's fire from lunch was still smoldering, so I coaxed it back to life to make a pot of tea. The monk upstairs was chanting and I climbed the stairs with a cup of tea and gently knocked on his door. His chant stopped and he bid me to enter. He was sitting cross-legged on a cushion with the loose-paged book in two neatly stacked piles before him. The pile with the hand-lettered Tibetan writing face up he was yet to read, and the pile with the lettering face down he had already been through. Each pile was six inches high. I marveled at his steady determination. And this was only one volume of the Prajnaparamita; the other volumes lay wrapped in silk by the window. I placed the cup of tea on the floor by his side.

"Toshe," he said, the Tibetan word for thank you. This was the only Tibetan word I knew. So I smiled. He smiled back and we were at an impasse we had been at many times before. I stood a moment longer, then pressed my palms together. "Namaste," I said, and stepped back toward the door. He bowed his head and lifted the cup. "Toshe," he said again. I stepped through the door and shut it behind me.

By the time I reached the door to my room he had resumed his chanting. Swinging the window wide open, I heard the soft monotone murmur occasionally interrupted by a loud slurp of tea.

28

When the sun began to dip toward the western horizon I left my room and walked toward the cliffs on the western side of Kasar Devi, as I did every afternoon.

There was no one path to the western cliffs. The paths were innumerable, following both the contours of the hill and rising and descending its slopes. This was true not only of Kasar Devi, but of every hill and valley I explored, no matter

Windblown Clouds Thomas K. Shor

how remote. Once my eye became sensitive, I could find a path that ascended a slope just where I wanted to reach higher ground and run level when I became tired of climbing. This was because villagers and their livestock had been living in these hills for millennia and every possible approach to the land had been taken and a way beaten down. There was no route I could take that had not already been taken by thousands before me. This seemed significant in a land so steeped in tradition. The philosophers of India teach that there is no one path to the summit. They teach that, though the paths are many, truth, like the mountain, is one.

    I was halfway to the western cliffs when I climbed a sharp promontory of rock and found myself next to the old Ladakhi monk. He was sitting on a mossy knoll with his back against the trunk of an ancient and gnarled tree. Gazing gently over the tops of the trees below, he worked the beads of his *maller* while muttering an ancient mantra. I often came upon him in unexpected places along the slopes of Kasar Devi, for his main duty was tending the cows. In the mornings he'd open the gate to the little barnyard just below the house and the cows would follow him down one of the many paths. They'd follow closely behind him without coaxing until he came upon a good place for them to forage beneath the trees, and there he'd stop, usually beside a prominent rock or cliff, where he'd sit all day reciting his mantra and working his *maller*. A few chapatis and perhaps a piece of fruit wrapped in a piece of cloth that hung from a chord over his shoulder would be his lunch. The cows would range far from where he sat, but he never had to chase after them, for when the sun began to set they'd come, one by one, out of the woods and gather around him. He'd stand, they'd follow him back to the barnyard, and he'd close them in for the night.

    When he saw me he moved over to make space on the moss. I sat beside him and he shared with me what he could— the silence of the mountainside and the soft murmur of his mantra. He pointed to the sun, which was just above the trees

Windblown Clouds

Thomas K. Shor

and shone on us with the first faint tint of its setting. Sighing contentedly, he closed his eyes. The sun's rays penetrated his deeply wrinkled skin and made it glow as if from the inside. I too closed my eyes and felt the soft warmth. This was a special day, for the clouds hadn't mounted in the sky and brought rain. For the first time in what seemed like ages the sun would set in all its glory. Looking at this monk, whose eyes were closed to feel the warmth of the sun and whose lower lip moved in time to his mantra, making the handful of long, wispy strands of a beard quiver, I couldn't help but wonder what his long life had been like and what those eyes had seen; but I knew his past would never be open to me. I knew him only by the present, by each moment as it passed.

Cows began appearing out of the woods. The sun was beginning to set. I bid the monk a silent good bye and hastened toward the west.

On the western side of Kasar Devi there was a ledge, actually a series of ledges, just wide enough to walk along, that led to a shelf of rock over the deep. Into the rock face the wind and rain had together carved a small cave, big enough to sit in, but shallow, rather like a half shell.

I loved the solitude of that spot, so totally out of this world. Eagles soared on the up-rushing wind and hung in the air so close to me that I could hear the wind rushing through their wings. The cave was on a head of land that dropped off to the bottom of the valley. The valley rose away from me toward the west. The sun set over this valley and draped it slowly in shadow. Out of the shadow flowed a river, glowing golden like a stream of liquid sun. Terraced fields on the valley walls cast shadows on thin strips of winter wheat and barley. Everything was so vast that I could feel the earth turning away from the sun. The scale was not the human scale. I merged, insignificant, into my tiny ledge of rock among many ledges on a hill surrounded by untold thousands of other hills and mountains. And this is how I ended my day, much as it began. My days on Kasar Devi were framed always with the silent celestial events of sunrise and sunset. They were the parentheses within which my days occurred.

~

When I made it back to Lama's house the brightest stars were just beginning to shine. Lama was lighting the lanterns to stave off the darkness, and Sonam and Pima were taking the dinner of rice and vegetables off the fire. We sat, all of us—Lama, Sonam, the children, the monks, and I—in a circle on the grass to eat. Talk was mainly of the Lusar festival two days hence. The next day they were going shopping in Almora for the Lusar feast, and I agreed to go with them to help carry the food.

~

I was asleep by eight, up by four, and on the peak of that distant hill by the time the sun rose fresh out of an unsullied sky. By ten o'clock I was on the road to Almora with Lama, Sonam, and the two Ladakhi monks. We were quite a crew, with the men in long ceremonial robes each with a *maller* with which to count their mantras and Sonam at the lead, walking determinedly with burlap sacks slung over her shoulder to fill with food at market. I had on my red plaid lumberman's jacket straight out of the Vermont woods and my orange pack was on my back.

Never have I seen anyone bargain as hard as Sonam. At the rice merchant's she insisted new sacks of rice be opened so she could inspect every available grade before deciding upon which she wanted. And since she was buying in bulk she considered the price—which was usually fixed—as open for negotiation. She accused the shopkeeper of having inflated the prices. As he defended himself she reached into the sack and came up with a piece of straw and a stone. She held them up for him to inspect. "Should I pay such prices for stones and sticks?" she asked, and as he tried to calm her she pulled out a thick wad of bills. Pointing the bills toward another stall she threatened to take her business elsewhere. Soon the rice merchant weighed kilos of rice at half the price marked on the sack and funneled it into one of Sonam's sacks.

Sonam bargained just as hard at every shop and stall we stopped at, and thus we worked our way through the market, our loads becoming heavier and heavier. My pack was filled with potatoes; with one hand I held a sack of flour for chapattis, and in the other hand I held a sack of cauliflower. When we could carry no more, we began our return journey back to Kasar Devi. Tired, panting, and sweating we finally reached the house. For over ten miles uphill we had transported enough food for an army.

That afternoon and evening excitement and anticipation for the next day's celebration of Lusar mounted within young and old alike as Sonam set tasks for each to do. There were mounds of potatoes to be washed and vegetables to be cut. A new fireplace had to be built to hold the big pots taken out of storage for the occasion, and firewood had to be gathered. The house was cleaned from top to bottom and the little yellow flowers from a flowering tree were hung from every doorway and placed in every niche. My task for most of the afternoon was to fetch buckets of water with the younger of the Ladakhi monks. We filled great wooden barrels whose levels were always diminishing as floors were washed, pans scoured, vegetables rinsed, and endless pots of Tibetan tea made for the workers. We took a break between every load and drank tea, offered advice for the building of the fireplace, and watched everything progress. The place was buzzing with the happiest sort of commotion until well after dark, when we all sat down for a meal. And sitting there under the stars, our faces lit by lanterns wavering in the breeze, I felt a mixture of exhaustion and elation. Everything was ready for the big day. One by one the children fell asleep. As Lama and Sonam carried them inside the monks and I walked through the dark to the temple and to our beds.

Sleep came only intermittently for me that night, for I was excited as a kid on Christmas Eve.

29

In the morning I awoke to daylight for the first time in months. There was a knock at my door. I rose to answer it, but no one was there. A steaming cup of tea was on the step, and I caught sight of the tail end of the old monk's robe as he rounded the corner to the front of the temple. The morning was cool and the tea was soothing. I drank it as I dressed then went quickly to the house.

I had some money to give Lama as an offering and I found him inside, alone, before the altar performing a puja, or ritual. An entire wall of the house's big room, where they all also slept, was taken up with an altar. Masks, sculptures, and paintings of Tibetan deities, guardians, Buddhas, bodhisattvas, and demons stared down from the wall. Butter lamps were lit in homage. Lama sat cross-legged on a raised platform, hitting with a long, cloth-tipped stick a large flat drum suspended from the ceiling. He was chanting from a sacred text. The room was infused with a presence. I felt it in my gut. Tibetan ritual works on the deepest level. It passes from gut to gut.

When Lama was through, he wrapped the book back in its silk cover and put it on a shelf with the others. As he turned to leave he saw me. I stood, pressed the money between my palms, and raised them to my forehead. Then I held the money out for him. He tried to refuse my offering. I insisted, and he placed it on the altar. Then he took a long white cotton scarf that had been hanging over one of the paintings on the altar and draped it over my shoulders. This is traditional among Tibetans and it is a show of respect and thanks. Then he bowed. I bowed, and we touched foreheads. I felt a rush of energy. "Come," he said. "It is Lusar," and with his arm over my shoulder we went outside.

The place was thronging with people and more were coming all the time, entire families dressed in their finest

Windblown Clouds

Thomas K. Shor

clothes. Heavy jewelry of silver and turquoise adorned men and women alike. Children romped and tumbled on the ground, soiling their clean holiday clothing. Soon their faces and hands, which had been scrubbed so clean, were smeared with dirt. When everyone had arrived—there must have been over sixty people—the women gravitated toward the fireplaces hung over with pots of boiling food and the men gathered around Lama and the two monks. Lama cradled a sacred text in his arms and the two monks each held a drum. The younger monk had a large wooden drum and a long curved stick and the older had a little, two-faced drum the size of a tennis ball cut in half and glued back to back. It was held on a stick and at the ends of two lengths of strings were tiny weights so when you twirled the stick back and forth the weights would hit the two drum surfaces simultaneously. He also held a little brass horn that sounded a single, low note.

    A line formed with Lama at its head. Behind him were the two monks, followed by the older Tibetan men. Then the other men fell into line and I joined their ranks. The big drum sounded and on the fourth beat we started marching down the hill towards the temple, leaving the women and children behind. Lama and the monks were chanting now, Lama reading a line from the text and the monks chanting a refrain. The drums would sound, the horn would blow, and Lama would read a line of text. We veered off the path and circled the *stupa* three times, keeping our right shoulders always to the center, as is the custom. Then we continued down the hill to the temple. We circled the temple three times then cut up through the woods toward the top of the hill. The chanting and drumming entered our bones. We walked in time to the beating drum, which called forth something ancient and far away yet as close as the beating of our hearts.

    We climbed to the rock plateau above the house where the high pole stood streaming with prayer flags. We circled it three times. Then Lama and the monks sat on the rocks at the edge of the precipice and took out a new text. Then the three of them started chanting together, their thunderous voices resounding. Boom, the drum sounded and all the leaves quivered. Boom, boom, boom—all of Kasar Devi shook with the sound. Whatever gods they called forth were present now and we were his arms, his legs, and his body. Some of us collected sticks for a fire as the rest of us loosened the stones that secured the pole. The pole teetered and together we lifted the pole from its hole and set it down. It was heavy and landed with a thud. We stripped the pole of its streamers of prayer flags, which were in tatters, having been through a year of storms. The strings attached to trees were broken so there were trees to climb and strings to be cut. These flags, usually regarded with such respect, were now torn from their places and thrown to the ground. The sacred pole was lying horizontal now. The old link to the realm in the sky was now broken and we all worked frantically to rid the pole of the old to make ready for the new. The feverish pitch of the chant was increased for at this, the most sacred moment between the years, evil could enter the world order. The pole stood stripped, denuded of the protective deities. If something should happen now a year of calamities could befall us all.

The last strings had been cut. The prayer flags lay heaped on the ground. The pile of sticks was two feet high. Someone struck a match and lit the fire. Then we threw the old flags and strings on the fire. Amid great rejoicing, the old was burned and reduced to ashes and smoke. Ashes and smoke were all that remained of the previous year. A breeze came and took the smoke away.

One man had carried a sack up the hill and now he opened it. It was filled with lengths of string and dozens of newly printed prayer flags. We attached the strings to the tip of the pole and the flags to the strings. We lashed flags along the length of the pole. And then together we hoisted the pole and set it back into the hole. We packed the hole with stones to secure the pole, and then we climbed trees to tie off the strings.

The world had been regenerated, the pole was secure and true, and the prayer flags waved pristine against the deep blue sky. We circled the pole three times then we broke the circle open. We crashed through the woods screaming and hooting with joy down to the house where the women had laid out an enormous celebration meal.

That night the old Tibetans drank *chang*, a homemade barley beer. They sang songs and danced under the stars and dreamed of their homeland on the other side of the mountains.

Epilogue

A journey is a movement from one place to another. In a true journey this movement in space is but a metaphor for an inner movement. That is the wonder of it: the fusing of the outer and the inner. That is the mystery.

And that is how it was in those days.

~

When I returned to Athens I went straight to the house in the Plaka where I had left my big pack.

The house was abandoned.

A neighbor lady told me that the young Greek couple that ran the place hadn't had a permit to run a hotel. When the police came to close them down the couple vanished into thin air, apparently out a back door while the police came in the front. They had neither owned the building nor had permission to be there from the man who did.

The house had the derelict feel of a house abandoned in the face of an oncoming army. It had been stripped clean. Not a stick of furniture remained. The front-hall closet door was ajar, and of course it was empty: my pack was gone. The people staying there had scattered with the four winds.

An eddy of time in an ancient city.

Many times since then I have returned to Athens, and I've had occasion to go down that street. It has remained derelict and that old house stands boarded up, flanked on either side by houses whose front doors and windows are also nailed shut by crude boards. Even the neighbor who told me of the house's demise is now gone, her house abandoned, its doors and windows nailed shut.

I feel like the last survivor from those times.

Memories of a place that is boarded up stand differently in memory from a place that was still full of people when you saw it last. It makes more acute the single direction of time's arrow. It places the past more irrevocably and wholly in the only place where the past truly lives—in memory.